D1202508

THE COST OF SUGAR

The Cost of Sugar *is dedicated to Helen Gray.*

*Without her friendship, willingness and patience
this book would never have been written.*

Cynthia McLeod

THE COST OF SUGAR

hoperoad : London

Published by HopeRoad
P O Box 55544
Exhibition Road
London SW7 2DB

www.hoperoadpublishing.com
http://twitter.com/hoperoadpublish
http://hoperoadpublishing.wordpress.com

Copyright © 1987 Cynthia McLeod
Translated from the Dutch © Gerald R. Mettam

This edition first published in Great Britain in 2013 by HopeRoad

ISBN 978 1 908446 27 5

eISBN 978 1 908446 01 5

Printed and bound by
Lightning Source

10 9 8 7 6 5 4 3 2 1

Mrs. McLeod has deliberately referred to the original version in Sranan, which in this translated edition is indicated by footnotes. During the period of slavery in Suriname the slaves were forbidden to know or speak Dutch. People always addressed the slaves in Nengre (which was referred to by the Dutch as Negro-English). This language developed originally as a pidgin or contact language from the mingling of African languages, Portuguese and English. It became the native language of the slaves born in Suriname. The language changed its name gradually to Sranan-tongo, and more recently to Sranan. Outsiders have sometimes called the language taki-taki, but this name is never used by Surinamers. In present-day Suriname thirteen languages are spoken. Dutch is the official language and is used in educational establishments. It is also the native language of the middle and upper classes, of whatever race. Sranan is, however, the national language, the lingua franca, and the only language spoken by practically everyone. It may surprise English-speakers how much of the language can be understood with a little imagination, but as mentioned, one of the source languages was English. (This in itself might seem surprising, but Suriname was first settled by the English [via Barbados] between 1651 and 1667, the first of three short occupations in its history.)

Terms specific to Suriname have been explained in footnotes, but most are also collated in a glossary, which in some cases offers an indication of pronunciation. This is to be found at the end of the book.

Dear Reader,

The Cost of Sugar was first published on 28 October 1987 and the first day of sale was on 30 October 1987. I still remember that a colleague from the high school where I was teaching said to me a few days before the presentation, "If five hundred copies of a book are sold in Suriname, it will be a bestseller." When I asked her over what period of time, she answered, "Oh, that doesn't matter, just if five hundred copies are sold, because Suriname doesn't have a reading tradition."

I felt troubled and sorry for the publisher, who had printed 3000 books. I already envisaged piles of unsold copies of the book in the bookstore. The facts have proven the contrary. Within six weeks the first printing was sold out and many reprints followed. Then in October 1994 the book was discovered by Dutch publisher Kees de Bakker from uitgeverij Conserve who published the book in the Netherlands under licence. Immediately after that, a German edition followed. And today we present this special edition in English.

Who could have imagined this? Not me! Who could have imagined that this book would remain the best-selling book in Suriname all these years and also the best-sold book of a Surinamer abroad? And who today would dare to say that Suriname doesn't have a reading tradition?

The Surinamese community has embraced, cuddled and cherished this book, and this in particular proves that a book, a work, can have a certain value for a community that extends far beyond a literary and/or commercial value. And especially for this I wish to thank all readers in and outside Suriname. The expressions of appreciation that I have received in abundance over these many years have always been heart-warming and an incentive to continue writing.

To my surprise I was honoured by all the bookshops of Paramaribo, led by Sylva Koemar, who organized a big party in November 2007 to celebrate the 20th anniversary of the publication of my book. It was a delightful evening.

In December 2011 the excellent theatre group 'Julius Leeft' made a theatre piece from 'Hoe duur was de Suiker, with music, songs, acting and dancing. It was a trilling experience to be in the audience and watch this. It was performed twice in the Amsterdamse Schouwburg with attendance of Prince and Princess Willem Alexander and Maxima. In July and August 2013 the performances were on Aruba and Curacao. In September 2013, the feature film, Hoe Duur Was De Suiker, directed by Jean van de Velde and producer Paul Voorthuysen, was released to celebrate the 150th anniversary since slavery was abolished in Surinam. I am also proud to say, The Cost of Sugar as well as a printed book, is now an e-book, both in English published by HopeRoad Publishing.

Thank you for your interest.
Cynthia McLeod, Paramaribo, September 2013

CHAPTER I

THE HÉBRON PLANTATION

Dawn is breaking on the Hébron Plantation, and while the eastern sky is blushing at the caress of the rising sun, the doors of the slave huts begin to open one by one, and small fires can be seen under their lean-to shelters. Faya watra is being made: hot water into which a shoot of molasses is stirred. Here and there an appetizing scent arises from a cooking pot, signalling the presence of an aniseed leaf or some herbs in the water.

Now, outside all the huts, men, women and children are standing, some talking, some just looking around. Eventually they make their way to the southern edge of the plantation, where a canal has been dug at right-angles to the river, serving for both the supply and the drainage of water. Alongside the boathouse, where the river shore slopes gently, they enter the water to bathe: the adults more serious, the children laughing gaily and splashing each other until they're wet through. With loincloths slung around their wet bodies they return to the huts, mostly in small groups, the children following on, naked. Now it's time to drink the faya watra. The leftovers from the previous evening's meal serve as breakfast.

In the hut where the fifteen-year-old Amimba is living with her mother, brothers and sisters, Mama Leida throws a handful of dried herbs into a gourd and pours boiling water over them. This is a drink for Amimba; as happens every month, she is suffering terrible abdominal pains. She has lain on her mat moaning and groaning the whole night through, tossing and turning, now lying, now sitting up. Now she is sleeping a little. Luckily. But Mama Leida herself has hardly caught a wink of sleep the past night.

After the faya watra and breakfast, people begin drifting in the direction of the warehouse, the occasional woman breast-feeding a baby, another with a baby already tied to her back. The warehouse doors are still closed, but it isn't long before the white overseer, Masra[1] Mekers, arrives with the keys. The rations for the evening are now distributed to each family head, and instructions are given for the day's work.

But first the roll-call. Where's Kofi? Oh yes, he has a sprained ankle and won't be going onto the land but will have to work in the carpenter's shop. Amimba with stomach-ache? What, again! No messing about! Come here and now, or be fetched with a whip. Why doesn't Afi have her baby with her? He was sick the whole night long with fever. Afi would prefer to leave him with the nurse today. She'll give him a herbal bath for the fever. Tenu? Where's Tenu? Come here! Basya[2] – five lashes of the whip for Tenu, thirteen years old, who sees to the chickens. He has stolen eggs. There were six too few yesterday, and the empty shells were still lying next to the chicken-run. Tenu protests vehemently. It's a lie; he's stolen no eggs. Didn't masra know that a huge sapakara[3] has been lurking around and has stolen the eggs? If he, Tenu, had indeed stolen eggs, then he wouldn't have been so stupid as to leave the empty shells lying around near the run, now would he! Even so, five lashes for Tenu! For isn't it his job to look after the chickens? How had a sapakara managed to steal six eggs if Tenu was there? Of course: because Tenu was not there! Hadn't he spent half the day yesterday fishing in the creek? Five lashes! And this evening not a single egg missing and Tenu to present the dead sapakara! Five lashes, too, for Kobi, a year older than Tenu and helping Felix look after the horses, mules and cows in the stalls. Kobi cut too little grass for the animals yesterday. And no wonder: he was sitting fishing at the water's edge along with Tenu! Five lashes, and this evening a double portion of grass to have been cut. That was all.

Once the basya has delivered the lashes the slaves can de-

1 Mister.
2 Negro foreman (himself a slave).
3 A large type of iguana that lives on eggs and small animals.

part. And after the whip has descended on Tenu and Kobi's slender, bare backs and the two boys stumble off tearfully to their workplaces, the group, about sixty strong, disperses. The field group, about forty in number, leaves first. This group begins to move off silently, most of the slaves chewing on an alanga tiki[4]. Two of them are carrying a bunch of bananas on their heads, another a bundle of various root crops for the meal to be cooked in the fields, in two huge iron pots. The basya, with a whip in one hand and a machete in the other, follows at the rear. Another group, comprising six slaves, goes to the sugar mill, a few others to the shed where the sugar is boiled up with water. Yet another group is off to the carpentry shop, two to the boat house, and two of the more elderly to the grounds around the plantation house to ensure, armed with rake, hoe and watering can, that everything there is neat and tidy. Five-or-so women and girls go towards this white house, too, as well as the domestic slaves and the errand boys, and Sydni, the master's personal slave. The house still presents a rather sleepy prospect, its doors and windows all closed. The overseer, Mekers, goes first to his own house, where his slave-girl has breakfast waiting.

Even before he arrives he is greeted by the mouth-watering odour of fried eggs and freshly made coffee from the laid table. A new day has dawned. For the slaves, a new day of hard labour, a new day in the endless progression of days devoid of the faintest ray of hope.

ELZA

At the front of the splendid Great House, however, not all windows are still closed. An upstairs window is open, and there stands Elza, seventeen years old. She is gazing out over the green lawn that extends from the front of the house right down to the edge of the wide, lazy Suriname River. A lovely morning, the beginning of a good day. Today, 11 October 1765, the family will travel to Joden[5]-Savanna for grandma's

4 A twig from a citrus tree.
5 Jews.

sixty-fifth birthday. That will be tomorrow, the twelfth of October and at the same time the eightieth anniversary of the synagogue at Joden-Savanna.

Grandma had always been proud that she had been born on 12 October 1700, the day on which the Beracha Ve Shalom (Blessing and Peace) Synagogue in her birthplace in Suriname was fifteen years old. Elza had been looking forward to the coming two weeks. Not so much because of grandma, but for the stay itself and all the parties there would be. Many friends and acquaintances would be there, and many a tent boat had recently sailed by. Sometimes the company had stopped off for a few hours at Hébron Plantation, or had even stayed overnight, since the plantation lay precisely half way between Paramaribo and Joden-Savanna and it was sometimes necessary to wait for high tide. The whole Jewish community in Suriname was in the habit of travelling to Joden-Savanna for a few days around high days and holidays. This year the Feast of Tabernacles fell in the same week as grandma's birthday. The parties were always enjoyable, even though Elza realized that her situation was rather different, having a Jewish father and a Jewish name, but not herself being Jewish. And there were enough types who were not always that congenial towards her. She often felt a sense of admiration for her father when she considered that he had managed twenty-five years ago to act against his mother's will. Of course, she wasn't born then, not by a long chalk, but she had heard the tales often enough, especially from Ashana, her mother's personal slave.

Levi Fernandez, now forty-five years old, had from the age of twelve, when his father died, been raised single-handedly by his strict mother. She ran the Hébron Plantation on her own, and decided and organized everything. She had everything and everybody beautifully under control: the plantation, the household, the slaves, her son ... Or at least that's what she thought, until he refused to marry Rachel Mozes de Meza, the Jewish girl whom it was assumed, from the very moment of her birth, would be Levi's wife. The twenty-year-old Levi had confronted his mother like a fiery young stallion. No way was he going to marry Rachel, the daughter of his mother's bosom friend, who was four years younger than he and whom he had known from childhood. He would not marry her because he was fond of someone else: the seventeen-year-old Elizabeth Smeets, daughter of an army officer, only two years in the colony, without money, without prospects and above all a Christian. That was the first time that Widow Fernandez failed to impose her will on her son. Immediately after Levi had married his Elizabeth, his mother had moved out, returning to Joden-Savanna, her birthplace. She left the Hébron Plantation, to which her son had been legally entitled since his eighteenth year ... 'Because it was not her intention to live under the same roof with that Christian person'.

It was nine years before she returned to the plantation, and that was on the occasion of the burial of her daughter-in-law Elizabeth. She had died a few days after the birth of her daughter, who received her name from Elizabeth, and was accordingly called Elza. Had the widow Fernandez perhaps hoped and believed that she might take up the reins of the Hébron Plantation again? Had she perhaps imagined herself holding sway over the slaves, her household, her son, the children, David, then eight, six-year-old Jonathan and baby Elza? That was, however, not to be. Levi treated his mother with politeness and propriety, but the plantation was his and his domineering mother could remain at Joden-Savanna. The children were well cared for by Ashana, Elizabeth's personal slave, and by Ashana's daughter, the eighteen-year-old Maisa. When Elizabeth died, Maisa was just starting to breast-feed her second son and so it was no problem to take on the misi's[6] newborn daughter, too. And so it was that the Hébron Plantation remained without a mistress for a good seven years, but with Ashana and Maisa there to look after everything.

Until in 1754 the second son, Jonathan, died at the age of

6 Mistress.

twelve. Such an insignificant mishap, a sharp, pointed stick in his foot. But it turned into something terrible, and Jonathan passed away. And Grandma Fernandez could claim that she had always thought something like that would happen. The children, after all, were being brought up by slaves, were running around the grounds barefooted, playing in the creeks, climbing trees, in short behaving not at all like neat and tidy, white plantation children. But what could you expect if slave women ruled the roost. They had no way of knowing how things should be in a white family. So Jonathan's death was his father Levi's fault.

Did Pa Levi give in to all these reproaches? Did he perhaps have real feelings of guilt? Be that as it may, a few months after Jonathan's death he married Rachel, the woman he should have married fifteen years earlier and who herself was now the widow of A'haron and had three daughters. And so it was that Aunt Rachel moved onto the Hébron Plantation along with daughters Esther, Rebecca and Sarith. Sarith and Elza were about the same age, and it was wonderful for the seven-year-old daughter of the house to enjoy the company of someone of the same age. And now Elza could hardly remember the time before Sarith.

Elza looked out of her window and breathed in the fresh morning air. How beautiful and fresh everything looked from the dew. In a few hours' time it would be dusty. It was the dry season and there had been no rain for three weeks now. Luckily the lawn was still green, and would remain so, for lo and behold there was the elderly slave Kwasi, already busy watering the lawn with buckets and watering cans. He walked to the jetty, lowering the bucket into the river and filling the watering cans from it. Elza turned round and called softly, "Sarith, Sarith, are you awake?"

"Hmmm, no, yes, oh Elza, let me sleep on a bit more," came Sarith's voice from a bed on the other side of the room. Sarith turned her back towards Elza and pulled the sheet over her head.

Soft footsteps in the corridor and a modest knock on the door.

"Yes, come on, Maisa, I've been up for ages."

Maisa entered with a tray with two cups of cocoa in one hand and a bucket of water in the other.

"O Maisa, isn't it a lovely day today?"

"Yes misi," answered Maisa with a smile while she placed the tray on the table and filled the water jugs on the two washstands with water. She then went to the cupboard and took out a light-green muslin dress and asked, "Will misi be wearing this?"[7]

A few moments later Elza had freshened up and was sitting on her bed with Maisa kneeling before her, drawing on her stockings one by one after having put her pantaloons on for her. Thin white cotton down to the ankles, with lace at the bottom by the legs. Thereafter a white cotton batiste blouse and two underskirts. Another discreet knock on the door. Upon hearing a "Yes" from Elza, a beautiful brown girl came in. This was Mini-mini, the fifteen-year-old slave-girl who would have to dress Sarith.

Elza peered at the bed, where there was still no sign of movement, and said, "Sarith, get up now: you know that papa wants us ready in time."

"Oh, blow – all this moaning and nagging, too."

Upon which the sheets were pulled aside in one single jerk and landed on the floor, and Sarith strode angrily towards the small room where the chamber pots stood. Elza and Maisa exchanged fleeting but meaningful glances and the timid Mini-mini remained standing near the wall while her head dropped and she shuffled submissively over the floor. Elza sighed. Sarith was in a bad mood again, as she had so often been of late. What was up with Sarith? In the past she told her everything, but now no more. But so be it, she wasn't going to let it worry her. Maisa motioned to Elza to sit down and she lit a candle on the table. Then she held a small curling iron in the flame and began carefully to curl her mistress' hair.

When Elza went into the dining room downstairs a little later, only her father was sitting at the breakfast table.

7   "Misi o weri disi?"

"Good morning, papa."

"Good morning, dear little miss; are you ready? We'll be leaving the moment the tide is right, and that's in three-quarters of an hour."

The elderly slave woman Ashana entered with a plate bearing freshly fried meat, eggs and bread. She set everything down in front of Elza and remarked with an approving nod, "Oh Misi Elza, aren't you looking pretty!"[8]

Soft footsteps could be heard, and Rebecca now came in from the rear veranda. Rebecca, twenty-one, was Aunt Rachel's second daughter. She was deaf. At the age of nine she had contracted typhoid fever. She had survived this, but since then could hardly hear anything. She could still speak, but in a monotone, and she spoke very little. Rebecca lived her own private life, quiet, withdrawn, mostly in her room, where she read, painted, drew and made dolls. Lovely dolls. Everyone who saw them said she could start a business with them. Just now and then Rebecca made a doll to order and accepted some money for it, but she often gave them as presents to people she knew and most of the dolls were simply displayed in her room. People didn't bother much with Rebecca. She hardly ever saw her mother and she said only what was really necessary to her sister Sarith and her stepsister Elza. The only people she did talk with were her stepfather Levi and her slave-girl Caro. When the widow Rachel A'haron had moved to Hébron Plantation ten years earlier she had brought with her a number of slaves: Kwasiba and her two daughters Caro and Mini-mini, who were at that time eight and five years old, and in addition her own personal slave-girl, Leida. Caro was Rebecca's slave-girl. She followed her mistress everywhere and helped with washing paintbrushes, mixing paint, sewing dolls' clothes and so forth. The fifteen-year-old Mini-mini was Kwasiba's pride and joy. Obviously of mixed blood, Kwasiba had never revealed who Mini-mini's father was, but people suspected that it must have been Rachel's late husband Jacob A'haron

8   "Ai misi Elza, yu moi baya!"

or his son Ishaak. In any event, Mini-mini had brown skin, slightly curled hair, a slender face and large, dark eyes. Mini-mini was Sarith's slave-girl, and no-one seeing them together could avoid the impression that there was a striking resemblance in face and figure.

Father Levi smiled at Rebecca as she took her place at the table. "Ready for the trip?" he asked, exaggerating the movement of his lips.

Rebecca shook her head. "I'm not going."

"Oh come, why not?" asked Pa Levi.

Something like "Don't want to" sounded as Rebecca shook her head again. Elza looked at Rebecca. She could well understand that Rebecca didn't feel like going. Why would a deaf person want to go to a party that comprised mainly chatting, gossiping and playing music? She would be able to follow nothing and would just end up feeling lonely. She often felt sorry for Rebecca; what could her future be? Even now, at twenty-one, she was an old spinster, and was destined to remain so for ever, for who would marry a deaf woman? Above all, she hardly ever encountered a young man.

Now from the rear veranda came Aunt Rachel's voice asking Maisa and Kwasiba if they had looked after everything for the misses. Entering the dining room, Rachel asked immediately, "Where's Sarith?"

"Oh, she'll be here," answered Elza. Whatever Sarith might do, Rachel never got angry with her, for she was her mother's darling. Elza had often thought that this was due to Aunt Rachel's surprise at having borne such a beautiful daughter. And now Sarith came dashing down the stairs. She had some rouge on her cheeks and looked really lovely in her light-yellow dress. The naturally black curls danced around her ears, but with an angry look she said to her mother, "That stupid Mini-mini: I told her to wash my pink gown, but she hasn't done it and now I can't wear it."

"You have plenty of others," replied her mother.

"Yes, but I wanted to put that one on."

And then impatiently to Kwasiba:

"I don't want that egg; take it away. I want pancakes."

"Yes misi," said Kwasiba, and she hurried off to the kitchen to tell Ashana that Misi Sarith wanted pancakes, not an egg. Pa Levi had in the meantime left the table and had gone to the waterside to see whether the boat was ready and the luggage properly loaded.

Elza got up and went to the rear veranda. She wanted to say farewell to Ashana before they departed. Standing on the veranda, she looked towards the outside kitchen at the back of the grounds where the cook was hastily making pancakes for Sarith. She wondered again what it was that was making Sarith so cross and bad-tempered lately. When a little later Kwasiba came towards the house with a plate of pancakes, Ashana emerged from the kitchen.

"Ashana, I wanted to say goodbye," called Elza. Ashana hurried to the veranda.

"Look after yourself well now, misi, I'll miss you."[9]

"Oh, it's only a few days, Ashana."

"Take good care of your father: I hope he won't quarrel with that old woman."[10]

Elza laughed. Just like Ashana, she knew that no-one could prevent grandma using her sharp tongue. But as always, papa would survive.

"I'll have Koki prepare a tasty banana soup when my misi returns,"[11] Ashana continued.

"Very good, Ashana, keep well," and Elza nodded to Ashana with a smile. At the door Elza turned for a moment and added, "Look after Misi Rebecca, won't you!"[12]

"Yes misi," replied Ashana. She would look after Rebecca; she liked her a lot. It was a very different story with Misi Rachel and Misi Sarith. As far as Ashana was concerned they could stay away for ever.

---

9 "Ai misi, luku bun yere, m'o firi mankeri fa mi misi n'o de."

10 "Luku yu p'pa yere, no meki a feti nanga a granmisi."

11 "M'o meki Koki bori wan switi griti bana gi mi misi t'ai kon baka."

12 "Sorgu misi Rebecca bun."

SARITH

The tent boat glided slowly over the Suriname River, powered by a crew of eight oarsmen. Under the canvas roof sat Uncle Levi, mother Rachel, Elza and Sarith. Behind Rachel, Kwasiba and Mini-mini were sitting, and in front of Elza and Sarith sat Maisa. Sydni, Uncle Levi's personal slave, sat near the stern of the boat and now and then conversed softly with Kofi, who was seated right at the back, steering the boat.

Sarith sat with her chin in her hands, gazing ahead. In fact, she had said nothing since their departure. Now and then Elza said something to Maisa or her father, and she occasionally cast a sideward glance towards Sarith, but she looked so cross that Elza found it better not to speak to her.

When Elza had called that morning, "Sarith, are you awake?" Sarith had replied, "Let me sleep on a bit more." She didn't want to sleep, however – she had long been awake – but she did want to think about what she would do today. She must get to speak to Nathan alone, but that would not be easy, since he would of course be in the constant company of his betrothed Leah, that pale, puny Leah. What was she in comparison with her, Sarith? She was a hundred times more beautiful than Leah. Oh yes, she was quite aware of that: she was beautiful, far more beautiful than all the young girls she knew. Everyone said it, and she knew from the way all the men, young and old, looked at her.

Nathan, the yellow-belly, was engaged to Leah after all. And again Sarith recalled what had happened rather more than a month ago. There had been a huge party at the Eden Plantation, near Paramaribo. That was the plantation belonging to Nathan's parents. The occasion was the Bar Mitzvah of the youngest son, the thirteen-year-old Joshua, Nathan's youngest brother. Many guests had lodged there for a week or more: the older couples in the plantation house, the young ladies with their slave-girls in the unoccupied overseer's lodge, and the young gentlemen in a warehouse that had been refitted especially for the occasion. The nineteen-year-old Nathan, the oldest son, had behaved as a real host and had made no secret of his amorous feelings towards Sarith. He and Sarith had spent several afternoons together in his room while everyone was resting. Many a time they had passionately kissed and hugged, and each time they both looked forward to the next moment they could be together. Nathan adored her. Infatuated, he had told her time upon time how much he loved her and that he wanted no-one else but her. But for the moment they would have to keep their liaison a secret, for it had already been decided by his parents that he should marry Leah Nassy. Sarith would have to grant him some time, and then he would make it clear to his parents that he could not marry Leah because he was in love with Sarith.

And Sarith had indeed given nothing away. With a surreptitious smile she had listened to the chatter of the other girls, especially Leah, and had seen how she blushed every time Nathan's name was mentioned. Children, they were all just children, and even Elza her stepsister was really just such a child. Now she, Sarith, knew much more about life. Nathan was not the first with whom she had played the game of love. From the age of thirteen she had lived for two years in the town[13] with Elza at the house of their sister, Esther. And then she had become friends with Charles van Henegouwen, the brother of one of her classmates at the French School. Many were the afternoons she had spent in the company of Charles. When his parents were out visiting, she and Charles had always managed to arrange to be alone in the house. Until his parents had found out, probably given away by one of the slave-girls. The result was armageddon. Esther was livid and had summoned mama. Sarith and Elza had to return immediately to the plantation and Charles was sent to Holland by his parents. Oh, she understood perfectly well why. She was a Jewess and Charles was not. Many well-to-do Christian plantation owners wanted as little as possible to do with Jews, as if they were an inferior type of person. Ridiculous: they were all whites, after all!

Once back at the plantation, mama had delivered a com-

13 Paramaribo, which is often referred to as 'the town'.

plete sermon and had tried to find out exactly what had been going on between her and Charles, but Sarith wasn't stupid enough to tell all. She could hardly admit to her mother that they had slept together on at least six occasions, and so she had said that they had just kissed. Mama had heaved a sigh and had said that a girl could never be too careful, and must absolutely not do anything stupid. Oh yes, that is how it was: men and boys could do anything and everything, but girls could do nothing. They had to take their place in the marriage bed as innocent and naïve angels.

After Charles there had been a young captain, who had been ordered to inspect a military post in the hinterland of Joden-Savanna. He had fallen ill there and had been taken to Jo-den-Savanna. A whole month he had lain there sick in her grandparents' house. During that period she and Elza had by chance lodged at Joden-Savanna for two weeks. At first they had both stayed with Grandma Fernandez, because Sarith's own grandmother Jezebel would not have two young girls sleeping in her house while the captain was lying there sick. But when the captain was beginning to recover, Sarith had visited him regularly and what in fact had begun as a bit of fun had ended as a full-blown love scene. Just once, for the captain had said afterwards that he regretted what had happened. He was married, had a wife and children, and he asked Sarith to forgive and forget him.

And a little more than a month ago it was Nathan. Nathan, who had told her that he would explain to his parents why he could not marry Leah. Two weeks earlier Uncle Levi had happened to be visiting Paramaribo for a few days and returned from town with the news that Nathan was officially engaged to Leah Nassy. Leah's parents had given an intimate dinner party for the family and a few friends. Since Uncle Levi was in town, he was also one of the guests, along with Sarith's sister Esther and brother-in-law Jacob. It would not be a long engagement, for Nathan and Leah would marry within two months. How furious Sarith was upon hearing all this! She had stormed to her room, had wept, smashed things, thrown the bedding on the floor, stamped with rage. In short, she was livid, and Mini-mini was more than once the unfortunate who suffered at first hand. Everything the slave-girl did in those days was wrong, and on several occasions she had suffered a resounding thick ear from her mistress. Amazed, Elza had asked time and again what was the matter, but each time Sarith had sullenly replied, "Nothing," or, "It's none of your business."

Now she would be seeing Nathan in a few hours' time, and then everything would turn out all right, because she would demand of him that he, there at Joden-Savanna, tell his family and everyone else that he loved her, Sarith. And he would do what she said, because he loved her. He simply had to do it, and that stupid, plain Leah would get a nasty surprise and perhaps burst into tears and faint. A pity that there was no chance in Suriname to elope with someone. In another country, in Europe for instance, you could run off, in a carriage or on a horse, far away to another town and get married there. But here, where could you go? Except for the town and the plantations it was all jungle. Scary jungle with dangerous wild animals and Maroons – escaped slaves who murdered white people.[14] But all right, once Nathan saw her he would of course be so in love with her that he would do what she said and everything would turn out as it should. That was the reason she had really wanted to put her pink dress on that morning. Mini-mini must wash that dress as soon as they landed at Joden-Savanna, and then she could wear it tomorrow, on the feast-day itself.

When, some hours later, the boat moored at the jetty at Joden-Savanna and the company was being welcomed by the many guests who were already there, Sarith looked around straightaway to see whether she could see Nathan. But she saw neither him nor Leah. Leah's parents she did see, and they told her enthusiastically that Leah together with Nathan would arrive only the next day, since they had stopped off at Rama Plantation and would spend the night there.

14 In Suriname the term Marron is used.

Rama was scarcely an hour away from Joden-Savanna, and a cousin of Nathan's was the owner there. Leah and Nathan would be at Joden-Savanna the next day well before the start of the service in the synagogue. Until that time, Sarith would just have to be patient. Now, at any rate that gave her time to think over carefully everything she would say to Nathan.

JODEN-SAVANNA

When the boat bearing Nathan and Leah moored at the jetty at around 9 o'clock the next morning, there turned out to be other guests on it: Nathan's cousin, who was the owner of the Rama Plantation, and Rutger le Chasseur, a young man who had been in the colony only a few weeks, appointed as assistant-administrator for a well-known Amsterdam bank. Sarith was dressed in her beautiful pink gown, pink slippers of shiny satin on her feet. When a surprised Elza had seen Mini-mini carefully lowering the exquisite gown over Sarith's head early that morning, she had asked her stepsister whether it would not be better to let the dress hang ready for the ball that evening. But Sarith had retorted with a short, "No," and then asked, "Are you coming along to the water-front?" When the boat moored, Sarith was standing there provocatively on the very end of the jetty. Nathan had turned extremely red when he saw her standing there, but Sarith had no chance to talk with him. Leah's parents herded the complete company along, first to the house where they would be staying and then to the synagogue. In the synagogue there was not the slightest chance for Sarith to exchange a single word with Nathan, for the women and men sat in separate sections to follow the service.

ELZA

Since all the Jews had gone into the synagogue, Elza just wandered around outside. She had just decided to go and sit on the front veranda of her grandmother's house when suddenly an unfamiliar man stood before her.

"Shouldn't you be inside, Miss, uh ..."

"Fernandez," said Elza, "I am Elza Fernandez, and no, I don't belong there, I'm not a Jew, and you are apparently also not Jewish."

"No, indeed, me neither, but you do have a Jewish name, don't you?"

"Yes, that's because my father is Jewish but my mother is not, and as you may know, under Jewish law only children of a Jewish mother are regarded as being Jewish."

"Well I never," the young man continued, "I had never expected to find something as enlightened as a mixed marriage in this far-off Suriname."

"Maybe you'll come across a lot more enlightenment during your time here, Mister ..."

"Le Chasseur, Rutger le Chasseur is my name; please excuse me for not having introduced myself earlier."

"How long have you been in the colony?" asked Elza.

"Oh, not so long, about three months."

"And how has it been so far?"

"Hot, very hot," answered Rutger. Elza laughed,

"Oh yes, these past months are usually the hottest of the year, though at Joden-Savanna it's usually not too bad. It's higher than Paramaribo, you see."

"Oh yes, I have noticed that. And how do I find it for the rest? Beautiful! Paramaribo is such a lovely, bright town, not large, but pretty, fresh and clean. I'm already beginning to feel a bit at home. Shall we wander down to the river?"

Together they walked and he told Elza how he had come to Suriname as assistant-administrator. His great-uncle, who was the owner of a bank in Amsterdam and also of several plantations in Suriname and Berbice[15], had decreed that he, Rutger, should learn the trade of administrator. When Elza remarked that that uncle must be extremely wealthy, Rutger had laughed and confirmed that his great-uncle was indeed very rich. He, Rutger, belonged to the poor branch of the family and was also no heir, since great-uncle had four daughters. His grandmother, who was a sister of his great-

15 Now a region of Guyana.

uncle, had been married to an exiled Huguenot, which explained his French surname.

Elza in turn recounted how she lived on the Hébron Plantation together with her father, stepmother Rachel and stepsisters Rebecca and Sarith. Her own brother David was already married and had a plantation on the Para River.

"Was that pretty girl who stood next to you on the jetty one of the stepsisters?"

"Yes, that was Sarith," said Elza.

"What a pretty girl that was," remarked Rutger. Elza nodded. Yes, Sarith was certainly pretty. Everyone was always saying that. Everywhere they went it was Sarith who was noticed first, and time and time again it was remarked how attractive she was. Yesterday, when they had arrived, everyone had yet again admired her beauty. Aunt Jezebel, Sarith's grandmother, had said this on many occasions to grandma; Aunt Sarah, Aunt Rachel's sister, had mentioned it, and Aunt Rachel beamed with pride every time she heard how beautiful everyone found her youngest daughter. The eyes of all the men beheld Sarith with wonder, and one of the older ladies had remarked that Sarith was already fully a young lady, while Elza, of the same age, was still only a girl.

"Do you come to Joden-Savanna very often?" Rutger was asking.

"Oh, at least once a year. It's my grandmother's birthday today, and it's important to her that everyone knows that she and the synagogue share the same birthday, and very often this coincides with the Feast of Tabernacles, you see. And so it goes."

"And do you always have to wait outside when there's a service in the synagogue?" Rutger repeated.

"Yes, always, but it really doesn't matter," answered Elza. "We ourselves have been baptized as Lutherans, because my mother was Lutheran, and as children Pa always dropped us off in the town at Christmas, to stay with our grandfather, our mother's father. But Grandfather died five years ago, and since then we've never been in the church in Paramaribo at Christmas."

"But isn't it difficult being Jewish as well as Christian?" asked Rutger admiringly.

"Oh, all that fuss about nothing. I think that it doesn't matter to God whether people are Jewish or Protestant or Catholic as long as they lead a good life and do no harm to other people."

"What a wise and well-considered remark for a young girl," said Rutger, looking at her amusedly.

"Are wise remarks always reserved for men and old women, then?" asked Elza.

"Of course not, but you don't fit in so well with the young ladies," replied Rutger.

"At least, the men think that," said Elza sharply.

Now Rutger laughed out loud: "Miss Elza, I think you're exceptionally quick-witted."

As they walked back, Elza showed him how the village was constructed, as a square with four streets across. The houses in the corners of this square were large and comfortable, the others sometimes simpler, but everything was very attractive. Most of the houses had gardens on the slopes. And in the middle of all this, the lovely synagogue, built of bricks, about thirty metres long, fourteen metres wide and eleven metres high. If possible, she would let him look inside later. There was a beautifully decorated ceiling and a huge cedarwood ark with lovely carvings in which the Torah scrolls were kept. Silver chandeliers, large candelabra and various candlesticks.

Jews and gentiles were in agreement: this synagogue was one of Suriname's real gems. It was a pity, however, that many rich Jews had left or now lived elsewhere on plantations, whereby Joden-Savanna had gone into steep decline and was inhabited mainly by the elderly such as her grandmother and Aunt Rachel's parents.

Near the synagogue was the great tabernacle. A little further along the valley a few smaller huts had been built by men who appreciated having their own tabernacle.

Once the service had finished, everyone left the synagogue and went to sit on benches at long tables that had been set up in the hut. This was the high point of the Feast of Tabernacles. Three huge, round loaves, baked specially for the occasion, lay on the table. The rabbi said a prayer, broke the bread and distributed it among those present, after which the wine was poured and distributed.

After this traditional ceremony, dishes were brought by the slave-boys and slave-girls from the houses and the feast could begin. Rutger had as a matter of course come to sit next to Elza, and when father Levi had taken a place at the same table and had made Rutger's acquaintance, a congenial round of conversation arose among all those seated there. Elza looked around once to see where Sarith was, but she wasn't at any of the tables. Was she perhaps still busy changing? She really didn't know what the matter was with Sarith, but, all right, perhaps she didn't feel like eating at the moment and would come along later.

The conversation at the table was not always congenial, for there soon arose talk of the colony's problems. The attacks by the escapees. Only recently they had raided several plantations. They had made it as far as the Temptatie, where they had killed the Jewish owner and his wife, as well as the overseer. They had freed the slaves, who had immediately joined them, and they had set the plantation house on fire as well as the sugarcane in the field.

Some weeks earlier they had raided the Jukemombo Plantation on the Boven[16]-Commewijne River. The owner, Master Biertempel, was away at that moment. His wife was murdered and his three children were wounded. The raiders had taken everything, even the children's clothes. When the father had hastened back home the following day, he had found his children, half-naked, weeping over their mother's corpse. The colonists were now well and truly frightened. A stop would have to be put to this!

Rutger remarked that in his opinion it would be better for the government to make peace with the Maroons and not

16 Upper.

persecute them any longer. Suriname was so large, and nobody
used the hinterland. That could be the free negroes domain.
Many of the guests turned on Rutger. He was still new in the
colony and didn't know what he was talking about. The
government had already made peace with the bush-negroes.
Some years ago there had been a huge fuss because the government had made peace with the escapees on the Boven-Suriname River. Did Rutger perhaps think that peace must be made
every time a wild group appeared in the hinterland? Then you
could just keep on doing that and very soon the whole of Suriname would be portioned off to those devil's children.

A corpulent women in a dress of black silk declared that
she believed that an uprising wasn't far off. Everyone could
surely remember the terrible uprising in Berbice a few years
ago. Well, they could expect something like that here. An uprising in which all the whites would be murdered or forced
into slavery by the negroes.

"Would it not then be better if all slave owners treated
their slaves well?" Rutger asked, "Without the terrible punishments that are handed out. Is it not the fear of these bru-
talities, such as being hung on a meat hook, a hand or a foot
being hacked off, a savage beating, burning alive, that makes
slaves run away?"

Pa Levi nodded in agreement when Rutger made this remark, but most of the guests at the table laughed heartily.
Rutger really was a naïve newcomer. Punishment was the
only way to treat slaves: they were stupid and lazy. If you
didn't terrify them with heavy and cruel punishment, they
would get the idea that they could do what they liked. And
in any case, were they not created by our Lord to sweat and
toil for the whites? Rutger wanted to remark that he would
gladly like to hear how it was so unequivocally known that
negroes had been created to this end, but Elza whispered to
him, "Oh, Rutger, say nothing now. These folks are real fa-
natics. You'll fall so out of grace with them if you share your
opinion that slaves must be treated well."

So Rutger had said nothing further. He was after all a
guest there.

SARITH

But Sarith was not resting in her grandparents' house. She had seized an opportunity that had presented itself as everyone was leaving the synagogue, had sidled up to Nathan and said, "Come now, I must talk to you."

"Must that be now?" Nathan had asked apprehensively.

"Yes, now," Sarith replied, "And if you don't come this minute, I will scream, and I will do it right here and loudly."

Nathan then told Leah that she should carry on to the tabernacle because he had to go and fetch something, and he walked off in the other direction with Sarith, to the back of her grandparents' house where the garden overlooked the valley.

"Nathan, you said that you loved me! I was really the one you wanted to marry. And then I suddenly hear that you are engaged to Leah. How can you, Nathan?" Sarith almost stumbled over her words, so quickly did she utter them.

"Oh, Sarith, Sarith." Nathan held both her hands. "I really do love you, but I have no choice, don't you see. This was decided long ago by my parents."

"You knew that then, but you would explain everything, that's what you said."

"It simply cannot be, Sarith, really not. My father is heavily in debt. He could lose the plantation. There are another three children after me, and Leah is an only child and the heiress, and that plantation is so huge and, uh ..."

"So it's about the money. I should have known." Sarith pulled her hands away. "But still you loved me. Have you forgotten what happened between us?"

"No, Sarith, no, I shall never forget that. I shall keep it in my heart as my most cherished memory."

"That's a lot of good to me, isn't it," said Sarith cynically.

"Oh Sarith, you just have to understand. A person doesn't always marry the one he or she really loves."

Nathan looked at her and wanted to stroke her cheek, but she knocked his hand aside and said, "What if I were pregnant now? What if I were to tell everyone here what has happened between us?"

"Oh no, Sarith, no, you mustn't do that. Everyone would … everyone would think so badly of you."

"Of me, eh? Of me?" Now Sarith was screaming. "Of me, not of you, eh? You coward. Oh you vile, vile coward. I hate you!"

"Sarith, calm down."

Nathan wanted to take hold of her hand. He hesitated, however. This was a very different Sarith from the sweet, cooing young thing he had had in his bed. This petite ball of fire scared him. She knocked his hand aside and before he knew it she had slapped his face hard, screaming, "Don't you dare touch me, you coward! I hate you! Leave me – go away, go to your Leah!"

She turned and ran off through the back door of her grandparents' house. Nathan remained a while, pensively rubbing his cheek, before returning slowly to where the guests were at table.

The tears rolled over Sarith's cheeks as she stormed up-stairs and threw herself on a bed in one of the bedrooms, sobbing uncontrollably, her head pounding the pillow. But wait … she would have Nathan. She would let him see how all the men wanted her. She would show him, really show him. She called to one of her grandmother's slaves, since she didn't know where Mini-mini was, and ordered her to fetch a basin of cold water so that she could freshen up.

When Sarith went and sat at the long table a quarter of an hour later, there was no trace of what had just happened. She was exceptionally happy, joked and laughed with everyone and pouted and flirted with all the men, young and old. Every time her laugh rang out she saw Nathan looking her way, embarrassed or concerned, but she pretended not to no-tice him. Could he not see how charmed all the men were with her? During the afternoon all the ladies went to have a rest. Some men also rested, but many remained sitting in the shade of the large trees, or had slave-boys hang hammocks up, and then chatted, smoked and drank rum punch. Sarith did not go to rest with the other ladies, but remained in the company of the men and chatted nineteen to the dozen while she sat, now with the one, now with the other, briefly in a hammock and even taking a sip from some glass or other.

In the evening a ball was held. The estate was decorated with Chinese-style lanterns, all alight, and with the ladies in their wonderful evening gowns and the men in their evening suits the evening took on a most festive air. Elza danced and chatted mainly with Rutger. Dressing for the ball, Elza had told Sarith with a blush that the new assistant administrator was so pleasant and easy to talk with. Sarith had wondered for a moment whether she should extend her flirtations to this new young man, but had decided against it. It was Nathan she wanted to hurt, not Elza, and it was not every day that men showed some interest in Elza. And above all, she, Sarith, wasn't at all interested in some poor office clerk, especially one who wasn't all that handsome anyway.

Sarith passed laughing and cooing from the one pair of male hands to the other. She was merry, even provocative, and not seldom was an angry glance cast in her direction by a wife or fiancée. Elza was too preoccupied with keeping Rutger engaged to pay much attention to Sarith. She had seen Rutger now and then glance amusedly in Sarith's direction and he had remarked, "What a pretty girl your stepsister is, and how jolly."

Then Elza had noticed how Sarith was especially enjoying herself in the company of the widower Robles de Medina. The thirty-three-year-old Julius Robles de Medina had lost his wife and a child in a smallpox epidemic the previous year, and was left with two daughters of ten and eight years. This was the first time since the loss of his wife and child that he had travelled with his two daughters from his plantation on the Boven-Commewijne River to Joden-Savanna to attend the feast.

Elza noted with considerable amazement how her stepsister was now flirting with 'Noso' and how provocatively she was behaving with him. She and Sarith had never liked Julius Robles de Medina or his wife very much, and as little girls they had given him the nickname 'Noso' because he had such an enormous nose. In recent years they had always kept out of his way at parties because Sarith considered him such a bore, always wanting to talk about his beautiful Klein Paradijs[17] Plantation. And now that same Sarith was sitting so close to him and talking and laughing while she teasingly stroked his hair and told him how handsome he was. Elza couldn't understand at all what was the matter with Sarith.

Most of the company remained for almost a week at Joden-Savanna, and Sarith's behaviour did not change. When she and Elza went to bed at night, Elza got no chance to talk with her stepsister because Leah was sleeping in the same room, as was one of Nathan's sisters. And while Sarith was being undressed by Mini-mini she would hum merrily or make a remark along the lines of, "Some people can't get a man themselves and have to be married off."

After five days or so, Nathan departed with his parents, brothers and little sister. Nathan's cousin from the Rama Plantation and Rutger went in the same boat, too. Two days later Pa Levi, mother Rachel and the girls left. Rachel, above all, was pleased that the stay was coming to an end. She could not help noticing that both young and old ladies had been looking disapprovingly at Sarith and uneasily at their husbands. One of the ladies had even remarked that Sarith was behaving like any old coloured concubine. But when her mother-in-law, the widow Fernandez, had said to her that Sarith was behaving far too provocatively and freely with all the men, Rachel had answered that the poor child certainly meant no harm by it. It was just a young girl's fun and pleasure. Although in her heart she agreed with her mother-in-law, she could not permit anyone to say something hurtful about the apple of her eye.

Sitting in the boat, she now looked at her daughter, who was no longer the happy, flirtatious young girl, but was rather just looking straight ahead with a bored expression. And mother Rachel wondered and worried about what was going on in her daughter's pretty head.

17 Little Paradise.

CHAPTER II

RUTGER LE CHASSEUR

It was a journey of many hours from Joden-Savanna to Paramaribo in the tent boat rowed by ten slaves. When the tide started coming in they broke the journey at a plantation and spent the night there. The following day on the ebb tide they continued the journey. When the boat arrived in Paramaribo the sun was already setting and Rutger looked out from the boat at the beautiful white town that came ever closer. Now that he was approaching it from the land side, of course he saw it from different angle as compared to a good three months ago, when he had sailed in from the sea. Didn't it look crisp and cared-for. Totally different from Amsterdam, where he came from and where the narrow streets were paved with cobblestones. The streets of Paramaribo were planted with orange blossom, and this gave it a floral feel overall. Rutger could not help thinking that Governor Mauricius, who had caused considerable upheaval about fifteen years earlier, had in the end achieved good results with his measures to improve the town. Not only Paramaribo but the whole colony had made great strides forward under the rule of this enterprising governor, despite his having been thwarted by a group of rich, conservative planters who simply would not understand that better treatment of the slaves and making peace with the Maroons could only be to their advantage. Plagued and tormented by these planters and in the end wrongly impeached, Governor Mauricius had been forced to leave the colony. Although his name was cleared in Holland, he did not return to Suriname to finish what he had begun as his life's work. Luckily, this well cared-for and bright town was a permanent reminder of his good intentions.

Rutger le Chasseur was lodging with his patron, the administrator Van Omhoog, who occupied a spacious house in the Gravenstraat. One of the rooms on the ground floor served as an office. Rutger still recalled his surprise at seeing this beautiful mansion for the first time. He hadn't expected to find such houses in a faraway colony. Now he knew that there were many of these houses in Paramaribo. All were built and furnished in more or less the same way.

In front of the building was a large, high veranda that ran the whole breadth of the house. You entered through a renaissance-style door with a highly polished copper doorknocker and came immediately into the large front hall, with its own particular style of furnishing, typical of the colony. Usually there stood on the one side a piano, above which hung a large mirror with a heavily gilded frame; in the middle a huge mahogany table with a sizeable chandelier hanging above it, to be lit by candles. Around the table four rocking chairs and often along the wall another set of mahogany chairs. Two sofas stood opposite each other, and in one of the four corners there would be a large mahogany wall unit, a chiffonier or tallboy, on which would be standing all kinds of objects in glass and earthenware and also crystal glasses, smaller glasses and carafes with wine, liqueur and Madeira. In its cupboards glittered the expensive porcelain and silver tableware. On the walls hung paintings, a pendulum clock and candlesticks with finely chamfered glass reflectors. The windows had Venetian blinds and were spanned with green gauze. Magnificent curtains of silk or cotton were tied with loops and bows along the sides of the windows.

At the Van Omhoogs' there was, next to the front hall, a sitting room that served as an office. Behind that there was a second sitting room. The dining room was behind the front hall. At the back of the house there ran a wide gallery where tea or coffee was taken. At the end of the gallery the minor cooking quarters were to be found: a pantry and the inside kitchen itself. A large selection of plates stood in long rows along the walls, and under the open sink were the copper pans and baking dishes. The staircase leading to the upper floor also opened onto the rear gallery. On the upper floor there were four spacious rooms. In the bedrooms stood large, high mahogany bedsteads decorated with copper bands and globes. In the grounds of the house stood the kitchen in which the real cooking was done, the large wash-house and the building used for storage. Then, a little further away, stood the slaves' dwellings, in two rows facing each other. In between there was the brick-lined well, and nearer the house there was also a large rainwater tank. Behind the slaves' dwellings there was yet another garden with all kinds of fruit trees.

When the boat landed near the Platte Brug[18], Rutger bade everyone a warm farewell and walked through the Molen-straat and the Kerkstraat to his lodgings, followed by his slave Alex. When Rutger had arrived in Suriname, to be greeted by administrator Van Omhoog on the waterside, Van Omhoog had the sixteen-year-old Alex there with him and had told his young assistant that Alex was his and that he would have to see to it that the boy attended to his slightest whim and accompanied him constantly. From that moment on, Alex literally followed him all the time, helped him with dressing and undressing, put his shoes on and took them off, stood ready with drinks, pipe and tobacco, and when Rutger was going out, had his hat and walking stick ready. Now, too, he walked behind Rutger, pushing the case with his mas-ter's clothes on a hired wheelbarrow.

Mrs van Omhoog was pleased to see her lodger after an absence of almost a month. He had gone to visit two planta-tions along the Suriname River that fell under the office's jurisdiction, and she had understood that, his being so close to Joden-Savanna, he would be a guest at the annual Feast of Tabernacles. The Van Omhoogs had no children of their own, and the lady of the house found it very pleasing to have this young gentleman in her home. She at least had someone to talk to, for Mr van Omhoog was a quite a taciturn indi-

18 'Flat Bridge'.

vidual. She also had plenty of time on her hands, for there were four slave-girls, three slave-boys and an errand boy around the house. Mr van Omhoog had been in the colony for fifteen years now as representative of an Amsterdam merchant banking firm, and in a few years' time, as he had some time previously written to his director in Holland, he wanted very much to be able to retire and enjoy some well-earned rest. The director had sent his nephew to the colony as assistant to Mr van Omhoog with the intention that Rutger would take over from him when he stopped working at some time in the future.

There was certainly a lot to learn. Rutger had to go through the books of past years to get an overall impression of how things were. In the beginning it was especially difficult to get a grip on the prices of things, since everything had previously been expressed in pounds of sugar. A few years earlier, card money had been introduced to Suriname: a kind of bank note with an official stamp, coat-of-arms and seal, in denominations of 1 guilder, 2 guilders 50 cents, and 10 guilders. Remarkably, the card money was made in the form of playing cards bearing images of diamonds and clubs, kings and jacks. Upon seeing this money for the first time, Rutger had asked Van Omhoog the reason for these illustrations, and received the answer that the government had probably arranged for this as an aid for the many illiterates.

The day after Rutger's return, he sat in his patron's office, and Mr van Omhoog wanted to know all about his experiences. How were things on the plantations Mijn Geluk and De Goede Verwachting?[19] Those were the plantations Rutger had had to visit. And what were his impressions of Joden-Savanna? Had there been many guests present? Of course, mainly Jews. And Rutger recounted how he had enjoyed the people's hospitality and how he had already made many new friends. He had become especially friendly with Elza Fernandez and her father Levi Fernandez, owner

19 'My Happiness' and 'The Great Expectations'.

of the Hébron Plantation. Mr van Omhoog naturally knew who Levi Fernandez was. Did Rutger realize, however, that it was better not to become too friendly with the Jews? They formed such a closed, individual circle, and in recent years there had arisen considerable 'anti' feelings among the Christians with respect to the Jewish community. Rutger did not really understand this. Had it not been the Jews who had been the founders of this colony and had set a good example with the plantations and so forth? Why, then, all the antagonism? Administrator Van Omhoog did not know this, either, but those feelings did exist, even to the extent that there was talk of housing the Jews in a separate part of the town. A kind of ghetto, so to speak. Rutger shrugged: "Small-minded colonial palaver! I'm man enough to choose my own friends and won't let myself be misled by the prejudices of others."

"Of course, the position of the Fernandez girl is somewhat different," the administrator continued. "She herself isn't a Jewess because her mother was Lutheran, but, well, she does have a Jewish name."

Rutger remarked that, as far as he had observed, the Fernandez girl had very good judgement when it came to matters of Jew and gentile, Christian and non-Christian: really refreshing amongst all this small-mindedness. Mister van Omhoog could not help laughing at what Rutger was – somewhat curtly – saying, but he still found that it would be better to avoid being too intimate with the Fernandez family. As far as female company was concerned, if Rutger needed a woman, the administrator could provide a pretty mulatto girl. Almost all whites had a mulatto woman as mistress or concubine. This satisfied the needs of the man and carried absolutely no responsibility. For of course, no white man would ever be so stupid as to consider marrying one of these women. If such a woman had children by him, then a few guilders sufficed for their care and upbringing. He, Van Omhoog, himself had such a mistress. He had installed her in a small house on the road to the Oranje Cemetery on the edge of the town. She had had two children by him. There were even a few whites who gave such children their own family name, but he, Van Omhoog, certainly did not intend to do this. Many of these mulattos then began to get big ideas and started behaving as if they were white, but he would not be party to that.

Rutger listened in astonishment to his patron's words. It was not the first time he had heard this kind of thing. What double standards: use a woman, conceive children by her, and then look down on your own children because they were coloured. Rutger thought, "God help me never to become like this." When he heard the whites in Suriname going on like this about the negroes he wondered whether he really wanted to remain in this country, and he had often wondered whether he was the only one who thought this way. Of all the people he had met thus far, the sixteen-year-old Alex, his slave, was possibly the most intelligent. He had noticed that the predominant occupations of the colonists, as far as the men were concerned, were drinking, eating, playing cards and other games of chance, sleeping with various women, and indulging in so-called deep conversation, that always concerned money, the governor, attacks by the bush-negroes, and their own small circle. With the women it was no different: chatting, gossiping, complaining about the slaves' laziness, about their husbands' behaviour, endless nibbles, and yet more gossiping. And for the rest, all the showing off, partying, one-upmanship and displaying one's wealth and magnificence.

When Rutger had accompanied mister and mistress Van Omhoog in their carriage to church the first Sunday of his stay (even though the church was no more than a five-minute walk away, just around the corner, in a large hall above the town hall on the church square), he could not understand why two slave-boys, two slave-girls and his own Alex had to walk alongside the conveyance. Only upon their arrival at the town hall on the square did it become apparent what this was all about. The Van Omhoog couple were decked out in all their richest finery and the slaves, too, had beautiful clothes on, but naturally no shoes, for it was strictly forbidden for slaves to wear shoes. When the company alighted from the carriage, Mr van Omhoog's personal slave held a large parasol above his master's head while another slave walked behind him with the prayer book. This pattern was repeated for Mrs van Omhoog: a slave-girl with parasol, another with the prayer book. Since Rutger had no parasol, it was Alex who walked behind him with the prayer book. All the colonists had come to church in this manner, with or without a carriage, but always with five or six slaves in attendance. Rutger could barely restrain himself from laughing out loud at this comedy act. What a farce, what a stupid, vain show. And when you looked at the churchgoers' severe, deadpan faces, then you really wanted to burst out laughing. Just as all the feasts and parties: each wanted to outdo the other with rich attire and a superfluity of dishes.

And now such an invitation was delivered. It was from Governor Crommelin and his wife, to a spectacular ball that would be held in four weeks' time. Mr van Omhoog had told Rutger that the whole of 'high and white society' in Suriname would be attending the ball. Rutger very much hoped that Elza would be in Paramaribo at that time. He could then meet her at the Governor's Ball. Her family would also be invited.

What a hollow and vain existence it was in such a colony. Those who read and concerned themselves with things other than trivia were so few in number that it had come as a surprise to have met a girl such as Elza Fernandez. She lived on a plantation but knew a lot about books and had very definite views on particular matters. She was a marked exception to the women and girls he had met until then. Not once had she belittled a slave-girl, but to the contrary had said that, apart from her father, brother and stepsister, the two slave-women who had brought her up were the most important people in her life. He had noticed that she never spoke to a slave in a commanding tone of voice, but was always pleasant and friendly. He had thoroughly enjoyed her company. How they had talked about all kinds of things: books, slavery, the Maroons. And that stepsister, what an incorrigible flirt she was, a typical spoilt colonial girl who did just as she pleased. Rutger had to smile as he thought back on Elza's worried looks when her stepsister was carrying on like that. And Sarith had acted as if she had not noticed in the slightest all the women's hostile glances while she flirted with first the one, then the other man. Even so, Rutger wondered whether it had all been as innocent as it might have appeared.

ELZA

A few weeks later, the Fernandez family were indeed on their way by tent boat from the Hébron Plantation to Paramaribo. Father Levi, Aunt Rachel, Elza and Sarith would stay in the large house of Jacob de Ledesma, who was married to Aunt Rachel's eldest daughter, Esther. That couple had three little sons, the three-year-old twins Samuel and Joshua and a baby of a few months, Ezau. Everyone called Samuel and Joshua Sammy and Jossy because that was the way the slaves pronounced the names. Jacob de Ledesma was a very well-to-do businessman who, in addition to his businesses in Paramaribo, owned three plantations. Everything pointed to the family's good fortunes: a beautiful, large mansion on the Saramaccastraat blessed with vast grounds supporting lots of fruit trees, a vegetable garden and ten or more slave huts right at the back. In fact, thirty slaves worked in the house. The front hall and dining room were enhanced by superior furniture specially imported from Europe, silk curtains, expensive porcelain and silverware and large crystal chandeliers in which hundreds of candles could be lit to provide brilliant lighting at balls and feasts. This part of the house was normally forbidden territory for the two youngsters, who had the habit of terrorizing the whole household with their mischievous antics. Each had a slave-girl, a girl of fourteen or thereabouts, who did nothing all day but run after the little master to ensure he didn't have an accident or to take an object out of his hands. In addition there was a small errand boy who was constantly picking up discarded toys.

Aunt Rachel loved her two grandsons, but a little of their company was quite sufficient, for they soon got on her nerves with all their running and shouting, and given half the chance they would climb on her and attack her meticulously coiffured wig with their grabbing little fingers. If Elza and Sarith were lodging in the town and heard the patter of tiny feet running up the stairs, they would hastily lock the door, for, "If those Philistines should get in ..."

The lodgers had then installed themselves, and during the extensive meal put on for them, the feast at Joden-Savanna was recounted at length, whereafter the conversation turned to the supper ball that the governor would be holding in a few days' time and to which they, too, were naturally invited.

Rutger was one of the first to see Elza when she entered the great ground-floor hall of the Governor's palace. He went to her with outstretched hands, and it was clear that he was pleased to see her again. Elza was pleased, too. She had hoped to see him again and blushed when she saw that he appreciated her company so much. They were together the whole evening, talking, laughing, dancing. Sarith was the star of the evening. She looked lovely in a light-green gown, her black curls pinned up, her grey-green eyes sparkling with pleasure at all the male attention. All the men, young and old, wanted to dance with Sarith, and like a butterfly she was now here, now there, flirting and laughing. At a certain moment she was also near Elza and Rutger and said laughingly to Rutger that he surely must not spend the whole evening devoting his attention only to her sister; she was there, too. And smiling, she had led Rutger to the dance floor. Elza had watched how the two danced, one dance, and then another one, and she had also seen that there was just as much admiration at her beauty in Rutger's eyes as in those of all the other men. Shortly thereafter it was time for supper. As was the custom, the tables for the Jewish guests were in the upper hall. That was always the case in the governmental palace. At their special tables the Jews were served dishes that were prepared for them in their own kosher manner. Sarith therefore went upstairs together with her father, Aunt Rachel, Jacob, Esther and all the other Jews. Elza was pleased that the supper began at that moment, for she had wondered whether Sarith and Rutger would carry on dancing with each other for much longer.

A few days after the ball, an invitation was delivered to Elza in the Saramaccastraat. Her company was requested for a meal at the Van Omhoogs'. There was also an accompanying note for Mr and Mrs Fernandez in which the Van Omhoogs requested their permission to invite Elza.

This was the subject of much discussion in the family. Aunt Rachel had her objections. Was this done? After all, Rutger moved in very different circles from the Fernandez family. Would it not be preferable for Elza to choose a man from her own sphere? For Pa Levi everything was all right as it was. Elza might be his daughter, but she was not a Jewess. She was not really accepted within the Jewish community, after all. Would a Jewish man ever want to marry her? No, it was in fact a good thing that this newcomer to the colony was showing so much interest in his daughter. Elza blushed when all this was being discussed so openly, especially when Sarith remarked that it all seemed to be becoming quite serious.

The invitation was accepted and Rutger was pleased. In fact, Rutger would have preferred not only Elza but the whole Fernandez family to have been invited, but he understood well enough that that was something the Van Omhoogs would not readily do. He did not know that it had already cost Mr van Omhoog all his powers of persuasion to bring his wife round to agreeing to invite just Elza. So it was that Elza went to eat at the Van Omhoogs'. In front of her walked a slave with a lantern; two steps behind her followed Maisa.

Mrs van Omhoog found her guest, despite everything, to be a dear girl, so sensible and unassuming. The dinner was a complete success. Afterwards Rutger accompanied her home. Alex led the way with the lantern and behind the couple walked Maisa, who had waited the whole evening, seated on the back doorstep of the house.

In the days that followed, Elza and Rutger often walked and talked, sometimes dropping in on Mrs van Omhoog for a cool drink. Alex always walked in front of the couple and Maisa behind. Rutger wondered whether he would ever get used to the idea of slaves being constantly in his company, literally with every step he took.

In bed, late evenings, Elza and Sarith often talked extensively about Rutger. Yes, Sarith was certain: Elza was in love. Elza denied this at first, but come now, in Sarith's mind there could be no shadow of a doubt. Look how Elza could talk about nothing else but Rutger, and could think about nothing else. That was true love. When she had jokingly asked her stepsister whether Rutger had kissed her, Elza had responded indignantly, "Sarith, please!" – such things certainly never happened before you were married to someone. And Sarith had laughed at such naïvety. She was happy for Elza that she had this young man, of course. He was certainly most agreeable, but it would not be someone for her. She wanted a rich man with money and plantations.

The De Ledesmas threw a grand dinner on New Year's Eve, followed by a ball. There were many guests, including Elza's brother, David, who had come to Paramaribo for a week with his wife Suzanna and their two small boys from their plantation on the Para River. They were lodging with Suzanna's sister on the Malebatrumstraat. Rutger was naturally one of the invitees. He and Elza danced a lot, but also spent a lot of time talking outside on the large, wide veranda, it being very hot inside.

When the Fernandez family returned to Hébron a few weeks later, it was taken for granted that Rutger would soon be paying a visit to the plantation. That he did, and during that visit he asked Pa Levi for Elza's hand in marriage. Pa Levi was most impressed with this respectable young man. He wasn't rich, but would undoubtedly be a good husband for Elza.

Ashana and Maisa were happy with Elza's choice. Yes, Masra Rutger was a good person. And when Rutger was at the plantation he was spoilt outrageously. Ashana had to know what his favourite dishes were and Maisa was always seeing to it that his clothes were perfectly washed and ironed and that Alex could always bring him something to drink. A busy period now ensued for Aunt Rachel. Elza's trousseau had to be prepared. Twenty-four sheets, twenty-four pillow-slips, hand-towels, bath-towels and so forth. As soon as they could be spared, Caro, Mini-mini and some other slave-girls were to be found in the sewing-room, hemming, sewing and embroidering.

When Rutger was there, he got involved with everybody. He talked with Rebecca, looked at her drawings and paintings and discussed books with her, and it was clear that Rebecca felt at ease with him. Sarith talked and joked a lot, too. She was in her element again. At the Vooruitzicht[20] Plantation, which was only 90 minutes' journey from Hébron, three young men were lodging who were paying her a lot of attention, and the young ladies and gentlemen were constantly coming and going between the various plantations. But Sarith could not help flirting with Rutger, too. When Elza noticed the amused looks Sarith was getting from Rutger, she wondered whether he didn't perhaps find her dull and boring.

One afternoon Elza and Rutger were sitting on a bench on the river bank near the boathouse. It was a peaceful afternoon and they looked out over the river to the green of the rainforest on the other side. Elza was a bit quiet. They and Sarith had just been playing cards and Sarith had laughed and talked so much with Rutger. Now Sarith had gone indoors. Rutger's eyes had followed her admiringly, and he had said, "How pretty she is, eh?"

Elza asked softly, "Would you perhaps rather marry such a beautiful woman?"

Rutger looked at her amusedly and said, "Elza, you're not jealous, are you?"

Elza said nothing and shrugged her shoulders, and Rutger continued, "Listen, Elza. I would never want to marry your stepsister. I admire her beauty in the same way that I admire a beautiful flower or bird or a painting, but marry her? No,

20 Prospect.

absolutely not. A beautiful woman is a difficult possession, and a beautiful woman with Sarith's temperament would be a difficult and dangerous possession. I would soon find myself in the position of having to fight duels, and that is nothing for me. But Elza, you must promise me one thing: never be jealous. I find men who have jealous wives always so pitiful and I would never want to be like that. Trust me: I love you and will always love you, always."

Elza smiled at him: "That sounds good."

Rutger said pensively, "This land is sometimes so odd. There are sometimes such strange customs. Promise me, Elza, that you'll never get angry with me over another woman. That even if I get involved with another woman on occasion – you never know – you must even then trust me and know that I will always love you and never will leave you."

"Involved with another woman?" said Elza, while reflecting that such things were commonplace in this colony. So many men had, in addition to their lawfully wedded wife, a mistress or a concubine, and these latter were usually mulatto or even slaves. Did Rutger intend this, too?

"Are you intending to take a mistress, Rutger?" she asked.

"Intending? No, certainly not!" cried Rutger. "Oh no, but you never know how life goes, and I want you to know that I will always remain true to you, even if, for instance, I have a brief something or a short affair with another woman. Do you understand that? Promise me that you won't be angry or think that you must have your revenge with another man."

"Yes, I promise," said Elza, "But if, if ..." she hesitated.

"If what?" asked Rutger.

"Such an incident or short affair – that would surely not happen in my house?"

"Oh, come now, Elza!" Rutger laughed. "Certainly not, my darling. Were you afraid of that?"

"Oh, rain, rain, come my dearest, inside, quickly; hurry."

It had suddenly started to rain, and within a few seconds it was pouring down. He brought Elza quickly to her feet and they raced indoors, followed by Alex, who took the empty glasses and plates to the kitchen.

When Rutger was again at the plantation a few weeks later, Elza saw immediately that there was something amiss. He looked strained and tense; it seemed as if something was restraining him. "What's the matter, Rutger," she asked softly when the two of them were sitting on the veranda.

"Van Omhoog wants me gradually to take over his position in the Court of Civil Justice," Rutger replied.

"But surely that's wonderful, Rutger, a real honour and so good for your career," thought Elza.

"Perhaps, but still I think I won't do it. It's always swimming against the tide. I went along to one of the sittings, and after that I got the chance to read various papers. It was terrible, Elza, terrible what I read there. It was mostly about the cruel punishments the slaves received. I couldn't believe my eyes. And do you imagine for one moment that the owners were punished? They got a telling-off! You ask yourself how it is possible that people can think up such atrocities. You know, I read about a certain Basdow. A few years ago he had a slave's fingers hacked off one by one, and then he forced the slave to eat the first few fingers that had been cut off!" Rutger shivered as he recounted this.

"Oh, terrible!" cried Elza.

"Wait, that's not all," Rutger continued. "He wanted to have the same slave burned alive, and when they couldn't get the fire hot enough, he had him buried alive. It is surely that wretch himself that should be well and truly punished?"

"Who should be well and truly punished?" asked Sarith, who had come onto the veranda and had heard the last few words.

"A certain Basdow who wanted a slave to be cruelly punished," said Elza.

"But the slave will have deserved it," said Sarith.

"No-one can deserve the punishment of being first forced to eat his hacked-off fingers and then being buried alive." Rutger was furious as he said this.

"Oh, Rutger," cried Sarith, "You seem not to have understood that slaves need to be severely punished. If we didn't do that, they could quite easily murder us!"

"I don't call this punishment," retorted Rutger. "A punishment must offer the chance for improvement, and these atrocities most certainly do not do that."

"Oh come, you make it sound as if you can compare slaves with ordinary people. Slaves are negroes. You punish one to scare the others. Don't you understand that?" Sarith went and sat in the rocking chair while she said this.

"Do you know what I think?" Rutger went on. "I think that people who invent such horrible things as hanging on a meat hook, scorching lips and tongues and burning alive – those creatures don't deserve to be called people. Even in the animal world you see that creatures kill other sorts only for food. Even animals don't treat their victims in this way." Rutger was getting all workedd up. Elza looked at him: his face was red and a small artery pulsed in his neck.

Sarith rocked slowly to and fro in the rocking chair. "Rutger," she said, "What do you know of slaves? You've not been here long enough to be able to judge. When you've been here longer, you'll talk differently." Then she called out, "Mini-mini, I want something to drink."[21]

"What Rutger is saying has nothing to do with being here for a long or a short time," said Elza. "He's right: the slaves are simply mistreated. On some plantations they get an extreme beating or a hundred lashes for the slightest thing. Have you heard what Susanna Duplessis has done now? She has had a child drowned before its mother's eyes. Even children get a cruel, cruel beating under her."

"Then at least they learn to work from a young age," said Sarith. "If Uncle Levi allowed the slaves to be treated more strictly, then the plantation would produce much more, that's what everyone says." And then she shouted out loudly, "Mini-mini, come on! And why are you always grumbling about the slaves," she sneered. "Don't you have nicer things to talk about?"

At that moment came the sound of a bell from the riverside.

21 "Mini-mini mi wani dringi."

"A boat, a boat! Who is it?" Sarith had sprung up. "Oh look, visitors!"

Two gentlemen walked up from the riverside. One was Joshua de Miranda, the eldest son from the Ephrata Plantation, and the other was a stranger. Arriving on the veranda, Joshua explained, "This is Moshe Bueno de Mesquita. He's just arrived from Amsterdam. He has come to lodge with us as of yesterday. We've come to ask whether the ladies and gentleman would like to come home with us for a pleasant afternoon."

Sarith was excited. Of course she wanted to go along. There was nothing to do here, after all. She had got bored long ago. Rutger, however, was not all that keen, and therefore Elza also preferred to stay at home of course.

When Sarith returned towards evening, she was cheerful and even elated. They had had such a good time. Later in the evening she described excitedly to Elza how obviously charmed by her the newcomer Mosche Bueno de Mesquita had been. Actually he was destined for Joshua's niece, Naomi, but he couldn't take his eyes off Sarith, and that Naomi, she had looked increasingly miserable and annoyed. Now, Sarith had in any case had a really wonderful time!

"And Elza, what have you been doing all afternoon?" asked Sarith, before she prepared to go to sleep. That Rutger had got so worked up about such unimportant matters as slaves' punishments and all that nonsense. Was Elza sure that she wanted to marry such a moaner? And, already yawning, Sarith declared, "When you are married I won't visit you very often; there won't be very much happening. Hmm, I can see it already: a dull couple you'll become, really boring."

CHAPTER III

ELZA

The wedding of Elza and Rutger took place on Sunday 14 August 1766. The weeks running up to the great day were filled with many and varied activities, for bride as well as groom. Rutger had been able to rent a house on the Wagenwegstraat: a pleasant place with extensive grounds and adequate slave accommodation on the property. Pa Levi had been exceedingly generous and had seen to it that the furnishing was impeccable. He had paid for the furniture in the front hall and for the equipping of the kitchens, also for the beautiful silk curtains, while Rutger himself had taken care of the dining room and had had a cabinet maker make the large mahogany four-poster bed and the large mahogany mirrored dressing cabinets.

The last two weeks Elza had been in her future home every day, ensuring that everything was put in its proper place: the elegant porcelain service, the silverware and the crystal glass. While Maisa put neat piles of crisp linen in the cupboard, Sarith and Elza would walk around the house, stopping yet again in front of an open cupboard and looking out from one of the windows over the grounds.

In the bedroom Sarith demonstrated how Elza would from now on be a fashionable lady, drinking chocolate with the other fashionable ladies, how she would run her household and direct the slaves. Bursting with laughter at Sarith's play-acting, both girls landed on the bed, and when the laughter had subsided Sarith said suddenly and softly, "Oh Elza, I will miss you so much."

Elza replied, "I'll miss you, too, Sarith. I can't imagine being without you."

"You won't miss me – you have Rutger, remember," Sarith

smiled, but Elza shook her head, "That is different. Sarith; promise me that you'll often come and stay with me."

"I'll certainly come to stay, but not too often, because I think your husband won't want me around all the time and above all I'd feel like a third wheel on the wagon."

"Oh no, Sarith, Rutger isn't like that; promise me that you'll visit a lot," said Elza, giving her stepsister a warm hug.

The wedding ceremony took place on the Saturday afternoon in the Lutheran Church. There was no reception afterwards, since at 8 o'clock on the Sunday morning the whole company would depart for Hébron to celebrate there with a huge feast. The Jewish guests were not present in the Lutheran Church, but many had already travelled to Hébron on the Friday, or would arrive there during the Sunday morning.

The last Friday, and also the Saturday, Elza still lodged at the home of Esther and Jacob de Ledesma, together with her father Levi and with Sarith. It was a merry gathering at the waterside that Sunday morning, where a multitude of guests stood near the Platte Brug, all in their finest finery, with slaves holding parasols above their misis' heads. A loud cheer went up as the newly-weds stepped from their carriage and went to take their place in the beautifully decorated Hébron tent boat. A whole fleet of tent boats with flags flying could shortly afterwards be seen making its way along the Suriname River towards the wedding feast.

Hébron Plantation was all hustle and bustle. Everything was prepared; everywhere there were decorations, on the large green lawn were wooden benches and tables under open shelters with leaf roofs. Over a hundred lamps hung in trees and on ropes to provide the lighting, since there would be a great ball that evening. The slaves were all wearing pretty loincloths and had been instructed to come as soon as the great bell sounded.

When the boats had moored and the great bell had rung, the slaves went to stand in two rows as a guard of honour from the jetty to the plantation house. Everyone waved palm branches and the slave children threw flowers and rice. With flushed cheeks, Elza and Rutger walked through the human archway, almost deafened by the greetings shouted by the well-wishers. On the doorstep of the house Pa Levi stood waiting with a large bag of coins. Now Elza and Rutger threw the coins with generous hands, and all the slaves cheered and scrambled. After that the slaves returned to their own quarters, shouting their best wishes again as they departed. Elza had insisted that the slaves be given two free days for the celebrations.

For many days now, everyone had been hard at work getting everything ready: pom[22], pasties, various cakes such as fiadu, keksi and inglish boru,[23] different wines and ginger beer. The slaves had extra salted fish and eggs. All the men had received dram[24] and there were little cakes for the slave children.

The main dinner was eaten at tables that had been pushed together on the wide veranda at the back of the house. It lasted two hours and was marked with regular bursts of laughter at all the poems that had been written in the couple's honour. In the evening, the ball. The orchestra played, the green lawn spectacularly lit with all the lovely, coloured lanterns, and the ladies in their wonderful evening creations, each hair-do seemingly more elegant than the next, slaves in the background constantly busy ensuring everyone was served, and ready with fans after each dance.

At a certain moment both Elza and Rutger had left the festivities, for Elza wanted Rutger to see something of the slaves' celebrations. He must witness a genuine winti dansi, a ritual negro dance. This would be his only chance to see this, for the negroes did not usually appreciate whites coming to look at their dances, and such things were in fact for-

22 A warm dish based on grated taro stem, with chicken and vegetables, eaten mainly on festive occasions.
23 Fiadu (fiadoe or viadoe) is a (pastry) tart filled with raisins, almond slivers, amongst other things. Keksi is a sponge-cake, but also with raisins and currents. Inglish boru (or Engris buru, Ingris boroe), similar to keksi but sometimes with pineapple.
24 A brew with a very high alcohol content.

bidden on all the plantations. Elza had told her father that she was intending to go to the slaves' party with Rutger, and Levi had approved on condition that her brother David and Maisa could go, too. He knew that the slaves would not mind his children being there. They had done this on various occasions in the past. Aunt Rachel's arrival on the plantation had put an abrupt stop to this, because in her eyes it was inappropriate, and it was better that the children knew nothing of it.

When Elza, Rutger and David had withdrawn from the rest of the company, they encountered Sarith, who wanted to go along, too, for she had never witnessed anything like this, and asked whether her companion, the young teacher at the Yeshiva (Jewish school) who had been in the colony only three weeks, could also go.

The five, accompanied by Maisa and the old slave Felix, made their way silently to the open space in the rainforest where the slaves were holding their celebrations. The beating of the drums could be heard from far away. As they approached they saw all the dark, half-naked bodies, lit by the flames of the large fire that was burning in the middle of the clearing. They were not noticed, for at that moment a slave was busy dancing with a small bench between his legs. His feet moved ever faster to the beat of the drums, but not for one second did the bench drop. A woman now went into a trance. Her body began to shudder. She began to dance while the onlookers sang loudly. Rutger could not believe his eyes. The new Jewish teacher, too, looked at the sight with eyes wide open. Then another man who, while dancing, suddenly, before anyone realized what was happening, jumped into the fire and danced for at least two minutes on the red-hot embers before a woman pulled him out.

The drums beat out their ceaseless rhythm, and all the negroes around the fire were moving their bodies one way or another to the beat of the music. David looked sideways at Sarith. She had a strange look in her eyes and also began to move her body, slowly but surely towards the slaves. David caught Sarith by the arm. She had such a strange expression and heard nothing of David's cry to her. The movements of her body became increasingly violent. The teacher and Rutger now also looked at Sarith. Without another word, David grabbed Sarith by the shoulder and said, "Rutger, help me: we've got to get her away."

As David and Rutger walked away with Sarith between them, Maisa said to Elza, "It is better for misi herself to leave, too."[25]

And so they all returned to the ball, where some guest or other who had partaken somewhat liberally of the drinks called another toast to the couple. He was, however, so drunk that he almost swallowed his tongue. Whatever the wish might have been that he expressed, no-one could understand it, especially since he had even forgotten the names of the newly-weds.

OCTOBER 1766

Elza and Rutger had lived for two months now in their house on the Wagenwegstraat. Maisa, Amimba and Ta Dani had accompanied them from Hébron. When Elza was still at home and it was being discussed which slaves should go with her, she had said straightaway at the beginning of the conversation, "Maisa is going," and everyone had laughed out loud. Papa said teasingly, "Imagine if Maisa did not go with you, that would be the end for both of you," referring to the fact that from the day Elza was born, Maisa had never left her side. Hesitatingly, Elza said, "And Ashana?"

But papa answered immediately, "No, my dearest. You know I'd like to grant you everything in the world, but Ashana isn't leaving." Elza had asked nothing more. She had tried her best, but she had known in advance that papa would never let Ashana go. Ashana was after all the only link he still kept with his late darling Elizabeth. Both he and Ashana had seen Elizabeth die and it was Ashana who looked after papa and did everything for him: keeping an eye on his food and his clothes, massaging his back when he re-

25 "A betre misi srefi gowe tu."

turned weary from a long day in the tent boat or a journey
on horseback. She knew precisely how he wanted his bath-
water, how the pillows on his bed should be arranged. In
short, Ashana cared for her masra as nobody else ever could.

No, Elza could take Amimba. She was in principle a slave-
woman for the fields, but she was in fact too weak for that
work, but still young. Under Maisa's gentle instruction she
could certainly become a good house-slave. Ta Dani was an
elderly slave who worked in the timber store. He had come
from Africa as a salt-water negro[26] and was at Hébron even
before Levi had married Elizabeth. He was now old and infirm
and could not really be used for the plantation, but he could do
minor repair work for Elza and keep an eye on the grounds.

Rutger's Alex was there too, of course, and Rutger had
furthermore bought a strong, young slave named Kwasi, a
Karboeger-negro[27], and when Rutger had said that he was
still looking for a cook, Kwasi had asked his new boss to buy
his wife, Lena, also a Karboeger, who could cook really well.

So now Elza was living in her new house with her husband
and six slaves. Maisa slept in the house, in a small room behind the pantry, and the other five slaves slept in the accommodation in the grounds.

Since Rutger was away at the office during the day, Elza
had naturally very little to do. Maisa ensured that the household ran smoothly. So Elza would go and visit former classmates from the French school, the majority of whom were
now also married, some already having a child. Or she went
to visit Mrs van Omhoog, or received visitors herself. But
most of all she went to visit Esther de Ledesma. In that
house, where she herself had lived for two years as a girl, she
always felt at ease. Although – it was a very different household from when she and Sarith had lived there some years
earlier. The twins, now four years old, terrorized everyone
with their roguish antics, and their little brother, Ezau, now

26 Brought directly from Africa, or born during the voyage.
27 Three-quarters negro, one-quarter white, or the a child of a ne-
    gro and an indian.

just one year old, tended to be almost forgotten amongst all the fuss surrounding Masra Sammy and Masra Jossy.

Ezau was a pleasant little boy, playing sweetly in his bed for hours on end, or sitting on the nursery floor, playing happily with a rag doll or some toy bricks. Elza had a real soft spot for him, and always made a point of busying herself with the little, forgotten Ezau whenever she was visiting.

On 21 October the population of Suriname experienced a heavy earthquake. The citizens of Paramaribo heard around five in the morning a loud underground rumbling that was followed by a number of violent shocks, lasting about five minutes in total. Elza and Rutger were lying in bed and were both woken by the rumbling. But before they could say a word about the rumble and what it might be, the whole house began to shudder and sway. Elza stammered, "It's an earthquake."

Rutger took one leap out of bed, dragged Elza over the edge of the bed and threw himself on the floor, pulling Elza with him. A second later they both lay under the heavy mahogany four-poster. "Oh Rutger, what on earth is happening?"

Teeth chattering, she was holding onto him tightly. "Why must we stay under the bed?"

"This is the safest place to be," answered Rutger. Then Maisa was at the top of the stairs, shouting, "Oh my God, Misi Elza, what is going on?"[28]

Elza called, "Here Maisa, under the bed."

And then Maisa bent down and Rutger pulled her under the bed with them. The three of them lay there while the house shuddered and creaked and now and then even swung to and fro. Doors and windows banged open and closed, and outside in the well and the rainwater butt the water splashed around. They heard the slaves shouting and screaming. Maisa had only moaned and whined, eyes tightly closed, expecting at any moment to have the house coming down on her head.

28 "Misi, o, mi Tata, misi Elza, san eh pesa?"

When, after about ten minutes, everything seemed to be over and the last rumbling receded into in the distance, the three went cautiously downstairs. There they found the other slaves in a state of panic. Amimba was weeping loudly and crying that she wanted to go to her mother. Maisa had to give her a thorough shaking to calm her down. Alex was talking nineteen to the dozen in his agitation. He knew all about it, it was an earthquake, he could explain exactly how it had come about. But Maisa said sharply that he could shut up or people would come to believe that the whole earthquake was of his making.

In the meantime it was light and the streets had filled with people. Everyone wanted to recount his or her experiences, his or her fears. Many were convinced that the world was ending and the slaves knew for certain that their ancestors' spirits had finally risen to seek revenge and to have justice done at last. Just wait: the whites would pay at long last for all the atrocities they had wreaked on the negroes.

For days and indeed weeks on end there was no other topic of conversation, especially since further heavy shocks were felt in the night of 25 October.

There were fortunately no personal accidents or injuries. The only exception was a Mister Daniel Forques, a civil servant, who had sprung out of a first-floor window in panic and had landed on his head. He lost consciousness for several hours, and when he eventually came round he was convinced that he was in heaven, but found that heaven looked amazingly like his own house.

The incident that attracted most attention, however, was the fact that His Excellency the Governor and Mrs Crommelin had fled barefoot and in their night-attire out of the palace and onto the street. Governor Crommelin had not the slightest problem admitting that this was indeed the case. He and his wife had been terrified. When they had felt the tremors, had heard cracking sounds and had seen a huge crack open in the wall, they could not get their old, fat bodies fast enough down the stairs and out of the building, so certain they were that the whole palace was on the point of coming down about their ears. For the first few days nothing could persuade them to return to the palace, and slaves had to fetch their clothes and other necessities while they themselves stayed two doors further along in Mr Jean Nepveu's large mansion.

The governor was so thankful that he and all Surinamers had survived, that 29 October was declared a day of general thanksgiving and prayer.

ELZA

There suddenly came a big surprise in the first week of December. One afternoon, Papa, Aunt Rachel and Sarith stood at the door. They got the warmest of welcomes from Elza, who, in her new role of hostess, urged Maisa to prepare food and drink for everyone. How was everybody, how were things on the plantation, how was Ashana? Papa and Aunt Rachel smiled. Everything was fine. How were things with Elza and with Rutger? The family had arrived a few hours earlier and, having freshened up and rested in the Saramac-castraat, had come straight to Elza. Would they not stay here with her, Elza had asked. No, Papa and Aunt Rachel were lodging as always with Esther and Jacob; they had their own room there. But if Sarith wished to stay … Elza was over-joyed: of course Sarith must stay here. They could send Sarith's luggage on later. But everyone would stay until Rutger had arrived. He had a business meeting and would be home in about an hour. Rutger, too, was surprised to see his in-laws. And of course Sarith must stay here. It would be so pleasant for Elza when he was away during the day.

In the days that followed, Elza and Sarith indeed had much to tell each other. About the earthquake, about Sarith's latest admirers. Did Elza remember the Jewish teacher who was with them at the wedding, Abraham Cohen? He was also present at Joden-Savanna for the recent Feast of Tabernacles. He was a little shy, but Sarith had clearly seen that she had made a considerable impression on him. Did Elza know that the slaves had not worked for a whole week after the earth-quake? They were terrified that if they were working in the

fields a huge crack would open up and swallow them. Uncle
Levi had not forced them to work, even though overseer
Mekers would have had it differently. But on many other
plantations where the slaves also were scared, they had been
whipped back to work. What kinds of things did Elza do all
day? Did she and Rutger go out a lot? Just like old times the
two had again chatted and laughed together, and Rutger had
often looked on amusedly and listened to the merry chatter.
He was the complete host, so attentive to both Elza and
Sarith.

As always, there were in December and January many
feasts and parties, and several times each week the three of
them walked off somewhere to a feast or a sociable evening
out, always preceded by Alex with a lamp in his hand.

A few weeks later – it was early February – Elza sat one
morning in the dining room near the window. Amimba was
busy rubbing the floor and wall with bitter oranges, cut in
half.[29] That happened once a week in all houses. The floors
then remained nice and shiny, it was a tried and tested reme-
dy against pests, and there was always a fresh ambience in
the house.

Elza looked towards Amimba without really seeing her,
for she was deep in thought. She had every reason to be.
Something had gradually changed. At first she had thought
that it was just an idea of hers, but now it was so patently
obvious that with the best will in the world she could not
pass it off as a delusion. Rutger and Sarith were getting involved. Oh, Elza had seen it coming. The attentions that
were first directed towards both her and Sarith, but of late
more towards Sarith. The way he sometimes took Sarith's
hand or arm if they had to step up or down along the road.
And she, Elza, then walked behind and seemed to have been
forgotten. And Sarith, no longer at parties the butterfly flit-
ting from one man to the other, but staying constantly in
their company. At first Rutger had always danced with both
of them, but recently he had been dancing much more fre-

29 This was a bitter citrus fruit that was used for many purposes.

quently with Sarith, and she had sat there ignored, or to be eventually invited by some other man to dance.

And now Sarith was suddenly interested in serious conversations. She, who previously had not concerned herself with anything outside her immediate field of vision, was suddenly interested in all kinds of things and even wanted to read in order to be able to converse with Rutger. On the evenings when they weren't going out, the three of them would sit for hours in the front room talking. It was often getting late and then Rutger would say, "Elza, if you want to go to bed, do go, and I'll be along shortly," and she had understood that he wanted to be alone with Sarith. Without speaking another word she would get up and go upstairs. When Maisa had undressed her and had helped her into bed it had sometimes been more than an hour before Rutger had joined her.

Yesterday evening had been such an occasion. Rutger had said that she should go upstairs, but after Maisa had gone to her own room, Elza had got up quietly and had gone downstairs again; very carefully, so that no tread would creak. On the rear veranda where a lamp shed light up to the staircase she had seen Mini-mini sleeping on the ground. That poor child, Elza had thought, for of course Mini-mini had to remain up all that time in order to help her mistress undress before she herself could go to her room in the grounds.

Elza had crept on tiptoe to the back room which Rutger had furnished as his office and where a writing bureau and his bookshelves stood. Without making a sound she had leaned forward and had looked through the keyhole of the door between the front room and this back room. And she had seen what she already had suspected. In the clear light of the large crystal chandelier she had seen how Sarith sat on the arm of Rutger's chair and stroked his hair. He had looked up and there followed a long, loving kiss. Oh, appalling! Elza had left, running up the stairs, now not worrying whether a step creaked or not. Tears streaming over her cheeks, she had lain on the bed and had pretended to be asleep, her back turned towards Rutger as he came to lie next to her half an hour later.

How could Sarith do such a thing? Sarith, of all people! How could Rutger do such a thing? What was happening? She must and she would talk about this with Rutger. But how? There was hardly a moment when she was alone with him. She could not talk alone with Sarith, either, for she had noticed for quite a time now that Sarith always saw to it that she wasn't alone with Elza. In the morning she slept on, and Mini-mini often had to bring her breakfast in her room. When, and when, around ten o'clock, she was dressed and ready, she would go out – Elza often not knowing where to – and she would always come back late when it was time for lunch and Rutger himself was just home or would be coming home. After lunch everyone went to rest, and Rutger always fell asleep as soon as his head touched the pillow, to wake again at half past three, in time to take his bath and so be fresh and alert at the office with Mr van Omhoog at four.

She must talk with Rutger about this, but didn't know how. But there must be some way for a wife to talk with her own husband.

That Sarith! Why couldn't something happen to make her clear off back to the Hébron Plantation or somewhere else. Elza actually did think that there was someone else in the house who knew precisely what was going on: this was Maisa. She had noticed the way Maisa sometimes shook her head as Sarith entered the room, or the way Maisa looked at Sarith when she was excitedly recounting something. If only she could talk with Maisa about this. She wanted so much to be able to fling her arms around Maisa, weep copiously on her shoulder and feel the dear, comforting hand over her head that she had so often felt as a child, when she had gone to Maisa or Ashana with all her sorrows. But now she was a lady, and had to behave with propriety. And above all, how would she talk about such a difficult subject? She knew, too, that Maisa would never initiate a conversation about this. Some things were the subject of an unwritten code, and a slave would never begin to talk about a delicate matter, even if she had breast-fed her mistress and had cared for her as a mother from birth onwards.

Elza sighed, then heard a commotion and voices at the front door and the excited voice of Amimba, who had opened the door, and there in the dining room stood her father.

"Oh papa," Elza threw her arms round his neck, "Dear papa," and, feeling the tears welling in her eyes, said to herself, "Don't cry: he mustn't notice anything." To avoid his seeing her face she went quickly to the rear veranda, where she dried her tears and called, "Maisa, Maisa, come now, papa is here."

Maisa, too, was happy to see the masra. How was everyone, how was Ashana? And papa told them that Ashana missed them both a lot and complained daily that the house was so dull now all the children were away. Amimba and Mini-mini had to know, too, that their mothers were doing well and sent their love.

"Where's Sarith?" asked papa eventually, and when Elza told him that she was still asleep, papa remarked with a laugh that he had thought that in a town with so many diversions Sarith would be up early. He had a message for Sarith. Her mother wanted her back home. She was expecting a lodger on the plantation very shortly. Even Pa Levi was in the town for only two days. He had arrived yesterday afternoon and would return the next day.

Mini-mini was sent upstairs by Elza to report that she was awaited down below. When Sarith appeared half an hour later and had greeted Uncle Levi sweetly, he told her that her mother wanted her at Hébron. In a few days' time the new Jewish teacher, Abraham Cohen, would come to lodge with them. A few weeks earlier, on his way to Joden-Savanna, he had already spent a good week at Hébron and had then enquired after Sarith. On the return journey from Joden-Savanna to Paramaribo he would be their guest again for five days or so. Sarith declared that she would certainly like to return to Hébron if Abraham Cohen was going to stay there. Hadn't he got bored when he had stayed there a whole week with no-one to keep him company?

"Rebecca was there, you know," father Levi replied.

"Rebecca," Sarith sneered, as if to make it clear that Rebecca didn't count.

Elza closed her eyes briefly. What a relief! Sarith was leaving. What a deliverance! Of course papa stayed for lunch, and Maisa went to the kitchen in the grounds to tell Lena that she would have to cook a little more because the misi's father had arrived.

Rutger came home from the office at half past twelve and found to his surprise that his father-in-law was there. When he heard that Sarith would be leaving he said what a pity that was and how they would miss her. Like a bad toothache, thought Elza. Father thought that it would be better for Sarith to go with him immediately after lunch to Esther's house, since they would have to leave at seven the following morning. But Sarith protested. No, that was impossible. There was so much to pack and she must ensure that Mini-mini forgot nothing. Rutger also protested. No, Sarith must still sleep here tonight and he would himself ensure that she was there at the Platte Brug at seven the next morning together with Mini-mini and all her luggage. That evening everyone went to bed early. After all, the peace had been disturbed by father's visit, and everyone would have to be up very early the next morning.

When Elza lay next to her husband in the large bed, she thought that it would after all be better to say nothing. Everything had solved itself. Sarith was leaving. Rutger would be hers again. Thank God!

SARITH

Sarith was very quiet during the long journey to the Hébron Plantation. Fortunately, Uncle Levi had other company: a new white officer, destined for a nearby plantation, travelled along with him. He was completely new to the colony and Uncle Levi could tell him everything.

Sarith had certainly noticed how this blond young man, fresh from Holland, still with rosy cheeks, had looked in her direction on several occasions. She had greeted him with a slight nod early that morning when Rutger had set her down near the Platte Brug.

She did not feel like talking: she had too much to think about. What kind of situation had she got herself into? Was she in love with Elza's husband? She would certainly not wish to upset Elza, not Elza of all people. They had always been such good friends. But how, then, had it happened that Rutger had so obviously fallen victim to her charms? Had she encouraged him? No, she thought not, or perhaps she had? In any case, she did have to admit to herself that she had not discouraged him. Oh, as always it had begun as a game, but because she was constantly in his company, it had of itself become more serious. But, well, fortunately nothing dramatic had happened: a few passionate kisses, nothing more.

She had, however, noticed that Elza had also seen what was going on, and because of this she had felt less at ease the past few weeks. She had remained in her room in the morning, going out immediately and staying out until Rutger would be back. In this way she avoided being alone with Elza. It made no sense, in fact, his being married to Elza. If she had wanted, he would have been married to her if she had paid more attention to him when he was getting to know them both. But, in fact, she didn't really have an office assistant in her sights: that was all right for girls who were less pretty than her, such as Elza. She wanted a plantation owner. Although, Rutger had the chance to become administrator, of course, but heaven knows how long that would take. She would not want to live in a simple house with front hall, dining room, two bedrooms and only six slaves, and not even a carriage. But fine – now the Jewish teacher would be coming to stay at Hébron. That was something different. A Jewish teacher who was also assistant-rabbi and would later be rabbi. That was someone with prestige and position. The teacher's house on the corner of the Heerenstraat and Klipstenenstraat was a beautiful dwelling, and his annual earnings would be quite respectable, too. For of course Abraham would succumb to her charms and she would certainly see to it that he asked her to marry him. She was, after all, nineteen years old – just, the previous month. No, it was now really time to get married. Just imagine that she might be left on the shelf, the most beautiful of all the girls of her age.

During the hottest part of the day she occasionally dozed off. Mini-mini sat in front of her with a large fan made of feathers and now and then poured her something to drink from the large basket with food and drink that was always well filled on journeys.

Once at Hébron and while sitting with her mother in the front room after their afternoon rest, Sarith had to recount everything she had been doing during her two months in town, and in her turn she had asked her mother when precisely Abraham Cohen would be arriving and had he not got bored during the previous visit.

Mama answered, "Apparently not, otherwise he would not want to come along during the return journey and stay here," but she said nothing more about this. She said only that he was so pleasant and so considerate, so full of interest in everything, and how she had thought then what a pity it was that Sarith wasn't there to keep him company.

A few days later the tent boat of the Jewish authorities came and moored. Sarith was already standing on the jetty. Rebecca, too, was standing at the waterside. Sarith had noticed this and was surprised, since Rebecca hardly ever bothered herself with lodgers or strangers, but she gave it no further thought. With a smile Abraham Cohen came towards her.

"Oh Miss Sarith, you're at home, what a pleasant surprise."

"Is that so?" Sarith asked with a provocative laugh.

Abraham looked at her briefly, laughing, and then turned and had walked with outstretched arms towards Rebecca.

"Rebecca, how wonderful to see you again."

He then took her arm and together they walked back towards the house, stopping occasionally so that he could talk to her while looking her in the face.

Sarith was astounded. Was this the shy, inhibited Rebecca, who hardly ever said anything? She saw a young woman in the bloom of her existence, without a trace of shyness, but rather talking and laughing and not worrying at all about her monotonous voice. So it was Rebecca Abraham had returned to see, can you imagine. Now that Sarith looked more closely she saw that Rebecca was wearing a new, pretty gown and that her hair was elegantly styled. And Abraham, who was enjoying Rebecca's company so much as she walked alongside him, cast not a glance at Sarith.

Oh, thought Sarith, of course this was all because there had been no-one else at the plantation when he was here the previous time. But now Sarith was there, it would be a real disappointment for Rebecca, for of course he would prefer to be with Sarith. Who would want a deaf woman?

But in the days that followed, the situation remained the same. Abraham was interested only in Rebecca. They talked about books and about the Torah. She showed him all her dolls and paintings. They walked together and sat now and then, sometimes on the bench at the waterside, sometimes on the front veranda. Occasionally they would take a trip on the river, and if Sarith was with them, Abraham appeared hardly to notice her. A cursory word exchanged with her and he was back with his full attention for Rebecca. And Sarith became increasingly annoyed. Was it for this she had come to Hébron? Did Abraham not see how beautiful she was? Did he not know that she was every man's lust object, but that she would be his were he only to ask? She really would have to make him look at and listen to her.

One afternoon when they were sitting outside and Rebecca had gone indoors for a moment, Sarith remarked, "You are really paying her a lot of attention, aren't you? Are you really serious about this?"

"Am I serious about it?" asked Abraham, "But of course I'm serious; I find her the most fascinating lady I've ever encountered."

"But she's deaf," cried Sarith.

"So what? That makes her even more fascinating. I believe that the time I've been spending with her has been the happiest of my life."

The reply could not be clearer, and Sarith reflected with not a little resentment that it was indeed for this that she had returned.

When, after ten days or so, Abraham returned to Paramaribo with the promise to return immediately after the Jewish Passover feast, Sarith wanted to travel with him to the town to stay again with Elza and Rutger. It would in any case be better than remaining here. But she didn't know how to arrange this, especially with Passover on the horizon and the knowledge that Esther, Jacob and the three boys would be spending a week at Hébron. So she remained on the plantation, sometimes bored, sometimes less bored, for there was enough diversion. Many tent boats put in at the plantation to 'bide the tide' as they would say. For all river journeys, people took serious account of the tide. You left Paramaribo if at all possible with the flood tide. When the tide turned, you stopped at a plantation and waited for six hours. If night had fallen in the meantime, then you stayed overnight. Everyone took all this for granted, and at every plantation a welcome awaited all tent boat passengers. Plantation owners invited white guests to their table. Bedrooms and bathrooms were at their disposal. Were there insufficient beds, then the guest could always hang up his hammock, inside if he so chose, or in the daytime outside in the shadow of some large trees. Slaves could lodge with the plantation slaves.

During these weeks, Rebecca went around the house with a happy smile on her lips. She was now interested in things other than painting and making dolls, and sometimes she even went to look in the kitchen with Ashana and Kokkie.

Abraham indeed returned after the Passover feast, and what everyone had anticipated now happened: he asked Levi for Rebecca's hand in marriage. Levi was all smiles. He was so happy for her. He had watched that silent child growing into a lonely young woman and he was delighted that she had still found her way in life despite her handicap. Abraham himself looked so rosy and cheerful, mother Rachel was pleased, and Sarith looked into space with a fixed gaze.

When Abraham travelled back after a few weeks, Ma Rachel, Rebecca and Sarith were also in the boat. The first two were going to Paramaribo to buy everything that would now be needed: cotton for sheets, pillow-slips, bath towels and so forth. That had to happen quickly now, for Abraham wanted to get married in three months' time. Sarith went along determined to continue her stay with Rutger and Elza.

ELZA

It had been a happy time for Elza. She sang and hummed and was cheerful. She had never spoken with Rutger about what she had seen through the keyhole that evening. They had, however, talked frequently about Sarith. Early on, Rutger had said one evening, "I miss Sarith; she was always so lively."

Elza had then asked softly, "Do you love her, Rutger?"

"Oh, yes, I think so, just a little bit, in the same way I love everyone, and she is beautiful, isn't she?"

But for the rest they were very happy together as a couple. They talked about all kinds of things, went out frequently and often received visitors themselves. And then suddenly – it was already May – Aunt Rachel, Rebecca and Sarith appeared on the doorstep, the latter accompanied by Mini-mini and one of the De Ledesma's errand boys with a wheelbarrow bearing Sarith's luggage. With a sigh, Elza realized that all was not over, as she had hoped, but rather that things would just carry on as before. Aunt Rachel told the good news in great excitement: "Rebecca is engaged to the Jewish teacher Abraham Cohen."

Rebecca herself looked on with a blissful smile, and then walked through the house to look at everything. Sarith asked whether it was all right to have the errand boy take her things upstairs and ordered Mini-mini to unpack for her. She had taken it for granted that she could stay in Elza's house whenever she chose.

When Rutger returned home, Aunt Rachel and Rebecca had already left. He was clearly surprised to see Sarith and made no secret of it. He gave her a warm hug and told her time upon time how he had missed her. After lunch everyone took a siesta. Rutger usually went for his afternoon nap and was already in bed when Elza came upstairs, since he had to be at the office again at four to go to the stock exchange with

Mr van Omhoog. Today, however, Elza waited alone, with no sign of Rutger. Where could he be for such a long time, Elza wondered. He would surely not want to miss his afternoon nap, especially as they were going out that evening. She got out of bed, intending to go downstairs to see where Rutger had got to, and walked along the passage. But when she was passing the guest bedroom, where Sarith slept, on the other side of the passage, near the stairs, she heard voices in that room. She heard clearly Rutger's voice and then Sarith's cooing titters, and then Rutger's voice again.

"Oh God, no, not that." Elza had been expecting anything and everything, but not this. She suppressed the urge to look through the keyhole, for she knew full well what she would see if she did. She hurried back to her own room. The tears burning her eyes, she lay on her bed, thinking: how low, how dreadful; how could Rutger do such a thing! How could Sarith do such a thing! It was as if she suddenly heard Rutger's words that Sunday afternoon at Hébron: "Promise me one thing: never be jealous." She had promised, but this she had never expected. Who on earth could have anticipated something like this? She knew, too, that she had said that afternoon, "That would surely not happen in my house?"

Had he not promised that? What had he answered when she asked that? She didn't know any more. But no, this was simply not acceptable, and she would tell him so, too. This was too much. Wait – as soon as he left the room she would tell him. But Rutger did not come to her room. She heard him a little while later whistling as he went outside to the bathhouse, and as always Alex had laid his clothes out in the small office downstairs, near the outer door, and from there he went away. She heard the front door closing.

When Elza sat in the front room around six o'clock waiting for Rutger, Sarith also came into the room as soon as he arrived home. Elza was silent during the visit they were paying to acquaintances that evening. Rutger talked with the host and Sarith giggled a lot and talked sweet nothings with the lady of the house, now and then involving Elza in the conversation.

Was Rutger tired out due to his having missed his siesta? Or was it feelings of guilt that made him say, on arrival back home, "We're going straight to bed, Sarith; sleep tight."

In their own room, Elza thought, it's now or never, and said, "Rutger, you were with Sarith in her room this afternoon."

Rutger denied nothing, saying, "Yes, I was there."

"And you went to bed with her," said Elza.

"Yes, hmmm, well yes," replied Rutger.

"Oh Rutger, how could you; how could you do such a thing?"

"Listen, Elza, you promised that you would not be a jealous woman, remember?"

"Yes, I promised that ... but this ..."

Rutger continued, "Oh dear girl, don't take it so seriously. Look, I didn't want this, but she wanted it so much; she pretty well forced me into it."

"Rutger, how despicable: how vile of you to say such a thing. You know full well it's not true." Elza was livid.

"What do you mean, not true? It is the truth. I didn't want it," said Rutger.

"An innocent young girl can never force a man into such a thing." Elza was now really incensed.

"An innocent young girl?" Now it was Rutger's turn to be angry. "An innocent young girl? Do you really think that Sarith is an innocent young girl? Dear child, she is an experienced woman. You are an innocent girl, but she? Do you think I'm the first man she's had in her bed? If that was the case I would certainly not have done it, but darling, you seem to know your stepsister hardly at all. She has certainly had three or four other men."

"Oh no, that's impossible." Elza couldn't believe her ears. "I thought ... I always thought ..."

"Listen Elza, and believe me: she wanted this so much, and when I said that it was better not to, she told me herself that she had first had a certain Charles van Hennegouwen, and then a captain and then still someone whose name she didn't want to mention because it is someone I know and she found it rather painful."

Elza sat on the bed. The conversation had taken a completely unexpected turn. Sarith an experienced woman, she thought. Rutger was right: she didn't know her stepsister after all. She had thought that they knew everything about each other, but she knew nothing about her.

"Come now, my little one," said Rutger. "This kind of thing blows over. Don't be angry. Look – this doesn't mean so much to a man. I don't love Sarith, I love you. Believe me, this is nothing special. Be my loving wife again."

Laughing, he took her in his arms and began to hug her lovingly and tenderly. Elza allowed her mind to be put at ease. With a bit of luck it would be over after this one time. Perhaps Sarith would be so ashamed about it that she would leave. And Elza told Rutger what she had wanted to tell him earlier: that she thought she was pregnant. Rutger was delighted. He kissed her and said that he hoped the child would be as sweet and sensible as the mother.

The next day there was nothing to suggest that Sarith was ashamed of anything. She laughed and hummed around the house. Indeed never alone with Elza, but when Rutger was around she would talk sweetly and amicably, also with Elza. For a whole week nothing further happened, and Elza began to hope that what had happened that afternoon really was the end.

One evening, Rutger had an important meeting. At the instigation of Mr van Omhoog he had been appointed a Master of the Orphan Chamber, that ensured that the rights of orphans and the mentally handicapped concerning any inheritance were respected, and the Annual Meeting was now to be held. When he was leaving, just after dinner, he said at table, "You mustn't wait up for me: it will be a late evening."

After Rutger had left, Sarith said that she would go straight to bed, as she had a slight headache. Elza also went upstairs early on. A few hours later she heard Rutger come home and heard how he said something to Alex downstairs. She then heard him stop at the head of the stairs and say, "Oh Sarith, aren't you asleep?"

She heard nothing further after that, and understood that

Sarith had been waiting for him. More than an hour passed before Rutger came into their room. Elza was angry. So it was not all over, it wasn't just the one time. What a nasty situation. Oh Sarith, she thought, why on earth? Why all this? And Rutger? Why did he carry on despite everything? Yes, she had promised that she would not be a jealous wife, but had she really promised all this?

When Rutger had said that she should not be a jealous wife, she had thought in terms of a passing adventure with a half-breed girl, sleeping occasionally with a slave-girl, or a mulatto concubine if necessary. That was normal; every white man did it and all the ladies managed to live with it. But this? Sarith, of all people. Her stepsister, her bosom friend, the child she had grown up with, from whom from the age of seven she had been inseparable. How was this possible? Oh how she hated Sarith, yes, hated her, but even as she thought this, she saw in her mind's eye Sarith and herself as children. Always together, giggling and laughing, in the same room in the evening, whispering in bed. And then she knew that she could not bring herself to hate Sarith. So, then she would be angry with Rutger. It was he who had brought about this miserable situation; it was all his fault. But then she heard how he assured her that such things were of little significance to him. Elza simply did not know how she should feel. She was angry. And when Rutger came into the room after an hour or so, she pretended to be asleep.

The following morning Elza intended to say nothing at all, but Rutger himself began to talk about it. He stretched his arm out to her, drew her towards him, and said, "You are so sweet, will you always be so? Do you know that Sarith was waiting for me late yesterday evening?"

Elza said nothing. What was there to say?

A few days later on the Sunday morning, Rutger and Elza decided not to go to church. Elza was not feeling too well and had been sick. When Sarith came downstairs and found them, to her amazement, sitting in the front room, Rutger said, "We're just staying in. Elza isn't feeling too well and she needs to take things easy for a while, don't you, my little Elza?"

Sarith looked questioningly at Elza. When she saw a slight blush appear on Elza's cheeks, she understood what Rutger meant. Elza looked up and saw Sarith's gaze fixed on her. No bashful look, nor a gaze of understanding and sympathy, but two rock-hard, icy-green eyes looking at her. Elza saw this and realized with a shock: this is no little sister, but a rival, an enemy, that I have against me. And it was as if an ice-cold hand from inside had wrapped itself around her heart.

It was the end of May; June came along. Rain and still more rain. Hard rain; soft drizzly rain. Everything wet through. Now Sarith usually stayed in her room all morning. If the rain stopped she would go out after all. If not, she would come down again only when Rutger came home from the office. And it happened more often that Rutger failed to come for his siesta in the afternoon or that Elza was alone in the bedroom at night because he still had some matters to attend to. And then she knew that he was with Sarith. Elza sometimes felt like gouging her stepsister's eyes out. That Sarith – she could happily have done something to her. If only she would leave. But apparently Sarith had no plans whatsoever to depart. At the end of the day Elza knew one thing for certain: she did not intend to carry on in this way. But she was also aware that she did not know how she could put an end to the situation.

Each time she talked to Rutger about it, he assured her that it was nothing and that these things blow over of their own accord. She must be patient and above all remember that she had promised not to be a jealous wife. On each occasion Elza determined to talk to Sarith, but she never got the chance, for Sarith ensured that she was never alone with Elza.

Elza also noticed a gradual change in Sarith's attitude. If she had in the past taken care never to make an intimate move towards Rutger in Elza's presence, these days she had no problem with touching his hand, placing her hand on his shoulder, or even leaning on him when Elza was around and could observe everything. It was as if she were demonstrating, "He is mine." All the time there was that provocative laugh, and when the three of them were sitting in the front room, her hand would find its way often enough in Rutger's direction. When Elza was alone and contemplating the whole situation, she saw constantly before her those possessive little gestures and Sarith's triumphant gaze cast in her direction. Elza tried to talk to Rutger about this, but he said that Elza was imagining it all. How could Sarith be making covetous gestures? He most certainly was not hers! Nothing escaped Maisa's all-seeing eye. Elza heard how she often mumbled something in Sarith's presence. She hardly spoke to Sarith, and was usually very abrupt with Rutger. To Mini-mini she did make all kinds of remarks that clearly were not intended for Mini-mini but rather for her mistress.

One morning, Felix, the nine-year-old futuboi[30], Lena's son, was called by Mini-mini to run an errand. He must go and buy a few things for Misi Sarith from a shop in the Saramaccastraat. When Felix came downstairs, Maisa was waiting for him at the bottom. Maisa asked, "And where do you think you're going?"[31]

"I'm going to the shop,"[32] answered Felix.

"Is Misi Elza sending you?"[33] asked Maisa.

"No, the other misi,"[34] said Felix.

"You're going nowhere. This is Misi Elza's house and you are Misi Elza's futuboi. She and she alone can send you on an errand. Take the money back."[35]

Maisa's sturdy arm pointed upstairs. Felix hesitated: what must he do now? He knew full well that every slave in the house did what Maisa said, but now that white misi upstairs

---

30 A younger boy who would attend constantly to every whim and fancy of his master or mistress. In this respect the term is untranslatable, for this degree of servitude is these days inconceivable. 'Footboy' or 'footman' simply does not do justice to the concept.

31 "Dan pe y'e go?"

32 "M'e go na winkri."

33 "Na misi Elza seni yu?"

34 "Nono, na a tra misi."

35 "Yu n'e go no wan pe. Dyaso na misi Elza hoso, yu na misi Elza futuboi, na en wawán kan seni yu go du boskopu. Tyari a mono go baka."

had sent him on an errand: who should he obey? But Maisa, who had noticed the hesitation, grabbed him by the shoulder and shouted, "Get going – take the money back, or I'll throw you against the wall so hard that you'll be knocked into the middle of next week."[36]

And she gave him a push, so that he flew upstairs. It could not be said that Maisa had spoken softly. At the top of the stairs stood Mini-mini. She took the money back from Felix. Sarith, in her room, had also heard everything that had been said, as had Elza, in the front room. When Felix came downstairs again, Maisa took his ear between her thumb and index finger and said, still very loudly, "Listen well, boy. If I ever again see that someone else is sending you on an errand, I'll give you such a good hiding that you'll not be able to sit down for three days."[37]

Elza smiled briefly in the front room, for she knew that Maisa wasn't at all angry with Felix: it was her way of making it clear to Sarith that she, Sarith, had no authority in this home and that Elza alone was the lady of the house. Felix would probably now get an extra large biscuit from Maisa in the kitchen to show that she wasn't angry with him.

Upstairs, Mini-mini slowly entered her mistress' room. Now she would have to go to the shop in the Saramacca-straat, and that was something she did not do willingly, for she was scared of all the men, white and coloured, who were always making remarks and all kinds of suggestions to her. Even before she was in the room, she was greeted with Misi Sarith's words:

"What are you doing, still here? Hurry up and come straight back or I'll make you pay."

Since there was no-one else on whom Misi Sarith could vent her anger, Mini-mini knew full well that she ran a good chance of getting a thick ear, and so hurried off.

36 "Mars go tyari a moni baka, noso m'é hipsi yu meki na sé wan-ti naki yu di fu tu."
37 "Hartyi bun boi if wan tra leisi m'é si taki tra sma seni yu go du wan boskopu, m'e fon yu yere, m'e fon fy tak' dri dei yu no man sidon."

CHAPTER IV

RUTGER

When Rutger arrived at his office one morning in the last week of June, Mr van Omhoog was waiting for him impatiently. The administrator had been visited the previous evening by Daniel Jeremiah, owner of the Jericho Plantation on the Cottica River.

An uprising had broken out among the slaves on this plantation two weeks earlier. They had set the cane in the fields on fire, as well as the warehouse and the sugar mill. The damage had been limited to a section of the fields. The warehouse had been burnt down; the sugar mill had been saved. This had been due to the timely arrival of soldiers and to the fact that overseer Vredelings had immediately shot and killed the instigators. The main instigator's head had been displayed on a stake in the middle of the slave village as a deterrent. The owner Daniel Jeremiah had now travelled to Paramaribo to ask administrator Van Omhoog for a bank loan.

Mr van Omhoog wanted Rutger's advice. Daniel Jeremiah already had a considerable debt at the bank. The total debt was greater than the value of the plantation. The owner was known as someone who was more often drunk than sober and who spent most of his time playing dice.

What should be done now?

"Don't give any further loan," advised Rutger. "Take the plantation and either improve it or sell it." That might well be the best thing to do, Mr van Omhoog also thought, but then the undertaking might not earn all its money back, and could one in fact do such a thing? It would mean that Mr Jeremiah would be made bankrupt in his old age, with no plantation and no income.

"That is his own fault," said Rutger.

Mr van Omhoog hesitated. "He will say that I have refused him a loan because he is Jewish. You know how these things go here: people are always ready to find fault."

For the rest, Mr van Omhoog had the feeling that there was something not quite right with Mr Jeremiah's story. He had claimed that the uprising was due to the Boni-negroes having raided the Voorspoed en Uitzicht[38] Plantation on the Cottica River about three weeks previously. They had killed the owner and overseer, but had left the wife and children unharmed. Most of the slaves had, however, joined the raiders and they had taken with them everything they could use from the plantation. The uprising on the Jericho Plantation was, according to the owner, inspired by this raid, but Mr van Omhoog had a strong impression that there was more behind it.

He had told Daniel Jeremiah that he would have to discuss the matter with his colleague. In fact, what he really wanted was for Rutger to travel to Jericho to see things for himself before they made a decision. How the plantation was looking, the state of the fields, what the white supervisor was like. Answers to these questions were necessary before the company could grant a loan.

A little later, Daniel Jeremiah came into the office. What a shabby type, thought Rutger, looking at the carelessly dressed individual, and how suitable his name is! For Mr van Omhoog began the conversation by saying that the company could really not grant the loan in view of the huge debts that were already on the books. Upon hearing this, Mr Jeremiah immediately started whining. Had he then worked so hard all his life for nothing? Would he have to end his days as a beggar?

He should have drunk and gambled less, thought Rutger, looking at the fat, sloppy individual and at Mr van Omhoog, who was not at all impressed with the man's crocodile tears, but rather continued calmly to explain that Mr le Chasseur would travel back with him to Jericho to see whether the company might still be able to do something.

"Be on your guard there, Rutger, for the man is a sly

38 'Prosperity and Prospect'.

type," said Mr van Omhoog once Daniel Jeremiah had departed, relieved.

At table that lunchtime, Rutger told Elza and Sarith that he would be travelling to Jericho in two days' time.

"Can't we come along?" Sarith asked. But Rutger answered, "Absolutely not. It will certainly not be a pleasant journey. It's a three-day journey before we're there, and it's raining so much. Who knows what I'll find there. And in any case it would be far too tiring for Elza. You stay here and amuse yourselves. I'll be away for only a week or two."

Two weeks alone with Elza was something that Sarith could obviously do without, and she thought that it would then be better simply to return to Hébron. Thank goodness, thought Elza, hoping that Sarith would remain at Hébron a lot longer than two weeks! Sarith left the very next day, on the tent boat of a plantation that lay a lot further than Hébron along the Suriname River.

Daniel Jeremiah had done everything within his powers to make the journey as pleasant as possible for the man who would have to decide whether or not the bank would increase his loan. The tent boat was supplied with different wines, rum, fruit and various roast meats. It was thus a considerable disappointment to him when Rutger kindly refused the drinks and said that he enjoyed something with a kick, but never drank before evening.

Before they left home, Rutger had told Alex to use his eyes and ears well. He must try to learn from the slaves on the plantation how things were there, and he should keep a constant watch on the overseer. Rutger knew he could depend on Alex. From the moment he had been given this young slave, when he had just arrived in Suriname, he had realized what an intelligent youngster he had. For a start he understood everything in Dutch and could speak it, too. As the child of the Van Omhoog's kitchen slave he had virtually grown up in their home, but he had always been wise enough not to let on that he understood everything they said.

Rutger had, however, realized this very quickly, and had made it common practice always to speak Dutch with Alex when they were alone together. When it became apparent that Alex was so interested in everything, Rutger had taught him to read and write. Within a few months, Alex could read fluently, and Rutger often handed him a book. If Alex wanted to know something and asked about it, Rutger would give him a book and would say, "Read about it for yourself and we'll talk about it later."

When Rutger refused his host's drinks in the boat, he looked at Alex with a wink. The tent boat sailed from Paramaribo first to the other side of the river, then along the various plantations to Fort Nieuw Amsterdam, where they could navigate the bend that would take them into the Commewijne River. The tide was favourable. They had sailed on the ebb tide down to the mouth of the river and could now take advantage of the flood tide to sail up the Commewijne. The boat cruised along various plantations: everything looking really fine. A grand plantation house and other buildings; very often pleasant summerhouses at the waterside in which you frequently saw people sitting who would always look up and wave to the passing company. At five in the afternoon they arrived at the Mon Trésor Plantation, where they stopped for the night.

Even by noon, Daniel Jeremiah had drunk so much that he looked really drowsy and was slurring his words. The small slave-boy whose job it was to provide him constantly with drinks had his ear twisted now and then when the glass was not filled quickly enough. Over and over again Daniel told Rutger that in past times the plantation had been a feast for the eyes. Oh yes, in the past, when his wife was still alive. Those were different times, those were. She had always cared for everything so well. Not that it was a dilapidated pile now, oh no, Rutger mustn't imagine that. But even so, the household missed a woman's touch. Women a'plenty for the other, that wasn't the problem; he could have a different one every night if he wished. But women, black or white, were still the cause of most problems, didn't Rutger agree?

The next day passed like the previous one. They departed on the flood tide and sailed on further upriver. Still plantations on both sides, but also large stretches of rainforest in between, and in some places slaves hard at work where new plantations were being laid out. Suriname gold, Rutger contemplated as he sailed along all the plantations and could sometimes see all the labour from the river. Yes, the explorers had been right. There was gold in South America. Not the yellow gold that they had first sought after, but the fertile ground that could produce goods for which there was so much demand: sugar, and now coffee, cocoa, tobacco and cotton. A golden era for the plantation owners and for the bankers in the Netherlands who generously provided credit and got richer and richer. Were the handsome mansions along Amsterdam's famous canals not a striking proof of this? Did the owners of these fine houses have the slightest idea of how that gold was come by? Did they know anything at all about the despicable lives led by so many of the slaves?

The boat could sail as far as La Felicité Plantation on the Cottica River, where they would have to wait for the tide. La Felicité's owners were delighted to be able to welcome the assistant of the well-know administrator's office as a guest on their plantation. When Alex was with Rutger that evening in the bedroom, he said that they would need to sail for only two-and-a-half hours the next day. He had seen how Masra Jeremiah had sent two of his rowers on ahead in a small boat to Jericho to tell the white supervisor that everything must be properly prepared to receive an important guest.

Jericho was a sugar plantation, very large, with more than a hundred slaves. When the tent boat arrived around noon the following day, everything was indeed ready and could easily have fed a company of ten. Grilled chickens, bread, bananas, roasted meats, many kinds of vegetables and fruit. After lunch, for which they had been joined by the white supervisor, Mr Vredelings, Rutger's host insisted that he should take a rest. A nice slave-girl would show him to his room. That evening the gentlemen would play some rounds of cards. The director and white supervisor from a neighbour-

ing plantation had already been invited. The following day
would be soon enough for the inspection to commence.

After his rest in the afternoon and with his host still fast
asleep, Rutger went for a walk outside. He took a look along
the waterfront at the boathouse, then walked along the half-
burnt-out warehouse and into the slave village. It struck him
how quiet everything was. On the other plantations he had
always seen children laughing and playing. Not here.

He was still walking in the village when the slaves returned home from working in the fields. An emaciated,
gaunt group of individuals. No-one laughed, no-one talked.
All silent. When he approached, the group stopped, shuffling
along with bowed heads and mumbling, "Greetings, masra,"
and waited until he had passed.

At cards that evening there was much drinking, shouting
and laughing and the odds were amazingly high. The breasts
and buttocks of beautiful slave-girls who had had to stay up
to serve the masra and his company were pinched on several
occasions, while the two boys got a regular kick up their
backsides. Rutger said little and ensured that he drank little,
and for the card games, with their high odds, he remained a
patient onlooker. He was glad when the evening was over
and he could go to bed. His host had said that he could
choose one of the slave-girls for the night. When Rutger
had answered, "Thank you, but no," Daniel Jeremiah had
laughingly asked whether he perhaps wanted a different one
– there was enough choice on the plantation. He had only to
say the word and overseer Vredelings would see to it. Rutger
had amicably but firmly refused.

The next morning when Rutger awoke and opened the
door to let Alex in, Alex wasn't lying on his mat right next to
the door where he always slept when they were travelling
and staying the night somewhere. He was standing some distance away along the passage and was looking intently out
through the window.

"Look, masra," he said, and pointed into the distance
when Rutger had come to stand next to him. There hung

three naked figures on a large tree, hands bound together with the rope fastened to a branch. The overseer stood alongside and watched how the basya dealt out whip lashes to one of the hanging figures.

"Come, quickly," said Rutger, and, still in his night attire and slippers, he ran down the stairs and into the open, followed by Alex.

"Stop!" called Rutger, when he had reached the spot. The basya looked at the overseer, who nodded briefly, and then stopped with the flogging.

"Release them," ordered Rutger.

The basya looked again at the overseer and began, once he had nodded, to lower the hanging bodies and cut them loose. The overseer's face was strained. He did not like this interference with his business and usually the owner let him have his way. But on this occasion the owner had said that every effort must be made to please Rutger.

"Why the flogging?" Rutger now asked the overseer.

"They deserve it. That one there," and he pointed to the negro who had just been whipped, "has stolen dram, and that one" (pointing to the other) "is more lazy than tired; and this here," poking his stick into the girl's breast, for the third figure was a girl of perhaps sixteen, "has insulted me."

"Insulted you?" asked Rutger, amazed. "How so?"

"She spat in my face."

"Oh yes, and when?"

Rutger looked towards the girl, who, her hands still bound, was looking at her feet.

"Yesterday evening, uh, night," retorted the overseer curtly.

"Hmmm, then your face was certainly very close to hers," remarked Rutger calmly.

"Why have you been stealing?"[39] he asked the slave who was supposed to have been stealing dram.

"I haven't been stealing, masra. It fell on the ground,"[40] came the answer in a whisper.

39 "Yu, san ede yu fufuru?"
40 "Mi no fufuru, masra, ma a fadon na gron."

"And you, you won't work?"[41]

The man turned around in silence and showed Rutger his back. From top to bottom it was covered with huge gashes and festering wheals. The result of a previous flogging.

"You aren't working today," said Rutger to him. "Go to the medicine man."[42]

"Well, enough flogging for today," continued Rutger, now addressing the overseer. "Have they had their daily rations yet?"

"No, not yet," came the answer.

"Well, wait with their distribution; I want to be there. Come along, Alex." And with great strides Rutger returned to the house.

Half an hour later at the ration distribution, he looked at what the slaves received.

"Is that all?" he asked, pointing to the few pieces of sweet potato and the miniscule pieces of fish. "No wonder they're so thin and cannot work. Quadruple the portions and give more fish."

"There is no more fish: after all, it was they themselves who set fire to the warehouse." The overseer made it clear that he wasn't enamoured with Rutger's interference.

"Well, give them eggs, then. There are eggs. And give milk for all small children and pregnant mothers."

"Milk and eggs?" The overseer could not believe his ears.

"Yes, and hurry up." And then pointing to the young slave, "Go to the kitchen and fetch the cook."[43] When the astonished cook arrived, Rutger said to her, "Are there milk and eggs in the kitchen?"[44]

"Yes masra," said the woman with a slight bow.

"Have them brought here."[45]

Everything else passed without a fuss.

An iron pan with milk was brought and a basket of eggs,

41 "En yu, yu no wani wroko?"
42 "Yu n'e wroko tidé, go meki a dresi nengre luku yu."
43 "Yu go na kukru go kari a koki."
44 "Merki nanga eksi de na kukru?"
45 "Seni den kon dyaso."

and everything was distributed among the slaves, who could hardly conceal their astonishment. At the breakfast table Mr Jeremiah said to Rutger that he hoped he would not mind going alone with the overseer into the fields, as he himself did not ride a horse any more.

During the journey on horseback through the cane fields, Rutger tried to get overseer Vredelings talking. He enquired how he found working on the plantation.

"It's all right," Vredelings mumbled. "Far from the town, but, well, the boss doesn't bother himself much with things. Of course it would be better if that black rubbish would work harder and not be so untrustworthy."

"I have heard that there was recently a kind of uprising or something of the sort," said Rutger now, in the hope that Vredelings would respond. But he said only, "They did try, but we soon dealt with them and got even with the leaders. You have to do it that way, or you'll be finished."

Rutger realized that he would not get much further with the overseer. He was curious as to whether Alex would ever get the chance to hear something from the slaves. No, if he really wanted to know what had happened, he would have to think of something else. What if he tried with one of the slave-girls who had so generously been offered to him yesterday evening. That was an idea.

The sun was burning, the journey long. Everywhere they went there was a silent group working hard, and the basya stood on the side with a whip in one hand and a machete in the other. No-one looked up; no-one stopped working.

Returning from the journey round the fields, they stopped off at the sugar mill. There the cane was crushed between three cylindrical rollers, through which each stem passed twice. The sap was collected and channelled off to the boiler house, to be received in a huge wooden vat. From there it was strained off into a large iron pan, known as a kapa. It was boiled, and impurities were removed before it was led into the following kapa, with further boiling and purifying. It was then boiled to double thickness and a kind of acid was added to promote crystallization. Thereafter the mass was boiled more and more to thicken. When it passed finally into the wooden coolers, it was all constantly stirred and shaken. After that, the thick, syrupy liquid would pass into a hogshead. Through small openings it was given a final drying. This liquid was called molasses. After this last processing, the sugar was ready to be shipped to Europe, where it would be refined and moulded in large blocks. In those days around 10 000 tonnes of sugar was transported to Amsterdam each year. Molasses were usually shipped to North America.

Rutger walked around, going from the sugar mill, which was powered by a waterwheel, to the kitchen, to look around there. No-one said anything; no-one stopped working.

When he was back in the sugar mill and happened to be looking through the window, he suddenly heard a coarse scream behind him. He jerked round. Murmuring, shouting, calling from the direction of the slaves. He heard the basya shout something angrily, and as he looked again, he saw a severed black hand between the rollers. The man who had been tending the crushing machine stood wide-eyed, gazing at his wrist, from which blood was pouring and to which there was no longer a hand attached. A few seconds later he fell to the ground in a faint. What had happened? A moment's inattention on the part of the slave. But working with the crusher was extremely dangerous. If only a finger got caught between the cylinders, the whole hand and then the arm and then the whole body of the unfortunate would be dragged in and crushed before anyone could stop the cogwheel. To prevent this happening, the solution was to cut off the hand or arm. Therefore, there was always a basya standing with a razor-sharp axe next to the crusher.

Rutger was dumb with horror. He looked at the black hand between the rollers and at the man who lay there bleeding on the ground.

"Get up, man, get up,"[46] the basya called, kicking at the motionless body.

46 "Opo, dan, opo."

"Mr Vredelings," Rutger shouted.

Vredelings came in, and when he saw what had happened, said calmly, "What an idiot. Stop the cogwheel."

A slave had already run outside to stop the wheel. Mr Vredelings said to the basya, "Remove the hand, or the sugar will be spoilt,"[47] and to his errand boy he said, "Call the medicine man."[48] The medicine man came and the still unconscious body was dragged outside. Water was thrown on his face and he was given some dram to drink. Then he was taken by another man to the slave huts to be further attended to there by the medicine man.

All this time Rutger had said nothing. He could only look at the hand on the crusher, at the man on the ground and at all that blood. Only one thought went through his mind: all this for sugar, and a pound of sugar cost five cents! Five cents for a pound of sugar, and how many hands, arms, legs and human lives were sacrificed for this! He looked towards Mr Vredelings, for whom such a thing was apparently completely normal, for as soon as the victim had been removed from the building he called another slave to the crusher, saying roughly, "And take more care, you."[49]

And everything carried on as if nothing had happened.

During lunch the incident came up in conversation, and Jeremiah's only comment was, "Those ruffians should simply pay more attention."

When they were leaving the table, Rutger said to his host, "You know, Mr Jeremiah, I would very much like to take you up on your offer of that slave-girl for this evening."

Mr Jeremiah looked pleasantly surprised. "Ah, that is good. Do you perhaps have a preference?" "Well, not really. I'll be pleased to leave the choice completely to the experienced judgement of your overseer," responded Rutger, with a nod towards Mr Vredelings. He pushed his chair back and stood up, saying, "With your permission I'll take my nap now."

That evening there were no visitors from the neighbouring

47 "Puru a anu, noso a o pori na sukru."
48 "Go kari a dresi nengre."
49 "Yu betre luku bun yere."

plantation. The three men sat talking, and the conversation concerned mainly the economic situation in the colony. Sugar was a much sought-after commodity on the European market, coffee and cocoa, too. Things were looking good for all the plantation owners. The banks in the Netherlands were generous with credit. If only that black rabble would work a bit harder. They were quite capable of this. They were strong, and after all, God had created the negro race solely for the purpose of working as slaves for the whites. When Rutger asked the men how they knew this so surely, Jeremiah replied, "Come, come, young man: it is written at length in the Torah."

"Well," retorted Rutger, "I have read the Old Testament from beginning to end, and I have never come across that passage. But perhaps your Torah and my Old Testament are not one and the same."

Rutger went to his room early. After he had undressed and Alex had taken his boots with him, he lay on the large bed with his hands folded under his head. He watched a kamra-wintje, a small salamander, which was creeping along the ceiling looking for mosquitoes. Suddenly there came a timid knock at the door, and upon his "Yes" a girl was pushed inside. Rutger sat up. He was shocked. He had expected a girl, a young woman, but what was standing by the door was a child, a thin, small girl, thirteen or at the most fourteen years old. She hung her head and was terrified. You could see this from her trembling fingers, creasing the lower edge of her loincloth. So, the overseer had clearly thought to do him a favour by sending him an untouched little virgin. The bastard! And then suddenly again the image of the crushed hand in the rollers. Now this scared child, and this all for the sugar.

"What's your name, girl?"[50] asked Rutger now.

Very softly came, "Afanaisa, masra."

"Afanaisa," said Rutger softly, and again, "Afanaisa." He looked at the child, shook his head slowly, and then stretched out his hand and told her, "You don't need to be

50 "Fa den kari yu pikin?"

afraid. I'm not going to do anything. Come here."[51] The child shuffled a few steps nearer, but still stayed out of reach. Now he said, "Who has sent you here?"[52]

"The basya, masra," came the whispered answer.

So, the overseer had left it to the basya to take care of this little job. Bastards, those bastards, thought Rutger again.

"Do you know what you have to do here?"[53] Rutger asked.

"I don't know, masra,"[54] was the answer, but Rutger suspected that she knew very well what it was all about.

"Have you ever slept with a man?"[55] asked Rutger.

The girl glanced at him: "No masra."

"What does your mother think about this?"[56] asked Rutger.

"I have no mother, masra."[57]

"Afanaisa, you can go back. I shall do nothing to you."[58] Rutger had stood up and was next to the girl, but she did not leave. She remained standing there, looking at her feet. "You really may go," Rutger repeated.

Really softly she now asked, "Is the masra not going to break me in?"[59]

"No, child, I shall not do that."[60]

Still she did not leave, but whispered in great embarrassment, "It would be better for the masra to do that."[61]

Rutger understood nothing of this. Did the child know what she was saying? With a finger he lifted the girl's chin so that he could look into her face. Tears were in her eyes and

51 "Yu n'afu frede, mi n'o du yu noti. Kon."
52 "Suma seni yu kon dyaso?"
53 "Yu sabi san yu mus kon du dyaso?"
54 "Mi no sabi, masra."
55 "Yu sribi nanga wan man, kaba?"
56 "Sa yu m'ma taki dan."
57 "Mi no habi m'ma, masra."
58 "Afanaisa, yu kan gowe baka yere, mi n'o du yu noti."
59 "Masra n'o broko mi dan?"
60 "No no pikin, mi n'o du dati."
61 "A moro betre masra broko mi."

she blinked briefly. "Why do you want me to break you in?"[62] Rutger now asked gently. While the child answered, a tear rolled down her cheek. "Otherwise the basya will thrash me."[63]

Now it was clear to Rutger. He also understood immediately how the Basya would discover this. Oh bastards, rotten bastards. What should he now do with the child? He was absolutely not intending to misuse her, but neither could she go back. Would he have to keep her there in his room the whole night through? Not knowing what to do, he began pacing up and down the room. Then he went to sit on the bed again and said to the girl, pointing to the floor opposite the bed, "Sit down."

The child sat on the floor. Rutger now said, "I shan't do anything to you, Afanaisa. You don't have to be afraid. No-one will know what happened here, not even the basya; I'll take care of that. But I'm going to ask you a few questions and you must give me exact answers. Is that good?"[64]

The child nodded. And so Rutger came to hear what exactly had caused the uprising.

Overseer Vredelings would have all young women come to spend a few nights with him in his home. At a certain moment he had set eyes on a certain Sylvia, the wife of a large negro man named Kwaku. This Kwaku had said to his wife that she must ignore the white supervisor Vredelings' order and not go to him. When the overseer realized this, he had several basyas tie Kwaku to a tree and had him watch while he raped Sylvia. Not once, but three times.

When Kwaku was released he had been unable to do anything, for the white supervisor walked round with a gun and there were always two basyas with him with razor-sharp axes. Even so, two of Kwaku's friends had managed to talk

62 "Fu san-ede yu wani mi broko yu?"
63 "Bika a basya o sabi en dan a fon mi."
64 "Mi n'o du yu noti, Afanaisa, yu no afu frede, no wan sma e go sabi san e pesa dyaso. Basya n'o sabi, mi e go sorgu fu dati. Ma luku, mi o aksi yu wan tu sani, dan yu musu piki mi. A bun?"

to him, and the three of them would run away with Sylvia. But before they did that, they would start fires. They began in the warehouse. A large group joined them, but Vredelings had smelled trouble, and Kwaku and Sylvia had been shot dead immediately. Help had arrived from a military camp in the neighbourhood, and once the slaves had seen the soldiers with their weapons they had stopped everything out of fear. Because it was not known precisely who had and who had not taken part in the uprising, punishment was meted out by depriving all slaves of food for two whole days and giving all the men a whipping.

Afanaisa was saying nothing without prompting. Rutger had constantly to ask questions, and she would answer precisely the question that had been asked, and nothing more, before falling silent again. But even so, Rutger eventually came to know everything. Around eleven o'clock – the girl had been in his room for about two hours – Rutger had Alex come in. He said that Alex must take the girl back to her hut and say there that no-one must approach her.

She must return the next day. When he saw Alex looking at him somewhat reproachfully, he said quickly in Dutch, "I haven't touched her, Alex, but she is scared of the basya."

When Alex left the girl at her hut, he said to the woman who opened the door, "Masra says that no man must touch her, otherwise he'll get a beating."[65]

And so it was that every evening thereafter, Afanaisa came to the masra's room, and every evening she sat on the floor and answered the questions. After a few evenings she dared to reveal more, and so Rutger came to know a lot about Jericho.

While Mr Jeremiah's wife was still alive it had indeed been a prim plantation and a decent household. Perhaps not pleasant or amicable as far as the slaves were concerned, for Mrs Jeremiah was also a merciless mistress who did not spare the whip. But in those days the slaves always had

65 "Masra taki no wan man no mag fasi en, noso a dati o kisi wan pansboko."

enough to eat and she saw to it that the sick were properly tended. Children and pregnant women were cared for exceptionally well, for the misi knew well that they were her best investment. The masra had always been indifferent, and had drunk and played cards a lot. Everything had gone really wrong only when, two years ago, the previous white supervisor had left and Mr Vredelings had come in his place.

When, after ten days or so, Rutger told Afanaisa that he was grateful to her and wanted to give her a coin, she began to weep and pleaded, "Please, masra, take me with you, please take me with you. The basya will whip me. I implore you, masra."[66]

The following morning Rutger took his leave of Masra Jeremiah and said, "You will hear from us very quickly, Mr Jeremiah. It seems best to me that you come to the office in a week or two's time. And, oh, yes, I'll buy that slave-girl from you."

Mr Jeremiah's semi-toothless mouth opened in a wide grin when he heard this, and he said with a raised finger, "Didn't I tell you, Le Chasseur, that my girls would be to your liking?"

Three weeks later, Daniel Jeremiah stood once again in Mr van Omhoog's office. Mr van Omhoog told him that he and his companion had decided on the following. The company would extend Jeremiah's loan under certain conditions. The white supervisor Mr Vredelings must be replaced.

Mr Jeremiah had absolutely no objection to this. He had always suspected that Mr Vredelings was not that good a white supervisor. While saying this he contentedly rubbed his fat hands together. Mr van Omhoog went on, "The new overseer will remain in the service of this administrators' office. He will report monthly to this office, will receive his salary directly from us, and will carry out the orders given by this office. We will find another plantation for Vredelings. There are always plantations needing a white supervisor."

66 "Ke masra, tyari mi gew no, teki mi, tyari mi gwe; a basya, a o fon mi, m'e begi yu masra."

If Mr Jeremiah was in agreement with everything, he could meet the new overseer straightaway. He could then travel back with him and he could send Vredelings back. Mr Jeremiah was in agreement with everything. This was a load off his mind. Le Chasseur was not so bad after all. He had obviously enjoyed the delicious meals and the delicious women on the plantation.

"Just a moment. You shall meet your new overseer. I'll just go and fetch him," said Rutger, leaving the room. A little bit later he returned, followed by a dark man, and said, "Mr Jeremiah, this is Mr Rozenblad, your new overseer."

Daniel Jeremiah's mouth fell open in amazement. A mulatto? Did they want to give him a negro as overseer on his plantation?

"This is impossible," he stammered.

"What is impossible?" asked Rutger with a stern face.

"A mulatto, a nigger as overseer?"

"A capable, very cultured man, Mr Jeremiah," said Rutger calmly.

Daniel Jeremiah was angry. What a mean trick this was. And he could not refuse, otherwise the loan would certainly not go through.

"So you want to saddle me with a mulatto, eh?"

"You can refuse," said Rutger. "No Mr Rozenblad, no loan."

"And of course I'll have to invite him to my table. What are you playing at?" Mr Jeremiah was no longer speaking quietly.

Rutger remained exceedingly composed, as did Rozenblad and Van Omhoog, and said calmly, "Who says that Mr Rozenblad would want to join you at table? He is used to moving in highly civilized circles."

"I shall write to your patron in the Netherlands about this." Jeremiah's face had turned a deep shade of crimson.

"Do that indeed, Mr Jeremiah. I am sure that Mr Rozenblad will be able to help you in that. He has a fine hand and makes no spelling mistakes. He is also an expert book-keeper. If you would now inform him as to when he is expected at the jetty to leave for your plantation, then our business is completed."

When, ten minutes later, a still angry Daniel Jeremiah had left the office, Rutger laughed out loud. Mr van Omhoog had in the first place not seen much virtue in Rutger's plan, but he had had to admit that a new overseer would be the best solution, and what was there against Mr Rozenblad? The colour of his skin? Rutger placed his hand on Mr Rozenblad's shoulder and said, "Do you still dare to take this on, good friend? Don't let yourself be intimidated; don't be afraid. Do what you think is best."

"I'm never afraid," answered Stanley Rozenblad calmly. "I know what to expect and I'm up to it."

CHAPTER V

ELZA

It was by now the beginning of August, and time for the marriage of Rebecca and Abraham Cohen. Although Rebecca herself did not want a huge celebration, Aunt Rachel felt that it should be a real happening, especially because the groom was not just anybody. A learned man, teacher, assistant rabbi for the moment, head of the Yeshiva, the Jewish school to which all Orthodox parents sent their sons and where they studied the Talmud under his guidance.

When Elza received the message that the wedding of Rebecca and Abraham would be celebrated at Hébron in the week 15–20 August, she and Rutger made plans to stay at the plantation for ten days or so. She would be happy to be home again, to see Ashana and all familiar things around. But how would it be with Sarith? When Rutger had returned from his Jericho journey he had been exceedingly loving and caring. They often laughed at his tales about Daniel Jeremiah. She had shared his anger and indignation at the mishandling of the slaves.

Maisa had immediately taken Afanaisa into her care. She said that the child would need extra feeding, and when she saw what a dear, diligent girl Afanaisa was, so willing to learn, she said to Elza that Afanaisa would make a good nanny once the baby had arrived. Everything in the home was pleasant and peaceful. How would it be when they were at Hébron? Would Rutger again fall under Sarith's spell? And imagine that something were to happen? Would everyone get to know about it? How would she feel then?

Maisa looked forward enormously to the stay, and so did Amimba, for she was going along especially to be able to spend a week with her mother.

The guests for the wedding at Hébron were predominantly Jewish. The ceremony itself had taken place on the previous Sabbath at Joden-Savanna. That had been Abraham's wish. The Sunday after, the couple travelled to Hébron, where all the guests were awaiting them. Rutger and Elza had not gone to Joden-Savanna, but rather had arrived at Hébron two days earlier.

When Elza saw Ashana, she threw herself literally into her arms and cried, "Ashana, oh Ashana, how I've missed you!" Then she toured the whole house to see whether everything was still the same. Of course she didn't sleep in her old room, which she had in the past shared with Sarith, but she and Rutger were to sleep in the room next to Rebecca's: 'the bridal wing of the house,' Aunt Rachel had laughingly called it.

During those first days before the guests arrived for the celebrations, as well as Elza and Rutger, Esther and Jacob de Ledesma were in the house with their three sons, as were David and Suzanna and their two children. How did it happen that Rutger always finished up sitting across the table from Sarith? How did it happen that Sarith was there during every walk they went for and every boat trip on the river? Sometimes she would be recounting something excitedly and would tug his arm as if there were no-one else around, and she even on occasion threw her arm round his shoulder and pressed her cheek to his. It seemed as if she wanted to make a statement to Elza.

When the guests arrived on the Sunday and the great feast began, Sarith's attitude changed. She was really friendly towards Elza and behaved just normally with Rutger. All the guests were interested in Elza. How well she was looking! And, whisper whisper, was there a baby on the way? What a lovely little woman she was, and so pleasant. Didn't that threesome get along with each other so well. Elza and Sarith had always been such good friends. How lovely for Elza that Sarith travelled so often to Paramaribo and stayed with her to keep her company. And Elza wanted to cry out in the face of all that chatter, "Does no-one see what is really happening? Are you all blind? Does no-one see how she's luring him away from me?" But of course she did not do that, but rather nodded and confirmed how nice it was that Sarith kept her company in Paramaribo.

There was nothing to arouse an outsider's suspicions that Sarith had a special interest in Rutger. She behaved normally with Elza. Just as had happened when they were girls, she would often look at Elza and exchange a comment about some guest or other. Exploding with laughter, "Have you seen Aunt There Blows the Wind? She has at least three on today."

'Aunt There Blows the Wind' was a cousin of Rachel's, an enormously rich Jewish widow who always wore broad silken dresses. At every movement she made, the silk skirts would rustle so that it sounded as if the wind was blowing through the house. That was why the girls had given her the nickname 'There Blows the Wind'. Or Sarith would whisper in Elza's ear, with a giggle, "Have you seen Noso? His nose is looking extra large today and he's always wanting to hold my hand." And then Elza understood that Sarith did this only so as not to arouse suspicion. Aunt Rachel had decreed that there must be a large ball, for what was a celebration without a ball? And so there was dancing on the third day there.

The musicians played. Just as at Elza's wedding, everywhere was lit with Chinese-style lanterns and the guests sat at tables on wooden benches, the ladies in beautiful gowns and with artificially exaggerated hair-do's, the gentlemen in their most formal evening attire. Elza saw how Sarith stood near to Rutger at the beginning of every dance, and said something to him, whereupon they would go and dance together.

Elza went to the house and sat on the veranda, watching the dancing couple. When the music stopped and most of the people went to sit down, she saw how Rutger remained standing and began a conversation with a number of men. Five men were standing there in a circle, deep in conversation. Watching her husband, it struck Elza how quickly Rutger had adapted to this country. He's become a real Suriname man, she thought, and when she looked who the men were who were talking with Rutger, she realized that they all had more than one woman. Each of them had a concubine or mistress somewhere in Paramaribo alongside his legally wedded partner. Bitterly she thought – yes, in this, too, he is a real Suriname man: he has two women as well.

The music began again and she saw how Sarith approached the circle of men and said something funny, for they all started laughing. Elza saw, too, how Sarith took Rutger's hand and pulled him in the direction of the dancers, calling back to the group, "I'll take this one for the time being."

Elza closed her eyes briefly and went indoors. She went through the large front hall into the rear of the house and went to stand there on the back veranda. In the distance she could see the faint lights in the slave huts and hear the dull beat of the drums. In the corner of the rear veranda she saw the old hammock that had been hanging for years and years between two posts. That was the corner where she and Sarith had always been sitting or lying together in the hammock, talking, laughing, giggling, telling each other stories or things that had been happening. How many hours had they spent together in that hammock? Sarith and Elza, Elza and Sarith, the inseparable pair.

Elza lay her head dejectedly against one of the posts, when suddenly she felt a hand on her shoulder and a voice saying, "What's up with my little misi, then?"[67]

"Ashana, oh Ashana!" Elza lay her head on Ashana's shoulder and wrapped her arms around her. Tears rolled down her cheeks. She couldn't contain herself any longer, but could only sob, "Ashana, Ashana!"

Ashana led her to the old rocking chair that stood on the other side of the veranda, sat down and sat Elza on her broad lap. The same rocking chair where Ashana had rocked

67 "San de fu du nanga mi pikin misi dan?"

her misi to sleep as a small child; the same rocking chair where she had always sat with her misi on her lap, when she was sad or in pain, or just wanted to feel secure. Now she sat again in this rocking chair, and rocked and soothed her misi. No question here of mistress and slave, just a child who was sad and who sought love and security in the arms of she who, she knew, had always provided that: the most trusted, the most cherished, her Ashana. Here was simply a mother who wanted to watch over her most adored child and protect her, who wanted to banish all sadness and all perils from this child's life. "Shush, my darling, calm yourself now,"[68] came Ashana's soothing tones. Elza would never know how much Ashana really knew and how much she just assumed, but that did not matter. The fact was that she felt Ashana's arms around her, ever trusted and ever loving.

"Elza, Elza, where are you now?"

That was Rutger's voice. With long strides he came through the front room.

"Here,"[69] called Ashana. Rutger came onto the lighted rear veranda and looked on the scene with amazement. Elza like a little girl on Ashana's lap? He was just about to tease her when he saw that she was weeping.

"You're crying," he said, taken aback. "Why are you crying, Elza? What's the matter? Are you ill?"

When she shook her head in denial he said to Ashana, "What's up with Misi Elza, Ashana?"[70]

Ashana looked him straight in the eye and said tensely, "Perhaps you alone can know what's up with her."[71] With these words she nudged Elza from her lap, saying, "Go to your husband, my treasure; he must care for you."[72]

And Ashana went inside. Rutger put his arm around Elza, and said, "Are you crying about me, Elza, is it about me? Tell me!"

68 "Tantiri, ke ba, mi gudu, tantiri ba."
69 "Dyaso."
70 "San du misi Elza, Ashana?"
71 "Kan de na en masra wan kan sabi san du en, masra Rutger."
72 "Go nay u masra, mi gudu misi, na en musu luku yu."

Elza sobbed and sobbed again and said, "Rutger, I know I promised not to be a jealous wife, but when I see you and Sarith like that, I just don't know any more. I can't help it, really."

"Elza, don't cry on my account, not for that: you know that Sarith means nothing to me. Really not. Believe me. But when she comes to dance with me and so on, can I refuse? Can a gentleman snub a lady in such a way? But believe me, Elza, I really care nothing about her. Don't cry any more. Look, I was searching for you all over the place. Let's go and dance."

And with his handkerchief he dried her tears and then he kissed her, first on the eyes, then on the mouth. Then he took her outside to join the dancing company.

The rest of the evening he stayed with Elza and danced only with her. Sarith cast a glance in their direction now and then, but when she saw them sitting so closely to each other, holding each other's hand, she didn't come near, but danced with all the other men, one by one.

When the stay was drawing to an end and the guests were leaving in small groups, Sarith announced that she would return to the town with Elza and Rutger. O heavens, thought Elza, here we go again. But what could she say? How could she say that Sarith was not welcome in her house? No-one would understand. And so it was that Sarith travelled back to Paramaribo and installed herself in the room that was no longer called the guest room, but rather 'Misi Sarith's room'.

Had Rutger perhaps realized how much he hurt Elza by his intimacy with Sarith? In any case, in these weeks following Rebecca's wedding he did not respond to Sarith's advances, and the latter became increasingly restless. She would snap at Elza in answer to a question, or retained a sullen silence with a disgruntled expression. Elza found that the atmosphere in the house was suffering, and wished that Sarith would leave. Poor Mini-mini was really on the receiving end. A twisted ear or a push in the back was almost the order of the day.

One Sunday the threesome was invited to a party at the Lobo's, a Jewish family. A baby had just been born. On the eighth day, the day of the bris milah (the boy's circumcision), guests were invited. After the ceremony, which was performed by the rabbi, there was plenty to eat and drink and some even danced. All the guests brought presents, and although the mother was still confined to bed, this did not influence the degree of feasting downstairs. While Elza was upstairs with the mother in her room, admiring all the baby clothes and hearing about everything she should and should not do in her condition, Sarith danced with Rutger down below, and asked him why he had been avoiding her.

"Oh, I haven't been avoiding you, Sarith, but don't you think that all this must come to an end. It really upsets Elza, and that is something I simply don't want."

It seemed as if from that moment on Sarith's mood changed. When they returned home she was no longer cheerful and chatty, but miserable and pathetic. If she was alone in a room with Rutger, she would ensure that a tear rolled down her cheek. He had to ask her why she was crying, and then came the answer, "Because you don't care about me and you show that so clearly, while I, I love you Rutger, I love you so much."

Rutger was completely disoriented by this situation, and when Sarith waited for him at the door of her room one evening and called him in, he could not help but concede.

Of course Elza had noticed what was happening and realized what Sarith's tactics were. What could she do? Oh, how she hated Sarith, but every time she thought that, she saw Sarith and herself as children again, as girls, always inseparable. How was it possible that it had become like this?

A few weeks later, around the end of September, there came a message from Esther that Sarith would have to travel with them to Hébron at the end of the week, to continue on to the Feast of Tabernacles at Joden-Savanna. Rutger and Elza did not go along. Rutger found that the journey would be too tiring for Elza, and she thanked her lucky stars that her stepsister could end her stay in this way.

But Elza's respite was short-lived, for barely four weeks later
Sarith returned. As a matter of course she installed herself in
'her' room. Maisa could hardly conceal her displeasure. It
was now as if Sarith had decided to win Rutger over completely. Time upon time she contrived ways to be alone with
him and tell him how much she loved him. He should never
have married Elza, but her. Wasn't she so much prettier than
Elza. Did he realize how many men would gladly have had
her, but she had brushed them off, for she wanted only him,
just Rutger.

Although Rutger himself found the situation highly
painful – he was after all married to Elza and loved her – still
it tickled his pride that this beautiful Sarith admitted openly
that she loved only him. Despite his knowing that it hurt
Elza, he found his way often enough to Sarith's room to give
in to passionate love-making. As he saw it, he was the one
who was having a difficult time of all this. If he was with
Elza, then Sarith was unhappy, and oh how easily she could
start sobbing. If he was with Sarith, then it was Elza who
was despondent.

Elza said little. She often sat silently in her room, looking
in the mirror and seeing how the child grew within her, how
her belly got bigger and bigger. How differently she had
imagined all this. She often wondered whether she would
have married Rutger if she had known that this was how it
would turn out. Frequently she heard within herself a voice,
as she had heard him that afternoon at Hébron, "Promise me
that you'll not become a jealous wife? Even if, for instance, I
have a brief something or a short affair with another
woman, promise me that you won't be angry."

And she had asked, "Such an incident or short affair,
that would surely not happen in my house?" How had he
answered? Had he not promised? He must have, surely! And
where was 'this incident' happening, this relationship? Was it
not here in her own home?

But the worst thing of all was that it was Sarith. Sarith of
all people, her best friend, her sister, her playmate. Everything from the past was intertwined with Sarith, who was

now her greatest rival. How confusing, everything, how difficult.

Often enough, Elza asked herself, too, how she would have managed if the roles had been reversed, but she also knew that the answer would always be the same. She would never have done such a thing. Never! She would never steal the husband of the person she regarded as her best friend.

Maisa had a busy time making baby clothes. She taught Afanaisa how to do this, and in the afternoon she would sit with Afanaisa and Amimba on the back steps, and those two sewed and embroidered what Maisa had cut out. Maisa was angry with Rutger as well as with Sarith. She was often very abrupt with him, and if she knew that Rutger had been with Sarith in her room, she would avoid him for the next two days, muttering about 'people who behave like dogs.'[73]

Then, at the end of November, Elza's father came to the town. He stayed only briefly. He wanted to see how Elza was faring, but he had also come to fetch Sarith. They would have to go to Joden-Savanna. Her grandmother, Grandma Mozes de Meza, was seriously ill. She would not be around much longer and Sarith must go there with her mother. After all, she was Grandma's favourite grand-daughter. Sarith departed. Elza hoped above hope that Grandma Mozes de Meza would survive a few weeks on her deathbed before passing away. But this was not the case, and after about a week Sarith's grandmother died and was buried. Aunt Rachel was, however, of the opinion that it was not possible for Sarith to go to Paramaribo during the period of mourning. It was inappropriate to go to dances when your grandmother had died only recently, and the De Ledesmas' traditional ball was also cancelled due to this bereavement. The De Ledesmas spent New Year at Hébron, and this was reason enough for Sarith to stay peacefully at home.

During the night of 10 January 1768 Elza's baby was born. Everything went very well and very easily. Maisa had got

73 "Libisma san e du, leki den na dagu."

really worried, and with the first signs the evening before, Alex was sent to fetch the midwife. Rutger spent a tense night in his small office, and around three in the morning he heard faint crying. Half an hour later Maisa called him and he could see his joyful Elza, her hair still wet with sweat, but with a benign smile on her lips while she gazed at the little boy lying next to her.

Rutger looked at the little head, and, despite the midwife's protests, drew the sheet aside to check that everything was present and correct with his little son. Kissing Elza on her forehead, he said, "All the happiness in the world be yours, my darling, for we have a fine son. What shall we call him?"

"You say it – what name did you have in mind?" replied Elza.

"What do you think to Gideon?" asked Rutger. "That was my grandfather's name."

"Then he'll be called Gideon Rutger," said Elza.

Then Maisa came in bearing a tray with cups of cocoa, and Rutger was sent packing to the guest room where he would have to sleep that night, for, as she put it, it was high time that Misi Elza got some sleep at last.[74]

74 "En nanga misi Elza b'o go sribi now."

CHAPTER VI

SARITH

A few days later a tent boat stopped off at Hébron on its way to a plantation on the Boven-Suriname River. The boat's bell rang, and an errand boy rushed to the jetty to see what was going on. Waving a letter, he dashed back to the house, where Masra Levi was already waiting on the veranda to receive it. Just a little later the house rang to excited shouts and chatter. The letter was from Rutger, and told that a few days earlier Elza had given birth to a son. A hefty, healthy boy, almost seven pounds. Mother and child were doing very well. A beaming Levi told his wife, Sarith and Ashana, who had come running. Within a few moments the whole plantation knew. Ashana wanted to know more. What was the child's name? Whom did he most resemble? Had everything gone smoothly? Was there really nothing further in the letter? Did the child have any hair? What was the colour of his eyes? Uncle Levi had to laugh at Ashana, "I really don't know, Ashana, but we'll go to the town to see him. Come with us and then you can see them for yourself."[75] And Ashana, who hardly ever left the plantation and had been in the town only once or twice, decided to go along to see her misi and her son when the family left for Paramaribo in a few days' time.

During all the lively talking and decision making, Sarith went outside and sat in the summer house. With a book on her lap, which she did not read, she sat gazing into space. So, the baby was born. Elza had a son. No, Elza and Rutger had a son. Rutger! In what kind of situation had the three of

---

75 "Tru tu Ashana, mi no sabi, ma luku w'é go na foto, fu luku den, kon nanga wi, dan yu srefi kan si."

them landed? In fact, she herself did not really understand how things could have gone as they had, but the facts spoke for themselves.

During the past weeks at Hébron she had had ample opportunity to think things through. She had dreamt of the possibility of everything turning out all right for her, and that would happen if Elza died in childbirth. Of course that was possible. So many women die in childbirth. Hadn't Elza's own mother died in this way? Then Rutger would be free and would marry her. At first she had thought that it would be better if the baby died, too, but later on her imagination wandered towards the idea that it would be better if it survived, because with a baby it was obvious that Rutger would have to remarry. And wouldn't people think how sweet it was of her to become the mother of her stepsister's child. And a baby wasn't a problem: enough slaves to look after it and feed it. And of course in that case she would not keep Maisa, but she would quite probably not want to stay anyway if her beloved Misi Elza were no longer around, or perhaps she would, because of the baby. Well, that remained to be seen. And now the baby was born, but not the slightest mention of illness in the letter; on the contrary, mother and child doing fine. But well, anything was still possible.

Sarith had often wondered whether she really loved Rutger. She had told him so, but did she truly love him? In fact, she had to admit to herself that he wasn't really her type, and she sometimes considered him tiresome when he started talking about all kinds of things and when he became angry about the punishments dealt out to slaves and the injustice of slavery. Nonsense, of course. Everyone knew that negroes were put on this earth to be slaves, and you must well and truly punish slaves to keep them on the straight and narrow. But when, on the other hand, she saw how charming he could be and how full of courtesy and concern he was for Elza, then she felt jealousy stabbing at her heart and wanted him just for herself. She sometimes felt like going to their bedroom, slinging Elza out of the marriage bed and going to lie down next to Rutger.

She, too, sometimes wondered how Elza would have reacted had the roles been reversed. But time and time again she had to admit that she knew full well that Elza would not have behaved like this were she in her position. If she were married to Rutger, or anyone else for that matter, Elza would never have come to influence and steal her husband. It was simply not in her nature.

Every time Sarith considered that Elza was married, Rebecca was married, and so were all the other girls of her age, she got annoyed. How was this possible? After all, she was more beautiful than all the others. Men had always considered her attractive. Right from an early age she was admired by everyone for her beauty, and look now – twenty years old and unmarried; an old spinster. The coming week, on the twenty-second of January, she would be twenty. Was there ever a woman of twenty in this colony still unmarried? And that it should be her of all people, she, Sarith A'haron, the most beautiful of them all. When all this crossed her mind she became angry and defiant. This must change. But how? – she herself had no idea.

Three days later they were in Paramaribo. Uncle Levi's luggage and that of her mother was taken to the De Ledesmas', but Sarith's was taken on a wheelbarrow from the De Ledesmas' to the Wagenwegstraat where she would naturally be staying. What a surprise to find the whole family there. The room was suddenly full. Everyone just had to admire the baby, and Elza felt tears welling in her eyes when she saw Ashana. To think that Ashana had travelled to the town specially to see her child. Maisa proclaimed triumphantly that Misi Elza was doing really well, exceptionally well, almost indecently well. A new mother was supposed to be ill for at least two weeks, but this was not so in Elza's case. In fact, if it were left to her, she would be up and around, but Maisa and the midwife would not hear of it. All new mothers stayed in bed for at least two weeks. Who had ever heard of a white woman being out of bed only a week after giving birth.

When Ma Rachel asked whether a good wet-nurse had been found, Maisa laughed. No question of a wet nurse – Misi Elza was feeding the baby herself. She had enough milk, was insistent on doing it herself, and Masra Rutger was in total agreement. There we go again, interfering in everything, saying that Elza was so well and that there could be nothing better for his son than the milk of a healthy mother, and who knows what diseases could be passed from a wet-nurse to the child. And that Masra Rutger there, so pleased with his son. Did Misi Rachel know that he went to lie on the bed with mother and child and found it marvellous to see how the baby was fed? Maisa's dark face was beaming while she was recounting all this, and Sarith got a strong impression that she told it so proudly in order to stress to her, Sarith, that everything was fine between her misi and masra.

Sarith herself hugged Elza warmly to congratulate her on her son's birth. She stood next to the cot and turned to say, "Oh Elza, he's beautiful."

Mini-mini came in a little later bearing a large bouquet with a label, 'Wishing you all happiness on the birth of Gideon Rutger'. With the family around, she just shook hands with Rutger, saying, "Congratulations on your son."

But in the evening, when she met Rutger in the passage on the way to his bedroom, she said, "So, you're a father then." She had intended to make a more sarcastic remark, but that was unsuccessful, for Rutger, with his hand on the door-knob, replied, "Yes, isn't it wonderful?" and went into the bedroom, where Elza was lying with her baby in her arms, and closed the door behind him.

ELZA

Pa Levi could not stay in the town for long. He had come by to see Elza a few times, but had to return to the plantation after a few days because it would be overseer Meker's annual holiday. Of course Ashana returned with him. When Sarith had been in town for a few days – the baby was then ten days old – Rutger said that he had to go to a party that evening. The invitation had arrived two weeks previously. Of course Elza could not go, but he would go with Sarith. Elza had said nothing. Of course she would not be going and she knew that Sarith would be only too pleased to be going alone with Rutger.

When they came home, Elza listened nervously whether Rutger would go to Sarith's room. She rather expected this, but she had heard the front door open had heard the footsteps on the stairs, and had then heard how Rutger said at Sarith's door, "Well, good night then," and the next moment was in their room. She heard Sarith downstairs calling, "Mini-mini, where are you?"[76]

"Oh, you're still awake," Rutger said, and began to describe how nice it had been, that the Lobo sisters were there, girls of fifteen and sixteen. Elza knew them well. Now, they had sung so beautifully. All kinds of songs – French, English, Dutch and especially Portuguese folk songs, and all so sweetly and charmingly. Well, he, Rutger, had thought that it would be good for them to throw a party, too.

In two days' time, on the twenty-second, it would be Sarith's birthday. She would be twenty, and wouldn't that be a good occasion for a party, and everyone could see the baby.

"A party," Elza cried in astonishment, "But Rutger, I'm still confined to bed. How is it possible?"

"Oh Elza, you need do nothing yourself. Maisa will see to everything. I'll give her some extra money to buy everything. I've already arranged for the musicians, and along with Alex I'll see to it myself that the lighting and tables and chairs and everything else is all right."

"But how can I receive the guests if I'm still in bed, Rutger?" Elza sounded really upset.

"That's quite normal here, nothing exceptional. When there's a bris milah for a Jewish baby, the mother is in bed, and the party carries on in the house just the same. I've already invited a group of people from this evening's do, and it will be nice for Sarith to have a party for her birthday."

"For Sarith, of course for Sarith," said Elza tearfully.

"Oh darling, don't be angry." Rutger leant over and gave

76 "Mini-mini pé yu de?"

his wife a kiss on her forehead. "Let's do this for her. Look, you have a fantastic son, but what does she have, in fact? It's surely not all that terrible to give a party for her. She'll feel content and flattered and will only be kinder to you."

Elza said nothing further. Perhaps Rutger was right. Perhaps everything was over between Sarith and him. After all, he had come directly to her.

The next day it was all hustle and bustle in the house. Sarith herself went to Esther and Rebecca to tell them that there would be a party for her twentieth birthday. Aunt Rachel, who was still in the town, had objected briefly: it was, after all, still quite soon after the death of Grandma Mozes de Meza. But all right – the party was at Elza's, and she wasn't a relative of the deceased.

Elza had continually asked Maisa whether she really could not get up. She felt fine. But Maisa was adamant. A white lady simply could not leave her bed before the sixteenth day. Who could guess what consequences that might have. And when Elza complained that most slaves were up and around with their babies after only three days; what was the difference – a woman was a woman, surely – Maisa had asserted brusquely, "Negroes are negroes."[77]

On the twenty-second itself it was really hectic there in the house. Rutger had taken a day off specially. Elza lay in the bedroom with a contemplative expression and heard the footsteps coming and going downstairs. Chairs were set out in the front hall. The long table in the dining room would be used for the supper, with all the porcelain, crystal and silver being polished up by Amimba and Afanaisa.

When Rutger, amidst all the goings-on, paid a brief visit to her in the room and saw her lying on the pillows, he said, "How upset you're looking, Elza."

"Oh," answered Elza with a shrug of her shoulders, "Isn't this just typical of what is going on in this house. A party is being given in another woman's honour, and I can just lie here upstairs in bed."

---

77 "Nengre na Nengre."

"Oh dearest, are you feeling a bit neglected? Please don't feel that way. Look, the party is for our son, too. And who has had this wonderful son, well you, of course! So do cheer up." Rutger looked her in the eye while teasingly lifting her chin with his finger. "But you know what? To make sure you don't feel neglected, we'll come and have lunch here with you in this room, all right?" And he called Maisa from the stairs to set a small table in Misi Elza's room so that they could eat there.

Maisa did so, grumbling, "There'll soon be ants on the baby."[78] But she was nevertheless pleased that Masra Rutger wanted to be with his wife so much that he wanted to have lunch in the room with her. Sarith did not come to eat with them, however. Mini-mini came to say that Misi Sarith wasn't hungry, and so Rutger and Elza ate alone, and Elza was cheerful again.

After lunch, when Rutger was already lying on the bed for his afternoon nap, wearing only thin pyjama trousers, and Elza was half asleep, there came a timid knock at the door. It was Mini-mini coming to say that Misi Sarith had asked whether Masra Rutger could come along briefly.

Rutger left the room. Elza waited and waited. Rutger did not return. Half an hour passed, then an hour. Where could he be? He couldn't be with Sarith all this time. Elza became furious. This was too much. She had to know whether Rutger was with Sarith in her room. She would get up. She let her feet glide from the bed; slowly she stood up. Oh what an unpleasant feeling she had in her legs and feet. It felt as if there were a thousand needles in her feet, and her legs were so limp. Perhaps Maisa was right: it was bad to get up before the sixteenth day. But she had to, just had to. Step by prickly step she began walking cautiously, first to the door and then along the passage, softly, step by step. Oh those feet, those pins and needles. There she was by the door of Sarith's room. She heard nothing. Perhaps Rutger wasn't there; perhaps he was downstairs. Should she call downstairs? But then she suddenly heard soft voices coming from the room.

78 "Dyonsro mira e kon na a pikin."

She bent down, looked through the keyhole, and could just see a part of the bed. She saw Rutger's bare shoulder and she saw Sarith's bare arm thrown round Rutger and her black hair lying over the pillow and across his shoulder.

Elza felt a sharp pain in her chest. Oh, how low, how vile; my Rutger, how could he! And she had thought that everything was now all right, that it was all over between him and Sarith. Sarith: she could happily murder her. She felt faint. It was as if her legs could no longer support her, and there she was gliding away. But at the same moment she felt a strong arm around her, supporting her at the waist, and a voice next to her saying, "Come, my little misi, come."[79] It was Maisa.

Elza didn't know how Maisa had realized that she was there by the door, but the sturdy arm was around her and guided her back to her room. Even before she had reached the bed, Elza was weeping, and sobbed on Maisa's shoulder. Maisa said little at first, but helped her misi into bed and remained, shaking her head, looking at the little lady weeping in front of her, her head in the pillow.

When the sobs had subsided, Maisa began to speak. "We have brought you up, Ashana and I. We have taught you what we thought was good for a white girl. We have taught you to be a dear, sweet woman, to be kind and gentle towards others, to do good. But we shouldn't have taught you these things. We should have taught you to be a nasty, mean woman. Look what's happening now. You're sweet, you're good. But others, they aren't good, they aren't sweet: they're mean and they let you weep. Don't be good any longer, no longer the sweet Misi Elza. Be nasty like they are. Send that woman away. Have her disappear from your house."[80]

"How can I send her away, Maisa," sobbed Elza. "Everyone thinks that we're like two sisters. I can't send her away."[81]

"You must send her away. Let people know that she isn't your sister. No, she isn't your sister. She doesn't love you, she's never loved you, I can tell you that. This is no longer the

79 "Kon baya, mi pikin misi, kon."

time to think in terms of sisters, Misi Elza. Now you must fight, yes, fight."[82]

Maisa looked sternly at Elza. Then she went to the cot where the baby was sleeping, drew aside the curtain and took the child out, who, woken from his sleep, starting crying in protest. With the weeping child in her arms she went back to the bed and said to Elza, "Look: if you won't fight for yourself, then fight for him. Don't allow that vampire to suck his father dry."[83]

Elza was now silent. She dried her tears with the corner of the sheet. It was good that she could speak about this with Maisa. But it was alright her talking. How could she possibly fight Sarith; how could she expel her? What would Rutger say about it all?

"How shall I fight then, Maisa."[84] Elza looked despairingly at Maisa, who had returned the baby to his cot.

Maisa turned and came back to the bed, saying, "If you say that you want to fight, then I, Maisa, will help you."[85]

---

80 "Un kweki yu, mi nanga Ashana, un kweki yu, leri yu ala sani san un ben denki taki bakra misi musu sabi, un leri yu fu de wan switi umasma, fu lobi trawan, fu dun bun gi trawan. Ma a no dati un ben musu leri yu; luku fa wi meki fowtu, un ben musu leri yu fu de wan takru sma, bika luku san e pesa nanga yu now. Yu bun, yu switi, ma tra sma, den no bun, den no switi, den takru, den meki yu krei. No de bun moro, no de a switi misi Elza moro, kon takru leki su, seni na uma gowe, seni en gowé, meki a mars komopo na yu oso."

81 "Fa mi kan seni en gowe Maisa? Ala sma e denkti dati un de leki tu sisa, mi no kan seni en gowe."

82 "Yu musu fu seni en gowe, meki sma sabi taki en a no yu sisa, a no yu sisa nono, a no lobi yu srefi srefi, noiti a no ben lobi yu, mi kan taigi yu dati. Now a no ten fu prakseri sisatori misi Elza, now yu musu feti, ai feti."

83 "Luku, efu yu no wani feti gi yu srefi, dan feti gi en. No meki a asema soigi en p'pa."

84 "Fa mi o feti dan Maisa?"

85 "Taigi mi dati yu wani feti, dan mi Maisa o yepi yu."

"But you're not going to use any wisi[86], Maisa?"[87]

"Never fear; I'm no witch,"[88] answered Maisa calmly. She shook Elza's pillow, picked up a fan and, going to sit next to the bed, said, "Now just get some sleep."[89]

Elza didn't see Rutger again that afternoon. When she awoke later, she heard him talking to Alex downstairs, and he came into the room again only when the first guests had arrived and he was bringing them upstairs to say hello to Elza and see the baby.

A few hours later the party was in full swing. People danced, drank, ate. Upstairs in her room Elza did not get bored, for there were always some guests, mainly the ladies, in her room, sitting with her for a while, chatting and especially wanting to know how everything had gone with the baby. At a certain moment, a silence fell downstairs, and the ladies upstairs heard the Lobo sisters singing. Really sweet voices. And so they sang various songs, each time to loud applause, and shortly afterwards they came upstairs with Rutger, one of the violin players, and some more of the ladies.

Rutger said that they had come to sing for Elza, and they sang song after song. Rutger sat next to Elza on the bed, looking at the girls and at his wife. "Well, Elza, what do you say to that: your own serenade. There are not many women who can say that they have had a serenade in bed just after giving birth." And he caressed her hair fondly.

After singing, the girls wanted to stay upstairs a while to chat with Elza. They sat in the cane bedroom chairs and Rutger sat on the bed next to Elza. Everyone was laughing and chatting. More and more people came upstairs. The room was full with laughing and chatting guests. Downstairs people went on dancing. Rutger went downstairs to dance with one lady, then another. When he was about to return

86 Black magic.
87 "Ma yu n'o du wisi toch Maisa?"
88 "Yu no afu frede, mi a no wisiman."
89 "Dan sribi now."

upstairs with one of the Lobo sisters on his arm, an angry Sarith suddenly appeared in front of him.

"Where have you been? I've not seen you at all. You're neglecting me," she snapped.

"Me, neglecting you?" cried Rutger in surprise. "My dear child. This whole party is in your honour. How can you possibly say that I'm neglecting you?"

And he went on upstairs, to come down a little later with the other Lobo sister on his arm.

Sarith was furious. Rutger had not had a single dance with her the whole evening. He seemed to be particularly enchanted by the little singers and for the rest had spent almost the whole evening with Elza in her room. That wasn't how she had imagined the evening. When she had enticed Rutger into her room that afternoon and had pretty well seduced him, she had imagined how she would be dancing with him the whole evening while Elza remained alone in her room. And now everyone was continually going upstairs to Elza. Oh, plenty of men who wanted to dance with her, but not Rutger. Angrily she went into the front hall. In any event, she did not go upstairs.

The party went its lively way, the company upstairs increasing all the time. It was well after midnight when the guests took their leave and departed in small groups, some in carriages, some on foot, led by various slaves bearing lanterns. The slaves who had accompanied their masters had spent the whole evening in the grounds near the slave quarters and had also had food and drink.

The Lobo sisters were among the last guests to depart. In his role as gallant host, Rutger escorted them to their carriage, which stood in front of the door. As he returned indoors, Sarith stood at the open front door.

"And, Sarith, were you pleased with your party?" asked Rutger amicably.

"Pleased? Pleased?" Sarith's voice was shrill. "The whole evening Annètje and Meta, Meta and Annètje" – this came with a tone that sounded as if she was imitating someone – "I know what you're after, you're certainly in love with one of them: just admit it."

Rutger gazed in astonishment at the irate creature opposite him.

"Oh Sarith, don't be so absurd," and walked on. But Sarith followed him.

"Oh yes, now I'm absurd, eh? That's what you think of me."

"Go to bed Sarith, you must be tired," said Rutger calmly.

Rutger went upstairs. Sarith followed him and her voice became increasingly more piercing.

"I know what you want, you want one of them, and you want to cast me aside."

While she said this, she grabbed Rutger's hand. Now he got angry. He knocked her hand aside, saying curtly, "How can I cast you aside, you aren't even mine. Don't set yourself up like this."

"So, I'm not yours, eh, not yours!" Sarith was now screaming.

"No, you're not mine. My wife is here inside."

With these words Rutger opened the door of the room, went inside and slammed the door in Sarith's face.

"Shhh, if you're not careful you'll wake the baby," said Elza, who had heard everything. Secretly she was rejoicing. Rutger and Sarith were fighting. Wonderful! She had wanted to say something to Rutger about what she had seen that afternoon, but this was much better.

"Can you imagine," said Rutger, "that creature making such a jealous scene?"

"Hmmm," said Elza placidly, "perhaps she regards it as her right."

"Right? She has no right whatsoever."

Angry, Rutger began to undress.

"Quiet there; think of the baby," said Elza soothingly.

Rutger must certainly not be angry with her. When he came to lie next to her, she said, "How sweetly those girls sang, eh? We must invite them more often, we're sure to become good friends." And she thought to herself that this might be the best way to get rid of Sarith.

MAISA

The morning after the party, really early, while everyone was still asleep and even the slaves' quarters in the grounds were shut tight, Maisa went out through the negroes' gate into the street. She went to the market in the Oude Oranjetuin. Here the slave market was held and all kinds of provisions could be bought. Arriving at the market, which was already quite busy, she first talked with a woman selling fruit, bought a few large mangoes and was directed to an old woman selling dried fish, sitting behind her wares with a small stone pipe in her mouth. Maisa bought a few pieces of fish from her and struck up a conversation with the old woman. She took the pipe from her mouth, spat copiously behind her on the ground, and began to explain something in detail to Maisa.

Shortly thereafter, Maisa left the market, going with quick steps in the direction of the Saramaccastraat. She had a long walk ahead of her, for she was going to Kau-Knie. There she would visit Ma Akuba. Nene[90] Duseisi, the fishmongress, had just explained to her where she could find Ma Akuba: someone who would help her beloved Misi Elza and free her from the cursed Misi Sarith.

Among the slaves it was well known that this Ma Akuba was familiar with everything to do with magic, and she lived together with Ta Agosu, who was a magician. When she arrived at the small, unsightly house that stood on an open, uncultivated plot of land, she stood by the door and called out, "Good morning, Ma Akuba."[91]

"Who's wishing me good morning?"[92] came a voice from within.

"It's me, Maisa, I've come to ask Ma Akuba something."[93]

The door was pushed open. On a small bench inside sat Ma Akuba, an elderly negress, heavily built, with a rugged face and sharp, piercing eyes. Her hair was completely greyish yellow with old age. She had all kinds of incisions on her face, shoulders and back, and was dressed in a wrap that was fastened under her breasts.

She looked severely at Maisa, who stood outside in the

grounds, took a small pipe out of her mouth and said, "Who is Maisa? I don't know you."[94]

"I'm Misi le Chasseur's slave. I used to live on the plantation and am new in the town, but Ma Akuba's friend Nene Duseisi, she has sent me."[95]

"Well, sit down, then,"[96] Ma Akuba grumbled in response, waving towards the doorstep. "Tell me what's the matter."[97]

Maisa began to speak, and talked about her misi and her husband, between whom everything was in fact all right, and about the other woman who was influencing her misi's husband and enticing him away from his wife. The old woman went into a small room and came out again with a small jug of water, an earthenware dish, a candle and a small mirror. She sat down, poured some water from the jug into the dish, lit the candle and held the mirror in front of it. Looking intently into the mirror, she mumbled a few words. Then she blew out the candle, closed her eyes and remained sitting like that for a while. After that she poured the water from the dish back into the jug and held the empty dish in front of Maisa. Maisa hurriedly pulled a knotted handkerchief from the pocket of her dress and placed a guilder in the dish. Ma Akuba said, "I shall make something for you, but then you must bring a chicken, three eggs, a bottle of sweet rum and a piece of clothing belonging to your masra and one from the other woman. Bring these tomorrow evening."[98]

"Thank you, Ma Akuba, thank you so much!"[99]

Maisa stood up and left the grounds hastily, for in fact she

94 "Dan suma na Maisa dan, mi no sabi yu."
95 "Mi na misi Le Chasseur srafu. Mi ben libi na pernasi fosi. Na pas-pas mi kon a foto, ma na Ma Akuba mati, Néné Duseisi seni mi dyaso."
96 "Hmmm, we sidon dan."
97 "Taigi mi san de fu du."
98 "Mi o meki wan sani gi yu, ma dan yu musu tyari wan fowru, dri eksi, wan batra switi sopi, nanga wan pis krosi fu yu masra nanga wan fu na tra uma. Tyari den kon tamara neti."
99 "Gran tanyi baya Ma Akuba, gran tanyi."

found the whole business exceptionally creepy, but she would do anything to see her Misi Elza happy.

When she arrived home everyone was already up and there was much whispering and giggling between Afanaisa, Amimba and Mini-mini. What was going on? The three girls couldn't wait to tell Maisa that Misi Sarith and Masra Rutger had had a quarrel. This morning, when Masra Rutger was having breakfast, Misi Sarith had come into the dining room, still in her nightclothes, and had said all kinds of nasty things to him. He had become angry, had got up from the table and had said that he could do what he liked in his own home and if Misi Sarith didn't like it, she could leave. With these words he had left, and she had gone upstairs almost in tears. After that she had Mini-mini massage her back, and Mini-mini could see that she was crying. Excellent, thought Maisa, that's going well. Every slave in the house knew, of course, what was going on, and everyone, even Mini-mini, who was after all Sarith's slave-girl, was on Elza's side.

Maisa hoped that this would be enough to precipitate Misi Sarith's departure, but leave she did not. She remained in her room the whole day, sulking, and had Mini-mini bring her food and drink. Maisa pondered how she would get hold of one of Misi Sarith's items of clothing. She told Mini-mini to bring Misi Sarith's dirty clothes downstairs and told her later that Lena had scorched one of Misi Sarith's blouses while doing the ironing. Mini-mini didn't have to be afraid, she, Maisa, would tell Misi Sarith herself. A little later she knocked on Sarith's door. When Sarith called out, "Enter," she was shocked to see Maisa standing there. She was scared of Maisa, for she knew that she was so fond of Elza. Perhaps Maisa had come to send her packing. When Maisa apologized for the scorched blouse, Sarith was greatly relieved. "It's nothing, Maisa, let it be," she said. What was a scorched blouse to her: there were far worse things in the world.

ELZA

The next day Maisa finally allowed Elza to get up. Before she was dressed, Maisa wound several cloth bands around her waist, quite tightly, to ensure that she would keep her figure. Then she went step by step downstairs to the dining room, where she was installed in a rocking-chair next to the window.

Sarith had remained sulking in her room for two whole days, but seemed eventually to have come to terms with the fact that she was after all a guest in the house and really could not behave in this way. She came downstairs, spoke with Elza and also with Rutger, and then went on to read a book. Elza thought that it would be good for Rutger and Sarith to remain angry with each other, and considered how she could manage this.

In bed that evening she asked Rutger what he thought of having a few guests round for lunch the following Sunday.

"Won't it be too tiring for you," Rutger asked.

"No, it would be fine to have some people around me on the first Sunday I'm up and about. After all, I'm not actually ill. What would you think of the Van Schaiks and the Lobo girls, and perhaps Chaim and Hanna Lobo with their baby?"

Rutger was in agreement. In the morning – it would be Friday already – he would send Alex to the various addresses with a message.

In the meantime Maisa had taken the various things to Ma Akuba the evening after her first visit and had heard that she should come on Saturday to collect what was necessary. After she had donated another guilder that Saturday evening, she received a drink in a small black bottle, with the express command to add half a teaspoonful to the bad woman's first drink of the day.

Sarith was now being extremely pleasant and sweet to Rutger. She had realized that she would not get much further by being angry with him, and had conceived a plan. She had been invited to the country home of the De Miranda's in the Combé. She would go there with Rutger, but would tell him only on Sunday morning, since she was afraid that he would otherwise talk it over with Elza, and she would say that he must remain with her.

Sunday morning Rutger had gone to church alone and Sarith was up early. Mini-mini was making a cup of coffee for her mistress in the kitchen. While she was doing this, Maisa sent her, with great urgency, to fetch a bucket of water from the rainwater butt. While Mini-mini was away, Maisa added the drink to Sarith's coffee.

When Rutger returned from church, Elza was already sitting in the dining room. Sarith came in a little later. She was dressed prettily in a white muslin dress decorated with small pink bows. Sweetly she began, "Rutger, I've been invited for a meal at the De Mirandas' country house. I thought it would be nice for you to come along with me. You'll just be sitting here at home otherwise."

"That won't be possible," said Rutger, looking at her, "We ourselves are having guests for lunch here. Didn't you know that?"

Sarith had not expected this at all.

"Oh, didn't you know, Sarith," said Elza, "We're having guests, yes, the Van Schaiks and Meta and Annètje Lobo. Rutger is going to pick them up shortly in the Van Omhoogs' carriage."

Sarith was angry: those Lobo girls again. Of course Elza had deliberately contrived this just to annoy her.

"Of course, the Lobo girls! So you're not going with me," she screamed at Rutger.

"No, I'll stay here with my guests," came the calm answer. Sarith was furious and looked for words to offend both Elza and Rutger. She said to Rutger, "Oh, of course, I know what you're after. Of course you want to get them into bed."

Rutger turned crimson and replied icily, "That kind of thing I leave completely to you, Sarith."

"You're out to tease me, eh?" Sarith stamped her foot angrily. "I know you can do without my company. I'm not staying here a minute longer. I'm leaving."

"Do feel free to go," said Rutger, "You're certainly not pleasant company."

Sarith stormed out of the room, called Mini-mini and rushed out of the front door, slamming it behind her.

In the kitchen quarters near the back door all the slaves had been following this scene. Maisa danced around the veranda. It was working, the drink was working! Misi Sarith had left the house in a temper. When, a little later, she sent Afanaisa upstairs to clean up Misi Sarith's room, since Mini-mini was also away, she saw Afanaisa come down again with a full cup of coffee. Maisa then understood that Misi Sarith had not drunk any of the coffee. Well, that meant that the drink was so powerful that just its presence had influenced Misi Sarith.

CHAPTER VII

SARITH

An angry Sarith walked along the street, so fast that Mini-mini, who was holding a parasol above Sarith's head, almost had to run to keep up with her. When she left the house she had no idea where she was going. She had wondered for a moment whether it might not be better to go to Rebecca's, which was just around the corner. But she had immediately thought better of that. Rebecca and Abraham were real sweethearts, focused entirely on each other. They would certainly be amazed if Sarith suddenly appeared like this. No, she went to Esther's. Her mother was still staying there. As she continued walking along in the direction of the Saramaccastraat her anger steadily increased. "Do feel free to go," Rutger had said. If only he were here this minute! She would gouge his eyes out! She no longer felt like going visiting. When she arrived at the De Ledesmas' it turned out that her mother Rachel was planning to leave for Hébron in about two hours' time, taking her son-in-law's boat when the tide began to come in. Her mother assumed that Sarith knew that she was leaving and had come to say goodbye. Sarith left it at that.

"Aren't you staying at Elza's any more?" asked a curious Esther when, after Rachel had departed, she heard Sarith telling Mini-mini that after the afternoon rest period she must go with an errand boy to fetch her belongings from the Le Chasseurs'.

"No, I prefer to stay here," replied Sarith, "I can't sleep because of the baby's yelling."

And so she remained at Esther's for a few days; here and there a visit, now and then with Esther and Jacob to a party or an evening with acquaintances.

When one morning she was at Rebecca's and heard that Abraham and his wife would be going to Joden-Savanna the next day and would stay some days at Hébron, Sarith decided to go with them. Once at Hébron she didn't carry on to Joden-Savanna, but stayed at home, bored and getting irritated and grumbling about anything and everything. Since there was no-one to talk with, she talked with Mini-mini. Mini-mini had to give her a massage every day and time and time again answer the question: wasn't her Misi Sarith oh so beautiful. Patiently, Mini-mini would say each time, "Yes Misi Sarith, you are beautiful."[100]

Now and then she would go by boat to a neighbouring plantation or go visiting with her mother for a few hours. Sometimes there were visitors at Hébron itself: passing tent boats that had to wait for the tide, passengers who sometimes stayed overnight. But in general it was pretty dull. Sarith was continually worrying. She was twenty years old, exquisitely beautiful, unmarried, not even engaged, and could not really think of anyone she would readily marry. And then you had Elza and Rutger playing the happy young couple with their baby there in that little house on the Wagenwegstraat. But wait a moment: she would change her tactics. She would return to Paramaribo and be really sweet to Rutger. Of course he would fall completely for her charms, and once she had him well and truly caught, she would make it plain that the role of happy father was nothing for him.

ELZA

Little Gideon was growing apace. He was now four months old, a high-spirited baby who hardly ever cried and often lay playing in his cot. Elza still fed him herself. When Rutger came home from work he would often spend hours playing with his son on the large bed. Elza often had to laugh, moved as she was at how convinced Rutger was that there was no child more handsome and intelligent than his.

Coming home from the office one afternoon, Rutger

100   "Yia misi Sarith, yu moi ba."

asked Elza while they were eating, "Who do you think came by the office today?"

When Elza asked who that was, he answered, "Sarith."

"Sarith? What did she want at your office?"

"She came to apologize for her behaviour recently and to ask whether she could come to stay with us again."

"And what did you tell her?" asked Elza.

"That it was all right, of course," replied Rutger, and, looking at his wife, "There was nothing else I could do!"

Elza said nothing, but thought to herself how stupid she had been to have imagined that they were now rid of Sarith. She would return and everything would just start up again.

Early that evening, around six, when Elza and Rutger were sitting in the front room, Sarith indeed appeared. She behaved as if nothing had ever happened, greeting Elza and Rutger sweetly and telling Mini-mini to take her things upstairs and unpack. In the days that followed she was exceptionally friendly towards both Rutger and Elza, though she hardly glanced at the baby.

Once when she saw Rutger alone in the dining room sitting on a rocking-chair with his son, she sneered, "So, you're playing the role of devoted father very well."

"I'm not playing a role: I am a devoted father," said Rutger, and he continued talking to his child and paid no further attention to Sarith, who realized that if she was to win Rutger over again she would have to try different tactics. She decided that from now on she would pay all the more attention to the child and take every opportunity to say how handsome and sweet he was.

When she came downstairs the next afternoon, she saw Afanaisa standing on the back step with the baby on her arm. She went to the child and tickled his chin, and when he began to laugh she wanted to take him from Afanaisa, but Maisa's stern tones rang out from the stairs, "Afanaisa, bring the young masra here: his nappy needs changing."[101]

---

101 "Afanaisa, tyari a yongu masra kon dya, a musu kenki en pisiduku."

At the top of the stairs Maisa took the baby from Afanaisa and disappeared into the room with him. There she said to Elza, "If you don't want your child to get fyo-fyo[102], don't let that woman touch him."[103]

Elza started. Fyo-fyo! She didn't know what it was precisely, but it was in any case something really terrible. Babies and small children could die from it. She thought of Maisa's words when Gideon was born. She would have to fight for him. Well, she was prepared to fight for him. With everything, if necessary.

Sarith continued being sweet and affectionate towards Rutger. She tried everything: laughed with him, even wanted to pour coffee for him when they sat eating. Elza saw all this and also noted how Sarith was becoming increasingly unfriendly towards her, often saying nothing to her the whole day long, or perhaps just making a snide remark.

One afternoon, around the time that Rutger usually arrived home, the baby lay on a mat on the dining room floor, while Afanaisa sat next to him on the ground. Sarith came into the room, looked at the child, bent down, picked him up and went with him in her arms to stand on the porch in front of the house. Elza came into the dining room, saw that the child wasn't there, and asked Afanaisa, "Where is Masra Gideon?"[104]

"Misi Sarith has taken him with her, to the front veranda,"[105] came the answer.

Elza flew outside onto the veranda, grabbed the child from Sarith's arms and snarled, "Keep away from him; he's my child." Once indoors, she passed the child to Afanaisa, saying, "Take him upstairs."[106]

Sarith could say nothing. She had wanted to set a tender

102 In Creole folklore the belief is held that arguments between parents and/or relatives can influence a child's health.

103 "Misi Elza, luku dya: Efu yu no wani yu pikin kisi fyo-fyo, nomeki na uma fasi en."

104 "Pe masra Gideon de?"

105 "Misi Sarith teki en tyari go na mofodoro."

106 "Tyari en go na sodro."

little scene for Rutger when he came home, but hadn't reckoned with Elza's reaction.

After lunch, when they had already retired to their room for the afternoon nap, there came a gentle knock on the door. It was Mini-mini: "Misi Sarith is asking whether Masra Rutger can come to hear something."[107]

Rutger left the room. Elza was furious. On edge, she waited to see whether Rutger would return or whether he would stay with Sarith in her room as on the previous occasion. In Sarith's room, Rutger stood in the doorway. "What's up, Sarith?" he asked.

"Oh, Rutger, could you just look at my back? I think some insect or other has bitten me there." Rutger gazed at the pretty young woman standing there with her hair hanging carelessly over her shoulders, dressed in only a very thin batiste shirt. He knew what her intentions were and said calmly, "I think it would be better for Mini-mini to take a look at you. Will that be all?" and made to turn around. This was something Sarith had not expected. With one leap she was upon him, grabbed him by the arm and pushed the door closed. "Oh Rutger, what is it? Don't you love me any more; don't you want me?" She put her arms round him and lay her head on his chest.

He loosened her grip and said steadily, "No, Sarith, not this, not any more," and left the room.

"What did Sarith want?" asked Elza when, to her relief, Rutger returned promptly.

"Oh, she wanted me to look at something or other on her back."

"It just never stops, does it, hey?" said a now angry Elza, "And next time she'll succeed in getting you so far."

"Elza, Elza, think about your promise that you'll not be a jealous wife," said Rutger. Now or never, thought Elza. I must – absolutely must – act now, and she thought of what Maisa had said about fighting. If she couldn't remember ex-

107 "Misi Sarith seni aksi efu masra Rutger kan kon yere wan sani."

actly how Rutger had replied when she had asked that such a relationship should not happen in her own house, then Rutger probably did not remember, either. "Why must I keep to my promise when you don't?" she asked sharply.

"What do you mean?" Rutger had already lain down, but sat up again.

"Don't you remember, when you said I must promise not to be a jealous wife? Then I asked that such an incident or relationship should not happen in my house. And what did you say?"

"I will have said no, it wouldn't," replied Rutger.

"Don't you have to do what you promise, then? Is the relationship with Sarith not in this house, or is this not my house?"

"Of course this is your house, Elza," replied Rutger, now thinking that she was in fact quite right: the conversation had gone like that. And, indeed, he had not kept his word.

"Well, since this is my house, I don't want Sarith lodging here any longer, and especially I don't want my child to get fyo-fyo."

"Oh, stuff and nonsense, that fyo-fyo. Don't start believing in all this black superstitious nonsense."

"Superstition or not, I don't want Sarith staying here any longer." Elza sounded most decisive.

"Tell her, then," said Rutger calmly.

"No, absolutely not: it's you who must tell her. After all, it's you she's here for."

Rutger got out of the bed and said, "All right. I'll have her called right now." He opened the door and called to Mini-mini, who was sitting at the top of the stairs, "Mini-mini, ask Misi Sarith to come here."[108]

A little later Sarith stood there with them in the room, still dressed in the thin shirt. "Sarith, Elza does not want you to stay here any longer," said Rutger.

Sarith looked at them both and then said to Rutger, "And what do you think?"

108 "Mini-mini taigi misi Sarith mek' a kon dyaso."

"Well, I think my wife is right," said Rutger.

Sarith's inside froze with anger. So she was being sent away, simply expelled. "Right, I shall go. I shall go right now and never come back. Of course everyone will be astonished, and will wonder why I'm suddenly no longer welcome in the house of my dear stepsister." The last words were spoken really hatefully.

"Tell them the truth, Sarith." Elza sounded really calm. "Just tell them the truth. Tell them that your dear stepsister doesn't want you in the house any more because you keep trying to get her husband into bed. Tell them that, and then everyone will understand."

Furious, Sarith turned away and left the room.

Voices had been decidedly not soft, and Maisa and Mini-mini had heard everything from the stairs. Maisa danced down the stairs. "Just what she deserves. Misi Elza has got that skunk good and proper now."[109]

From her room, Sarith called Mini-mini to pack her things, and she herself made so much noise throwing things around that no-one got any rest that afternoon.

When Rutger came out of his room later that afternoon for his bath, she was waiting for him in the passage, and said, "Rutger, when I'm somewhere else, will you come and visit me?"

"Certainly not, Sarith, that's something I shall not do."

"So I won't see you again?" Sarith's voice was tearful.

"Oh, Paramaribo is so small, we'll be sure to see each other."

"But you're sending me away. Everything's over and done for, isn't it?"

"I think this is better for all concerned. Good bye, Sarith." And Rutger hastened towards the bath-house.

An hour later Sarith left the house in the Wagenwegstraat. She had never felt so humiliated. Oh, she would get her own back. She would find a way to repay this rejection and insult.

109 "Hai hai, kisi en moi. Misi Elza kisi na sakasaka."

SARITH

Still angry, Sarith arrived back at Hébron Plantation a few days later. Mother Rachel was surprised to see her daughter back at the plantation so soon, but, used to the girl's whimsical nature, she enquired no further. Sarith grumbled around the house, threw things around in her bedroom, continuously scolded Mini-mini, who could do nothing right. In short, she was abominable.

Ashana rejoiced. She had heard exactly what had happened. Mini-mini had told her mother, Kwasiba, everything, and Kwasiba had in turn told Ashana. Although Kwasiba and Mini-mini were in fact mother Rachel's slaves, they really liked Elza because she treated them so pleasantly, quite unlike the spoilt Sarith, who regarded slaves just as creatures who must serve her and always be there for her, never taking into account that they were people, too, and people with feelings. The domestic slave-girls knew what had been going on and all had taken Misi Elza's side.

Sarith had now been back at home a few days and was sitting at the breakfast table one morning. She was alone. Her mother was upstairs and Uncle Levi had left on the boat, visiting a plantation further upriver. She had given Mini-mini a thick ear because she came to say that there were no oranges to make juice. Ashana came in, and hearing Sarith going on, said, "The pig says: what's yours remains yours."[110]

"What did you say, Ashana?"[111] cried Sarith, realizing that this was meant for her.

Ashana repeated what she had said.

"What do you mean by that?"

Ashana replied really calmly, "I'm happy that Misi Elza has come to her senses and has chased the scorpion out of her house. Tyakun, tyakun, what's hers is hers."[112]

110 "Agu, taki, tyakun tyakun, fu yu na fu yu." These last words (tyakun …) are in fact a saying : " That is the nature of the beast."

111 "San wan taki dati?"

112 "Mi breti dati misi Elza kisi en srefi, yagi na kruktutere na en hoso, tyakun tyakun fu en na fu en."

Before Ashana had finished speaking Sarith sprung up and gave Ashana two mighty slaps in the face. "You foul nigger woman: how dare you insult me like that, how dare you!"

She grabbed Ashana by her smock and shook her. But Ashana was a sturdy woman and stood firmly on her feet. She looked fixedly at Sarith and said, "It is never good to do evil."[113]

Sarith became increasingly furious and began to scream, "You wretched slave, just wait, I'll ... whatever are you thinking ... I'll make sure you're punished for this. Punished, I say."

She rushed to the rear veranda and said to a small errand boy sitting on the doorstep, "Boy, call the basya, and hurry."[114]

When the basya came a little later, Sarith pointed to Ashana and said, "Basya, tie this woman to a tree and give her a whipping."[115]

Shocked, the basya took a step back. "No misi," he said, shaking his head. In his view this was impossible. How could he whip Ashana – Ashana who was as it were head of the household, with almost more authority than the misi herself. Ashana, who had never ever been whipped? The masra would certainly not agree to this.

But Sarith grabbed the whip from his hand and gave him two cutting lashes, screaming, "Whip her, basya, do what I say, or I'll have a few strong nigger boys whip you."[116]

All the tumult had brought Mother Rachel downstairs. She saw her incensed, yelling daughter standing there with a whip in her hand, ordering the basya to whip Ashana. "What is going on, Sarith, calm down now."

But Sarith did not calm down. She screamed, "This nigger woman, she's insulted me, insulted me. She shall be punished; I swear she'll be punished."

113   "Du ogri noiti no bun."
114   "Boi kari a basya kon, esi esi."
115   "Basya tai a uma disi n'a bon, dan yu fon en."
116   "Fon en, basya, du san mi taki, noso mi o meki wan tu basi nengre fon yu."

"Is this really necessary?" asked Mother Rachel, recalling with some trepidation that this was Ashana, whom everyone in the household respected, and that Levi Fernandez would certainly be most angry.

"Is that all right, then, mother? Can a slave insult me? Are you going to allow that? What will become of us if that can just happen?" Sarith screamed, shouted and stamped her foot. "Go inside, mother, and don't interfere."

Mother Rachel thought that this might indeed be best. She had never been a match for her daughter, and of course Sarith was right: as a white you could certainly not permit a slave to insult you. Just imagine!

The basya took Ashana outside and took her to a tree. The small errand boy had to get rope from the warehouse to tie her so that she would hang with her feet just above the ground.

Sarith herself began to tear the clothes from Ashana's body, so that she ended up standing in front of her in just a small loincloth knotted round her waist.

When Mini-mini saw that Ashana really was tied up she threw herself weeping at her mistress' feet, threw her arms around her legs and sobbed, "Oh no, misi, I beg you, don't whip Ashana, don't let Ashana be beaten."[117]

But Sarith remained adamant. She tried to kick Mini-mini, and when she didn't let go of Sarith's legs, Sarith took the whip from the errand boy's hand and gave Mini-mini a lash in her face. Mini-mini let go, covered the bleeding wheal on her face with her hands, and turned away to avoid seeing how the elderly Ashana was whipped.

From the kitchen in the grounds, Kwasiba and the cook gazed in silence on the scene, lips pursed and looks that conveyed nothing but disgust. The basya began to whip. By the tenth lash Ashana's back was cut completely open and blood was streaming from the wounds. Sarith watched and counted the lashes herself. When she had reached twenty-eight, Ashana collapsed, and the basya, totally desperate, threw the

117   "Ke poti, misi, mi e begi yu, no fon Ashana; ke, no meki Ashana kisi fonfón."

whip down and threw himself on the ground, shouting, "I can't do this any more; whip me if you must, misi."[118]

Sarith decided that enough was enough. "Untie her,"[119] she said. She turned and went into the house, followed by Mini-mini, still weeping.

When she had gone, Kwasiba and the cook ran to the tree to help the basya untie Ashana. The errand boy was sent to fetch the medicine woman. Still unconscious, Ashana was laid on the ground. The medicine woman washed her face and her back, and another woman fetched water from the well.

When Ashana came round, the women wanted to take her into the house, but with a faint voice she said, "No, don't take me into the house; take me to the slaves' quarters."

FATHER LEVI

Levi Fernandez returned home that afternoon. He was tired. It had rained. He had got soaking wet while riding through his friend's fields on horseback. He had pain in his back and was stiff from sitting so long in the boat with his wet clothes on. He was so looking forward to a warm bath and a sturdy massage from Ashana, who could get rid of his back pain with her nimble fingers. When he went through the house to the rear veranda, where he always found Ashana waiting for him in the old rocking chair, she wasn't there. "Where is Ashana?" he asked his wife, surprised.

"Ashana is ill," came the answer.

"Ashana ill?" That never happened. He started to walk towards Ashana's room, which was next to the kitchen, but Rachel said, "She isn't there. She's in one of the slave huts. Kwasiba has seen to your water and towel and if you want she can give you a massage, too."

"No, don't bother," said Levi. It was Ashana's massage that did him good, and if she was ill today he could wait until tomorrow. He asked no more questions, and went to bed early that evening.

118 "Mi no man moro, we misi fon mi dan."
119 "Lusu en."

The following morning he was up early. He noticed that it was not Ashana but Kwasiba who brought him his coffee. Later he would go and see what was the matter with Ashana.

He walked towards the waterfront, and his own slave, Sydni, who was always at his side, came and stood next to him. Sydni said softly, "Masra really doesn't know what has happened to Ashana?"[120]

"No, what has happened?"[121] asked Levi. He had thought that Ashana simply did not feel well.

"Misi Sarith has had her whipped. The basya had to tie her up and whip her. The basya didn't want to do it, but Sarith whipped him, too."[122]

"What!" cried Levi. "Where is Ashana now?"[123]

"She is at the medicine woman's."[124]

As quickly as his feet could carry him, Levi went to the medicine woman's hut, threw open the door, and went into the small room, where he saw Ashana lying moaning on a mat in the corner.

In one step he was at her side and knelt down. He saw the totally raw, bloody back and whispered, "Ashana, oh Ashana."

Ashana, who had been lying facing the wall, now turned her head and said softly, "Masra, you've come to me, masra."[125]

The medicine woman had left the room silently.

"Ashana, why has she whipped you? What have you done?"[126]

"Leave it, masra, it is done. Water, I need water."[127]

Levi looked around and saw in another corner a gourd

120 "Masra no sabi no san pasa nanga Ashana?"
121 "No, san pasa dan?"
122 "Misi Sarith meki a kisi pansboko, a basya tai en na wan bon, dan a fon en, a basya no ben wani, ma misi Sarith fon en tu."
123 "Pe Ashana de now?"
124 "A de na a dresimama."
125 "Masra, yu kon no, ke masra."
126 "Ashana, ke Ashana, san hede a fon yu, san yu du dan?"
127 "Libi en masra, a pasa kaba. Watra, mi wani watra."

containing some water. With a smaller gourd he took some of the water and gave it to her to drink. With his hand covering his mouth he looked at the terrible wounds covering Ashana's back from top to bottom. All kinds of thoughts and emotions raced through his mind as he stood there. He felt confused, but above all he was angry with that child, that Sarith, who had done this, and with his wife, who had told him nothing but had just said, "Ashana is ill." He called the medicine woman and said to her, "Do everything for her and make her better."[128]

The medicine woman bowed and nodded, "Yes, masra, I will do whatever I can."[129]

Levi went into his house. With great strides he went up the stairs and burst into Sarith's room, not stopping to knock.

"Why have you done this?" he shouted at Sarith, who was still in bed.

A shocked Sarith realized immediately that this was about Ashana. When she gave no answer, he grabbed her by the shoulder and shook her, shouting, "Why, Sarith, why?"

Rebecca came hurrying in, and Sarith screamed, "Let go of me! She insulted me. That's why. She insulted me!"

"What insult can possibly be so bad that you need to have her thrashed like this? Tell me, what insult?"

He still had Sarith by the shoulder, shaking her. The top of her nightdress slipped from her shoulder.

"Levi, stop it, stop it!" Rachel stood in the doorway.

Levi suddenly realized that he was in his stepdaughter's bedroom, with her almost half naked in bed. Shaking his head, he went towards the door.

Sarith called, "She's a slave. I won't be insulted by a slave. Just know that. And if it were to happen again, I'd do the same thing again. Then she'd realize that she's a nigger woman, a slave, no more and no less!"

Levi went past his wife out of the room. Ashana was a slave. Yes, a slave. Could he ever have explained to someone

128 "Du ala san gi en, meki a kon betre."
129 "Iya masra, m'e du san mi kan."

else what this slave had meant to him throughout his life? How she had loved his children, cared for his wife; how she, despite her own sorrow, had consoled him when his wife died; how she had cared for his children with all the love that was within her, and how she was always there for them, from early morning to deep in the night? He could still see her, sitting there with his son Jonathan in her arms, trying everything to prevent his passing away. How he, Levi, eventually had to take the dead child from her arms.

Downstairs on the rear veranda he looked at the old rocking chair. How many nights had he heard the sound of that chair, because, for instance, Elza could not sleep and lay in Ashana's lap on that rocking chair. And Ashana just rocking and singing songs. How on earth could he ever explain all that to anyone else? Ashana the slave. Elizabeth's Ashana. Ashana who was love personified for his children, now lying there in the slave hut with a totally lacerated back. Levi Fernandez had never in years felt so lonely and abandoned. He walked to the waterfront and sat on the bench by the water.

Sydni came to him and asked gently, "Has the masra seen Ashana?"[130]

Levi gave a slight nod. He remained the whole day sitting there by the water. Now and then Sydni poured him something to drink. Ashana would die. Had he ever let her know how much he valued her? No, of course not: she was just a slave! All slave labour was simply taken for granted. Not working was a misdemeanour. But all that love, that warmth, that consolation, Levi wondered: was that work, too? Was that to be taken for granted?

During the afternoon an errand boy came to tell him that the medicine woman was asking if he could come to Ashana. When he was sitting next to her in the hut, she asked whether he could have the package brought to her that was in an old case in her room. Sydni fetched it. Ashana told the masra to open it. It contained two necklaces, one of red

130   "Masra si Ashana?"

coral, the other of pomegranate pearls. Both necklaces had belonged to his wife, Elizabeth. One she had given Ashana herself and the other he had given her when Elizabeth died. Ashana gave him the necklaces, saying, "Masra, you must give one to Misi Elza and one to Maisa. Tell Misi Elza to look after her child well and her husband, too."[131]

"This money you must give to Maisa."[132] She pointed weakly to a little money wrapped in a cloth. She had saved all the money that she had ever received from the masra. "Masra must give my regards to Misi Elza and Masra David and Maisa."[133]

"Ashana, oh Ashana." Levi didn't know what more he could say. "No, Ashana, you'll get better." [134]

But Ashana shook her head and said, "Don't be sad, masra, I'm going home, and in my home there is no slavery; don't be sad."[135]

That was the last time Levi saw Ashana, for she died during the night and he was not there when the slaves took their leave of her with their own traditional ceremonies and rituals. And there was certainly no-one from the Grand House there when a small procession took Ashana to her last resting place. A nameless grave in an opening in the rainforest next to the other graves of hundreds of nameless slaves.

A few days later, Levi Fernandez was at his daughter's in the Wagenwegstraat. He had come specially to Paramaribo to tell Elza and Maisa that Ashana had died, and he intended to continue on to Suzanna's Lust on the Para River, to spend a few days there with his son David.

131   "Masra yu musi gi misi Elza wan, nanga Maisa wan. Taigi misi Elza a musu sorgu en pikin nanga en masra bun."
132   "A moni disi yu musi gi Maisa."
133   "Masra musu taigi misi Elza nanga masra David nanga Maisa adyosi yere."
134   "No no Ashana, y'e kon betre."
135   "No sari masra, m'e go na hoso, mi hoso na sabi katibo, no sari."

Elza was pleased to see her father, but when she saw his grave expression, she realized that something was wrong.

"Ashana is dead," said Pa Levi simply.

Elza took hold of his hand and said, "No papa, surely not. How can Ashana have died? She was never ill." She understood the sorrow this must be causing him and thought immediately of Maisa, too. Maisa would have to be told that her mother had died.

When she went into the kitchen and saw Maisa sitting at the table, weeping, she realized that she already knew. "Oh Maisa, she is dead, eh; oh Maisa my dearest."

Elza put her arms round Maisa and lay her head on her shoulder. Maisa nodded and cried out suddenly, "That devil, that damned, foul devil. Just wait: she'll be punished."[136]

Shocked, Elza lifted her head and looked at Maisa. Why was Maisa saying this? Why was she talking about Ashana like this?

Maisa, seeing Elza's amazed expression, cried, "Oh misi, you don't know, do you? It was Misi Sarith that killed Ashana. She had the basya tie Ashana up and whip her 'til she passed out, the vampire."[137]

"No, no!" With her hand over her mouth, Elza started backwards. "That can't possibly be true?" With a scream she stormed into the dining room and shouted, "Papa, it can't be true, say it's not true, that Sarith has done this, that she had Ashana beaten?"

"Yes, my child, yes." Pa Levi shook his head and said to Rutger, who was looking in amazement from his wife to her father, "Sarith had Ashana tied up and whipped, and she died from her injuries."

Elza now sobbed out loud, her head in her arms on the table, weeping uncontrollably.

136 "Na didibri, na frufruktu, a saka-saka, ma watki a o kisi en strafu."

137 "Tan, misi, yu no sabi no, na misi Sarith kiri Ashana, a meki a basya tai Ashana na wan bon, fon en te a flaw, na takru ase- ma dati."

"How could Sarith do such a thing?" said Rutger, softly.

But Elza raised her head and screamed, "She had her beaten to death."

And as she looked at him so completely wretchedly, he understood that others might ask the whys and wherefores, but they both knew why Sarith had done this. Elza just wept and wept as the realization grew that Ashana was dead: the person from whom she had had the most love in all her life. The person who had cared for her, who had cherished her, for whom nothing was too much. This Ashana had died, not surrounded by love and affection, but rather as she had been all her life, a slave. She could forgive Sarith many things, but this, no, for this she could never forgive Sarith.

CHAPTER VIII

RUTGER

It was happening more frequently that people in the town were shocked by the news that yet another plantation had been raided. It appeared that the escapees were becoming increasingly bolder. Rutger wondered whether one could still talk of escapees. In his view they were well-organized groups.

On every occasion you heard that the group was led by a certain Boni, and in the town people were already using the term Boni-negroes.

There were already more than eight hundred military personnel in the country, sent by the Society[138] in the Netherlands at the repeated request of the colonial government. In addition there were at least three hundred men of the colonial troops. But even so, this relatively large army had not succeeded in defeating the Boni-negroes. Now and then a group of militia managed to capture a few. These would then be taken into captivity and brought to the town with appropriate pomp and circumstance. But after that it seemed that the Maroons were attacking with still more violence and getting closer. The colonists were getting increasingly scared. The devils would soon be in the town itself! Most of the plantation owners were also angry and indignant. Each year a hefty sum had to be paid into the escapee fund, and in recent years this sum was increasing regularly. So much money

138   The Licensed Society of Suriname (Geoctroyeerde Sociëteit van Suriname) was established in 1683 by the Dutch West India Company, the City of Amsterdam and Cornelis van Aerssen van Sommelsdijck to manage the new colony, which had been exchanged for Nieuw Amsterdam (later New York) through the Treaty of Breda, 1667. The society was disbanded in 1795 and a colonial government was instituted.

for nothing, since all those soldiers who were costing so much money were obviously able to do nothing against the bunch of wild savages there in the bush.

One morning three gentlemen came to the administrator's office. They were officer candidate Goedkoop, a sub-lieutenant serving in Captain Joo's regiment, the planter Van Bemmelen, owner of the Groot-Vertier Plantation, and his white overseer. The three visitors looked extremely dejected. After sitting down and being given drinks by Alex, Sub-lieutenant Goedkoop began to describe how the Maroons had raided the Groot-Vertier Plantation and had taken everything as spoil. Van Bemmelen, his family and his white overseer had fled and had been received on a nearby plantation. Because they were so afraid, they had had a military escort to the town. Van Bemmelen was at his wits' end. His wife did not want to return to the plantation. He had come to the administrator's office to request a loan. The plantation had to be re-established. Otherwise, how could he live with no plantation and no slaves?

Mr van Omhoog expressed his amazement at how it was possible for a handful of wild negroes to get the better of the soldiers. Sub-lieutenant Goedkoop explained that the colonial government could no longer think of the bush-negroes as a group of negro savages hiding in the jungle and now and then raiding to get what they needed. In the town, the government had thought that the escapees would be forced to give themselves up. If the military forces did not succeed, then hunger would drive them from the bush. But it was turning out to be quite the opposite.

The bush-negroes on the Cottica had succeeded in establishing a complete community. They called themselves the Aluku Tribe. They planned and laid out fields for growing food and created food stores, and put to good use their knowledge of carpentry and metalworking. Raids on plantations were carried out following a strategic plan. Also, the negroes didn't simply kill all the whites, but targeted mainly those who had caused them suffering. They left children largely untouched. Boni was one of the great leaders from the Cottica area, and the other important leader was Baron.

The government was doing everything possible to make hunting the escapees attractive. Soldiers were sent out. Slaves and indians were encouraged by means of prize money to organize patrols to catch escapees. The negroes were usually too clever for the soldiers. The soldiers would very often find a village, but no people. For they knew that the soldiers were coming and had gone into hiding.

Once they had escaped from the plantations and had joined their fellows, they shook off all the submissiveness that had been forced upon them by the whites. They could again become the self-assured, proud folk that was their true nature. Their freedom and self-confidence were the main motives for maintaining the struggle against a group of whites who in principle held all the cards. They were outnumbered by the whites, who had weapons and gunpowder and enough to eat. Even so, the whites were usually on the losing side. Fair enough, they sometimes found the villages, which had names such as 'Stay away from me', 'Hide me', 'Hold me' or 'God knows'[139], but the negroes themselves were by then invisible.

In 1768 the bush-negroes had carried out a well-planned raid on the 's-Hagenbosch Plantation. As a result of this, a commando was sent out under the leadership of Captain Joo. He found two villages. The larger village comprised thirty-two houses, plots for food crops, fruit trees, from which it was evident that the village had existed for some considerable time, a complete blacksmith's shop with a large amount of ironwork, and a poultry stock that included five hundred chickens. The inhabitants he did not find, however. What he did find was a written message to the effect that the whites need not dream that they would ever catch the negroes. If it pleased the negroes they would eliminate all the whites.

As was the military's practice in all such situations, they destroyed the village completely. Everything was set on fire;

139   'No meri mi', 'Kibri mi', 'Holi mi', 'Gado Sabi'.

they burnt the crops and food stores once they had taken what they themselves needed. In this case they had first eaten one hundred and eighty chickens before setting the rest on fire.

But still the Maroons succeeded in surviving and continuing the battle. They knew the bush much better than did the soldiers. Despite everything, they managed often enough even to raid a military post, take weapons and send the soldiers packing in total humiliation. The government became increasingly apprehensive. They were actually no match for the bush-negroes, who were no longer just escapees, but rather trained guerrillas who would have to be combated by all means available. They were in fact dealing with excellent, tough men and women, and Rutger thought he noticed a certain degree of admiration and even jealousy in the words of Sub-lieutenant Goedkoop.

"It is almost unbelievable, but they really are capable warriors," said Rutger.

"Monsters, they are, devil's children," sighed Van Bemmelen. "There's nothing to be done against them, because they're working with black magic."

After Mr van Omhoog had discussed a few formal details of the loan with his client, the group departed. Mr van Omhoog went upstairs, and Rutger stood a while deep in thought near the window. Alex came in to clear away the used cups and heard Rutger talking to himself. "Boni, always Boni. Why don't they make sure they get him first?"

"They can never catch Boni, masra," said Alex. "Never. He has an enormous tapu[140]. No bullet can touch him and no person can catch him."

"It would seem that you're right," said Rutger. "Who is this Boni, anyway? I'd very much like to know from which plantation he came."

"Boni does not come from a plantation, masra. He has never been a slave. He was born free in the bush," said Alex. "I could tell you everything about Boni."

140 Protection through magical forces.

"How do you know all this?" asked Rutger. Alex smiled. "I listen, masra," he said. "I listen when others speak. Would masra like to hear about it?"

"Of course I'd like to hear it," said Rutger. "Tell me, tell me everything about Boni."

Alex recounted.

"Boni was not born into slavery. He is proud to be able to say that he is a genuine bush-negro. Boni's mother was a slave on the plantation of a rich Jewish family in the time of Governor Mauricius. This family was very well known in Paramaribo. They belonged to the top of the Cabal[141], the group of wealthy people who had given Governor Mauricius so much trouble. They owned various plantations on the Boven-Cottica. The wife was a cruel and merciless person. The husband was a lecherous type who often misused slave-girls. Now, it happened that his eye had fallen on a pretty young slave-girl, who would later be Boni's mother.

"When it later turned out that she was pregnant, the jealous and brutish wife began to scheme revenge. She bided her time until her husband was away on a journey for a few days, and then had the slave-girl come to her, remarking, "I see you are pregnant. Who is the father of your child?" When the girl answered that she had a man-friend and that he was the father of the child, she had the man in question sent for.

She asked him, "Is this your woman; have you made her pregnant?"

The man answered that this was indeed the case, and the mistress then said, "She is my slave-girl. Who gave you the right to use my property like this? I'll teach you a lesson!"

And with those words she took a razor-sharp knife and cut off the man's genitals. To the woman she said, "You're pregnant. Your breasts are so large and beautiful that one will certainly suffice to feed your child."

With the same knife she cut off one of the woman's breasts. She then said to the heavily bleeding couple, "Now get out of my sight. I never want to see you again!"

141 In Suriname, Cabale.

She was reckoning that they would not get very far with such injuries. When her husband came home two days later and at lunch lifted the lid from the plate that was set before him, he was confronted with the breast of a negro woman, and his wife said, with a mean laugh, "You obviously find negresses' breasts so tasty: bon appetit!"

"In the meantime, the two slaves had left and had fled into the bush, where the man died from his injuries. Helped by some other escapees, the woman ended up in the negro camp in the Cottica region. There she gave birth to twins: two boys.

"The children realized soon enough that they were different from the other negroes. For a start they were not black, but brown, and they had red curly hair. They asked their mother why they were different and why she had only one breast. Time and time again their mother told her story, and time and time again the brothers swore revenge: for their mother and for the man who should have been their father. When one of the boys died at the age of twelve as a result of a shot from a soldier's gun, this gave the survivor Boni all the more reason to seek revenge."

Alex fell silent. Rutger gazed into space, deep in thought.

ELZA

Paramaribo was buzzing with rumours. Governor Crommelin wanted to quit. He had been governor of the colony since 1748. Because he had taken the governor's side in the struggle between Governor Mauricius and the Cabal, he was certainly not loved by many of the more prominent residents, and these people had made life difficult for him once he himself had taken over as governor. For a year now, Crommelin had been requesting the governors of the Society in the Netherlands to allow him to retire. He wanted to travel to the Netherlands and thereafter enjoy a well-earned rest. This would now be permitted, but the governor did not leave immediately, remaining for some time in Suriname as a private citizen, while Jean Nepveu was appointed interim governor.

Mr van Omhoog, too, longed for peace and quiet and wanted to retire. He had said this much in a letter to his patron, Rutger's great-uncle.

Uncle Frederik found it necessary, however, for Rutger first to travel to the Netherlands to acquaint himself with various matters before being appointed administrator. Uncle Frederik also realized, however, that his nephew would not wish to be separated from his wife and son for such a long time, and therefore suggested that Elza and little Gideon should also make the journey to the Netherlands. At least, if Elza dared to do this. For everyone knew that the journey to the Netherlands and back was not without danger. Apart from storms and hurricanes, there were also the pirates and, in times of war, enemy ships. Above all, the eight-week stay on board could not be described as pleasant. Cramped quarters, bad food and disease were the order of the day.

Rutger received the letter with his uncle's proposition in November 1768. Elza wasn't afraid to make the journey with Rutger. It was not a good idea to arrive in Holland in the middle of winter, so the family would board in January so as to land around the end of March. They would then stay six months with Uncle Frederik, who lived in a fine mansion on the Keizersgracht in Amsterdam.

There was much to do in preparation for the journey. Alex, Maisa and Afanaisa would go along, for how on earth would Elza survive in Holland without her slaves around her, who always did everything for her. The other slaves would remain in the grounds and keep the house in good order until the family returned towards the end of the year.

When they all departed, little Gideon was already one year old. He was about the house, walking, running and of course falling all over the place, playing on the back veranda and going into the grounds with Afanaisa's guiding hand. He was a happy child, rarely cried, and had everyone laughing at his mischievous antics. On 28 January the family left Paramaribo, and on 29 May Pa Levi Fernandez, who was by chance in the town for a week, staying with the De Ledesmas, received the following letter.

Amsterdam, 2 April 1769

Dear Papa,
Here is the first letter I'm writing to you from this cold land,
for oh isn't it cold and wet here. I could never have imagined
anything like it. But wait: I'll begin at the beginning. During
the first weeks the voyage went well. The sea was calm, the
wind was favourable, and so the voyage went quickly. Rut-
ger, Gideon and I had good accommodation in the stern of
the ship, where the officers also had their quarters. The
slaves would be sleeping in the forecastle along with the
sailors, but Maisa and Afanaisa were so unhappy there that
even the first night we took them in with us and let them
sleep in a corner of our cabin. After crossing the ocean, and
after we had landed on Madeira, the sea became rougher and
it began to get cold, too. The further north we sailed, the
worse it became. We had to remain inside, and the portholes
were nailed shut. So we got very little fresh air. It was stuffy
and smelly. This made Gideon peevish and fidgety.

Fortunately, it did not make him ill. The goat that we had
brought on board gave us enough milk each day to be able to
make his porridge, and the large store of oranges and lemons
ensured that we did not get scurvy or diarrhoea. We could
even give some to the crew. The chickens and eggs were also
most useful. Maisa went to cook our meal every day in the
galley. She found it so dirty that she dared not leave anything
around, not even a fork. When she had finished she brought
everything back to us in a large basket. We experienced a few
heavy storms, and to tell the truth I was frightened to death,
but everything turned out all right in the end, and after
seven weeks, on 22 March, very early, we were able to sail up
the IJ.[142] *And Papa: it snowed! Really: it snowed! I was*
woken by a frightened cry from Afanaisa. She stood at the
door and called, "Misi, something like cotton is falling from

142 The river running past Amsterdam and into the North Sea. It
     served as Amsterdam's harbour.

the sky and it's burning."[143] *When we approached the town it was a wonderful sight, but oh so cold.*

How fortunate I was to be able to borrow Mrs Tallans' winter clothing, for then I at least had warm shawls for myself and the slave-girls. We dressed Gideon in a lot of clothes, all of them far too large, for the Tallans' youngest child is four. Gideon looked like a round barrel with all that stuff on, and he didn't like it one bit. And then of course there was the problem of the shoes, for of course the slaves could not walk around in bare feet in all that cold. Now, Rutger explained that they would have to wear shoes. Since they were not in Suriname, the Suriname rules no longer applied. Maisa refused: she had no intention of putting those things on.

"I'll have no white person being angry with me,"[144] *she said, and no matter what we said, she didn't want to know.*

Luckily, Rutger was able to get a pair of goat-hair socks from one of the officers, and these she did agree to wear. Afanaisa didn't dare take a single step in shoes. She held onto the wall and swayed as if she were afraid to topple over at any moment. Alex, in contrast, put the boots on, turned on his heels, and walked away as if he'd been wearing boots all his life.

Carriage and driver were waiting for us when we disembarked, and in the house Great-uncle Frederik was waiting for us along with niece Marie, who lives with her father. We saw the other three nieces the same evening, because I think everyone wanted to see what I looked like. I think they were rather disappointed that 'the girl from the colony' appeared to be such a normal girl, but they couldn't take their eyes off the slaves and burst out laughing when they heard me talking with Maisa. Maisa is finding everything most frightening. She doesn't set foot out of doors. On the other hand, there's enough for her to do around the house. There is also a kitchen maid here, and a general maid, a house girl and a

---

143   "Misi, misi wan sani leki katun a fadon komopo na loktu, ai bron!"

144   "No wan bakra mus kon mandi nanga mi."

houseboy. Well, Papa, you could have knocked Alex, Maisa and Afanaisa over with a feather when they realized that white people actually work here! Afanaisa still gets the giggles about this. When she sees the maid with a mop and pail she has to turn her head so as not to laugh out loud.

Maisa is most put out that the girls find it terrible that she baths Gideon every day, and will herself not go to bed until she has washed herself from top to toe. And she's always complaining, "How is it that these whites are so filthy?"[145]

The day before yesterday a huge family dinner was held in our honour. As well as Great-uncle Frederik's daughters and their husbands, various other nieces and nephews had been invited. They all have the strangest ideas about our country.

Some of them think that you have to feel under the bed each morning to check that there are no tigers or giant snakes there. Others believe that there are headless indians living in the bush. They have heard that the ground is so fertile that if you plant a stick today, in two weeks you'll have a large tree full of ripe fruit. One asked me whether it was really true that paper would catch fire if the sun shone on it. And of course they had to see the slaves: we had to call them in. They were most surprised when it appeared that Alex spoke perfect Dutch. A great-aunt of mine asked me whether I wasn't frightened at home, with all those negroes around. I answered that I would be frightened if there weren't all those negroes around, and I could see that she didn't understand this at all and in fact found me rather strange.

It is still cold and it rains a lot: not a heavy shower like at home, but a really dreary rain. Everyone in the house is so happy when the sun shines. They say to us, "The sun is shining: wonderful, isn't it!" and we look at each other and wonder what is so great about that. Their sun gives them hardly any warmth, but everyone is saying that spring is here. There are already small leaves appearing on the trees, and then it will be warm, too, they say. Let's just hope so!

Papa, could you send Sydni along to the Wagenwegstraat

when you're in town? I would really like our slaves to know that all is well with us, and Sydni can stress to them that they should go to Mr van Omhoog if they need anything. I'm worried about Amimba, who's expecting her baby. She mustn't try to do too much. Could you perhaps miss her mother at Hébron for a few weeks? Then she could be in the town when it's time for the birth. Amimba would be much more at ease if her mother was with her. Especially now that Maisa is not there. So that was it for the moment. Despite all the care and being wrapped up so well, Gideon has managed to catch a cold and is now coughing. Nothing serious, and he doesn't have any fever, but of course Maisa is worried about him, especially because she can't boil up any calabash syrup for him. Rutger sends his warmest greetings. Please accept these from me, too, for everyone, and especially Aunt Rachel, the sisters, David and his family and everyone at Hébron. Do look after yourself, and a big kiss on your fore-head ...

from Elza

SARITH

Uncle Levi was really happy with Elza's letter. He read it at table so that everyone could hear everything, and then he gave a detailed account to any friends or acquaintances who asked whether he had heard anything from his daughter. Sarith had not let anything slip while Uncle Levi was reading the letter after dinner. She sat playing with a knife rest, her eyes fixed on the table. Oh what she could have done to those two, Elza and Rutger!

When she had heard that they were to go on their journey, she had imagined the ship sinking in a storm or being over-run by pirates. And now there came this letter for Uncle Levi from his dear Elza, who was now in Holland and was experiencing all kinds of new things. No ship sunk or captured by pirates. How unjust! It seemed that Elza was getting everything in this world that Sarith would have liked to have had. A husband, a child, loved by everyone, and now in Holland, where Rutger's family would certainly be speaking of her as 'that dear Elza'. And she, Sarith, what did she have? Oh yes, she was beautiful, very beautiful, but she would have gladly sacrificed some of her beauty to be in Elza's place, now in Holland, instead of in this stupid colony where nothing special ever happened. What did she have here – a party now and then where it was in any case all just chatting and gossiping? Just like the past two weeks. She had gone to a party and then on three occasions to friends for an evening. And what was the talk about? Always the same things …

Mrs Crommelin was being very rude to Jean Nepveu. In the past they had been good friends, but since he had become interim governor she was very unfriendly towards him. The Crommelins had been granted leave, but were still in Suriname and were still living in the governor's palace, where Jean Nepveu had to work every day in the office. Governor Crommelin himself had turned into a grumpy old man, and the staff and slaves in the palace didn't know where they stood. Should they obey Misi Crommelin or the new governor?

Oh, yes, and have you heard how Klaas Doesburgh's coloured concubine managed to send her slave to the Doesburgh's house on the Waterfront with the message that Klaas must go straightaway to the concubine's house because one of her children was ill, and he had gone, too, to the great annoyance of Mrs Doesburgh. What an impertinence of that coloured! It gets worse and worse with those types. And Sarith got bored and annoyed at these parties. She didn't feel like them any more. She wanted a man; she wanted to get married! She was twenty-one already. An old spinster, without a husband on the horizon. How was it possible for her to be in this situation when she was so much prettier than all the others?

A few months later, at the end of September, Uncle Levi received a last letter from Elza from Holland, which went as follows …

Amsterdam, 2 August 1769

Dearest Papa,
When you receive this letter we will be just about to leave or will already be at sea. We board in the first week of October. In this way we'll be out of these parts before the autumn storms begin. If everything goes well, we'll arrive in Paramaribo the last week of November or the first week of December. I shall be very glad to be back in our own home, especially since Gideon will be getting a little brother or sister around the middle of January. I don't mind which, as long as he or she is healthy. Oh, Papa, you must congratulate Esther and Jacob on the birth of their fourth son. For Esther's sake I had hoped that it would be a daughter this time round, but well, four sons is also quite something. And what a worthy kaddish they'll have said for them later on! How are things with Rebecca and Abraham and their little Zipporah? Is Rebecca already expecting again? It was really fine that you were able, after all, to send Leida to the town for two months to be with Amimba. Have you seen Amimba's son yet? Rutger and I had a good laugh when we read in your letter that the child has been named Rutty, after Rutger.

It has been really hot here, sometimes hotter than at home. I stayed for three weeks with Gideon at Annette and her husband's country house. Annette is Great-uncle Frederik's third daughter. They have four children, from four to eleven years old. We went there in a carriage: a huge country house near Bussum. Really nice. Sometimes I felt I was at home, at Hébron.

Gideon has kept himself amused. The nieces and nephews played with him a lot, and it was usually so warm that he could wander around in next to nothing, just as at home. He really liked that – he so hates all those clothes on his body.

He's now beginning to talk and says, amongst other things, something like 'Masha'. Both Maisa and Afanaisa claim that it is her name he's saying. Rutger was also in the country for two weeks. Niece Marie is sorry that we're leaving. She says that the house will feel empty without us. I think that Alex is also sorry that we are returning. Rutger sometimes allowed him to go out on his own. I think he knows Amsterdam like the back of his hand. He will miss all the conversations with the acquaintances he's made here. He's been so happy to have been able to speak to a white person without anyone disapproving, and to be able to come and go wherever he wants. When you hear him talk, he seems like a real Amsterdammer.

Well, Papa, that was it then. Do greet the whole family, have a big kiss from me, and goodbye for now.

From your Elza

Uncle Levi was staying along with Rachel and Sarith at the house of Jacob and Esther de Ledesma, on the occasion of Yom Kippur. That was traditionally a day of fasting followed in the evening by an extensive dinner. For this the table would be covered with a beautiful Jewish table cloth. The best porcelain, crystal and silverware were brought out and polished up for the day. Everything bright and shiny. The table bore so many plates and dishes that a hundred people could have feasted. Elza's letter was again the talk of the day, especially that she would soon be returning and was expecting another baby.

Sarith sat with a vexed look on her face, staring straight ahead. She was getting irritated, and every time Elza's name was mentioned she wanted to scream. Now Sarith knew one thing for certain: that she must be married by the time Elza and Rutger returned. She didn't know yet to whom, but it didn't really matter to whom, she just had to have a man and be married. Just had to!

When the family went to Joden-Savanna two weeks later for the Feast of Tabernacles, she saw upon arrival, among all the other guests, Julius Robles de Medina. He had been a widower for five years now. That was a suitable candidate. Oh, she knew well that she and Elza had always laughed at him in the past and had called him 'Noso' because of his large nose, but that didn't matter. Well, she would use all her feminine cunning to ensure that he fell in love with her and would ask her to marry him. All this must happen during these days that they were here at Joden-Savanna.

Julius didn't know what had hit him when Sarith A'haron suddenly showed so much interest in him. She was always near him, spoke really sweetly and pleasantly to him and was oh so interested in his two daughters, who were now twelve and fourteen. It had begun with her sitting next to him on the very first day, and telling him how good he looked, as always. He had asked her how things were with her stepsister in Holland. He expected that Sarith would be very pleased that Elza was returning soon, for she must miss her sister a lot. He still remembered how they were inseparable as growing girls, always together, smiling and giggling, yes, he remembered it well. And how this lovely pair had grown up to be such beautiful ladies, especially she, Sarith, was particularly enchanting. Sarith had sweetly and charmingly answered that of course he himself had such a lovely twosome in his daughters Miriam and Hannah. Wasn't it difficult for him to bring up these two lovely children alone, without a mother? Julius had sighed that it was indeed difficult, but that they were mostly in the town at their aunt's, their mother's sister. They attended the French school. Was it not dull for him, alone on the plantation, Sarith had asked, and Julius could only reply in the affirmative. Yes, it was often dull, alone on his plantation, Klein Paradijs, on the Boven-Commewijne River.

Time and time again Sarith was at his side, full of interest in his plantation, in him, in his daughters. She also talked a lot with his two daughters, who soon came to regard her as a really pleasant person. Within a week Julius Robles de Medina could no longer think of anything but Sarith A'haron. How wrong he had been. He had always thought that she was a frivolous girl, rather too merry and too easy, but she wasn't like that after all. Now he had come to know her better, he realized what a noble and honourable person she was; a good woman. Should he ask her to marry him? But he didn't dare, for she appeared to be very fond of going out, and how could he ask such a beautiful young woman, who loved to go out and about, to marry him and go to live on Klein Paradijs, a two-day journey from Paramaribo? When, however, Sarith said to him that there was nothing better than the peace of a distant plantation, he thought that he had better try it, anyway. Timidly, he asked her whether she would like to share the peace with him on such a distant plantation. And he couldn't believe his luck when she agreed. She had said 'yes'! This fantastically beautiful young woman, who could set all men's heads spinning and all male hearts beating, wanted to marry him, Julius!

Uncle Levi and Ma Rachel couldn't believe their ears when Julius spoke with them and told them that Sarith had agreed to be his wife. He wasn't exactly the man that Ma Rachel might have had in mind for her prettiest daughter, but, well, Sarith was twenty-one and had been so moody and surly of late. Rather Julius Robles de Medina with his large nose than no man at all. The engagement party was held immediately there at Joden-Savanna, and Sarith herself said to Julius that there was no point in waiting too long to marry. Why should they? A long engagement was usually needed for the partners to get to know each other better, but that wasn't necessary in this case. They had known each other for years. And so it was decided that the wedding would take place in four weeks' time at Klein Paradijs, and all the guests at Joden-Savanna were immediately invited.

The next four weeks passed quickly. Everything was hastily prepared, and in the third week of November the tent boat left Hébron. Sarith departed from the plantation where she had lived for almost fourteen years. Mother and Uncle Levi went along, as did Kwasiba and Mini-mini.

Sarith had managed to persuade her mother to let Kwasiba remain with her as well. She had never been to Klein Paradijs and was in fact a little afraid of the unknown. With the familiar Kwasiba and Mini-mini she would feel at ease more quickly. Kwasiba was simply happy that she could be with her daughter Mini-mini in the future, too. They remained in the town for a few days, where the rest of the family joined them, and then they all left for the plantation that would be Sarith's home. Klein Paradijs was a coffee plantation. The house was pleasant but not all that large. Far too small, thought Sarith, disappointed.

After the wedding most of the guests stayed on for a week or so and Sarith enjoyed herself tremendously with all the parties that were laid on in her honour. She was afraid of the first night alone with Julius. She did not love him, that she knew full well. She had used him for her own ends. But she would do her best to be nice to him. After their first union, when Julius had naturally discovered that she was certainly no virgin, he was of the opinion that he had the right to know who his predecessor had been. Sarith told him about Charles van Hennegouwen. She spun the tale that she was a naïve girl of fifteen, who believed that a love affair was the real thing, and Charles himself, being still young and knowing no better, had taken advantage of this. She even managed a few tears while recounting that if she had known how it would all turn out, it would never have happened, but could Julius please forgive her? That he did readily. She should quickly forget it all. He, Julius, would never lay any blame. He was just happy that she now loved him.

When Elza and Rutger arrived back in Paramaribo on 30 November, to be awaited by the rest of the family, the first news they heard was that Sarith was married to Julius Robles de Medina and now lived at Klein Paradijs on the Boven-Commewijne. Elza was astonished. Sarith married to 'Noso'? The same Noso whom they had always ridiculed and who according to Sarith was such a bore? Well, she must have been extremely desperate to have come to such a decision.

ELZA

It was really fine to be back home again, thought Elza, and the first day she went through the whole house to see all the familiar things again. She also went in the grounds to the slaves' huts to see Amimba's little son, who was a chubby, sturdy baby, and she gave Amimba some of Gideon's cast-off blouses. Maisa, Afanaisa and Alex had their hands full these early days recounting everything. The others wanted to know everything, and Elza often saw them all at the threshold of Alex's or Amimba's room, sitting in a circle around the narrators. The favourite topic to be recounted was how in Holland the whites actually did manual labour.

The others had not believed this at first. Maisa and Afanaisa were trying to take them for a ride! Even when Alex confirmed it, they could not believe it, and Misi Elza had to intervene and confirm that it really was the case: in Holland the whites worked. And the slaves rolled around laughing, roaring their heads off with tears in their eyes. Really true?

Did the whites actually know how to work with their hands? And time and time again Afanaisa and Maisa had to imitate the kitchen maid peeling the potatoes, the housemaid with broom and pail and how the coachman kept the stalls and the animals clean in the stables. And everyone laughed. Oh, that was a really priceless joke! Whites working with their hands. They never tired of this story, and from then on in this household whenever anyone came with a tall story, the reaction was, "Next you'll be trying to tell me that whites work with their hands!"[146]

Elza's second child, another son, was born on 17 January, just a week after his brother's second birthday. He was called Jonathan. Just as on the first occasion, everything went fine. Elza fed the child herself and felt completely fit again after just a few days, but was kept in bed again by Maisa, who still insisted that getting up before the sixteenth day was fraught with danger. After that things got busy, for Mr and Mrs van Omhoog would leave Suriname on 27 February, and in the first week of March the Le Chasseur family would move from the Wagenwegstraat into the large mansion on the Gravenstraat.

SARITH

In the meantime Sarith was finding Klein Paradijs to be a totally dull and boring spot. She got annoyed, was surly and moody. Julius was exceptionally loving and attentive, but all

146 "No kon taigi mi dati bakra sabi wroko nanga den anu."

that loving stuff on his part irritated her and she often re-strained herself with difficulty from snapping at him. Sarith had thought that they would go to Paramaribo around New Year, so as to attend the various festivities, such as that of Es-ther and Jacob. But when she suggested this to Julius, it turned out that he had a totally different plan. He had had to spend so many New Years at parties. No, he wanted some-thing different. He wanted to remain cosily with his darling little wife alone on their own plantation. And so it turned out, too. How angry Sarith was to be sitting there on her own with Julius while all those parties were going on in Paramari-bo. Oh how she hoped that there would very soon be some good reason for her to go to town, urgently and for a longer period. To pass the time, Mini-mini had to give her a massage very often. Sarith noticed something about Mini-mini. Was it just her idea, or was she very much down in the dumps? And then suddenly, around the middle of January, Sarith realized what was up with Mini-mini: she was expecting!

Sarith was surprised. She had never seen the girl together with a man. Mini-mini herself was very beautiful, but not the provocative type, in fact rather shy. Sarith had noticed often enough how men looked at Mini-mini, and she knew that some of Uncle Levi's guests at Hébron had on occasion asked whether they might not receive that beautiful slave-girl in their room. Uncle Levi had always answered that he had no authority over Mini-mini because she was his step-daughter's slave-girl. Sarith had occasionally asked Mini-mini whether she would like to sleep with such a person, and Mini-mini had always replied, "Me? No misi, I don't want to."[147]

Now, of course, Sarith was really curious as to who was the father of Mini-mini's child. Mini-mini told her that around the beginning of the year, when Sarith was staying so frequently in the town, she had got to know a young man. Also of mixed race, but a free man. He was called Hendrik de Mees. She had initially seen him frequently around the Saramaccastraat, where the De Ledesmas lived, and later he

147   "Mi? No no misi, mi no wani."

had admitted that it was for her that he was so often there. He was the child of a white man who had bought his slave-girl into freedom and kept her as a concubine in a small house in the Gemene Weide[148] area. The father had cared well for mother and child, but had died when the boy was four years old.

The mother had managed to raise the boy by selling small cakes. They were poor but they were free. Hendrik had also learnt to read and write, and at the age of fourteen he became apprenticed to a cabinet-maker. He was still working there and didn't earn very much, but enough to be able to keep himself and his mother and also enough for a wife. After their first meeting he had visited her on many occasions and had secretly spent the night with her (secretly, for it was forbidden for free mulattos to consort with the slaves). She had also visited him on occasion, on Sunday, when his mother wasn't at home. He had promised that he would save up so that he could buy her into freedom and then she could go to live with him, but that would take some time yet.

"And now you're already expecting his child?" said Sarith, when she had heard the whole story. "Yes, misi," said an embarrassed Mini-mini, and Sarith realized with a shock that she would lose Mini-mini if she were bought into freedom by her beloved. But, come now, that was still a long way off, and she generously promised the girl that if she were freed, she could take the child with her without having to pay for it.

Mini-mini was glad she had told all this. Perhaps that misi of hers wasn't so bad after all. The new masra was really nice. He was crazy about his wife, that was obvious to Mini-mini. She could also see that her misi did not love the masra. She could only hope that the misi would not do anything stupid, as she had with Masra Rutger. The masra sometimes gave her and Kwasiba a coin. Kwasiba usually bought tobacco, but Mini-mini saved everything she received so as to be able to help towards buying her freedom.

148   In English this would refer to a common or village green.

At the beginning of February 1770 it was announced that Governor Crommelin would retire and that the interim governor, Jean Nepveu, would now be appointed governor. The official installation would take place on 8 March. To mark the occasion an extensive dinner would be held in the palace that evening, with a spectacular ball the next day.

When the invitation for this arrived, Sarith was beside herself with joy. Something at last! Finally a party at which Sarith could make her mark. She would have to go to Paramaribo as quickly as possible to make all the necessary preparations. Bemused, Julius wondered why that all had to happen right now, since the festivities were still five weeks away. But Sarith managed to persuade him that it was absolutely necessary. After all, she needed to see to her clothes and have her ball gown made. He certainly wouldn't want her to be going in an old ball gown that everyone knew already? People would be sure to make remarks and think that he didn't want to give her a new gown. Julius had not thought of that, and so Sarith departed for the town four whole weeks in advance of the festivities, installing herself as before in the De Ledesmas' house.

Mini-mini was also pleased to be going to the town. She would be able to see her beloved Hendrik. Hardly had they arrived in the town when she asked Misi Sarith's permission to send an errand boy to Hendrik. He came to her that evening. Was he pleased to see her? Was she expecting a child, he asked. Already? He'd not really reckoned on that. Yes, he was already saving up, but it was a slow business.

A few days before the eighth of March Julius came to join his wife in the town. How exuberant and merry she was! She joked with him, laughed a lot. He couldn't tire of looking at this lovely creation that was now his wife. Ecstatic, he bought her everything she wanted.

A really huge dinner was given in the palace. Hundreds of guests sat at festively adorned tables, with the Jewish guests separated as always due to their kosher dishes. People lower down the social ladder had also been invited, such as the skippers of merchant vessels and other residents. For them tables had been laid out in a shed that was fifty metres long, built specially for the occasion. There was a superfluity of food and drink, exquisitely served, and that day the feast was rounded off with a marvellous firework display.

The next day was the day of the grand ball. It was preceded by a reception especially for the ladies, which was held in the house of Governor Nepveu in the Gravenstraat. After this, all the ladies, dressed in their finery, went to the governor's palace to join their husbands for the ball. It happened that at that moment the warship 'Castor' lay in the harbour, and the captain, Hoogwerf, who was naturally among the guests, as were his officers, could not believe his eyes when he saw all this splendour. The seamen had never expected to see such a display in the West Indies, and could only conclude that the people in Suriname were very well off indeed.

Sarith managed to avoid meeting Rutger and Elza. The first day, this was easy, since the Jews were sitting upstairs. The next day it was rather more difficult.

At Mrs Nepveu's she indeed saw Elza in the distance and she also saw a circle of ladies around her, but she ensured that she didn't come near her. In the palace, however, during a break in the dancing, Julius came to Rutger and Elza with extended hands. He was so pleased to see them. How were they getting on? He turned, and asked in surprise, "Where has Sarith got to? We were together when we came towards you. Oh well, she'll have been held up somewhere and will be along in a minute." Julius recounted in detail how sweet Sarith was. He patted Rutger on the shoulder and said that he and Rutger would often be seeing each other, since the two ladies were not only sisters but also inseparable friends. They must travel to Klein Paradijs as soon as possible and be their guests for a week or two.

Rutger smiled and said that was fine, but in the meantime he and Elza would like to invite Julius and Sarith to a feast in their new house in the Gravenstraat to mark Rutger's appointment as administrator. The feast would be in ten days' time. They would still be in town then? Sarith had absolutely no intention of going to a feast at Rutger and Elza's. The whole family was invited, as were many other friends, but Sarith decided not to tell Julius that she wasn't going, because he would then want to know why.

In the afternoon of the twentieth of March, the day before the feast, Sarith suddenly had an oh so unbearable headache. Oh what a headache she had; she could hardly open her eyes. She had to lie in a darkened room and Mini-mini had to lay wet compresses on her forehead. A concerned Julius sat by her bed. Did she want the surgeon to come? But no, Sarith didn't want that. She just wanted rest on her own. Of course she couldn't attend the feast: she was far too ill for that. When Julius asked if had better remain with her, she answered that it would be better if he went. In any case, she could not talk and didn't want any noise, either. Staying alone with Mini-mini was best. Julius therefore excused his wife and told the host and hostess that poor Sarith had such a terrible headache. In bed that evening, Elza said to Rutger, "Have you noticed how Sarith is avoiding us?"

"Oh, don't let it worry you. She'll come round," said Rutger.

Elza thought that as far as she was concerned Sarith need never come round. Even so, when she thought of Sarith, she felt a twinge of sorrow, of nostalgia. Every time she realized that she had lost her playmate, the bosom friend of her childhood years, she felt sorry for a relationship that could have been so wonderful but was now ruined beyond repair.

MINI-MINI

In the late afternoon of the ninth of March, the day of the major ball in the governor's palace, Mini-mini sat in the doorway of her room in the grounds of the house in the Saramaccastraat. She was tired. She had had to run around for a whole two hours helping her misi to get dressed, or kneeling to adjust something at the front or at the back. Then the hair-do, first like this, then like that, finishing up as a decorative bouffant couture with something like a jib of precious stones at the top. Finally she had to bend to give the silver buckles on the slippers an extra polish.

This was not good when you were five months pregnant.

Now she sat to wait for Hendrik. He was late. When he finally appeared, the eight o'clock gun had fired. He said that he had gone to take a look in the Gravenstraat. In the Oranjestraat, across from Jean Nepveu's house, a crowd of people had gathered, mostly free coloureds and slaves. Everyone wanted to see the sparkling display of all those ladies in their elaborate clothes and all their trimmings of precious stones, gold and silver. Now, that had been a sight! How rich those whites were! Hendrik added bitterly that all that wealth was gained at the cost of the slaves' sweat and toil. Naturally Hendrik spent the night with Mini-mini.

Being with her loved one in these circumstances wasn't how Mini-mini had seen it in her dreams. She slept in a small room that she shared with three other young slave-girls who were the children's nannies in the house. Fortunately, you couldn't see anything in the dark, but from all the shuffling and bumping on the floor, it was obvious to them what was going on, and they kept making derisory remarks to Mini-mini, who they had always regarded as a quiet, retiring type. If you were a slave, something like privacy just didn't exist. And everything had to happen in such secrecy because he was a free man. None of the whites in the house except for her misi knew that Hendrik was spending the night there.

Mini-mini lay on the mat. She could not sleep, feeling the child moving within her. Hendrik was asleep next to her. Mini-mini dreamed of her future as a free woman with Hendrik. How she loved him, and he her. And now they would soon have a child. It would be a long time before he had saved up enough, but she would be patient and would save up, too. She was so thankful that not a single masra had had her before Hendrik. Didn't that always happen with pretty slave-girls? And she was pretty; she knew that. From her earliest years she had always heard people saying so. She understood that 'beautiful' was used mainly when someone had white blood, and after all she had a white father. Her mother had told her that both Masra Jacob A'haron and his eighteen-year-old son had been sleeping with her at that time. One of the two was her father, but it didn't make any difference to Mini-mini: she was simply a slave-girl. What did being beautiful matter if you were a slave, anyway? And it was certainly not only her light skin that caused people to remark on her beauty; she had a good figure, small round breasts, finely cut features, pure white teeth and large dark-brown eyes. Her hair was black, with curls, and hung to half way down her back. She usually had it in a plait. How often had men, white and coloured, gazed at her hungrily. But fortunately, due to the fact that she was Misi Sarith's property, not a single man had ever been able to take advantage of her. At least for that she was thankful to the misi. This could have changed, of course, now that the misi had a masra, but he was a good and fair person. He loved his wife so much that he would certainly not interfere with a slave-girl. And luckily she now had her Hendrik.

Mini-mini heard the carriage ride into the grounds and realized that the family was returning home. She got up quickly, fastened a shawl around herself and hastened to the house, where her misi and masra were just going upstairs.

Misi Sarith was so happy. She told Mini-mini that she was dead tired. She had danced so much. It had been wonderful, everything so beautiful, and everyone had found her so beautiful and she had had so many compliments about her ingenious hair-do. Mini-mini had done that so beautifully. She would reward her for that in the morning. Masra Julius looked smilingly at his wife, who was so content and happy, felt in his pocket and gave Mini-mini a coin, saying, "Here Mini-mini, your reward, because the misi might well forget it in the morning."[149]

When Mini-mini returned to her room in the grounds Hendrik wasn't there. Perhaps he had gone to the loo in the grounds? But when he still had not returned a while later, she went looking for him.

"Are you looking for your boyfriend?" asked Nestor, the

149 "Kande a mise e frigiti tamara."

slave who functioned as coachman and was busy unshack-
ling the carriage. "He left."[150]

Mini-mini went inside again. Why had Hendrik gone?
Just like that, in the middle of the night? Oh, well, perhaps
he was afraid of oversleeping the next morning. She would
ask him tomorrow.

But Hendrik did not come the next evening, or the evening
after. Mini-mini sent an errand boy to his home with the
message that he must come to her quickly. The boy said that
he had delivered the message to Hendrik's mother, but still
Hendrik did not come. The following Sunday Mini-mini decided to go to the house herself. She knew that his mother
was usually away on Sundays. When she arrived at the house
she found everything shut. There was no-one at home.

A neighbour who was sitting at an open window and had
seen her walking around the house asked amicably, "Who
are you looking for?"[151]

"Hendrik," replied Mini-mini.

"Oh, he has just left with his woman,"[152] came the
answer.

"With his woman? Perhaps misi means his mother?"[153]

"No, not his mother, but Hendrik now has a woman, Misi
Meta, a nice mulatto girl. They went that way."[154]

Mini-mini felt as if she had just received a punch to the
face. Did Hendrik have a partner? Since when? She was his
woman. She walked slowly away from the house and in a
trance walked back to the Saramaccastraat, tear after tear
rolling down her cheeks. The whole day she just sat with her
head in her hands, just staring ahead, in such a way that even
Misi Sarith asked her, "What's the matter, Mini-mini, are
you ill? Go and sleep for a while."[155]

150 "Y'e suku yu mati no? A gowe yere."
151 "Dan suma y'e suku so dan?"
152 "Na di dyonsro de gowe, a gowe nanga en uma."
153 "Nanga en uma? Kande misi mene en m'ma?"
154 "No, no, e m'ma no de, ma Hendrik habi wan uma now, misi
      Meta, wan mooi malata uma, den gowe so sei."
155 "San de fu du Mini-mini, y'e siki no? We go sribi pikinso."

Mini-mini decided she just had to speak to Hendrik, and the next day she waited for him in the Steenbakkersgracht, where he worked at the cabinet maker's. When he came out to go home, she was suddenly there in front of him. "Mini-mini," he exclaimed, alarmed. Her voice soft, Mini-mini asked what truth there was in what the neighbour had told her, and why he was no longer coming to her.

Hendrik gave a sigh. Yes, it was true. He loved her, but she was a slave-girl. When would he ever get enough money together to buy her freedom? It would take years, and what would he do all those years? She on the plantation, now and then in the town for a week, and he alone here. He omitted to tell her how much his mother had been objecting and had told him how stupid she found him to have fallen in love with a slave-girl. Even if she was beautiful and a mulatto, she was still only a slave-girl, and he with his light skin and almost smooth hair could certainly attract so many other beautiful girls. It was his mother who engineered his meeting Meta. It wasn't long before she had come to live with them.

With downcast eyes Mini-mini heard what Hendrik had to say to her. She knew full well that any other woman would not have accepted this. She would have screamed, fought, gone to that Meta and slapped and hit her. But she, Mini-mini, could not do that. She was so timid and soft by nature and had never been able to cope with violence. She just turned and went away. So that was that. Exit Hendrik! Exit freedom! Everything had been just a dream. On her mat that night she wept. Yes, everything had been a dream. Except for the child. That was no dream; that was reality! She placed her hand on her stomach and felt the child moving. She resolved that, whatever it might take, she would ensure that that child would not be a slave. He or she would be born a slave, that was inevitable, but she would save every cent, and when the child was grown up she would buy his freedom to spare him all the humiliation and misery of slavery. For that is why Hendrik had rejected her. Because she was a slave-girl. Mini-mini thought back to what Hendrik had told her and to what the misi had said about the ball at the governor's, where all the whites had glistered with their gold and jewels, where the tables had groaned under all the food and drink. All the fantastic mansions in the town, carriages, expensive furnishings: everything obtained through slavery.

Slaves: people who were the property of a group of whites and who had to work and toil for them in order to produce these oh so necessary commodities. And Mini-mini asked herself whether these whites realized what they were drinking when they lifted that cup to their lips. Whether they ever for a second realized how costly this all was – what a price was paid for the coffee and for the sugar!

Julius had wanted to return to Klein Paradijs after the party, but Sarith did not want to. They couldn't possibly leave yet. On 16 March the new governor had been honoured at public worship in the synagogue in the Heerenstraat. This happening was specially in honour of Governor Nepveu, who was kindly disposed towards the Jews, in contrast to so many other whites who regarded Jews as second-rate citizens. The whites who had more recently arrived in Suriname appeared not to realize that it was precisely the Jews who had been the driving force behind the blossoming of this colony. They were the first substantial group to come here. They had settled here, mostly in the upper reaches of the rivers. They had started plantations, and with the money earned had paid huge sums to the government to provide for the colony's upkeep. Now things were going less well for the Jews. The land at their plantations, often in use for a hundred years or more, was becoming exhausted and infertile, and when they asked for land on the lower reaches of the rivers, where many plantations were being established, they were refused purely and simply because they were Jews. The whole Jewish community hoped that this would all change with the appointment of Jean Nepveu, and they very much wanted to demonstrate that they had every faith in him. The service in the synagogue was taking place in this context. Everything was beautifully decorated, including the complete entrance right down to the street. The whole coloured population stood once again to gape at this display of opulence. Carriages drove to and fro; pedestrians arrived, attended by slaves, all in their finest clothes.

Three weeks later, on 4 April, there was a reception at the house of Abraham Cohen, the Jewish teacher and assistant rabbi, in his house on the corner of the Klipstenenstraat and Heerenstraat. Now, Rebecca was after all Sarith's sister, and of course she and Julius could not possibly leave before the reception. They would really have to attend. Julius gave in to his wife, but then they really had to return. He must definitely be back on his plantation before the heavy rains set in.

When they returned to Klein Paradijs it was already raining. They arrived at the plantation in a heavy shower after a wet and tiring two-day journey. Mini-mini held the umbrella over Misi Sarith's head once they had disembarked. Misi Sarith walked so quickly that Mini-mini could hardly keep up with her. The wet clay was very slippery, and there Mini-mini lost her footing. With the umbrella in one hand and a large bag in the other she could not hold on to anything. With a great thump she landed on the ground.

"Oh Mini-mini," called Misi Sarith, and hurried on indoors. Mini-mini felt a sharp pain in her side. She tried to get up, but that proved impossible. The masra, who was still at the boat and had seen everything, came to help her stand up. He called Benny, his slave, and together they helped Mini-mini indoors. Once there, Kwasiba hurried to help her daughter.

That night Mini-mini's child was born, two months premature. He was already dead when he came into the world. Kwasiba said so softly, "The poor, poor dear!"[156] and wanted to take the child away before Mini-mini had seen him.

But Mini-mini sat up and said, "Let me look, mama."[157]

She gazed at the motionless little boy: a very light-brown skin with thin, black, downy hair across his head. She plant-

156　"Ké ba, ké poti."
157　"Meki mi si en, ma."

ed a kiss on his forehead, which was already turning cold, and gave him to her mother. Silently she lay down again. There were no tears. For such intense grief there were no tears any more.

SARITH

Sarith was considerably moved by what had happened to Mini-mini. She visited Mini-mini a few times in her room and stroked the girl's hand, lying there so silent. Poor Mini-mini. How terrible that she had lost her child.

Sarith had wanted to tell Mini-mini that for the past few weeks now she suspected that she was also pregnant. When she began to suspect this, she thought immediately how good it was that Mini-mini would herself have a child. She would then have a good wet-nurse for her own baby, and her child would have a playmate. If they were of the same sex she could give Mini-mini's child to hers. All this would now not happen. She didn't mention her own pregnancy to Mini-mini. Right now this would be too painful for the poor girl, lying silent and grieving on her mat. Mini-mini, however, knew her mistress' body better than did Sarith herself, and when, a week later, she was up and about again, and was helping her get dressed, she asked gently, "Is misi going to have a baby?"[158]

How happy Julius was when his wife told him she was expecting! He was immediately full of concern, however. She must now be very careful and must absolutely not get tired or exert herself. Alarmed, Sarith realized that he might mean by this that she should no longer go to the town. After about two months Sarith could not put up with it any longer. The silence and dullness of Klein Paradijs was driving her crazy. Nothing doing on the neighbouring plantations, either. Mostly older married couples; no feasts, no parties. Furthermore, she was scared, for the raids by the Maroons were getting steadily worse.

The Boni-negroes raided more and more plantations. Of-

158 "Misi, yu habi bere no?"

ten they murdered all the whites and set all the slaves free. It was really frightening. Sarith wanted to go to the town. She was scared. When she told Julius, he answered that she need not be afraid. These Bonis raided only those plantations where the masters mistreated the slaves. He had the reputation of being a good master. His slaves were faithful to him and no-one wanted to escape from the plantation. And even if there were a raid, all the slaves would fight for him. Furthermore, there were so many military posts in the neighbourhood. No Boni would ever dare come so far. Wasn't there even a military post near to their plantation?

When, however, it became known that the nearby military post had been raided by the Bonis, that five soldiers had been killed and others had fled, Sarith was no longer open to persuasion. She wept, wrung her hands and accused Julius of not loving her otherwise he would not expose her to such dangers and especially now that she was pregnant. All right: she could go to the town, and just for a few weeks, because the government would be sure to send reinforcements and set up a larger, stronger military post there. He himself could not go at this time, but he would send Benny with her. And so at the end of June Sarith left for the town, with no intention of returning to Klein Paradijs in the foreseeable future.

After six weeks or so, Julius did come to the town. He was missing his wife. Would she please go back with him? Everything was safe. The military had the situation well under control. Sarith agreed. She had come to the conclusion that she should be nice to him, for she had heard that the Jewish community would be holding a great feast at Joden-Savanna in October. This would be to mark the eighty-fifth anniversary of the synagogue, and the Feast of Tabernacles. Governor and Mrs Nepveu would be guests of honour. Well, Sarith must certainly be there, and so it was better to comply with Julius now and return to the plantation for a few weeks.

There she got bored, wandered around aimlessly, sat listlessly in an easy chair, while Mini-mini, Kwasiba and other domestic slave-girls were busy making clothes for the baby.

Sarith looked at her body, which was swelling, and thought that having a child was nice, but it was all the same a bother that it had to grow in its mother's body, with the ghastly things this did to her figure. To her horror she realized that in October, when the festivities would be taking place, her body would be even more gross and that she would then have nothing to wear. She must decidedly go again to Paramaribo to have gowns made that would to some degree disguise her condition. When she told Julius about this, he replied in amazement, "But Sarith, you've been back only three weeks. All that travelling to and fro can't be good for you?"

"But I must have new clothes for the feast; nothing fits any more," cried Sarith.

"Surely Kwasiba and Mini-mini can make something for you here?" remarked Julius.

"What? How could you dream for one second that I'd appear at the governor's feast dressed in gowns made by slaves? Do you really want me to be mocked and ridiculed by everyone there?" And she burst into tears again, because Julius didn't understand her and would have her be a figure of fun at such an important event. Julius could not cope with this feminine logic and gave in again.

And so Sarith went to the town again at the beginning of September and installed herself at her sister's, this time to have the best dress-makers create gowns. In the last week of September Julius also came to the town, to travel to Joden-Savanna with his wife and in-laws, but first to Hébron, where they would spend a few days before travelling on.

It was inevitable that Sarith and Elza would meet, now that they were all staying together at Hébron, but Sarith managed to arrange things so that she was never alone with Elza and Rutger. Although Rutger and Julius often spoke with each other, Sarith always had something else to do if Elza came into the front room or on the front veranda. If Elza came through one door into the dining room, Sarith would leave by another door. If Elza was with her children in the summerhouse, Sarith would be in her room or somewhere else indoors. Elza noticed all this, but said nothing. In fact, she would not know what to say to Sarith.

The families had agreed not to take the very little children to Joden-Savanna. Only Esther and Jacob's twins, who were now seven, went along. Esther's two other boys, as well as Elza's Gideon and Jonathan and Rebecca's Zipporah, stayed with their nannies at Hébron. In Elza's opinion that was more peaceful and certainly safer.

What superb festivities there were at the Savanna! After the service in the synagogue there were sumptuous meals and ball after ball. Despite her condition, Sarith managed to join in with nearly all the dancing. The seamstress had done her work well and had made marvellous gowns with full skirts or a satin jacket dropping over the hips, so that it was almost impossible to see that Sarith was seven months pregnant. She enjoyed herself and was still the desirable woman with whom all the men wanted to dance. In the governor's party there were several handsome captains and lieutenants who were paying her so much attention that Julius would now and then intervene and dance with her, to make it clear to everyone that she was his wife.

Elza and Rutger had wandered hand in hand through Joden-Savanna, recalling memories from five years previously when they had first met each other. "Do you still remember how annoyed you were when I said that you were really quite wise for a young girl?" asked Rutger with a laugh. "Yes, but you said it in such a way as to suggest that only men could be wise," answered Elza.

"Where has the time gone? Oh, yes, did you ever imagine that we would some day stand here again as man and wife?" asked Rutger again.

"Father and mother and two sons!" Elza laughed. She stopped and looked out over the valley. Rutger took her in his arms and gave her a kiss. As they walked back, Elza heard Sarith's laugh ring out. That was five years ago, too, she thought, but what has happened between us in the meantime no-one knows except the three of us.

After the governor and his entourage had departed, the

feasting went on for another week at Joden-Savanna, but Elza and Rutger did not stay to the end since Rutger's duties did not permit such a long absence from the office.

Sarith and Julius did stay until the end, at Sarith's insistence, and it was the last week of October when they arrived back in Paramaribo. After a few days at the De Ledesmas' in the Saramaccastraat Julius said, "Well Sarith, it's time for us to go back home."

"We?" asked Sarith, surprised, "Not we, Julius, because I'm not going!"

"What do you mean, you're not going? You surely cannot stay here? Your child will be born soon, and then you will certainly need to be at home."

"You can't possibly want me to travel to the Boven-Commewijne!" exclaimed Sarith. "You yourself said that I must take things quietly, and now you want me to make that tiring journey for two days in a boat!"

"It will be less tiring than all that dancing you've been doing of late. I'll have an easy chair with cushions installed in the boat," said Julius.

"But I'm not going. It's far too dangerous with all those Boni-negroes raiding plantations."

"They will certainly not raid our plantation."

"I don't want to go. No, no, no, I won't go. What if something goes wrong? There'll be no-one to help me!" By now Sarith was screaming.

"You don't need to worry about that. After all, you have Kwasiba and we also have an excellent midwife at the plantation – Nene Trude, who helps all the slave-girls with their births and everything always goes well."

"So you want her to attend to me, do you? What is good enough for slave-girls is good enough for your wife, too. I don't want that, I don't, I want my mother with me when that moment comes. Oh, you see, you don't love me or you'd never treat me like this." Sarith began to wail with rage.

"But oh my darling," Julius couldn't console his little woman quickly enough. "Of course your mother can come to you at Klein Paradijs. As far as I'm concerned she can stay with you, if that's what you want."

"Is that what you think? Do you think for one second that my mother would want to come to such a faraway place? My mother always wants to be in the town in December. Here in Paramaribo. She's here every year around this time." Sarith was now sobbing loudly, for she thought of all the parties that took place around New Year, and she would just die of misery if, as last year, she had to be on the plantation again in this period while everyone in the town was feasting away. "Don't you see," she wailed, now stamping her feet and thumping various objects around, "I won't go to the plantation, do you hear, I won't go. You never let me do anything; you don't even want me to be with my mother right now. You don't really love me." Sniffle, sniffle. Wailing and stamping and shouting "I want, I want" had always been tried and tested ways for her. As a thoroughly spoilt child she had always got her own way with such tantrums, and now, too, all this wailing and screaming worked, for Julius, totally put out by this outburst, knelt next to her and said soothingly, "No, dearest, I hadn't thought of all that, but you're right. Stay here if you wish. But aren't we putting too great a burden on the De Ledesmas? They might be family, but is this all all right?" Esther, however, said that they certainly had no objection to having her sister there. This house was after all almost like Sarith's parental home. They would look after Sarith well. He did not have to worry. And so Julius left for his plantation, thinking dejectedly that this was all turning out very differently from how he had imagined it.

On 4 December Sarith's baby was born. It was not an easy birth, mainly because Sarith herself was exceptionally scared of the unknown and behaved as if she was the first woman in the world ever to give birth. The whole house was in uproar that night. Kwasiba, who for safety's sake had also been sent by Julius to Paramaribo, was continually running up and down the stairs with hot water and complaining about this misi who was making everything so much worse by not being able to relax. Mini-mini knelt next to the bed, mopping her misi's forehead, holding her hand and speaking comforting words.

Only when the boy was born and had had his first good cry was Sarith finally at ease, and when she had the child lying next to her on the bed and Mini-mini had washed her face and combed her hair, she said, "He's beautiful, isn't he, Mini-mini?"[159]

And Mini-mini said quietly, "He is beautiful, yes misi,"[160] thinking sadly about another little boy who had been born a few months earlier and had not been granted an earthly existence.

Jacob de Ledesma ensured that his brother-in-law heard as quickly as possible that he had a son, and within just four days Julius was in town. He gazed happily on his wife. He was so pleased that he had a son again. "We'll call him Jethro," he said.

"Jethro, why Jethro?" asked Sarith. She was wanting another, much more modern, name.

"That's a really nice name from the Torah, full of significance," Julius replied. "You surely know that Jethro was the father-in-law of Moses, one of the founders of our people? And Jethro means great and wonderful, and that our son certainly will be."

Sarith was in total disagreement with that name. She regarded it as a stupid custom in many Jewish families, burdening all their children with all kinds of names from the Torah. Jethro! What a name! Almost as stupid as her own name, Sarith. Who was ever called Sarith?

When she had once asked her mother how on earth she had arrived at that name, her mother Rachel had explained that Sarith was called after her mother's sister, Sarah, and her little sister Judith, who had died young. Combining these two names had given rise to Sarith. Stupid, in fact. And now her own

159 "A moi no, Mini-mini?"
160 "A moi ya misi, a moi baya."

child, too, had been given such a name. Jethro, and that while there were so many nice names such as Edward and Arthur and Cedric. But well, she could not be opposed to everything her husband said, and so the child was given the name Jethro.

Following Jewish custom, the circumcision took place on precisely the eighth day. The rabbi came to perform the ritual, which took place in the large front hall. As with many Jewish traditions, this was predominantly a male happening. An uneven number of men stood in the room, all with their heads covered and looking towards the east. After various prayers had been said or sung and the rabbi had prepared everything, the child was brought in. The little Jethro lay on a white lace cushion with the lower part of his body uncovered and was brought in like this by Kwasiba. She lay the cushion on a small table in front of the rabbi and then went to stand outside the room. Jethro screamed really hard. His little face turned all shades of red and small drops of sweat appeared on his forehead. He had deliberately not been fed that morning. After the circumcision he would be very hungry and would suck away lustily. Exhausted and with a full stomach he would fall asleep, which would be best for the healing of the wound.

And of course all this was accompanied by a party. The De Ledesmas' house was full of people. Everyone was coming and going, and Sarith was really disappointed that she had to lie upstairs in bed. Elza and Rutger were also among the guests. Of course, the men did not have to visit the new mother's room, and Rutger could congratulate Julius downstairs on the birth of his son. For Elza it was more difficult. She could not stay away from Sarith's room, and in fact she wanted to get a good look at the little boy. She went in along with many other ladies, looked briefly in the cradle and remained standing by the wall while she placed a gift in Gideon's hands, with the instruction to give it to aunty in bed and to say, "Very best wishes." Gideon, now almost three, did this very nicely.

Julius understood full well that his wife could not travel, and he himself remained in the town. In the meantime it was the end of December. Sarith could get up, and at the New Year's celebrations she was already well enough to be able to dance, happy that her figure had not suffered and that she looked good again.

She did not feed the child herself. She didn't want to spoil her beautiful breasts with the suckling of a child. Luckily, the De Ledesmas had a slave-girl who herself had a baby and could therefore look after this. Around the middle of January Julius decided that it really was time to return to the plantation, but Sarith refused.

Julius did not understand this at all. She was surely strong enough. Everything was fine: look how she had been able to do all that dancing the past weeks. Sarith said that everything was well with her, but he obviously wasn't thinking of the child. Who would dream of undertaking such an arduous journey with a six-week-old child? And just look at all that rain. The child would most surely catch cold. Did he really want the child to catch cold and die?

"But we can pack him in well and he's lying in a cradle," Julius proposed.

"And feeding, then, the wet nurse? After all, that is Esther's slave-girl. How will the child be fed?" asked Sarith.

Julius thought that maybe he could buy the slave-girl.

"That won't be possible," answered Sarith. "Esther will never sell her; she needs her too badly herself."

Julius could not quite see how, in a household with perhaps thirty slaves, one slave-girl more or less would make a big difference, but all right, if Esther did not want to sell her, perhaps he could borrow her for a while. That was also not acceptable to Sarith, who began crying plaintively that Julius was really such a tyrant and always wanted to get his own way, never taking her into account and not even thinking of his own child. Julius therefore gave in yet again and travelled back alone to Klein Paradijs, leaving Sarith and Jethro behind.

Sarith continued her life just as in the past. She went out to feasts, to parties. Her child was fed by the wet nurse and further cared for by Mini-mini. But Esther, too, felt that Sarith's behaviour was not as it should be. She noted with some consternation how her sister was going from the one party to the next and seemed to have forgotten completely that she was now a married woman. When she remarked on this, Sarith thought that it was certainly better being in town than at Klein Paradijs, but having your sister's eye on you was not ideal, in fact. No, she would have to get her own house in Paramaribo. Julius would have to arrange this for her. A house of her own, with furniture and slaves. Then she would not have to rely on the hospitality of others and would be free to stay in town as long as she wanted. She would now have to be really sweet to Julius, and around a month later, when he visited the town again, she immediately agreed to return with him to Klein Paradijs.

CHAPTER IX

RUTGER

An invitation to a party at the Lust en Rust Plantation had just been delivered. Rutger sat in his office with the card in his hand. Yet another party. He didn't feel at all like it, for it meant another five days away from the office. And all these parties were so much of a muchness. They were all held for the sole purpose of flaunting one's wealth. The swagger of expensive clothing and jewellery, the houses with their finest furnishings, most extravagant crystal, silver and porcelain, an excess of food and drink. The planter was doing well! What prosperity; how things were flourishing!

All this wealth and splendour, all this extravagance, were, however, more fiction than fact, thought Rutger to himself. The City of Amsterdam had bought the Van Sommelsdijck family's shares in April 1770. This meant that two-thirds of the colony was now the property of Amsterdam, and one-third that of the West Indische Compagnie. Even in Governor Mauricius' time, many Amsterdam banks and merchant houses had been of the opinion that the plantations in the west represented the best investments. In the 1760's, sugar, coffee and cocoa commanded high prices. Most of the produce was transported to Amsterdam.

The annual turnover of these commodities could be counted in millions. Especially in Amsterdam huge profits were made, and it was no illusion that many of the wonderful mansions along the famous Amsterdam canals were built as a result of the era of slavery in Suriname and through the blood, sweat and toil of thousands of slaves.

In any event, the Amsterdam merchant houses were all too ready to pour money into the Suriname plantations. They sent agents who had the authority to arrange mortgages for the planters. If this was successful, then the agent would receive a percentage as commission. The colonists were completely dazzled by all this projected fortune. Everyone suddenly wanted to become a plantation owner: people who could hardly distinguish a cocoa plant from a coffee plant and who thought that crystals of sugar fell from the pressed sugarcane. Almost everyone, whether formerly a cobbler, a butcher or simply a good-for-nothing, everyone had to become a planter and saw himself as a rich plantation owner sitting in his easy chair on the veranda.

Others who had a small plantation wanted to expand it to three times its size. Still others wanted to sell the plantation they already had in order to establish another, larger one with better products. And this paid off, since you had money and wealth before the first sod of earth was dug. All kinds of methods were employed to gain more and more money. Bribed assessors valued plantations at three- or four-times their actual worth. Of course there were people who raised their voices in dissent, but who listened to them?

Rutger, himself an agent of an Amsterdam merchant company and administrator for several plantations, knew that this wasn't the normal way of doing things. He warned several friends not to accept the agents' proposals and especially not to get into debt, but as always when good advice is offered unsolicited, it was held against him. Some of his former good friends turned their backs on him, of the opinion that he was speaking only out of jealousy and resentment.

Rutger was still sitting with the card in his hand when Alex came in with a cup of coffee. Was something up with Alex, Rutger asked himself. He looked so down-in-the-mouth.

"What's up, Alex?" Rutger asked.

"Nothing, masra," Alex answered gently.

"Are you worried?" Rutger repeated. "Has something gone wrong with our agreement?"

Alex smiled briefly and said, "Not from my side, masra, but I don't know about masra."

Alex was saving up to be able to buy his freedom. When

they were returning from Holland a few years earlier, Rutger had had a serious talk with Alex on board ship. Alex had said to Rutger that in Holland everyone earned money by working. No-one was another's slave, no-one was someone else's property. Some people earned very little and were extremely poor, but they were free, and in Alex's eyes freedom was at the end of the day the greatest virtue. He could quite understand the Maroons, who preferred to face all the dangers of the bush rather than be slaves. Rutger had suggested to Alex that from that moment on he pay him, too, for his work; three guilders a week, and it was up to Alex what he did with the money. He could use it or give it back to Rutger for safe keeping, to be saved up until he had enough to buy his freedom. Alex was still saving. Just a few more months and he would have enough.

"So why are you looking so upset? Surely you're not ill?" asked Rutger.

"No masra, it's because of Caesar, masra."

"What's up with Caesar?" Rutger enquired.

Caesar was Alex's best friend. He was a slave of the Bueno de Mesquita family. Masra Bueno de Mesquita had died a few months earlier.

"His misi has sold him, masra," Alex continued, "to the government, for the Zwarte Jagers Corps."[161]

"But that's fine, surely," thought Rutger. "That means he'll gain his freedom in a while. That's promised to those people."

"But masra doesn't understand" said Alex. "Caesar will now have to fight his own people. They will regard him as a traitor. Caesar doesn't want that. He doesn't want to fight the Boni-negroes. He doesn't want to be a traitor. But what can he do? He's a slave, he doesn't even own himself, just like me. He must do what he's told, otherwise he'll be punished, severely punished."

Rutger looked at Alex thoughtfully. What could he say? Alex was right. No white would ever think about it from that point of view. They thought they were doing the slaves

161   Corps of Black Hunters or Black Rangers.

a great favour, for they were offering the chance of freedom. But listening to Alex, these negroes would in fact have a tough time.

The Zwarte Jagers Corps had just been inaugurated by Governor Nepveu. It was clear that white soldiers were not up to jungle warfare. Governor Nepveu had worked out that the escapees in the bush could best be opposed by negroes who were equally brave and strong as the bush-negroes. After true service they would be given their freedom and a plot of land. Now and then they could go to visit their wives and children on the plantations. How could these negroes refuse? They were slaves! In the army their uniform comprised knee-length shorts and a red cap. For this reason everyone was calling them Redi Musu (Red Hats).

Alex was sad because his friend Caesar would have to fight his own people against his will. What needless sorrow people caused each other!

"Masra, I want to ask masra something," came Alex's voice. Rutger started from his contemplations. He had totally forgotten that Alex was standing there.

"What do you want to ask, Alex," Rutger asked.

"May I visit Caesar this evening?" asked Alex.

"I'll give you a pass," said Rutger. "But be careful, lad, don't go doing anything stupid. I realize you sympathize with Caesar, but there's nothing you can do to help him."

There came a knock on the door and Mr van Ritter entered. Like Rutger, he was a member of the Court of Civil Justice. Alex went to sit outside near the door on his bench. Just as he had expected, the conversation was mainly about the soldiers' fight against the Boni-negroes. Masra van Ritter told Rutger that the governor was now corresponding with the Dutch State. The directors of the Society had been so angry with the governor in the past. Those gentlemen in Holland – they simply could not imagine what it was like here in Suriname.

Jean Nepveu had, however, done his very best. Since his inauguration in 1770 he had set up a corps of free negroes and mulattos. That this corps was ineffective in practice was not the governor's fault. The military themselves should have

seen to this. Every time the governor had requested reinforcements for the Dutch troops in the country, the gentlemen in the Netherlands were always so amazed that a corps
twelve hundred strong was not able to suppress a handful of
bush-negroes. They had sent the governor an extremely angry letter accusing him that there was total lack of discipline
in the ranks of the troops that were costing them so much
money, and that they were cowardly, lazy, incapable and
negligent.

The letter went on to demand of the governor, nay, to
compel him, to investigate thoroughly the behaviour of the
Dutch soldiers in the military posts and to react accordingly.
In addition, a list must be sent to Holland detailing the con-
crete evidence of the soldiers' behaviour, for it was a disgrace
that the good officers in the homeland were compared in the
same breath with the good-for-nothings and failures in Suriname who would sacrifice salary rather than go on expeditions. And one thing was for sure: they would not be sending
any new troops!

But now the governor had sent a desperate letter to His
Royal Highness the Prince. He had made it clear to him that
the situation was untenable. Everyone was scared. The
colonists were expecting that at any minute a general revolt
would break out among the slaves. The Dutch parliament had
decided to send state troops. These forces were recruited from
the various European countries. These mercenaries would be
under the command of the Swiss colonel Fourgeoud.

"And when are these troops coming, then?" asked Rutger.
"These are plans. It could take years before anything con-
crete happens."

Masra van Ritter thought not. "The parliament has clearly shown that it recognizes the seriousness of the situation,"
he believed. "In the meantime we'll have to fight with the
troops we have. The governor has high hopes for the Zwarte
Jagers. He wants to strengthen the corps. Do you perhaps
have a few good, strong negroes for sale? What about the
one who was here in the room just now? He seems to be a
good strong lad."

"Not a chance," said Rutger. "That is Alex. Alex is not for sale, for any price and to anyone except to himself. Good morning, Mr van Ritter."

And with his hand on the bell, he called out, "Alex, will you please see Masra van Ritter out?"

ALEX

The same evening Alex went to look for Caesar in the Zwarte Jagers' camp. He did not dare go in by the main entrance, but walked round and waited in a dark corner. He saw a few negroes and about four whites sitting on a bench near the entrance. Each of them was holding a weapon.

"Psst, Kwasi," whispered Alex when someone he knew came near, "Where is Caesar?"[162]

"Wait," said Kwasi softly. "Come with me."[163]

He took Alex to a small open camp a little further on where a group of about twenty men sat under a thatched shelter[164]. Caesar was surprised to see Alex. Alex didn't really know what to say, but Caesar began to speak of his own account. He had been in the camp for a few weeks now. There were always more than fifty Zwarte Jagers and some had already carried out several sorties. They were kept under tight supervision because several had deserted to the other side during the first sortie. They had pretended that they would fight, but when they had actually met the Alukus, they simply joined the side of Boni and his followers. Caesar wondered whether he should do that, too, but he had a wife and children. What would happen to them if he changed sides? Would they perhaps have to suffer?

The Alukus had quickly seen off the Redi Musus. It was a straight man-to-man fight. They were not all that bothered about the white soldiers, but could not accept that negroes were fighting against their own kind. They regarded the Redi Musus as traitors.

---

162   "Pe Caesar de?"
163   "Wakti. Kon nanga mi."
164   An open shelter with a roof of leaves.

And Caesar decided sadly that he did not know what to do for the best. He was no traitor, no more than the other Redi Musus. What could he do? If he wanted to leave the corps before the end of his period of service he would have to pay eight hundred or a thousand guilders. Where could a poor slave find that kind of money? He simply had no choice. Redi Musus were not traitors; they were just ordinary people whose situation was being readily taken advantage of.

Some men who had been in the corps since its foundation told about their experiences in the bush...

The Alukus had a real fort, one that was just as good as the whites'. This fort was called Buku[165], referring to the fact that the negroes themselves said they would rather 're-turn to the dust' than surrender. Fort Buku, under the leadership of Baron, lay in the middle of a swamp, completely surrounded by palisades and equipped with small canon. A flag bearing a black lion on a yellow background flew above the village, which they called 'Mi sa lasi' (I shall lose). There were other forts, too. For example, Gado Sabi (God Knows), which also lay in a swamp with extensive paddy fields having rows of felled trees in them which provided good cover for the guerrillas, for that is what the negroes were. Another Aluku fort was Pennenburg. The surrounding land was covered with sharp-pointed wooden stakes, which meant that the military could not get near.

The Alukus knew what they were doing. Maybe they did not have the weapons that the colonial army had, but they had all kinds of ways to make a fool of the enemy or frighten him off. They knew the military's strategies precisely, and put this knowledge to good use. Very often the army followed one of the Maroons' paths. The Bonis made all kinds of false tracks. For instance, a path would suddenly come to an end in the middle of the bush and then start again a few hundred metres further on, but the army did not know this. Often they would follow a path, only to find after struggling

165   Here, mould or mildew (more commonly, 'book').

on for two days that they had made a complete circle and were back where they started. There were many traps set, often with sharp-pointed stakes. A tuft of hair was attached to each point, and when the soldiers had managed to extract the points from their skin, the hair remained behind and ensured that infection set in.

The military could make no further progress at night, but the bush-negroes were experts in finding their way through the bush at night. They had very regular contact with the military's porters, who would provide all kinds of information. The Maroons hid themselves in the many swamps. If a troop of soldiers came on through such a swamp with their weapons in their upheld hands, the Maroons would shoot at them from their hideaways. The soldiers could return the fire only once, for it was then impossible for them to lower their arms in order to reload.

When raiding a military post the Maroons used the following tactics. They made a lot of noise outside the post at night. They took with them the bodies of soldiers that had been left behind after previous raids and treated them with herbs so that they did not decompose. When they raided a military post, they would throw these bodies down. The soldiers woke up, saw weapons pointed at them from all direction and dozens of bodies on the ground. A voice called to them that if they dared go for their weapons they would be shot dead. The soldiers would flee in panic, leaving everything behind. The weapons were, however, mock ones, made of wood, and when the soldiers had fled, the Maroons could triumphantly take possession of all the weapons, ammunition and food stocks that were left behind.

When the Alukus raided a plantation they would surround the buildings at night. All the buildings were set on fire simultaneously. If the plantation owner, manager or overseer was known as someone who mistreated slaves, then the Alukus made quick work of him. They usually left the white children unharmed. If they raided plantations where the owner did not have a bad reputation, they freed the slaves, took weapons and other tools, and did not harm the whites.

Because the negroes knew that the military were trying to starve them out by first stripping their farmlands and then destroying them, they laid these plots out a long way away from their villages. Sometimes such fields were one or even two days away from the village. Providing food was a job for the women. They cultivated the ground and laid up huge stores of food. It was painfully obvious that the eight hundred European soldiers with all their weapons were no match at all for the Alukus, about three hundred in number.

Three of the men who now belonged to the Zwarte Jagers had previously been porters. This meant that they had been in the army for five years now and had gone on many expeditions. They had a great deal to tell. Those white soldiers were in fact really stupid: you could almost take pity on them. What did those white kids know of the jungle? When they went on an expedition they just hoped for the best, with a compass in one hand and a machete in the other. For a four-week expedition a group would comprise three officers, six subalterns, three doctors and sixty-five soldiers. Such a group needed one hundred and eighty-three porters. These porters carried for the soldiers: one thousand and eighty pounds of meat, five hundred and forty loaves of bread, one thousand three hundred and fifty pints[166] of groats, thirty-six pints of dram (strong drink), six cases of cartridges, three cases of medical supplies, a hundred and fifty flints and seventy-five machetes. For the hundred and eighty-three porters themselves were taken: two thousand five hundred pounds of dried cod, twelve hundred loaves, one thousand seven hundred pints of groats. The paths were narrow, so they walked in single file, thus forming a long line. The vanguard comprised a few slaves who would have to hack the path free. Then came the troop itself, as a whole or in two parts. The porters walked in the middle. If they encountered Maroons or were attacked by them, all the soldiers had to form a tight circle round the porters, to ensure that they did not

166   The pint as used in Amsterdam at that time in the 18th century, equal to 0.5 litre.

desert. At the rear walked several more soldiers and an officer. Due to the huge distance between the front and rear of
this column, hardly any communication was possible, while
the Alukus had often detected them long in advance.

The bush itself held enough dangers for them. To begin
with there were the mosquitoes, ants, mites and so forth. Because their presence must not be detected, no 'smoke' pot (or
smudge pot) could be made. Sleeping in a hammock was almost impossible. Many soldiers simply slept on the ground
with their heads in a hollow, covered by a hammock. If they
came across a creek, it was crossed on felled tree trunks. A
swamp was more difficult. Since its extent was unknown,
they simply went through it. They were up to their waists in
water in which boa constrictors or crocodiles would be lurking. The most dangerous were the biri-biris – swamps covered with a thick crust on which grass and reeds were growing. You could therefore not see that there was such a swamp
until you were actually on it. Then the crust would break
and you or your companions would disappear into the deep.

During the previous five years the bush-negroes or Alukus
had raided more than thirty plantations and had been involved in heavy fighting with the colonial army on at least
twenty-five occasions. There was not the slightest question
of the troops actually knowing what they were doing. They
would go on an expedition lasting several weeks to the
Alukus' area in the hope of killing or catching a few. That
must be possible. Such dumb creatures as the negroes: no
problem at all. The men who were recounting all this had to
laugh. One of them said, "Whites think that the negroes are
stupid. Well, we let them see who's stupid."[167]

Caesar, Alex and all the others laughed, too, and answered, "Yes, we let them see who's stupid."[168]

It was long after midnight when Alex crept back home. In
his small room in the grounds in the Gravenstraat he lay
awake a long time, thinking back over everything he had

167   "Den bakra denki taki nengre don. We kon un si suma don!"
168   "Ayi, kon un si suma don."

heard that evening. What would Caesar do, he wondered. What would he do if he were in Caesar's position? He didn't know …

ALEX

The following evenings Alex went time and time again to the Zwarte Jagers' camp. The men sat talking for hours on end, usually in a whisper so that the white soldiers on duty would not hear them. Caesar himself said little, and Alex hardly spoke, either, but he listened intently to all the stories. Especially the porters, who sometimes secretly joined the Boni-negroes, had much to tell, and in this way Alex could form a good impression of what was happening there in the bush.

In April an extensive commando force had been sent out under the command of Captain Oorsinga and Lieutenant Keller. That was common knowledge. The order was to take the escapees' fort. At the beginning of May, Oorsinga had let it be known that they had reached the fort. It had then seemed that taking the fort would be just a question of days. It was now the end of June and the soldiers had still not succeeded. What had happened was that the seriously wounded Captain Oorsinga had been replaced by Captain Halthaus.

Then suddenly the news swept through Paramaribo that the group was returning, mission unaccomplished. Only half their original number, the others having succumbed to wounds or disease, they dribbled back to the town, starving and exhausted. They had had to abandon the siege. With the bush-negroes' howls of derision and calls of, "Shall we just come and lie in your arms?" ringing in their ears, they had undertaken the ignominious journey back to base. The slaves could not help laughing their heads off when they heard this story and saw the bedraggled troop of soldiers plodding along the streets. Ha, those bakras (whites) were getting their comeuppance. What had they expected?

The desperate government now decided to grant a general pardon to everyone who lay down his weapons and gave himself up to the whites. How Baron, Boni and Joli-Coeur and all their men and women laughed at this! Surrender, now it was so clear that they were on the winning hand? Never! They wanted no general pardon. They wanted real peace, on both sides, with demands from their side. If that were impossible, they would fight on until the whole country was freed from these wretched bakras.

In the camp Alex heard what had happened. This was narrated by some porters who had been on the expedition. Suppressed laughter, for the bakras must not notice anything. One of the men recounted ...

The soldiers had almost reached Buku but had been unable to get through the swamp that lay in front of the village. If they fired, then the Bonis returned the fire. Captain Oorsinga was hit in the neck by a bullet very early on. While the troops were stationed at the fort, the Alukus took the opportunity to carry out further raids on plantations. The Rozenbeek Plantation was raided, the whites were murdered and the slaves were freed. At the end of June it was the turn of the Poelwijk Plantation. All the ammunition and gunpowder were taken from Poelwijk, and Baron, who had been the leader of that attack, let it be known that all plantations in the Cottica and Boven-Commewijne area would disappear.

In the meantime the soldiers at Buku had been trying to construct a kind of bridge over the swamp. Much jeering from the Bonis from behind their fortifications. Every time a length of bridge was completed it was shot to bits, and several soldiers were wounded as well. And it rained and rained! Everything in the military camp was wet through. Not a thread of what the soldiers were wearing was dry. Those who were not wounded became ill. In addition, the food turned mouldy and rotted.

In the evening, the soldiers could hear the Bonis feasting, singing and dancing in their village. During the day they were always provoking the soldiers and ridiculing them. They asked, for example, whether they would like some of their gunpowder and guns to be able to shoot.

Twelve negroes from the Free Corps were allowed close to the village for negotiations. They were first offered the chance to join the Maroons. When they refused, eleven of them were shot dead. The twelfth was sent back with an ear and his hair cut off and the message that the bush-negroes feared neither the whites nor the Black Hunters.

Now the bakras were really and truly scared. You could see the fear in their eyes. In many households the head of the house went to bed with a pistol to hand. Some other families padlocked the doors and windows of the slave huts from the outside at night to prevent the slaves leaving. The whites were expecting an uprising any moment now. Men often came to talk with Masra Rutger at his office. Some of them wanted the masra to send Alex away from his seat near the door, but Rutger always answered that he saw no reason to do this.

Yet again a detachment was sent to the Marowijne-Cottica district. Governor Nepveu had placed all his hope in the Zwarte Jagers Corps. When Alex wanted to visit Caesar in the camp again, all the Redi Musus had departed. Caesar was also gone. The detachment was under the command of Captain Mayland and the hundred-and-eighty Zwarte Jagers or Redi Musus were under the command of the young lieutenant Frederici.

Everyone followed these events anxiously. In every house the slaves listened at the doors and tried to hear what the bakras thought was happening. In their secret language the slaves were able to pass messages to each other. In the grounds of every house there were whispers about those bush-negroes who were the bosses and would never be defeated by the bakras. Plans were made in secret. To well and truly defeat the bakras they would have to do what the bush-negroes had been doing.

Most of the plans were hatched on the plantations. Alex knew that in the town some slaves felt too attached to their owners to want to harm them. He knew for certain that none of the Le Chasseurs' slaves would turn against them, himself included. Misi Elza and Masra Rutger had always been good to them. If necessary, he would certainly help and protect them, but on the other hand he would take the side of his own people if it came to the crunch.

Then, all at once, in September, came the news ... Buku had fallen! Fort Buku was in the hands of the military. That was surely impossible? What a disappointment. The slaves could and would not believe it. Buku could never be taken. But it was true, Buku had fallen. The wretched bakras were so pleased. They had reason anew to feast, drink and laugh out loud and to make jokes about how the army had got those dumb negroes.

When the soldiers under Captain Mayland's command and the Zwarte Jagers under the leadership of Lieutenant Frederici returned they were given a heroes' welcome by the inhabitants of the town and very soon everyone in Paramaribo knew how Buku was captured. The story was told everywhere and was of course embellished often enough. The truth was this ...

The military had closed in on Buku. When Baron saw them, he hoisted a white flag next to the yellow one, not in surrender but as a sign of provocation. The Zwarte Jagers managed to find a path where the swamp was relatively shallow, only about the depth of a foot under the water. Captain Mayland staged a mock attack. Baron deployed all his forces at the focus of the attack. In the meantime Frederici with the Zwarte Jagers went along the newly discovered path on the other side and climbed over the palisades. A terrible bloodbath followed, with about forty negroes being killed and fifty being taken prisoner, including twenty-six women and nineteen children. A large proportion of the Bonis managed to escape, including the leaders Boni and Baron.

When Alex heard that the men had returned he hurried to the camp the same evening. There he looked for Caesar, but could not see him anywhere. Alex asked one of the men if he knew where Caesar was, but he answered, "I don't know."[169]

Where might Caesar be, Alex wondered. Had he returned, Alex asked another Redi Musu. This person answered that Caesar had definitely not returned. Alex then asked whether

169 "Mi no sabi."

Caesar was dead, to be given the answer again, "I don't know."

It was highly frustrating. Finally, Alex went looking for two men whom he knew had known Caesar well. One of them he did not find, hearing that he had succumbed to his injuries. The other sat silently in a corner with his arm in a sling. When Alex asked him what had happened to Caesar, he answered, "No-one knows. No-one has seen Caesar any more. We don't know whether he is dead, because no-one has seen his body. We also don't know whether he has deserted to join the bush-negroes. No-one saw anything. Since the time we arrived at Buku Caesar has never been seen again."[170]

Alex walked in silence back to his room. Caesar was gone, gone for ever. He did not know what to think, but he did know that he would never see his friend again. Later Alex heard that more than thirty Redi Musus had deserted to join the Boni-negroes during the first year, and in the case of a further twenty it was not known whether they were dead, had fled or had gone over to the Alukus.

Buku had fallen! Yes, Buku had fallen, but the Bonis were not yet beaten. The plantation owners would discover that soon enough.

RUTGER

The fall of Buku was the topic of conversation for several weeks. The colonists were relieved. Thank God! The wretches in the bush had been beaten. One could now continue peacefully with all the festivities and other pleasures. One feast after another was organized. There was money enough. No-one was as rich and affluent as the Suriname planter.

Feasts in Paramaribo and feasts on the plantations. On Sunday 27 September 1772 thanksgiving services were held

170 "No wan sma no sabi, no wan sma no si Caesar moro, un no sabi efu na dede Caesar dede, ma nowan sma no si na dede skin fu Caesar. No wan sma no si efu a go na businengre sei, no wan sma no si. Sinsi un doro kan na Buku no wan sma no si Caesar moro."

in the church to thank God for the defeat of Buku. The colonists and planters now had nothing more to fear. The few escaped negroes who wandered round the bush in small groups could no longer be a danger. No, every reason for festivities.

In the meantime the state troops had already been recruited in Europe, and by the time news of the fall of Buku reached the Netherlands they had already embarked and were on their way to Suriname: well-formed battalions of marines and two warships. Governor Nepveu and many inhabitants along with him now considered the troops to be superfluous, and while this was being discussed with the fatherland one of the warships already lay in the harbour of Paramaribo. It was then February 1773.

The commander-in-chief, Colonel Fourgeoud, and the officers were well received, but Fourgeoud and Nepveu soon came to disagree with each other, and as had happened in the past, various parties formed in the colony, one taking the side of Fourgeoud, who he claimed had received from the Prince of Orange command over all the armed forces in Suriname. This party saw Fourgeoud and his men as the saviours of Suriname. The other party took the side of the governor, who found Fourgeoud to be arrogant and regarded him and his troops as a burden on the colony because they were costing so much money.

The officers remained idle in Paramaribo and were soon welcome guests at the feasts and parties in the colony. They themselves decided that they had struck lucky in this way. At all gatherings there was talk of the expensive soldiers. The men would make sarcastic remarks about these lads who were just profiting from the money provided by their plantations. The ladies laughed up their sleeves and made furtive remarks that they would not normally have been able to make out loud.

Rutger was constantly annoyed at all these goings-on. Amongst friends and acquaintances he could not help but talk about colony's financial situation. The wealth was more pretence than reality. In his opinion catastrophe was just around the corner. He was ridiculed, considered a pessimist, a spoilsport. There was money enough and the wine flowed richly.

Rutger knew that the accumulated debts of the Suriname planters at the banks already totalled more than fifty million. This meant three million in interest annually, and the plantations could usually not produce this.

Then, all of a sudden, in 1773, the moment of truth dawned. The Amsterdam stock exchange crashed. Apparently, far too much credit had been accorded to the Suriname plantation owners. Plantations went bankrupt. The banks would never recover their money. What did happen was that many merchant houses suddenly found themselves to be plantation owners. A manager then had to be appointed, and in most cases this was the former plantation owner.

Rutger considered this to be not a very good solution, for the manager or overseer received his money whether the plantation made a profit or not. He employed another method. At his administrator's office the manager received a salary that was a fixed percentage of the profit. This naturally met with some opposition. The manager, who had previously himself been the plantation owner, could no longer flaunt his wealth, no longer give binge parties, and it was Le Chausseur's fault. Rutger and Elza were no longer invited to card evenings and parties by some families. At first Rutger found this most unfortunate for Elza, but after she had told him that it was no problem at all for her, he happily ignored all the gossip and went his own steady way.

CHAPTER X

SARITH

Sarith travelled with her husband and child to their home, Klein Paradijs, firmly resolved to persuade Julius to buy a house in town. That was nothing exceptional: so many plantation owners had a handsome mansion in town. She was extremely nice to Julius once they were back on the plantation, but oh how bored she became. It was one of the two rainy seasons. Heavy rain, everything wet and dreary, and no-one for any sociability. She herself had nothing to occupy her, for Mini-mini was taking care of the baby and Kwasiba saw to everything else in the household. Sarith rarely bothered about her baby. Now and then she saw him when he was lying on Mini-mini's lap or if Mini-mini was walking on the veranda with the baby in her arms. Julius did pay a lot of attention to his son. He did, of course, notice that Sarith had little interest in the child.

Then everyone became alarmed at the news that the Maroons had overrun a military post. Lieutenant Leppert, head of the military post at Patamacca, went out on a sortie because an escapees' camp had been discovered in that area. With about thirty soldiers he went into the bush. The Alukus lay in wait for him near a swamp through which the soldiers would have to pass. When the soldiers were up to their shoulders in the swamp they were fired upon. Leppert and ten soldiers were killed. The other twenty fled. Most of them got lost in the bush and only two returned.

After that, yet another plantation was raided, and this one was hardly an hour's journey from Klein Paradijs. Sarith began to put pressure on Julius to please buy a house in the town. They were not at all safe at Klein Paradijs. But Julius refused. Klein Paradijs was his home. He would not buy a house in the town. The Bonis would certainly not raid their plantation. Then rent a house for a while, asked Sarith. That he also did not want to do. And Sarith could insist, weep, stamp and shout "I want, I want" as much as she liked, Julius stood firm. He would not rent or buy a house in the town. His son would grow up on Klein Paradijs and not in Paramaribo.

Sarith tried the tack that it was necessary for his daughters, Miriam and Hannah. If they had a house in town the girls could live with her rather than at their aunt's. Julius replied that that certainly wasn't necessary. His daughters had become a part of their aunt's family to such an extent that they probably would not want to live with Sarith. Furthermore, they would soon be thinking of marriage. For those two it was certainly not needed.

Now Sarith began accusing him of thinking only of himself. He didn't take her into consideration and not even his own son. When Julius replied that he really wanted his son to become an excellent planter and therefore wanted him to grow up on the plantation, Sarith said that he was thinking of himself so much that it did not matter to him that he was exposing her to the risk of getting murdered.

"Well," said Julius, "If you're so scared, or if you're getting bored, feel free to go to the town for a few weeks. But no messing with the child: he stays here."

Sarith prepared to leave. Julius would send Benny along to ensure that she arrived safely. He heard her telling Mini-mini to look after everything well, and then said that Mini-mini was certainly not going as well.

Julius had realized for a long time now that it was Mini-mini who was bringing up the child. She fed him, washed him, rocked him to sleep. Hour after hour she would sit with him on her lap if he was crying, because, for instance, he was cutting his first teeth, and she was also the person towards whom he reached out as soon as he saw her.

"Mini-mini stays here. She has to care for Jethro," said Julius to his wife.

Surprised, Sarith asked how she would manage in the

town without Mini-mini. Julius said that she could take another slave with her – Kwasiba, for example, thinking along the lines that Kwasiba was Sarith's own slave and therefore familiar to her.

But Sarith did not want Kwasiba. She was afraid of Kwasiba's sharp, all-seeing eyes. Kwasiba had cared for her since she was little and therefore felt that she had the right to grumble at her mistress if she saw something that, in her eyes, was not right. No, Sarith could most certainly do without someone looking over her shoulder all the time. She did not say this to Julius, but remarked that Kwasiba was getting old and was not all that good with stairs any more. Sarith's room at Esther's was on the top floor.

No, she would take Nicolette. Nicolette was the cook's daughter, a girl of sixteen. Most certainly not a sweet and shy type like Mini-mini, but rather a small, slender fighting hen who always did most of the talking in the slaves' quarters and had her fists ready, too, if need be. You could always hear her talking and laughing above all the others. Mini-mini would have to teach Nicolette everything quickly: how to dress her mistress, make up her hair, and so forth.

Sarith left on the tent boat, accompanied by Benny, who would have to deliver her safely in the town, and an excited Nicolette, who was happy that she was going at long last to the town that she'd heard so much about and would see all the marvellous things there.

To Sarith's surprise, Mini-mini had said that she had no problem at all with staying at Klein Paradijs. She had even claimed that she found the plantation better than the town. Sarith did not know that Mini-mini had no interest in male company after being let down by Hendrik, and in the town there were so many men, white and coloured, who were interested in her. When she walked along the street on some errand or other for her misi, she had to bear the brunt of so many comments, and there were always the types who found it necessary to walk along next to her.

Sarith also saw that Julius was very pleased because Mini-mini cared for the child so well. Now, as far as Sarith was concerned, anything and everything was all right as long as she didn't have to stay at Klein Paradijs all the time.

And so Sarith was frequently in town. Sometimes she stayed for a whole three months on end because there were so many feasts and parties to attend and she couldn't really refuse, now could she. Now and then Julius would come to the town and could get her to return with him to the plantation. But she never stayed more than a few restless weeks. When in September 1772 the festivities took place around the fall of Buku, Sarith was in town, and when the first warship moored in February 1773 she was there, too. She soon met various lieutenants and officers at feasts and parties.

In December 1773 she was yet again in Paramaribo. After the Feast of Tabernacles at Joden-Savanna she had travelled back to Klein Paradijs with Julius to celebrate Jethro's third birthday at the beginning of December. Her sister Esther had come for a few days for the birthday, accompanied by all five of her sons and Rebecca with her daughter and tiny son, and yet another group of ladies and gentlemen, for Sarith wanted to make a great feast of her son's birthday. And that it was, too! All kinds of games were played with the children, lots of sweets, and there was much eating and drinking. Mini-mini, Kwasiba and all the other domestic slaves had their hands full. Fortunately, all the families and ladies had brought their own slaves with them. A week after the festivities everyone had departed, and Sarith, too, had left, in Esther's tent boat, because after all there were always so many parties around this time, and Esther and Jacob traditionally held a really grand ball at New Year.

It was at this ball that she first saw Lieutenant Reindert Andersma. He was new in the country, having arrived a few weeks previously. To his astonishment he was very quickly absorbed into a circle of people in which feast after feast was given. Everything in this land seemed so strange. All that bother with slaves everywhere around you. With a glass in his hand he stood by the window of the large front hall of the mansion in the Saramaccastraat. He had come to stand by the window especially because he simply found it too warm under the large crystal chandelier. He was looking out at the dark street and suddenly heard a merry voice next to him asking whether there were nicer things to see on the street than indoors. Reindert turned and found himself gazing into the laughing face of an exceptionally beautiful young woman.

Sarith looked at the blond man with sky-blue eyes. She considered him an extremely handsome figure. She had noticed him as soon as he came in, a tall blond man with an oh so fine moustache. A conversation ensued. He knew that she was one of the hostess' sisters. Upon arrival, the colleague with whom he had come had introduced him and had whispered in his ear, "A hot little filly," and so indeed she appeared. She wanted to know everything about him, and told him about herself. She was Mrs Robles de Medina, but suggested immediately that they should use an informal mode of address. Sarith, she was called. Well, he was Rein to his friends, was only just in the colony, and found this land quite an experience, very different from what he had imagined, and especially – hot.

All the time, Sarith's precocious laugh rang out. She danced a lot and enjoyed herself immensely. After that Sarith saw a lot of Reindert. Every time she was at a party, Lieutenant Andersma was there, too. When he missed her on one occasion and then saw her again, she explained that she had been at her plantation.

In the meantime it had become clear to the colonists that the Boni-negroes were anything but defeated. Plantations were raided, military posts overwhelmed and soldiers killed. Governor Nepveu and Colonel Fourgeoud bickered. Governor Nepveu had decided that a cordon of military defences must be established to act as defence against the Maroons. This would comprise a ten-metre-wide path through bush and swamp on which carriages could drive. Wooden bridges would be built over the creeks, and at approximately every five kilometres a military post would be established. This cordon path would stretch about a hundred kilometres from Joden-Savanna to Vredenburg on the Oranje Kreek.

At a party at the Levens' family home in April 1774 Rein Andersma told Sarith that he would be away from Paramaribo for a few weeks because he was in charge of the military posts that were to be established. Sarith and Rein had become good friends during the past months, and in fact it was already more than a friendship. Rein knew that he found this beautiful woman desirable and she made no secret of her being not indifferent to him. The way they looked at each other when they were together spoke volumes, and they had kissed several times when they thought no-one was looking.

Now that Rein said this particular evening that he would be leaving Paramaribo in a few days' time, she said what a pity that was. He said that he would like nothing better than to spend the remaining three days constantly in her company. Could she not come home with him after the party? Sarith knew she was playing with fire, but, oh, why not, no-one would need to know about it? They could simply pretend he was seeing her home. The lieutenant's house was in the Kleine Combéweg. Next door to Fort Zeelandia there were several houses reserved especially for captains and lieutenants.

Sarith rode along with him in the carriage, and once they had arrived in the house Rein dismissed his personal slave, who had been waiting for him on the rear veranda, telling him that he would not be needing him again that evening. As soon as they were in his room they were kissing each other passionately, and Rein slowly undressed this beautiful woman and undid her hair. When she stood before him like this, with her black hair falling over her breasts, his admiration for her boiled over in an amorous embrace which was completely mutual.

Nicolette waited for her mistress. She lay on the floor in front of the door in the Saramaccastraat and woke with a shock when she heard the six o'clock gun fire. Had she slept the whole night and not heard the misi come home? She could not understand it, for if misi came home late, she always kicked the sleeping Nicolette, who was then naturally wide awake and ready to help the misi undress. Cautiously she opened the door of the room and peeped inside, but the misi was not in bed. Where was she, then? Nicolette went downstairs, washed herself and went and sat on the rear porch.

When Sarith awoke in bed in a strange house, she suddenly wondered how on earth she could start the day without Nicolette. She woke Rein and said, "How can I get going without Nicolette?"

"Who is Nicolette?" grunted Rein.

"My slave-girl," whispered Sarith. Rein did not understand what she was on about.

"Do you have a slave-girl in the house?" she asked.

No, Rein did not. He had only male slaves and even those he held at a safe distance, for he could not stand having those people around him all the time, always watching what he was doing.

"But how can I get dressed, and what about my hair, how must I do my hair?" Sarith asked.

"Now, just do it yourself, of course!" Rein was amazed.

"But I can't. I don't know how to do it." Sarith was almost in tears.

Rein could not help himself and started laughing out loud. Just imagine, a grown-up woman, married and with a child, who didn't know how to dress herself and do her hair! That's a good joke. These colonial girls are quite something!

"Stop that laughing," cried Sarith, hitting him in the face with a cushion. A wild romp ensued, that ended again in love-making. "But really, I don't know what to do," said Sarith eventually.

"Can't I help you, then," said Rein, teasingly. "Come on, I'll be your slave-girl, just step in." Laughing, he took an item of underwear from the chair.

"No, stop it for heaven's sake," said Sarith. "Can't you send your slave to fetch Nicolette?"

"All right, that's possible."

Rein put on trousers and a dressing gown and went downstairs to explain to Kwasi, his slave, how and where he should fetch a certain Nicolette. When, almost an hour later, Nicolette was brought in by Kwasi, she understood immediately from Sarith's state and the presence of 'that white soldier'[171], what had been going on. She helped her mistress to wash, dressed her and did her hair up. Sarith then left for Esther's house, thinking that it would not be such a good idea to be away for so long. But before they went, she warned Nicolette, "If you dare say one word, I'll send you to get a good thrashing and I'll sell you to the Suynigheid Plantation."[172]

"No misi, I'll say nothing,"[173] Nicolette was quick to respond. She would most certainly say nothing. Sarith had in fact named a particularly cruel form of beating, which Nicolette most definitely wanted to avoid, and this also applied to being sold to the Suynigheid Plantation, infamous for the bad treatment of its slaves. At the house in the Saramaccastraat Sarith told Esther that she had spent the night at the home of a girl-friend who had been taken ill at the party.

The next day she said to Esther that she would spend the day with her girl-friend and would perhaps stay the night there. She told Nicolette to wait for her under a tree on the other side of the road from the lieutenant's house, for she knew that Rein did not like the idea of having slave-girls in his home.

However, at the gun that sounded for eight o'clock in the evening, all slaves had to be in their quarters. When evening began to fall and Nicolette had not yet seen her mistress emerging from the house, she began to get impatient. She paced up and down under the tree, and when the eight o'clock gun fired she went as quickly as possible to the Saramaccastraat because she was scared of being detained by a police officer. Early the next morning she returned to sit under the tree and waited until she saw Kwasi outside. When she helped her mistress, she asked Nicolette where she had spent the night.

171 Surdati Bakra.
172 "Efu yu prefuru fu taki wan sani, mi e seni yu fu wan pansboko en mi e seri yu go na pranasi Suynigheid."
173 "Nono Misi, mi no e taki noti."

Nicolette told her that she had waited until the eight o'clock gun and had then gone to the Saramaccastraat for fear of being arrested by the police.

"What did you say there?"[174] asked Sarith.

"Nothing, I said nothing."[175]

Now Sarith continued, "If you say anything, I'll cut out your tongue and I'll sell you."[176]

"No, misi, no." Eyes wide with fear, Nicolette pressed her lips together with a thumb and index finger, to assure the misi that she really would not say anything, and Sarith nodded. When they arrived back at Esther's house she gave the girl two pennies.

The next day Rein left the town for several weeks and Sarith decided simply to return to Klein Paradijs.

Julius was pleased when he saw his wife coming back just of her own accord. She said that she was happy to be with him again at home, and he thought how sweet she really was. After all, she was still young, and surely such a young woman needed some amusement. Well, as long as she remained his wife and always returned to him, he would certainly not deprive her of her feasts and parties.

At Klein Paradijs, Sarith had the idea of giving a feast herself at the plantation and inviting a group of friends to stay there. Soldiers also had the right to some leave, and most probably Rein would be able to take some weeks off. Julius agreed to a party at their plantation. It was a nice idea, and would give Sarith something to do. Sarith busied herself with the preparations and had of course to return to Paramaribo to see whether all the guests she wanted to invite would be able to come and stay in the early weeks of September. In the meantime Rein had returned from his expedition and Sarith again spent several nights with him.

According to Sarith, no-one knew anything about this, but of course all of Suriname already knew everything. And left, right and centre there was talk of that Sarith, who was

174   "San yu taki depe?"
175   "Noti, mi no taki noti."
176   "Efu yu taki wan sani, me e koti yu tongo en mi e seri yu."

carrying on with one of the lieutenants. Esther heard something of this, as well. She had suspected that there was something going on.

When, all of a sudden, Sarith was away staying with her friend Bella Levens, as she would have it, for three days on end, Esther went to visit this Bella Levens one morning. During a short conversation, Bella asked how things were with Sarith, and Esther knew enough. When Sarith returned around lunchtime that day, Esther first tried to get something out of Nicolette, but she played dumb – no, she knew nothing. Misi had been staying at the house of another misi and masra, but she, Nicolette, didn't know where. She hardly knew the town. Esther went to Sarith's room and asked her where she had been staying. When Sarith replied, "At Bella Levens'," Esther got angry and said, "Sarith, I was at Bella Levens' this morning and she asked how you were. She hadn't seen you in ages. Do you think I don't know where you've been? Everyone is talking about it – aren't you ashamed? What will your husband say if he hears about it?"

Like a little hellcat Sarith sprang up from the bed on which she had just lain down. Esther must mind her own business. Was it so terrible that she was with someone else now and then? Did anyone bother to consider what kind of life she was leading, there on that boring plantation, with just an old man and a child? And was her husband interested in anything else? No, only the plantation counted and whether the harvest was successful, and she, she had nothing. Esther had a house in the town, her husband liked going out, she had expensive clothes, carriages, everything, but she, Sarith, had nothing. Her husband wouldn't even grant her a house in town.

Esther looked and listened in astonishment at this outburst. Did Sarith ever think of anyone but herself? And even if she did? Did she not realize that she was endangering herself, too, her position? "But Sarith, don't you see that this simply cannot be, must not be. Consider for once what the consequences for you yourself might be. What will Julius say? How will he react if he gets to hear about this?"

"He won't get to hear about it, at least not so long as interfering busybody sisters just mind their own business." Sarith said this with a sharp glance towards Esther, who, with tightly pursed lips, turned and left the room.

There was simply no reasoning with this spoilt creature.

ELZA

It was the second week of October 1774. Elza was sitting on a rocking chair gazing out of the front hall window. The Gravenstraat was dry and dusty. It had not rained for almost four weeks. It was hot, too, very hot. For her, of course, even worse now that she was heavily pregnant. The baby was due any time now. She hoped it would be soon: it seemed to be taking ages. She had her feet on a small bench. Those were Maisa's orders, because her feet and ankles had swollen.

Downstairs she heard the voices of Alex and Gideon. Now and then she heard Gideon laugh. She would really have to tell Alex that he and Gideon must be quieter downstairs. At the end of the day, the office was there, and so many people were coming and going. She knew what the two were doing there. They made up little stories, drew pictures and wrote under the pictures what they had thought up. It was totally Alex's idea, and Rutger was delighted because it meant that Gideon was making such good progress with reading and writing. Alex was a born teacher.

Elza's thoughts went back to the Alex of bygone days. He had saved hard to buy his freedom and had been a free man for a year now. When he received the letter of manumission[177], Rutger had said to him, "Now you're a free person, Alex. What are you going to do now you're free?" And Alex had answered that he would really like to continue working for the masra. He was now the receptionist for the office downstairs. He let the people in, kept a record of appointments and that kind of thing. He sat at a small table next to the front door, always smartly dressed, with well-polished shoes. For that is what Alex had bought with the first mon-

177 Declaration of freedom.

ey he received: shoes. From the moment he was free, no-one had seen him without shoes. Gideon, who was now six and could already write a little, sat for hours on end on the other side of the table, and together the two of them wrote and drew.

It was often busy there below. Many plantation owners came along for loans. Often, nothing could be done for them. According to Rutger, things were not going at all well with the colony. Quite apart from the crash on the Amsterdam stock exchange the year before, it was the war in the interior that had been costing the country so much money. Rutger never stopped saying that the government had no choice but to make peace with the Maroons, to stop hunting them down and to grant them an area of land in the Marowijne region where they could settle and live as free people. But the governor and especially Colonel Fourgeoud, and also the directors of the Society in the Netherlands, thought differently. That rabble in the jungle must be eradicated.

There were yet again plans to send even more manpower to Suriname to reinforce the fifteen hundred who were already there. Increasingly large sums were demanded of the planters; increasingly large were the taxes that had to be paid into the escapees' fund. And even so, the thousand-or-so soldiers with all their weapons could not bring the Maroons to their knees. There were always reports of military posts and plantations being raided, buildings being set on fire and weapons and other equipment being seized.

Colonel Fourgeoud now had another tactic. He wanted to starve the bush-negroes out. If the bush were methodically burnt and all agricultural plots destroyed, then that riffraff would have to surrender.

The cordon path on which they were hard at work would serve to reach the bush-negroes wherever they might be. Every few kilometres there was a post with defences and every five kilometres there was a watch-tower where a horse was kept in order to be able to get a message through quickly if need be. And despite all this, the Alukus were not being defeated.

No, things were not going well in the colony. Elza gave a

sigh. She had nothing to complain about. Rutger was now administrator for no less than eight plantations. Four of these were plantations where the planters had been unable to pay their debts. These were now the bank's property, but Rutger had appointed the planters themselves as manager/overseers. On some plantations things were going along all right, on others not, for the manager still imagined himself to be the owner.

Elza heard footsteps on the stairs and Jonathan, who was playing on the rear veranda with Afanaisa, shouted, "Mama, here is an aunt."

Mia van Henegouwen came in. She was now Mrs Willemsen. Elza was pleased to see her. They were very good friends and had been right from the time that Elza and Sarith were attending the French School.

Mia said, "I thought you would already be lying in bed with a daughter next to you."

Elza laughed, "I wish that were the case, but it won't be long now and, yes, I am hoping for a daughter, with so many boys in the family. Esther has five of them, I myself two, my brother David three, Rebecca has two and Sarith one."

In this way the talk turned to Sarith. Did Elza know what was being said about Sarith? She had recently had various guests at Klein Paradijs, including Lieutenant Andersma and three friends, and even there under her husband's nose Sarith had managed to go with the lieutenant. Elza knew about it. Everyone was talking about it. She and Maisa had just been discussing it at length.

"Could you not talk to her, Elza?" asked Mia.

"Me, why me?" asked Elza, surprised.

"Oh, you were always such good friends and I always used to think that you had a good influence on her. You know, that time with Charles?"

Yes, Elza knew about that time with Charles. How Sarith was meeting him in secret, when everyone thought that the three girls were together, and how often she had asked Sarith not to do this. But that was all very long ago now.

"Oh no, not me," said Elza. "Oh, we were indeed very

good friends in the past, but now everyone has her own life to lead. In fact I have very little contact with Sarith. She has her own circle of friends, you see."

Yes, Mia understood that. "Can it be that her husband really knows nothing about it?" she asked again.

Elza did not know. Everyone was indeed talking about it, but as these things always go, the husband is the last person to hear. And this was also the case here. All Suriname knew that Sarith was having an affair with Lieutenant Andersma. Everyone knew about it, except Julius.

CHAPTER XI

FEBRUARY 1775: JAN

Eleven cannon shots resounded from Fort Zeelandia to greet the ship, and the ship responded likewise. Jan stood among the many soldiers on the ship and looked towards the white town that was coming closer and closer. So this was Paramaribo. It all looked so spick and span, but he would still have been pleased had it looked grey and filthy. Being confined in the small ship for sixty-one days amidst all these ruffians had been no picnic. They had left Amsterdam around the middle of December. They had first had their fill of rough weather. Waves as tall as houses had crashed continually over the ship. It had been cold and stuffy, because all the hatches had been battened down and heating was non-existent. Later the weather had become warmer and one could at least get some fresh air. The food had been terrible. No fresh meat, only salted peas. According to the captain, this was particularly good for the men, as they could get used to what they would be getting in the bush. But worst of all were the fights between the soldiers and the sailors. Time and time again this happened, and the punishments became increasingly severe.

One of the soldiers who had used a knife during a fight with a sailor was pinned to the main-mast with the knife. He had to remain there until he had freed himself. Both of them were then keelhauled and lost six months' pay. Two sailors caught having sex with each other were simply thrown overboard. Jan had stayed as much as possible out of the way of all these rough men and he was thanking God that he had survived all the diseases such as scurvy and diarrhoea and would soon be on dry land again.

He had had such expectations for his journey to Suriname. Not in the first place to fight – he was really no soldier – but because of the gold he was planning to find here. And while Jan looked at the steadily approaching, friendly, white little town, he thought back yet again to all the things he had heard about this marvellous country, and what had led him to decide to become a soldier, to fight the bush-negroes.

In Holland he had been living with his parents in a small farming community near Amsterdam. Father was a farm labourer. They were poor, for Pa wasn't a permanent farm-hand, but was taken on only when there was a lot to do: in the summer, for instance, for the haymaking and at harvest-time. In the winter he was often unemployed and then carved spoons and bowls out of willow. Sometimes his mother did have work in the winter, helping the farmer's wife with weaving or at the slaughter, working a whole day with nothing more than a pan of cooked peas or a side of bacon as payment.

It was by pure chance that Jan, then a lad of fourteen, had got a job as assistant to the stableman of a rich Amsterdam gentleman. One warm summer afternoon the gentleman had been driving through the village when one of the horses became lame through picking up a stone in a hoof. Jan, who had been sitting at the side of the ditch, had helped the coachman and had carefully worked the stone loose while talking comfortingly to the horse, which was at first very much on edge. As a reward he could come to work for the rich gentleman. It had been good work. There was always plenty to eat and he had a warm spot to sleep in the stable loft. The rich gentleman owned plantations in a land far away to the west, and the old stableman Joris had told Jan during the long winter evenings what a country that was: very warm, fantastic plantations, a land where all the whites were rich, simply because of being white. All the work was done by negro slaves: stupid, ignorant creatures who had been transported over from Africa and sold to the plantation owners. Those people were then set to work in the same way as horses or mules.

Joris knew all about this because he had been a seaman. As a sailor he had journeyed to those western parts. He had experienced everything, including pirates and privateers, and had lost an eye and three fingers. The finest tale, however, was about the gold, which was lying around in the huge forests there just for the taking. Of course, Joris had not found it. He was never there long enough to go and look for it himself. But it was there – he was sure of that.

Jan had listened open-mouthed to all these stories, and Joris had also said that in recent years soldiers were going to that country. Some of those negroes had fled to the bush because they no longer wanted to work on the plantations, and soldiers were being hired in from Amsterdam to catch them and bring them back to the plantations. Joris had said that he would certainly have gone had he been young enough. Jan, now eighteen, did want to go there. He could become a soldier, catching the negroes in the forests. Above all, he knew about the gold, so he could go looking for it. That would surely not be all that difficult. Yes, Jan knew for sure he would return to Holland as a rich man.

When he had made the two-hour trek to his village on his monthly Sunday off to tell his parents that he was going to Suriname as a soldier, they were at first most surprised. Was Jan leaving? Why on earth? He would never get such a good job again. And where was he going? Where was that strange land he was talking about? In the west? Was that perhaps somewhere near the east? Were there Chinamen there with those slant eyes? No, Jan answered patiently, no Chinese, but he would have to catch negroes, those black folks.

"Negroes?" his mother had cried, "Oh, Jan, but those people eat whites. Aren't they those wild people who cook whites in big pots and eat them, and stick bones through their noses as decoration?"

"No, mother, these are escaped slaves," Jan had explained, but Ma and Pa still thought that it was dangerous anyway, whether it was slant-eyes or negroes. All those types were really scary. And how was Jan planning to catch them? Jan had explained that it was child's play. Those folk had nothing and the soldiers had everything – guns, cannon, horses and so forth. But most important was the gold he would find there. He would be returning as a rich man. He would buy marvellous things for everyone, build a big house, keep his own horses and cows.

His little sisters had listened with eyes aglow and ears pricked up. Would Jan buy something nice for them, too, really nice? Indulgently Jan had promised: of course, they only had to say the word. Antje wanted shoes, real shoes with shiny buckles, and Miebetje wanted a dress, a new one from the shop. And mother? Well, for mother a warm skirt and a shawl; for father a new hat and a jacket. And for grandma? Grandma, who had been sitting mumbling in a corner of the room, hadn't the faintest idea what they were talking about, but the sisters had called out, "Grandma, you're getting a foot stove from Jan, a warm one for your feet, and a shawl."

Grandma mouthed toothlessly, "Where is it?"

The sisters had had a good laugh and shouted into grandma's deaf ears, "When he comes back from Suurvename and is rich."

So he had arrived in Suriname, and couldn't wait to get ashore. It was indeed hot – very hot!

A few weeks later Jan was on his first expedition. How different was the reality! It was truly terrible here in the jungle. Oppressive, dark, even in the middle of the day. They had been in the bush for twenty-seven days now. Progress was very slow. Every bit of path had first to be hacked clear. Negro porters carried everything they needed, and that was an awful lot! Captain Stoelman shouted orders, the officers gave orders, and the soldiers just trudged on. So far they had seen neither sight nor sound of a single negro. A strip of ground cleared in the forest had been found. Something people called farming land. It was planted with cassava and maize. Unfortunately, nothing was yet ripe, otherwise they could have used it. It would have been a welcome change from mouldy peas, groats and salted meat with the maggots crawling out. On the captain's orders the men had had to burn the field. Because everything was damp this did not work, and so the men had to dig everything out and cut it up, and then the resulting pile was burnt.

Jan felt totally wretched. In all the twenty-six nights he had not had one good night's sleep. Terrible, those mosquitoes. Now he always wrapped cloths around his head at night so as not to hear the humming and he would put his head in a hollow in the ground with his kit on top. His arms and legs were covered with infected boils. Every time he had been bitten by an insect he had scratched at the bite, and due to his dirty fingernails everything had festered. Worst of all was the pain in his groin. Mites had bitten him there. He had scratched away and everything had become infected and had festered. His uniform, dirty, stinking, wet from the rain, then dry, then wet again, made it even worse. Every step he took was torture. No, he had not imagined it like this. How dreadful! Hell itself could not be as awful as this.

At night everything was pitch black. You couldn't see your hand in front of your face and every sound could be a poisonous snake waiting to give you a fatal bite or a tiger lurking, ready to tear you to bits. All the men were more or less in the same state as he. All except the native porters, who appeared to have no trouble with all the insects and who seemed to be able to walk on their bare soles much more easily than the soldiers with their swollen feet in heavy boots.

There came a whisper that it was suspected that a group of Boni-negroes would be encountered. They would have to make as little noise as possible in order to surprise the negroes and capture them. If a group of negroes was captured, they would have to be shot straightaway. From each one a hand would be hacked off as proof back in town. The soldier would get a bonus for each hand. Should a chieftain be captured, his head would be cut off for display in the town.

Suddenly, shots rang out, and before the soldiers could prepare their weapons for firing, four of them lay bleeding on the ground. The porters had suddenly disappeared. More shots, noise, commotion. "Flee, flee, run for your life, get out of here!" Soldiers ran in all directions. No-one worried about anyone else, each of them just tried to save his own skin. Jan, too, ran, and ran, forcing his way through thorny bushes, scratching his face open, losing his hat, but going on. There lay a fallen tree trunk. He must get over it. He tried to jump, but caught his foot on something. A sharp pain, searing. He could go no further! With a cry he fell to the ground, piercing one hand on a pointed stick that protruded from the earth. Freeing his hand and looking with dread at the blood now pouring from it, he tried to stand up. He could not. His leg, what was wrong with his leg? With a shiver he looked at his left leg, which that lay under him at a strange angle. He began to realize that he would not be able to walk any further.

Trying with the one hand to compress the wound in the other, he called out loudly, "Help, help!" No reply. Everyone had disappeared. Again Jan screamed, "Help, help me, over here!" Nothing! Again he tried to stand and again he immediately collapsed onto the ground. He shuffled a little on his bottom so as to be able to lean with his back against a tree trunk. His hand was still bleeding. Dizzy, Jan closed his eyes. So this was it! He would remain here and die from loss of blood and from starvation. Perhaps torn apart by wild beasts. How stupid he had been when he had thought back there in Holland that he would come to this land, catch a few negroes and then still find gold. How stupid!

When Jan opened his eyes again he saw a large negro clad in only a loincloth standing about ten metres away from him. O God, a Maroon! His gun, where was his gun? But he had dropped his gun, and it lay on the ground close to the man. He would now pick up the gun and shoot him.

"Lord God in Heaven," Jan prayed with closed eyes, "Let me die straightaway. Let him shoot me in the heart or straight through my head. Don't let me suffer. Let me die instantly."

It was two, at the most three, minutes, but to Jan it was an eternity. Every moment he expected the shot. In a flash his village, his sisters, his parents, his grandma passed before his eyes. He heard grandma asking, "Where is it?" and his sisters replying, "When he comes back from Suurvename." Everything recalled in a flash. The shot, why no shot? He open his eyes briefly and saw that the man was now standing near him. Perhaps he wanted to shoot him from close by, to make sure he would die. But now Jan saw that the man had no weapon in his hands. The gun was propped up against a tree. The man leaned towards him. Perhaps he would rather strangle him or hack him to pieces with his machete? Jan raised his hands in defence. Still the one hand was bleeding.

"No," he cried, both hands in front of his face.

But the man said, "What's the matter? Get up, get up."[178]

Jan looked at his leg. Perhaps the man wanted to fight him. Then the man looked at the leg, too. He bent down and began carefully to undo Jan's boot. Jan groaned from the pain. When the boot was removed, Jan looked at the leg, which now had a large swelling at the site of the fracture. Now the man shook his head gently, saying something while trying cautiously to lay the leg in a better position. Then he went to a bush, cut off several branches with his machete and, after having stripped them, lay them on each side of Jan's leg. He said something again, but Jan could not understand what he meant.

Some way off lay his pack. The man went to it and got something out. It was his neck cloth. He tore several shreds off and began to fasten the sticks carefully along the leg. Jan could not understand. Was the man not going to murder him, then? It was after all one of the dreaded bush-negroes? The man said, "Don't be afraid, I'll be back soon."[179]

Then he went away. Even if he had wanted to, Jan could not have gone anywhere. The pain was too great and he was feeling totally exhausted.

A little later the man came back with another man. They had a kind of stretcher with them, bound together with lianas. They lay Jan very carefully on the stretcher and took him away.

178   "San de fu du? Opo no!"
179   "No frede, wakti m'e kon."

Perhaps they wanted to murder him in the village with a lot of show, thought Jan, but he couldn't care less. Nothing mattered any more. He would soon be dead, and how was not important. It seemed as if the men had to walk a long way. They sometimes weaved their way with difficulty through the thick bush and also went through a small creek, holding the stretcher up high so that it would not get wet. It seemed like hours. Jan closed his eyes and lost consciousness. When he came to, he was lying under a thatched roof. Someone was washing his face with fresh water. He saw negro faces looking at him, mostly women and children except for the two men who had carried him and some older men.

The women were not looking particularly friendly and he heard how some of them bickered with the two men. Jan could not understand them, but realized that the women were angry that he had been brought here to the village. One of the older men said something in a soothing tone of voice and appeared to be explaining something.

Later, the women left and an old man wrapped a dressing made of leaves and herbs very carefully around Jan's leg and bandaged it. Now it was less painful. Then he removed all Jan's clothes, washed him with fresh water containing herbs, and treated all his wounds and ulcers. While he was doing this he was constantly talking. Jan understood nothing, but everything felt very good and soothing. After that one of the women brought him a large calabash with a kind of delicious, strong soup, made from fish and pieces of cassava. The men lifted him carefully from the stretcher and lay him in a hammock. Wonderful, everything felt. What peace! His hand had been bandaged as well. A greasy liniment had been spread on the boils in his groin and he had been given a cloth for his shoulders. No damp, stinking, heavy clothes, no mosquitoes, no pain, what a blessing! At last he could sleep.

And sleep he did. It was late the following day before he opened his eyes again. The old man, whom everyone called Ta Jusu, came to tend to him again. Again he was given that delicious food. Jan had the feeling that he was now in paradise. Were these the dangerous negroes who had to be hunted and shot dead? Were these the people whose food crops had to be destroyed and burnt so that hunger would finally force them to surrender? Why, in fact? Because they had chosen for this life instead of slavery? There were no better or kinder people on earth, of that Jan was now convinced. Had a single soldier bothered about him for one second? No – everyone had thought only of himself.

Six weeks Jan stayed there in that village, six weeks of rest and heavenly bliss. He saw the women busy working, saw them baking loaves of cassava, drying and smoking fish, pounding rice, stripping maize. He had already understood that they were laying down large stores of food. Everything was communal, for everyone. Not that one had a lot and the other nothing. He saw how cleverly they knew how to make use of everything, making rope, roof covering, herbs for healing. He was ashamed to think that he had in the past been of the opinion that they were really stupid, because only whites had any brains. But all the whites put together could come and learn their lessons well from these negroes.

He now understood, too, how this small group of two hundred to three hundred souls managed to avoid being caught by the soldiers and always be one step ahead of the army. He saw how the women cared for the children, how they helped each other. They often stood near him while they were artfully plaiting their hair. Sometimes a child would come to him, show him something and laugh with him. And all the time Jan asked himself why. Why could they not live happily in their villages in the bush? He resolved never again to participate in the persecution and shooting of Boni-negroes.

Once when Ta Jusu was nursing him and carefully applying a liniment to his wounds, Jan asked why in fact those men had not killed him. He was, after all, the enemy. Ta Jusu had explained that in their view the soldiers were not the evil ones. They had just arrived from Holland and had not done anything to the negroes. They were simply being misused. The real enemies were the planters and the government and now also that wretched Swiss colonel, who had sworn to exterminate all the negroes in the bush.

When Jan's hand was completely healed, the old man allowed him to try to stand up. It was still difficult with his leg, but he was given a hefty stick that had been cut out of a thick branch and could try very carefully to walk a step or two. His leg was still being treated with herbs and leaves and was still bound with strips of cotton between the two branches. All wounds and ulcers on his body had healed, his clothes were freshly washed and clean, and he always had his shawl on.

After six weeks, when he could walk quite well, the old man told him that it was time for him to return. He was given a message that he had to pass on to that wretched Swiss man. Jan understood that this was Colonel Fourgeoud. The bush-negroes would never surrender, never. All they wanted was peace, and to be left alone. If they were no longer persecuted, then they would raid no more plantations, for then they would live peacefully here in their villages and live from what they planted and from what the bush provided. Becoming slaves again – never! Jan wanted to pass on the message, but how?

The next day the old man took him in a korjaal[180] along a small creek and set him down at the back of a plantation. He could simply follow the path and walk through the plantation until he came to the house towards the front of the estate. They would be sure to look after him there. The old man trusted that he would not betray them and say anything about the village. Jan would rather cut his tongue out than say anything about the village, Ta Jusu could be sure of that.

How amazed the slaves working in the fields were suddenly to see a soldier walking through the plantation, and how surprised, too, was the planter who awoke from his afternoon nap to find a soldier sitting on his veranda! This soldier told him in a matter-of-fact way that he had got lost in the bush and had become separated from the group. He had wandered around in the bush for about six weeks before ending up at the back of the plantation. Now, these new sol-

180   An advanced form of dug-out canoe (pronounced kor-yaal).

diers were obviously well trained men, for this was no starving, exhausted man standing in front of him, but someone who had endured all hardships and appeared fresh and lively. With such soldiers they would soon get the better of that rabble in the bush and this expensive war could end. The Dutch state had at long last sent some good men. Contented, the planter then sat with his guest and the family at dinner, intending to travel with Jan the following day in his tent boat to Paramaribo.

Captain Stoelman's commando was no less surprised when suddenly one of the soldiers stood before them who had been given up as dead. Who knows, more of them might return, although it was in fact certain that most of the thirty-two soldiers in that group had been killed or had drowned. Four of them they had buried themselves, since they had not survived their injuries. Jan was now allocated to the same commando as Lieutenant Reindert Andersma, which was under the command of Captain Hamel. This division was preparing for a twelve-week-long expedition. They would be responsible for the completion of a certain part of the cordon path and would have to set up watchtowers between the military post near to the devastated l'Esperance Plantation and the Tampoco Creek in the Boven-Commewijne district. From there they would also have to carry out raids against the Maroons in the region.

Jan wanted to pass on Ta Jusu's message. But how? And to whom? If he were to say that he had stayed six weeks with the Maroons, it would be demanded of him that he say where they were, and he would never betray them, never. With whom could he speak without putting himself in danger and endangering those good people?

That Lieutenant Andersma? He seemed a decent type. He was always cheerful and Jan had noticed that he spoke less roughly and harshly to the soldiers than did the other officers. He would talk to Lieutenant Andersma. Where would he do that? Not in the soldiers' quarters. That was too dangerous. Dare he visit him at home? In Fort Zeelandia?

During the days that followed, Jan was constantly in the

neighbourhood of the fort and watched the lieutenant's house. By the afternoon of the third day he had summoned up enough courage and was just about to knock on the door when he saw an elegant lady approaching with a slave two steps behind her. The lady had hardly reached the veranda when Lieutenant Andersma opened the door and came outside. With a laugh he put his arm around the lady and went inside with her. Jan understood very well that this was not the moment to knock and talk about the Maroons. But all right, he would wait until the lady had left. But by the time darkness fell and he knew that the lady was still indoors, he walked back to the soldiers' quarters.

Two days later he tried again. He now saw that the lieutenant was sitting on the veranda. Jan went straight up to him and asked if he might speak with him.

"What do you want to talk about, soldier?" asked Lieutenant Andersma, stretching out lazily in his chair and removing his feet from the foot-rest.

"About the Maroons, Lieutenant," said Jan submissively.

"Far too much has been said about them, lad," laughed Andersma. "But go ahead, tell me; perhaps I'll hear something new after all."

Jan began to relate what had happened to him. When he ended by saying that the Maroons had been so good and kind to him, Andersma burst out laughing. "Young man, that is a fine story, really good. Just save it for when you're back in Holland with your girls. Ha, ha: but you don't think I believe it, do you?"

"It is true, Lieutenant, really true, and the old man, that Ta Jusu, he said, he said ...." Jan stuttered with embarrassment.

"Ha, ha, soldier. Cut it out. Your story is great, really, and good for telling your friends around the campfire if they want to lose heart," laughed Andersma. "Ha, ha, this is certainly an original way of trying to get out of the service, eh?"

At that moment Jan saw the same lady as before approaching. When she was near the veranda, Andersma stood up and took a few steps towards her.

"Sarith, darling, come here. This soldier has been telling an amusing story."

Andersma put his arm in that of the lady and drew her towards him. "Guess what he is claiming? He says that he was rescued in the bush by the Boni-negroes and that they healed his broken leg. He's now trying to persuade me to be kind to those dear escapees there in the bush. Don't you find it great, dear? Shall we move into the bush and go and lie in a hammock with the Maroons? Ha, ha." The lady laughed, too, and said, "It will have happened in his dreams."

Still laughing, Andersma said, "Go and tell your tale to the captain, and he can have a good laugh, too. Good day."

Jan understood that the conversation was over and mumbled, "Good day, Lieutenant, madam." He turned and left the veranda. Well, now he knew. No-one was going to believe him. He would simply say nothing; it wouldn't help, anyway. If only he could get away from the army, it didn't matter where, but just away! Jan understood full well that refusing to go on an expedition meant, in military terms, deserting, and carried the death penalty. He therefore had no choice but to go along, but he knew for sure that he would never fire at a Maroon and in fact would even warn them or help them if he could.

Meanwhile, everyone in Paramaribo had again become mightily scared in the face of the raids by the Boni-negroes. Colonel Fourgeoud's men were suffering defeat after defeat. Time and time again came the frightening news that yet another plantation had been raided and whites had been murdered.

Within a short period the plantations Peron, Suynigheid and La Félicité fell. Even though the leaders Baron and Joli-Coeur had died a year earlier, their names were still mentioned in fear and trembling by the colonists. Joli-Coeur had raided the Rodenback Plantation with his group. They had succeeded in capturing the director, a certain Schulz, infamous for his atrocities against the negroes, and had hung him upside down by his feet. In the meantime the negroes ravaged through the plantation house, helping themselves to the wines and rum.

Schulz recognized Joli-Coeur, who was born on this same plantation and had lived there until fleeing at the age of twelve. Trembling, the director had called out, "Don't you recognize me, Joli-Coeur, don't you know any more who I am? I was good to you, wasn't I? I even gave you something from my own table when you were a child. Release me, please."

Joli-Coeur had answered, already dancing with delight, "I remember very well, Schulz. I remember especially the time you raped my mother and had my father whipped to death when he tried to help her. I remember all that. Yes, I'll release you."

And with those words he separated Schulz's head from his body with one stroke of his razor-sharp machete. Everyone knew this story, and it was embellished every time it was told. The one time Joli-Coeur had first thrown Schulz to the ground and all the negroes had danced on him. Then again, he had hung upside down for twenty-four hours, and when he had asked for something to drink, the negroes had emptied a bottle of wine just along the side of his mouth so that not a drop went into it. In any event, if a child was being naughty, the slave who was caring for him or her needed only to say, "Joli-Coeur is coming"[181], and the child would become good and sweet-tempered again.

Even before Reindert Andersma's group left, there came at the end of August the news that a commando comprising a hundred soldiers, thirty native rangers and the inevitable porters under the command of Captain Boltz had been attacked by the Maroons in a swamp. They had paid particular attention to the Black Rangers, whom they regarded as committing fratricide, and without bothering themselves too much with the Europeans they had unleashed a bloodbath among these negroes. Even so, only a few European soldiers, exhausted, starving and sick, managed to embark on the journey back to the town. The rest had already succumbed to exhaustion and disease.

The disagreement between Colonel Fourgeoud and Gov-

181   "Joli-Coeur e kon."

ernor Nepveu flared up again, because the latter was of the opinion that Fourgeoud was sacrificing human life needlessly by undertaking sorties during the rainy season.

Of the five hundred men who had arrived from Europe before 1775, there were no more than two hundred left. They had been sent to fight a small group of negroes. It was, however, a small but highly motivated group of negroes. They fought to achieve just one thing, the highest virtue: freedom, no longer to be enslaved. For the rest they wanted nothing from the whites; all they wanted was to live in freedom in the Suriname bush. Hundreds of innocent soldiers met their death in the jungles of Suriname, and not particularly at the hands of the Maroons. They died from disease, starvation and exhaustion, or from drowning in the swamps. Their fighting wasn't motivated. They were in fact playthings in the hands of the group of whites who misused them: the planters, the colonial government, the directors of the Society in the Netherlands. These individuals simply could not grasp that there was no question of fighting against people who waged a 'guerrilla' struggle just to be 'free'. They needed the slaves. Everything must be sacrificed for the production of the things that would bring them a pile of money: cotton, coffee and sugar.

Especially sugar ...

SARITH

When Sarith heard that Reindert Andersma would be spending several weeks on the Boven-Commewijne River between l'Esperance and Tampoco Creek, her enthusiasm knew no bounds. That was after all where Klein Paradijs was located. On the other side of the river, true, but that was no problem. Reindert had only to walk from where he was based through an abandoned plantation and he would be opposite them. She just needed to send a slave with a boat to the other side to collect him. Even before the military had left Paramaribo she was back on the plantation. She was really nice and sweet to Julius, who was glad that his wife was in such a good mood and had come back to the plantation of her own accord.

There were two reasons for Sarith's show of affection. In the first place she had discovered that she was pregnant, and she had to admit to herself in all honesty that she did not know whether Reindert or Julius was the father of the child she was expecting. But Julius must definitely not know of her doubts. Reindert had told her time upon time that she must not expect anything of him. He had a wife and children in Holland, and he did not want to jeopardize his position or that of Sarith. The other reason was that Julius should accept that the military who were encamped there should on occasion visit the plantation.

She therefore described to Julius how the poor lieutenants and officers were having such a tough time there in their camp. Now they were so close, he would certainly not mind if they came now and then to Klein Paradijs for a good meal, a good bath or a good night's sleep. Julius, as hospitable as all Surinamers, of course did not mind. The poor lads were having a difficult time and especially those who had stayed at the plantation the previous year were most welcome.

And therefore a boat often went to the other side of the river to collect an officer, but this officer was always Lieutenant Andersma. Sometimes when Julius returned from a journey or from a visit to a neighbouring plantation, he would hear that an officer had eaten there, or had rested in a bed for a time while Kwasiba washed and ironed his clothes.

Then Julius had to go to Paramaribo for a couple of weeks. It was mid-September. He would then travel on to Joden-Savanna for the annual Feast of Tabernacles. Of course Sarith would go along too, wouldn't she? But to Julius' amazement, Sarith refused. Julius simply could not understand this. Sarith, who grabbed at every opportunity to be away from the plantation, now did not want to go. "Oh, at this time of year it's so hot and dusty in town," she said. "No, I prefer to stay here."

"But aren't you afraid, then?" asked Julius. "You yourself have been saying how unsafe you feel here."

"Oh, not really," answered Sarith. "The Maroons will

most certainly not dare come round here. It's very well known that there are so many soldiers around."

Julius decided therefore to go alone, but not to travel on to Joden-Savanna, rather to return in about ten days' time, after completing his business.

A few days after Julius had departed, Sarith lay in her bedroom. Next to her in bed lay Reindert Andersma. He had left the group the day before, saying that he would be away for about three days, being on the track of something special. He would prefer to go alone, without soldiers or slaves. Sarith did not worry about what the slaves in the house thought of all this. Mini-mini just cared for Jethro. Nicolette she had already threatened enough. With Kwasiba, however, she did have to be careful. Kwasiba wasn't pleased with all this. She could see it from the way Kwasiba looked at her, and in addition Kwasiba wasn't treating Reindert with due subservience. She would always send one of the other slaves to pour him drinks or serve him. But Sarith resolved to give Kwasiba some money and so buy her silence.

It was siesta time. Around one o'clock they had lunched royally, and now it was half past three. Everything in the house was still silent. Next to her, Reindert also awoke. He looked at her, smiled and began to run a finger over her bare stomach.

"Rein, I think I'm expecting, did you know?" Sarith asked gently.

"Oh yes?" asked Rein. "Who do you think the father is?"

"I don't know. Terrible, eh?" said Sarith.

"We'll consider that your husband is the father. That will be best for all concerned," said Rein.

"Aren't I a really bad woman?" Sarith now asked.

"A fine, lovely, bad woman," laughed Rein, taking her in his arms.

Suddenly there was uproar outside. Shouting, screaming, "Oh heavens, bush-negroes, bush-negroes."[182]

182   "Mi Tata, Busi Nengre, Busi Nengre!"

Footsteps in the corridor downstairs. Rein was out of bed in one leap, pulling up the only piece of clothing he was wearing: thin pyjama trousers. He opened the bedroom door, ran onto the passage, and looked out of the window, that reached to his middle. At that same moment a shot rang out and he collapsed onto the floor of the passage, mortally wounded. Her eyes wide with fear, Sarith sat up in bed, pressing her thin batiste nightdress to her naked body. She had heard the shot. What had happened; where was Rein?

Then she heard Jethro crying and calling, "Mini-mini." The next moment Jethro was on Mini-mini's arm with her in the room, followed by Kwasiba, who, gasping, closed the door and whispered hoarsely, "Go and hide, my God misi, go and hide. The bush-negroes are here."[183]

She pulled Sarith from the bed, opened a cupboard door and pushed her, Mini-mini and Jethro in the cupboard, closed the door and quickly shoved a screen in front of it.

Immediately after that there was a lot of noise in the corridor and on the stairs, footsteps, shouting. The room door was flung open and five Alukus raced in.

"Where are they, where are the whites?"[184] one of them shouted to Kwasiba.

"Whites? There are no more whites. Haven't you killed him already?"[185] pointing to Rein's body that lay in the passage.

"The others, where are they hiding?"[186] they shouted again.

"There are no others; they're all in town."[187]

Kwasiba said this most calmly. Meanwhile a group of the plantation's slaves stood outside. One of the Maroons called from the window, next to which Rein's body lay, "All you

183 "Go kibri, mi Gado misi, go kibri, Busi Nengre dya!"
184 "Pe den dè, pe den bakra de?"
185 "Bakra? Bakra no de moro, yu kiri en kaba toch?"
186 "Den trawan, pe den e kibri?"
187 "Trawan no de, alamala go na foto."

slaves, we have killed the white man already. You can leave. Run away. You are free."[188]

A loud cheer rang out and the sound of running feet could be heard.

Suddenly a loud voice came, "Well, then I will sleep here tonight! Aren't you leaving, woman?"[189] "Oh, no," said Kwasiba. "If you are sleeping here then I can better stay, too, and you can eat a good meal."[190]

"Yes woman, you are right. Cook for me. Cook for all of us."[191]

"So who are you, brother?"[192] asked Kwasiba.

"I am Agosu."[193]

The slaves had often of late heard the name Agosu. He was one of the new leaders. When Kwasiba heard the name she was afraid, but she let nothing slip, and continued, "So you are Agosu, eh? I have heard your name. You are a great man."[194]

Agosu laughed, "You have heard it, eh? Well, now go and cook. The great man is hungry. I will stay here."[195]

Sarith and Mini-mini in the cupboard heard how Kwasiba left the room and they also heard Agosu pacing up and down the room, sometimes silent, sometimes talking to himself. They were both frightened to death. It was pitch dark in the cupboard. At first they stood up, trembling, Sarith still naked, with the nightgown pressed against her. Later she carefully put it on. Mini-mini had sat on the ground with

188　"Ala katibo nengre, un kiri a bakra kaba, yu kan gowe, lon gowe, yu fri."

189　"Ai dan m'o sribi dyaso tide neti. Yu dati yu n'e gowe ?"

190　"Nono ba, efu yu e tan sribi dyaso, a betre mi srefi e tan, dan mi kan bori gi yu fu yu kan nyan wan bun preti."

191　"Ai uma yi habi leti, we bori gi mi, bori gi un alamala."

192　"Suma na yu dan brada?"

193　"Mi na Agosu."

194　"So yu na Agosu no, ai mi yere yu nen, yu na wan bigi man."

195　"Yu yere no, we go bori dan, angri en kiri e bigi man, m'o wakti dya."

Jethro on her lap. She whispered very cautiously in his ear that he must keep deadly still, must make no noise and must not cry, or they would be discovered and murdered. Jethro, who was four years old, had already heard so much about those terrible Maroons who went around killing people that he understood that this was now a matter of life and death, and there wasn't a peep out of him. Sarith was so scared that she had to muster all her self-control to ensure that the sound of her teeth chattering would not be heard, or they would be discovered and murdered. It wasn't true, she kept trying to persuade herself. This wasn't really happening; it was a nightmare. Soon she would wake up and everything would be normal and safe again. But the nightmare went on. Now and then they heard footsteps, now and then the sound of a chair being moved and a voice saying something. And Rein, where was Rein; what had happened to him?

She didn't dare ask this of Mini-mini, afraid that her voice would be too loud. She began biting her fingers and had to force herself not to burst out sobbing. Mini-mini held Jethro pressed against her. Oh, as long as nothing happened to this child. If only this negro would leave. Perhaps they would all leave quickly now, now they believed that there were no further whites. That officer, the lad who was carrying on with the misi, was certainly dead. She had seen him lying there on the ground in a pool of blood. If they just remained dead still here in this cupboard, then the men might leave without discovering them. She understood that her mother was now busy cooking. Perhaps they would leave after they had eaten.

Every minute seemed like hours for Mini-mini and Sarith. After a while she heard Kwasiba coming. She said loudly that she had brought food and that all the men downstairs also had food. Agosu now opened the bedroom window, which had been closed all this time, and called, "All of you take the weapons away and come back to collect more."[196] After he had eaten he went and lay down on the bed, saying,

---

196 "Yu tyari den wroko sani gowe, dan un kon baka fu teki moro"

"It's already dark. I will stay here."[197] Kwasiba went and sat in the rocking chair and began talking to him. She asked him all kinds of things: how they worked in the bush, how they lived, and every time she said, "Yes, you all are right, you're getting them where it hurts, those infernal whites." [198]

When she had gone downstairs, Kwasiba had seen none of the people from the house. She understood very well that they would not all have fled, but that some of them had perhaps gone into hiding somewhere. She had thought that the best thing she could do in this situation would be to let the treacherous Agosu think that she was completely on his side. It was perhaps for the best that he wanted to stay upstairs, for then at least he would not set fire to the house, which so often happened.

Perhaps the soldiers would come. Perhaps they would come to ask where that one was, that one who loved the misi but who now lay dead on the ground. If only the three in the cupboard could remain immobile and not make any noise. For that reason she stayed in the room and talked with Agosu. She spoke loudly to signal that he was still in the room and also in the hope that he would not notice any sound that was made. She had to stay and talk to him, therefore, and so she asked him about everything and nothing while she rocked to and fro in the chair. Was it true what the people were saying about Joli-Coeur? Had he really hacked off the head of that wretch Schulz? Was it true what they did with those whites on the plantations?

Agosu spoke. Yes it was true. Sometimes they acted cruelly. But all the negroes' cruel acts totalled up would not come to one-thousandth of all the cruelty inflicted on the negroes by the whites. And in fact the negroes did not want to fight and murder whites at all. They just wanted their freedom. Freedom to live there in the bush. They wanted nothing from the planters or the government: just freedom. Because the

197 "A dungre keba, mi o tan dyaso."
198 "Ai, un habi leti baya, ai un kisi den moi, de bakra didibri."

whites seemed unable to grasp this, that was why they sometimes had to be cruel. But Kwasiba knew very well, in fact,
that negroes were not of themselves cruel. Every cruel act
they had first learnt from the whites. A negro would not be
cruel without due cause. For this reason they so often left the
white soldiers alone. They were, after all, innocent. No, a
negroe's faith would not permit him to treat cruelly someone
who was innocent. If he did that, then his kra (spirit) could
leave him. This was apparently very different for the whites,
who, it would seem, had no kra. Did Kwasiba know what
the soldiers did if they managed to capture an Aluku village?
Women and children were murdered, cruelly with a lance
pushed through the stomach and sometimes, yes sometimes,
and Agosu looked at Kwasiba with a look of steel while he
told her, "Soldiers have crushed our children in a mortar just
as you might crush bananas, until they were dead."[199]

"But I'll tell you this," Agosu stood up while he spoke. "If
I come across a white child, I let the mother watch and then
I take the child, I cut a finger off, then another finger, another one, then a hand, then a foot, the other foot, until I've cut
the child into pieces like this right before his mother's
eyes."[200]

In the cupboard, Sarith felt as if she would faint when she
heard this. This is what she could expect: that her child
would be cut to pieces in front of her eyes. Jethro had fallen
asleep in Mini-mini's lap. When she heard Agosu's words,
she clutched the child even more tightly and pressed her
hand on his free ear to prevent him from hearing any of this.
Sarith pressed herself completely against Mini-mini as if she
wanted to creep into Mini-mini's body.

199 "Surdati fon wi pikin na ini wan mata mata, te a dede, net
     leki fa y'e fon ton ton."
200 "Ma mi e taigi yu. Efu m'e miti nanga wan bakra pikin, m'o
     meki a m'ma luku, en dan m'e e teki a pikin, koti wan finga
     kmopo, dan ete wan finga, ete wan, dan en hanu, dan wan
     futu, tra futu, dan so mi e koti en na pisi-pisi, na en m'ma
     fesi."

Agosu and Kwasiba continued talking. Apparently he had gone to lie on the bed. Now and then it went quiet and you heard only the bump of the rocking chair. Then even that stopped occasionally. Hours passed. On the bed in the room Agosu slept with brief interruptions. In the rocking chair Kwasiba dozed off occasionally, as did Mini-mini in the cupboard. But Sarith did not sleep. She was wide awake. This was her punishment, that much she believed for sure. This is how God punished people who were bad. Was it not this very afternoon that she had asked Rein whether she wasn't perhaps a bad woman? This afternoon – it seemed like a hundred years ago. And Rein, what had happened to him? Had he managed to flee or was he dead? This had all happened because of her wickedness. In silence she prayed, "Lord God, allow this to pass, let them leave, have them not murder me and Jethro. I shall never be bad again, I promise." She thought over all the bad things she had done. Oh so many. Not only all this with Rein, but earlier, that with Rutger, when she had caused Elza so much sorrow. She had had Ashana whipped to death. And Julius, how bad she had been to Julius. In the first place she was married to him without being in love with him, and she had betrayed him. "Oh God forgive me," she prayed. "I shall not be bad any more, may he go without doing anything to us, I beg of you."

Day had broken. They heard Agosu talking again. They heard Kwasiba saying that she would get him something to eat, and some coffee. After that he paced up and down, looked out of the window now and then, sometimes shouted something below. In the cupboard they could see through a chink under the door that it had become light. Jethro woke up. Mini-mini whispered with her mouth right next to his ear that he still must be dead still. He badly needed to pee, but in that case how, and where? At her wits' end, Mini-mini took one of Julius' coats from the rack and rolled it up. Jethro would have to pee into that. In that way the urine could not stream out of the cupboard. Sarith was terribly thirsty. What would happen to them? Would they be saved? Would Agosu and his men leave of their own accord? Would he discover them?

The hours dragged by. In the middle of the day Kwasiba went again to cook something. Sarith, Mini-mini and Jethro could smell the food while Agosu was eating. Especially Jethro was very hungry, but most of all he was scared, oh so scared, and silently he cried with his face in Mini-mini's lap, who was holding him fast and stroking his hair. How many hours had passed? How long had they been sitting in the cupboard? It became warmer and more stuffy. How long would this torment last? Such uncertainty, not knowing what would happen the next moment. Now Jethro needed to do more than a pee. He whispered in Mini-mini's ear. She whispered back that it was impossible, he would have to keep it back. Sarith, too, hissed to her son that he must hold it back. But Jethro could not any more.

Then they heard Agosu shouting out of the window. They didn't understand, but then they heard, "Wait, I'm coming,"[201] and they heard the room door open and Agosu run onto the passage. Now Kwasiba was therefore alone in the room. Very carefully Mini-mini opened the door and whispered, "Psst." Kwasiba came closer. "My God, be quiet, do keep quiet there."[202]

Quickly Mini-mini whispered what the problem was. Now, quickly, then. Kwasiba took Jethro with her. He would have to be quick. In the small room where the chamber pots stood she took his trousers down and said, "Quick, quick!"

Jethro did his best and strained as quickly as possible on the night pot. Quickly she pulled his trousers up again and was intending to take him back to the cupboard, but she had taken just two steps into the room and there stood Agosu in the doorway. Kwasiba froze with shock and Jethro turned deathly white.

"Oh, so that's it. Where's the little white thing come from?"[203] and he came towards Jethro. Kwasiba stood in

201 "Wakti m'e kon."
202 "Mi Gado, un tantiri, un tan drape!"
203 "O na so no? Pe a pikin bakra disi kmopo?"

front of the child and held him tightly behind her, saying, "Leave him alone, oh, the poor boy, leave him."[204]

Agosu went towards the room with the chamber pots. "Where is his mother?"[205]

"He has no mother, she is already dead,"[206] said Kwasiba, turning with the boy still behind her, so that she was constantly between him and Agosu.

In the cupboard Sarith hung semiconscious onto Minimini. She had heard so much about hell, but now she knew: this was what she was experiencing, this was hell, and it was all happening as punishment for all the wicked things she had done. Yes, so it was: she was in hell and this was her retribution. Now it was going to happen. Now this ghastly negro would cut her child in pieces. Mini-mini wasn't even aware that her fingernails were biting into her misi's arms from the fright. Then they heard Agosu say, "Haven't I told you what I would do to a white child?"[207]

Jethro, pressing against Kwasiba's legs, suddenly saw a knife and screamed, "No, no!"

Kwasiba held her arms out against Agosu's approach, shouting, "Look, if you dare to do anything, then you will lose your kra. Surely you don't want that! You need your kra to fight. Leave the child alone, I beg you, leave him in peace."[208]

In the cupboard it felt to Sarith as if her heart had stopped. Mini-mini was ready to jump out of the cupboard. She didn't care any more. That awful Agosu could cut her fingers off, but not Jethro, oh no, not Jethro. Agosu took another step towards Kwasiba, the knife raised. At the same moment voices and footsteps sounded on the stairs and someone shouted, "Agosu, quick, quick, get away, boats are coming, boats full

204 "Libi en poti, libi en."
205 "P'e en m'ma de?"
206 "A no abi m'ma, en m'ma dede keba."
207 "Mi ben taigi yu san mi b'o du, nanga wan bakra pikin?"
208 "Luku, efu yu du wan sani, dan yu kra e go libi yu, yu habi yu kra fanodu fu feti. Libi na pikin, m'e begi yu, libi na pikin."

of soldiers and they're already at the jetty. Get away, all the others have already gone. Come on, Agosu."[209]

Agosu glanced again at Kwasiba, then turned and hurried away. From the cupboard they could hear his bare feet taking leaps down the stairs.

Commotion, then, and noise at the front. Shots fired, cries, whistles, men running around the house and then men's feet, fast, on the stairs.

"Sarith, Sarith, Jethro?" and a gasping Julius stood in the room. "Where is the misi?"[210] he cried, and the next moment the screen was pushed over and a semiconscious Sarith fell from the cupboard, followed by Mini-mini.

"So you're alive! Thank God, you're alive! Oh God, oh God!" and Julius sank onto the bed and looked at his wife, who was sitting in a stupor on the floor.

Kwasiba dumped the wailing child in his father's lap and, throwing herself onto the bed, cried, "Oh my God, my masra, oh my father,"[211] and began weeping and shouting uncontrollably.

Julius looked from the one to the other, but it was as if he didn't really see anything. He was conscious of only one thing: they were alive, his wife and child were alive. All those hours since three o'clock that morning when there had come a knock on the window in the Saramaccastraat and someone had shouted, "Masra, get up, the bush-negroes have raided Klein Paradijs,"[212] from that moment on he had expected nothing other than to find his wife and child murdered. He had left the town immediately, had made the oarsmen row against the tide, had himself rowed, and always with the one thought going through his head: what would he find when he got there? "God," he had prayed, "Let them live." It did

209 "Agosu, hesi hesi, kon un gowé, boto e kon, boto lai nanga surdati, den e kon na syoro keba, kon gowé, ala trawan gowé keba, Agosu, kon!"

210 "Pe a misi de?"

211 " O mi Gado, mi masra, mi Teta!"

212 "Masra, ke masra, opo; den busi nengre, den teki Klein Paradijs!"

not matter to him if his plantation was burnt out or destroyed, if only they survived. God had heard his prayers. But how? What had happened?

"Kwasiba," Sarith barely managed to whisper, "Kwasiba has saved us; it's thanks to Kwasiba that we're alive."

And now that the reality of what had happened penetrated her consciousness, she began weeping, not rebelliously and obtrusively, as she did when she wanted to get her own way, but softly, silently the tears dripped from her eyes. Mini-mini wept, too. She had drawn Jethro to her and held him fast with both arms while rocking her body back and forth.

"If Kwasiba hadn't been here, we would no longer be here, either; it's all thanks to Kwasiba," was all that Sarith could manage to say, and Julius looked at Kwasiba, still straddling the bed, shouting, "Those wretches, those devils!"[213]

Then everyone began talking at the same time. Jethro wanted to say something, Sarith wanted to say something, Kwasiba got up to make sugared water to calm everyone down. When they opened the door Julius suddenly noticed a foot belonging to the body that lay there on the passage. That young man, what was that man doing there? And suddenly everything welled up inside him, everything that in his anxiety had been suppressed. All the tales, all the gossip about his wife, and now that man, lying dead in the passage.

"Sarith, that lad, what was he doing here?"

"What lad?"

"That Andersma, the lieutenant, who's lying here dead."

"Dead, is he dead?" Sarith put her hand in front of her mouth. Rein was dead, and it was her fault. Oh, what should she do? What could she say?

"Yes, he's dead, and what was he doing here?"

Sarith gulped, "He was here to protect us."

Julius stood up and went to the door, asking, "Protect you, in his pyjamas?"

213   "Den frufruktu, den didibri!"

What he saw in the passage filled him with disgust. Three vultures were sitting on the window-sill near the corpse and two others were picking at it. One had an eye in its beak. Julius was about to go into the passage when he heard a thump behind him. Sarith, who had got up and was just behind him, had seen the same thing. Then she had fainted.

An hour later, Julius sat with Jethro on his knee in his office downstairs. He had called the soldiers to take the body away and bury it.

When Sarith had fainted, he had asked Mini-mini and Kwasiba to take care of the misi. He himself had gone downstairs with Jethro, covering the boy's eyes with his hand so that he would not see the disgusting spectacle. Kwasiba had gone to look for something edible. Almost everything was gone, but she could pull up some cassava somewhere and cook that. Jethro had lapped that up. Julius now understood that Sarith, Mini-mini and Jethro had sat for more than twenty-four hours in that cupboard while Kwasiba had kept that terrible Agosu talking and put him at his ease. That had meant that he had not searched any further.

But that other man, that gnawed at him. What he had heard in town. He had gone to Abraham and Rebecca's. By chance the previous rabbi was also visiting. He had asked where Julius' wife was. When he had answered that his wife had remained at Klein Paradijs, the rabbi had asked whether that was not dangerous. Julius had answered that Sarith herself found it not dangerous and above all there were so many soldiers in the area.

"That's precisely where the danger lies," the rabbi had answered.

Julius had looked at him incomprehensibly, and, noticing this, the old rabbi had said, in fatherly fashion, "My dear friend, I don't want to meddle in your affairs, but don't you know what the whole of Paramaribo is saying about your wife?"

Then the story was told, how Sarith was having an affair with that Andersma, was often even spending nights with him in his house. Everyone had been talking about it; it had been going on for some time. And he … he knew nothing. And now he had arrived after that fearful journey back, the first thing he had seen was that lad's corpse in the passage.

Jethro was talking. He said how scared he had been, the shooting had been really bad. He had heard shooting: "… like bang bang and I was scared papa. I shouted Mini-mini at the door and then Uncle Rein ran out of the bedroom and went to the window and then bang bang and boom, there he lay on the ground and was bleeding papa, blood, and I cried and Mini-mini came and …"

"Quiet now, my boy, quiet. It's all over; everything is safe. Don't think about it any more. Papa is here." Julius pressed the boy against him and then asked gently, "That Uncle Rein, was he often here?"

Jethro nodded. "Yes, lots of times, papa, and he had a gun papa, a really nice one, and if he had had it he would have shot first, and then bang bang the nasty men would be dead. But when he came out of mama's bedroom he did not have his gun, he just had his pyjamas on. A pity, eh?"

Julius nodded, "Yes, a pity. Was he often in mama's bedroom, then?" he enquired further.

"Oh yes. When he came he always went into mama's bedroom. Sometimes I only saw him when he went away. But he was very nice, papa; he gave me those things from his gun. Is he dead now, papa, and who will get his gun now? Because if you're dead you can't shoot any more, eh?"

"That's right: if you're dead you can't shoot any more," said Julius softly, stroking his child's head.

Hundreds of thoughts flashed through his mind. That was what Sarith had been doing, then. All that deceit. That's why she didn't want to come along when he went to the town. And he, the idiot, had known nothing, suspected nothing. He had even thought that Sarith was staying because she was happy at the plantation. Everyone had known everything; everyone except him.

Mini-mini came in. She came to collect Jethro. She wanted to bath him and put him to bed. So much had happened to him. Misi was quiet now. Kwasiba had brought her round with smelling salts and had given her strong sugared water to drink. She had wept at first, but had now calmed down. Julius looked at Mini-mini. Should he ask her what she knew about that Andersma and Sarith? But, oh, why put that poor girl in danger? After all, he already knew enough. He stayed a while in his office. Everything in the house was quiet. Outside he could hear the soldiers. At the house all the slaves had left except Kwasiba and Mini-mini. How many were left on the plantation as a whole he did not know. He stood up, went outside and told the soldiers that they could spend the night in the overseer's house. The troop leader said that the bush-negroes would certainly not return. They had taken everything they wanted: tools, food. He was lucky that they had not set fire to the house. They had buried Andersma at the edge of the forest. Julius wondered how much they knew about his wife and Andersma, but he said nothing. He went inside and paced up and down on the rear veranda. It was midnight by now.

He had to speak with Sarith. His common sense dictated waiting until the morning. But he could not manage to wait that long. He had to speak to her. Upstairs, he flung the bedroom door open. Sarith was lying on the bed, but she wasn't asleep.

"That Andersma, what was he doing here," Julius demanded harshly.

Sarith sat up with a shock. "He was here by chance and wanted to defend us," she said.

"In his pyjamas, of course?" Julius became angry. So, she was planning to lie to him. With a stride he came closer and yelled, "I want the truth. Don't lie to me. I know it all already. The whole town knows about it. Why was he here?"

Now Sarith dared say nothing. She looked at the furious man and closed her eyes.

Julius grabbed her by the shoulder of her nightdress and pulled her. "Just say it, you were carrying on with him, hey? You were sleeping with him, hey? Come on, just admit it."

When Sarith still said nothing he gave her a hard slap on the face, and then another. "Admit it, tell me, you were carrying on with him, hey?"

Sarith began wailing, "Yes, oh yes, but ..."

"But what, you slut?"

He smacked her again and then pushed her, so that she landed on the ground. Sarith screamed; now she was really afraid of him.

"No, oh no Julius, stop it!"

Julius' eyes were red with anger, foam was appearing on his lips. Trembling with rage he asked, "And how long is it now? A year, two years? How long have you been making a laughing stock of me, eh? Tell me!"

He came closer and put his hands round her throat. Sarith was now petrified: he was going to murder her, oh God, he was going to murder her.

"No," she screamed, "No, help, no!"

The next moment someone sprang between them and pushed Julius to one side and Sarith to the other. It was Kwasiba! She had heard all the commotion from downstairs. When she heard Sarith screaming like that, she had realized that something terrible was happening and had run upstairs. "Masra, stop it," she shouted. "The bush-negroes haven't murdered her. Do you want to kill her – are you out of your mind? Do you want to end up in prison?"[214]

Kwasiba was looking more at the masra, standing there beside himself with fury and with foam round his mouth. He had every reason to be livid, she was thinking. But she had to calm him down, she couldn't let him do something dire in a fit of rage.

"Come, masra, come with me," she said, taking his hand. "You're tired out, the way you've hurried here, you must be exhausted. Come, I'll give you a massage."[215]

214 "Masra keba, keba! Den busi nengre no kiri en, dan yu wan' kiri en? Yu law no, yu wan' koti strafu?"

215 "Kon masra, kon. Kon nanga mi, yu weri ba, luku fa yu lon kon dyaso, yu musu fu weri, kon mek' mi masi yu baka gi yu."

And she led him out of the room, and like an obedient child Julius went with her, overcome as he was by rage and humiliation.

In his office Kwasiba began to remove his shirt. She had him lie on the couch and began to massage his back. She very often did this. When he had made a long journey through the fields on horseback or had sat for hours in the boat, Kwasiba would always give him a massage. It felt good, calming, relaxing. Now, too, Kwasiba massaged him, calmly. Her old, strong fingers kneaded his back evenly, and she talked. As always when she did this, she talked. Now, however, not about all kinds of minor things to do with the plantation and the slaves, but about him and the misi. The misi was terribly in the wrong, yes, wicked and stupid. He was such a good masra to her, Kwasiba knew that. But now the misi was really sorry. She hadn't meant any harm. She was totally spoilt as a child and had always been able to do just what she wanted. Now Sarith knew he would not accept this, she would certainly do nothing like it again. He must forgive her, yes, he really had to. And the lad, he had had his punishment; he lay in his grave. But he, the masra must forgive misi. He must above all keep his calm. "Think of the children, do think of them."[216]

Julius was quiet, listening to what Kwasiba was saying.

"Children?" Then he asked her what she was talking about – after all, there was only Jethro. "Doesn't masra know, then; misi is expecting?"[217]

Oh, and now this, Sarith pregnant: a child with that soldier lad, no doubt. This too! Julius felt his anger welling up again, and cried, "A soldier's child."[218]

"No, masra, it is your child. I know it's your child."[219]

Kwasiba went on massaging and talking. Oh, she knew for certain that the misi would be a different person after all this. These events had affected her deeply. She would now be

216 "Prakseri den pikin baya, prakseri den."
217 "Masra no sabi dan, a misi habi bere?"
218 "Wan surdati pikin dan."
219 "No no masra, na yu pikin, mi sabi taki na yu pikin."

loving towards him, would not be seeking pleasure; a sweet, homely wife. Masra could certainly believe Kwasiba. She knew her misi so well.

When, after a good half hour, the massage was over, Julius stood up. He had to talk to Sarith again. "Don't go and fight with her, masra, I beg you."[220]

"No, I'll not fight."[221]

He went upstairs. Kwasiba stayed at the foot of the stairs, and when he went into the room, she went up quietly. In the room he said to Sarith, who was lying with her face in the pillow, "Sit up." She sat up, leaning against one of the bed-posts.

"Kwasiba says you're pregnant."

"Yes, I wanted to tell you myself once you were back here," said Sarith.

"What did you want to tell me: that you were pregnant with the lieutenant's child?"

"No Julius," Sarith began weeping again. "It is your child."

"How do you know that? How many times have you slept with him? Isn't there a far greater chance that it's his child? If you weren't Jethro's mother I'd throw you through the window, you whore. Now you'll not be hit, and I'm not throwing you out, understand me well. But don't expect anything from me – expect nothing, you hear. If you want to leave, then so much the better. If you stay, then it's because of Jethro. That other child, well, that is your business, but if you stay, you'll behave yourself, do you hear? Because otherwise, God help me, I'll strangle you with my own bare hands, slut."

He turned round and slammed the door shut behind him.

JULIUS

It was about a week later that Julius had finally taken stock of everything on the plantation. All those days he had sat in his office, brooding about Sarith, about himself, about how

220   "No go feti nanga en. Masra ke m'e begi masra."
221   "No, no mi no feti."

he should go further with his life. He had had Kwasiba bring bedding to the office and he slept on the couch. Sarith he hardly saw. Some of the slaves had returned. The domestic slaves, some of the older slaves who worked the land. Practically all the young men had gone, most of the young slave-girls, too. All in all he now had less than half of them. All the equipment was gone. He would certainly have to get thirty new slaves and everything else as well. The slaves' food plots were also empty. He would have to buy food.

He had no money. The last harvest had been bad. He had even run short and had had to call on his limited reserves. Where would he borrow money? The banks did not want to extend loans, and certainly not to Jews. If he did not borrow, how could he carry on with the plantation? What would they have to live on, and how would he be able to pay the huge sum for the escapees' fund? The annual planters' contribution was continually increasing, and all for nothing: all just to maintain an expensive army that had lads who carried on with your wife behind your back. Misery! Nothing but misery! Where could he borrow money?

And then he thought of Rutger. He would have to help him. It was common knowledge that Le Chasseur was an agent who did not readily extend loans, and certainly not in these times. But at the end of the day Rutger was his brother-in-law, Sarith and Elza were sisters, stepsisters perhaps, but sisters all the same, and Julius thought back to how they were virtually inseparable as girls, almost like twins. Well, it would be best if Sarith first spoke to Elza and explained the emergency. He would need Sarith, therefore. Now, if she still wanted to be his wife, she must be prepared to do something in return.

He went to Sarith's room. She had spent almost the whole week in there. Sarith got a fright when she saw her husband come in. Had he come to quarrel? Was he angry? But Julius began to explain in measured terms that the plantation was in a bad way. If he were to keep the plantation, then he must buy slaves and equipment urgently. He needed money and would therefore have to get a loan, and wanted to try that at

Rutger's bank in view of the fact that he would not get one anywhere else. For this reason it was necessary for Sarith to go to town and first explain to Elza that they were in desperate circumstances. Elza would certainly be able to talk her husband round.

"Me, go to Elza to ask for a loan? No, I won't do that." Sarith was indignant. With Elza of all people.

"Why not? She'll be sure to understand." Julius was already getting annoyed.

"No, I won't do it. You can ask everything of me, but not this, no, no," cried Sarith.

Now Julius was really angry. "Why not? What is the reason why you won't? Tell me, tell me." He held Sarith by her shoulder. "Why won't you? There is something, now that you mention it. You were always such good friends, but now you never go to her, in fact, and they've never been here. What is it? Tell me."

"Oh," Sarith shrugged, "Gossip and so forth."

"What kind of gossip, then. Who's telling tales? What gossip?"

Sarith said nothing, but Julius was livid. What was behind all this? What was all this secrecy about yet again?

"What kind of gossip, tell me," he yelled. Sarith was scared.

"Oh, from the past, long ago, that I, that I ... wanted to steal her husband."

Julius looked at his wife and said thoughtfully, "And that wasn't gossip, eh? That was the truth: yes, now I know. You tried to turn his head, yes, that's what it was."

Suddenly he saw in his mind's eye the scene at Hébron on the occasion of Rebecca's wedding. He remembered how he had seen Sarith standing at the side with Rutger, leaning against him, exercising all her charm, laughing.

"And who knows how far you got him, too, the husband of your sister, your bosom-friend. Oh what a monster you are!"

Furious, he went away.

That afternoon he saw her on the veranda and said, "Get

ready. Tomorrow we're going to town. Jethro and Mini-mini are going too. You don't need to go to Elza: I'll spare you that humiliation. But get one thing clear: you'll behave like the ideal wife and you'll come straight back with us."

In Paramaribo everyone had naturally known for a long time what had happened at Klein Paradijs. Everyone sympathized with Sarith: the terror she had experienced. Everyone was also full of admiration for Kwasiba's presence of mind and cleverness.

"She deserves a reward," said Esther. "She saved your life."

And Sarith thought, yes, twice in one day. But of course she could not say anything about what had happened between her and Julius after that. Naturally, everyone knew, too, what had happened to Andersma. People would not say it to Julius and Sarith, but everyone talked about it, and the story became increasingly juicy with the telling. Julius had found Andersma's naked body when he arrived home, and Sarith had rolled naked out of the cupboard, and so forth. Julius had the feeling that all the men were laughing at him, and when people asked him how his wife was and whether she had got over the shock, he thought peevishly, which shock were they referring to: the raid by Agosu or the death of her lover?

CHAPTER XII

JAN

When Lieutenant Andersma had left the military post, announcing that he was on the track of something special and would be gone about three days, the subalterns had had a good laugh behind his back. "Something special," Officer Bels had said, scornfully, "A special woman, no doubt?" The lieutenant must think they were mad. Perhaps he really did believe that no-one knew that he was carrying on with that little thing there on Klein Paradijs; and weren't they just a stone's throw away from the plantation? The soldiers had their own views on the matter, too. But all right, it didn't really matter to them one way or the other, and the longer they could stay on the post the better. They could at least sleep under one shelter in a hammock and make a smoke pot against the mosquitoes.

Jan was sorry that Lieutenant Andersma was leaving, even if it were for only three days, as he himself had said, for then the group was left to the mercy of the ruthless officer Bels, whom Jan regarded as the lowest of the low. And the subaltern had it in for him especially: he knew that all too well. That had all come about when they were only a few days away from the town, several weeks ago now.

After ten days some of the soldiers were already seriously ill. The negro porters had now to carry the sick men and their baggage as well as everything else. At a certain moment Officer Bels had forced yet another backpack on a porter who could even then hardly walk with everything he already had on his back. When the negro porter's knees collapsed under the weight, the subaltern had kicked him.

Jan, who had seen all this, had flared up at the subaltern, saying, "One man can't possibly carry all that."

"You carry it, then," replied the subaltern, and Jan had taken the extra pack over from the porter without further comment and had slung it over his shoulder. Lieutenant Andersma, who by chance had followed the whole incident, had said to the subaltern, "You can still learn something from a simple soldier about good army practice, Officer Bels!"

The subaltern had given Jan a look that could kill and had muttered a curse. From that moment on the subaltern had had it in for Jan. He had even almost pushed him in the creek, ostensibly by accident, and recently when Jan had stumbled over something, as far as he was concerned it wasn't over a sharp stake but over an extended foot: that of Officer Bels.

When the lieutenant had not returned after three days, the porters became worried. There were murmurings about a raid on Klein Paradijs. Officer Bels went there with two soldiers. They returned with the news that Lieutenant Andersma was dead, shot by the Bonis during a raid on the plantation. The plantation owner had not been there at the time. When he returned the next day he had found Andersma's body.

The group was therefore now under the command of Officer Bels. They must press on, more towards the Marowijne. After several days on the go they came across another commando at a post. This was a group under the command of Captain Mayland. They had discovered the Boni's village 'Gado Sabi', which was surrounded by agricultural land. The entrance to the village had been found by a few negroes from the Free Corps, but they had not been able to capture the village or take the Bonis prisoner, for as soon as the negroes had seen the military approaching, one of them had set fire to two houses at the front. The military fired, but the Bonis fired back, and while the military had been halted by the rain of bullets the Bonis had been able to get away. Then the fire had spread over part of the swamp and the military had had to withdraw. The Bonis had fled into the bush and the military had been unable to follow them.

It was, however, suspected that there were several other

small villages. It was now the task of Officer Bels' commando to look for them. Captain Mayland's group, already three months on the go, would carry on to 'Devils Harwar', where there was a military hospital. More than half the soldiers were on the verge of exhaustion.

The group under Officer Bels' command pressed on northwards. Jan was increasingly the object of the officer's bullying. He was often given all kinds of stupid tasks and dare not refuse, knowing that Bels would report him as a mutineer or objector. Now they came to a swamp. Would they have to go through it or try to walk round it?

"We need to send someone to find out whether we can get through," said the officer. "Go on Jan, you go through!"

"Me, why me?" Jan looked fearfully at the swamp. Wasn't that a crocodile? Some anacondas?

"Jan, come on, are you afraid?" The officer gave him a push in the back, and the next moment he was standing up to his knees in the swamp. The thick mud sucked at his feet so that it was with the utmost difficulty that he could make any progress, hoping that his mates on the bank would make enough noise to frighten away any crocodiles or snakes. He sunk ever deeper. He was now fifty metres from the edge, with no end in sight. Now the mud came up to his chest. He looked round. No-one was following him. Then he saw the officer signal left, and a soldier shouted, "Don't go any further, Jan, we're going round it."

He understood that this was yet another of the officer's tricks. He was probably never intending to go through the swamp in the first place. The whole day Jan had to struggle on further in his stinking, muddy clothes. Once again he had ulcers, wounds and blisters everywhere. He felt shivery, too, as if he were developing a fever.

Excitement in the vanguard. They had come across a field of food crops. Ripe corn, cassava and bananas. The soldiers plundered the field and they stopped for a while so that everyone could take enough for his own consumption. Then the crops were completely destroyed. Jan did not participate in the destruction. He tried to keep out of the way, noticing, however, that Officer Bels was keeping an eye on him. He pretended to be busy with his gun, which had got wet. He wanted no part in ruining the bush-negroes' produce.

During his time in the negroes' village, he had continually wondered why they had to be hunted and destroyed. It was so obvious that the Maroons really wanted peace and asked only to be allowed to live free in the bush. Jan could not understand what was so wrong with that. Now he understood that, if the government gave in to the bush-negroes, that could signal the end of slavery, for then even more slaves would flee. The plantations could not operate without slaves, and so they must stay, must be exploited, must be too scared to escape. Without the plantations there would, after all, be no coffee, cotton or sugar and therefore no wealth for the planters. The captured Boni-negroes had to serve as an example, frightening other refugees, and therefore they had to be punished severely. What a system! What misery! And to cap it all, the planters were convinced that they were good people. After all, they went to church on Sunday, praised and glorified God, who was so bountiful to them.

The next day they had to go looking for the village, which had to be nearby. Jan felt so sick that he had difficulty moving at all. At a certain moment they halted. The group had to spread out, everyone in a different direction. Jan went about a hundred metres through thick brushwood, saw fallen tree trunks and was about to climb over them when he saw a village, perhaps a hundred and fifty metres in front of him. Through the bush he saw roofs, women working outside the huts. He could picture the scene there: women preparing food, children playing. He had to get away, quickly, and no-one must come this way, no-one must see the village.

He went back as fast as he could, already shouting that there was nothing there, that it must be in the other direction, certainly in the other direction. The officer and other soldiers looked in amazement at the quiet, timid Jan, suddenly so talkative and insisting that the village was certainly on the other side. But then a few other soldiers came up who had gone in the same general direction as Jan. One of them had climbed a tree and had seen the village. There it was, and they would have to creep up on it and attack. And so it happened. A quarter of an hour later the women and children and a couple of old men were taken by surprise by a group of wild soldiers, shooting and hacking at everything in sight. A complete bloodbath followed. All fourteen villagers were murdered. Soldiers ran eagerly to and fro to hack off hands and so collect their bonuses in due course.

Jan did not take part in the massacre. Despondently he sat down by a tree, head in his hands. Was this really necessary? A group of excited soldiers had just returned from the village, swords and hands smeared with blood, when a faint cry was heard in the distance. The cry of a child. So there was still a child somewhere: find it and kill it; that was good. The soldiers set off again, and Officer Bels, who was still watching Jan, called, "Go on Jan, go for it, you can do it!"

"No," screamed Jan. "No, no!"

"Why not, Jan – are you scared?" shouted the officer.

Jan said nothing, putting his arm in front of his face and laying his head on his knees. The other soldiers had gone. Jan heard cries and muffled blows. "No," he choked into his arm, "No, oh please not this."

Then it was quiet for a while and he heard the officer saying, "Look Jan, look in front of you." When Jan looked up, he saw the bloody, smashed head of a small child. With a scream he sprang up, only to fall to the ground again the next moment. His head in his hands, he could no longer contain himself and started weeping uncontrollably, howling like a child.

The soldiers first stood watching, but then Officer Bels started laughing out loud, "Ha, ha, ha," and in no time the whole group was laughing, "Ha, ha, ha," and from left, right and centre, "Are you scared Jan? Jan, are you frightened? Are you afraid, Jan?"

From that moment on he was the laughing stock of all the soldiers. Everyone made him look stupid. Any moment a frog or a snake would be thrown at him, and if it startled him there came from all directions, "Are you frightened, Jan? Jan, are you scared?"

They forged ahead. The success had encouraged them. Perhaps they would find more villages. When Jan wanted to sleep at night, his hammock had disappeared or he found a snake on the spot. When he sat eating, a hacked-off negro hand would land in his bowl of peas. On one occasion it was the hand of that child. And every time there would be the laughter and the cries of, "Jan, are you scared?"

Jan felt increasingly ill. Sometimes he had fever and lay shivering on the ground. The next day the fever had gone, but he was so weak, he could not take a step further. And all the time he thought how stupid and naïve he had been, believing back home in Holland that could just go to Suriname to catch negroes and then simply find some gold and return wealthy. He would be lucky to get out of this green hell alive.

Finally, he could do nothing more. Now he was carried. The negro porter whom he had once helped was the only person to pay any attention to him, now and then giving him something to drink. The doctor in the group had already realized that Jan would not make it by a long chalk. Jan became delirious and started talking all kinds of nonsense. About gold, about peace, about good negroes, about grandma's shawl and a warm skirt. Before dying, he said to the porter who came to give him a can of water, "Tell them that there was no gold – no, no gold."

JULIUS

Sarith had decided to reward Kwasiba. She did not yet know how, but a reward she would certainly get. However, when the family returned to Klein Paradijs, Kwasiba was sick. She had high fever and chest pains, her cheeks were sunken and her eyes dim. "Kwasiba, what's wrong?"[222] asked Sarith, shocked. "Oh misi, I'm old, I'm tired,"[223] came the answer, weakly.

222 "Kwasiba, san de fu du?"
223 "Ai misi, mi grani kaba, mi skin weri."

"What can I give you? What can I do for you?"[224]

A faint smile appeared on Kwasiba's face as he said, "I want nothing. Where I'm going you can't take wealth along. Misi, I want nothing, but you and Masra Julius, you care for my child, care for my Mini-mini. Let her stay with you, look after her well. That's all I want."[225]

Sarith reflected that this was no reward for what Kwasiba had done for her, for it would be not the slightest trouble to keep Mini-mini. She would never be able to do without Mini-mini, such a loving and good person, so devoted to Jethro. No, she could have no better person than Mini-mini. Once Jethro was grown up, she thought, and she no longer needed Mini-mini, then she must certainly give Mini-mini her freedom. But only later, of course, for giving a slave freedom cost money, and that they didn't have right now.

A few days later Kwasiba died. Julius was not there when it happened. He had gone to the town to fetch the new slaves. When he returned and Sarith told him that Kwasiba had died, he said despondently, "And she never got that reward."

"She wanted no reward," said Sarith. "I asked her, but she didn't want anything, only that Mini-mini would stay with us and that we should be good to her."

The plantation was operating again. The new slaves were set to work. In the house there was more for Nicolette to do. She was one of the slaves who had returned, because she was expecting. The father was a slave who lived not far from the De Ledesmas in the Saramaccastraat. The cook, Freda, and Nicolette's sister were also in the house.

It was New Year. Sarith did not ask to go to town. She wanted to, but dared not ask for anything, and Julius paid hardly any attention to her and said only what was strictly necessary. Since the raid he had always slept in his office.

224   "San mi kan du gi yu, san mi kan gi yu dan?"
225   "Mi no wani noti baya, pe m'e go i no kan tyari gudu, misi mi no wani noti, ma yu nanga masra Julius, un luku mi pikin baya, un luku Mini-mini, meki a tan nanga yu, sorgu en bun, na dati nomo mi wani."

Sarith mainly remained in her room, where she lay in bed or just hung around, now her body was becoming ever greater with the child she was expecting.

It rained a lot. Julius arrived home after sitting half a day in the tent boat. He was tired and stiff and longed for a firm massage from Kwasiba, but Kwasiba was no more. He paced restlessly up and down the rear veranda and asked Sarith, who had just come down the steps, "Is there a slave-girl who can massage? I have back-ache."

"Mini-mini knows how to massage. Let her do it," said Sarith, and to Mini-mini, who was playing with Jethro on the front veranda, she said, "Mini-mini, go and massage the masra's back."[226]

It feels very different from what Kwasiba did, thought Julius as he lay on his stomach on the couch and felt Mini-mini's fingers on his back. Pleasant and much softer. He relaxed. He did miss Kwasiba's voice – she always spoke as she massaged – and he said to the girl, "Your mother always talked as she massaged. Tell me something."[227]

"I don't know what I could say, masra,"[228] said Mini-mini.

"Mini-mini: that is surely a name from the story of Koprokanu?"[229] remarked Julius.

"Yes, Mini-mini was the name of one of the children,"[230] agreed Mini-mini.

"Well, tell me that, then,"[231] said Julius.

Mini-mini laughed and with her soft, melodious voice she began to tell the Cinderella tale of the mother who had four children: Mini-mini, Fremantania, Fremanbonia and Koprokanu. She loved the first three, but not the fourth one, because she was not beautifully brown like the other three,

226 "Mini-mini go masi a masra en baka."
227 "Yu m'ma ben lobi fu taki te a ben masi mi baka, ferteri mi wan sani."
228 "Mi no sabi san fu ferteri, masra."
229 "Ya, a tori fu Mini-mini nanga Koprokanu."
230 "Ya, Mini-mini na a nem fu wan fu dem pikin."
231 "We, dan ferteri mi na tori fu yu nen."

but was more yellow in colour and had copper-red hair. And when Mini-mini sang the song that the mother would sing when she came home, her voice sounded so sweet that Julius felt a wave of happiness engulfing him. The tender fingers on his back, the lovely voice that narrated and sang so beautifully: oh how fine this was! This Mini-mini – how sweet she was. When the massage was over, he spent the rest of the evening thinking back on how wonderfully those fingers went over his back and how sweet her voice had sounded.

The next day he went into the fields on horseback. He came home wet through from the rain and again Mini-mini had to massage his back. Again he asked her to speak and sing to him. The next day, too. And so it continued, every day, so that it became a routine. But Julius noticed that he longed the whole day for that one hour that he would be lying alone with Mini-mini on the couch in his office, feeling her affectionate fingers passing over his back and hearing her soft, melodious voice. This was no massage, this was a caress, a delightful, fantastic caress that he hoped would never end. And then that voice, that sweet, soft voice.

Mini-mini knew no more stories, so he asked her just to sing. The songs she also sang to Jethro, so sweet, oh so sweet! Sometimes he turned over and asked her to massage his shoulders from the front. Then he would look at her. How beautiful she was, so delightful, so soft. He looked at her mouth, her large, dark eyes. Sometimes the headdress fell from her head and he saw the lovely thick plait that moved along with her. He could not help stretching a hand out and caressing her face and her bare shoulders.

He came to realize more and more that he was falling in love with Mini-mini! The whole day long he could think of nothing else but her. Every minute that he was away from her he felt a kind of longing, a deep desire to be lying on the couch, feeling her caring fingers and hearing that dulcet voice. This was true love. He loved her dearly.

It would have been easy for him to have taken her in his desire. He was, after all, her master. But that was something he didn't want. His feelings for her were too deep, too sincere for him to misuse her in that way. He wanted her, oh how he wanted her, but not like that. No, she would have to give herself in love or not at all. And of course, her master's feelings did not go unnoticed by Mini-mini, either. She, too, knew that he was far from indifferent to her: he was so good, so nice. But it was simply not in her nature to seduce a man, and in any case she was afraid, for what good would something like that do her.

In the meantime Julius decided that it was time for his son Jethro, now five years old, to begin to learn to read and write. In the early evening he would therefore sit with Jethro and Mini-mini in his office and teach the boy numbers and the alphabet. Because Mini-mini was always there with him, she learned, too. When the two were together during the day, they practised together, sometimes outside with a stick in the sand, sometimes on a slate with a chalk pencil. Every evening the three sat there in the lamplight, and when Sarith on occasion walked past the office and looked in, she noticed that there was a certain something between those three there, something intimate, something between the three of them in which she had no part. Three dark heads bent over the table in the lamplight. She would hear Jethro cry, "O Mini-mini, your a's look like tadpoles."[232] And Mini-mini would laugh and reply, with that soft voice of hers, "Those 2's of yours look a bit like ducks."[233] And then came Julius' voice, and the three of them bursting out laughing.

Every afternoon Mini-mini massaged the masra, and every afternoon he had to work hard to restrain himself from taking her in his arms, kissing her and returning her fond caresses.

Sarith had not been moaning any more about going to town. Perhaps she was ashamed about the child she was expecting? Or perhaps she realized that there was no money to be spent on all kinds of unnecessary purchases.

The baby was born in April. In the middle of the night,

232   "O, Mini-mini luku den 'a' fu yu, den gersi todo-bere."
233   "Den 'tu' fu masra Jethro gersi doksi."

during a heavy shower of rain, Mini-mini had to rush to the slave quarters to get women to help with the delivery. It was a girl, a stripling of a thing with a bald head. But when she opened her eyes for a second, they were blue. It was Mini-mini who went to the masra and insisted that he go to his wife. When he saw the child, he said only, "What's her name?" Sarith had no name for her daughter, nor did Julius: he couldn't care less what the child was called. So they decided to call her Eva.

Was it the new baby that reminded Julius that afternoon that Mini-mini had also once had a baby? When she was massaging him that afternoon, Julius said, "Today I want to hear the story of Mini-mini."[234]

The girl thought he meant the tale that she had told before, the story of Koprokanu, and so she said, "But I've told the masra that tale so often."[235]

"No, not the tale of Koprokanu – your story, Mini-mini, about the child you once bore, about his father and who your man was."[236]

With that mellow voice of hers, Mini-mini then told of Hendrik and her, his promise to save to buy her freedom, how he had rejected her, preferring another, free, woman, and the child whose lot it was not to live. With a sigh she told how stupid she had been to have believed that a free man would take a slave-girl; she was a slave, not good enough for a free man. When she said this, and Julius saw the tears in those beautiful dark eyes, he could no longer control himself.

He threw his arms around her and drew her towards him, whispering, "Never say that, Mini-mini. You're the loveliest, the best, the best, believe me. The best man in all the world is not good enough for you. If I could do that for you, give you someone like that, then believe me I would do it."

---

234   "Mini-mini tidé mi wan' yere a tori fu Mini-mini."
235   "Ma mi ferteri masra a tori dati someni lesi keba."
236   "No, no, a no Koprokanu mi wani yere, mi wani yere a tori fu yu, fu yu Mini-mini, a pikin san yu ben kisi, en p'pa, suma ben de yu mati?"

He kissed her on her tearful eyes, then on her mouth, caressing her, holding her. And she? She returned his kisses and caresses, for she loved him, too, and she knew well that there was no evil lurking in this man, that he had only good intentions towards her. What both of them had so long felt coming on and what both had tried to avoid, now happened. They loved each other, and they confirmed that love then and there, on the couch in the office. After this first time, it would happen very often.

Julius was totally besotted with Mini-mini. When she was massaging his back and he felt those fingers, the tender hands continually caressing him, he had the feeling that this was what he had been waiting for all his life. Every moment that he was not with her he was overwhelmed by an intense longing to run to her, throw his arms around her, hold her to him to be able to feel, stroke and caress her. He was almost jealous of Jethro because he could be with her nearly all the time, could sit on her lap and feel her arms around him. It was now so clear to Julius: he cared for no-one but her. He wanted to tell the whole world, shout it out loud: yes, he loved only Mini-mini.

SARITH

Sarith could survive no longer at Klein Paradijs. She had now been on the plantation for more than six consecutive months, for the first time since she was married. In the beginning the recent events, and especially the death of Rein Andersma, had cast their shadow over her such that amusement held no appeal forto her. She stayed in her room, thought things over a lot. She felt guilty that it was because of her that Rein was now dead. Often in the dead of night she would awake in terror, dreaming yet again of that ghastly day, shut up in the cupboard, that terrible Agosu pacing up and down in her room, and Rein lying dead in the passage. And then there was Julius. Julius, who was perhaps not angry any more, but just totally indifferent to her. She didn't know which was worse. He gave her hardly a glance. Now and then they had visitors on the plantation, people travelling to plantations further afield who would stop awhile. Her mother had also come just after the birth and had stayed a few weeks there.

She had also heard how Fourgeoud's forces, reinforced by the Zwarte Jagers Corps, had combed the Cottica region and had managed to destroy some villages and crops that were still left. The Bonis had left for the other side of the Marowijne River and were now in French Guyana. The colonists breathed a sigh of relief. At last! Finally they were rid of that rabble in the bush. They now had nothing more to fear, and that expensive army could be got rid of, and quickly. Away with all those soldiers, officers and lieutenants who were costing them money and were furthermore getting off with their women.

Julius never looked at the baby. It was Sarith's child, not his. When Sarith said in the month of June that she wanted to go to the town for a while, he said, "Just go, I don't care."

"I'll take the child with me, and Nicolette."

Julius replied, "Please yourself."

And so Sarith left and installed herself again on the top floor of her sister's house. Esther's boys found the baby great. Sarith began to go out again, seeking amusement in evenings out and visits here and there. She did, however, notice that she was no longer invited by some people, and that some of the rich plantation owners were most decidedly no longer rich. But she noticed most of all how people were whispering about her. Often people would ask after her little daughter, Eva. Eva was growing, and hair was growing over that little bald head: blond hair, while in neither her family nor that of Julius had blond hair and blue eyes ever been seen. No, everything was different now, and when it was becoming so hot and dusty in the town at the end of September, Sarith decided to return to Klein Paradijs.

When she arrived back home, she immediately noticed the intimacy between Julius, Jethro and Mini-mini. Jethro could already read quite well. He and Mini-mini would read happily together from a sheet on which Julius had written something, while he himself smiled along. One morning when Mini-mini was busy in Jethro's room and Sarith came in, she suddenly realized: Mini-mini was pregnant. "Hey, Mini-mini, are you expecting?"[237] asked Sarith in surprise.

With some embarrassment, the girl answered, "Yes misi."

"Who, then – who is the father?"[238] Sarith asked.

Mini-mini hung her head and remained silent.

"Who is the father – is it one of the slaves here?"[239]

"No misi, misi doesn't know him,"[240] came the sheepish answer.

Sarith assumed that it must anyway be one of the slaves, or a chance guest. Well, that Mini-mini – and she had always thought that she was so shy and withdrawing. She had obviously misjudged the girl.

But Sarith noticed more during the weeks that followed. If she had already suspected that there was something between those three people, something from which she was excluded, now she saw how Julius looked at Mini-mini and she had also seen on occasion how Mini-mini had returned the look. Those were no glances between master and slave, but between two lovers. At first the thought scared her. No, that was not possible. That was nothing for Julius. But she began to observe more closely, and noticed especially that Julius was massaged every afternoon and that he and Mini-mini spent a long time in the office. That would always happen around siesta time, when Mini-mini had first sat next to Jethro's bed with a fan, until he had fallen asleep.

Sarith was angry. She wanted to know the details. She waited for her chance, a moment when Julius and Mini-mini were together in the office. She went to the door and turned the knob silently, but the door was locked. She tried looking through the keyhole, but the key was in it and she could see nothing. She just had to know, had to know what was happening in there.

She left the rear veranda silently and walked round the

237 "San Mini-mini, yu habi bere?"
238 "Suma dan, suma na a p'pa?"
239 "Suma na a p'pa, na wan fu den srafu fu dya?"
240 "Nono, misi, misi no sabi en."

house. On the side there was the open window of the office, but it was too high for her to look in. What now? Then, still making no sound, she went inside again and upstairs. The office was under a small room that was hardly ever used and where various baskets and boxes with clothes and all kinds of things were piled up. Sarith looked at the floor. Fortunately for her there was a chink here and there between the floorboards. Very carefully she lay down on the floor and put an eye to one of the gaps. She saw the two of them on the couch and knew enough: so what she had suspected was true. She kept on looking. This was no wild Julius taking advantage of a slave-girl. No, this was tender cuddling, caressing and loving whispers.

Sarith was furious. That vile Mini-mini: just wait, she would get her. She said nothing about what she had seen, but waited until Julius was out inspecting the fields the next morning. Then she told Mini-mini that she must come to her room.

"Who made you pregnant?"[241] Sarith asked sharply.

Mini-mini said nothing, looking sheepishly at the floor.

"Tell me, who?"[242] said Sarith calmly.

Mini-mini still remained silent.

"I don't know him, eh? I obviously don't know my own husband! Is it not Masra Julius who's made you pregnant?"[243] Sarith was raising her voice. Beside her on the table lay a flat stick that was used in coffee roasting. She grabbed it and it landed with a thump on Mini-mini's shoulder, then in her face. But before Sarith could take a third swipe, a little figure flew at her and grabbed her hand.

"Don't hit Mini-mini, don't hit Mini-mini!" It was Jethro.

Sarith started in surprise, but recovered immediately and pushed the boy aside, shouting, "Scram, you!"

Jethro landed against the wall, but bounced back like a

241 "Suma gi yu bere?"
242 "Taigi mi, suma?"
243 "Mi no sabi en no? Mi no sabi mi eigi masra no? A no masra Julius gi yu bere? A no en?"

ball, now pummelling his mother with his little fists, screaming, "Don't hit her, don't hit Mini-mini." When he saw that
his mother was going to continue anyway, he turned and
threw himself against Mini-mini with both hands around her
neck, so that his own body acted as a shield for her. Crying,
he shouted, "Don't hit her, don't hit her."

Sarith shouted, "Get away, Jethro, let go. I'll teach that
bitch a lesson!"

"She's not a bitch, keep off her: you, you're the bitch," he
screamed.

Mini-mini, scared that Sarith would now even hit Jethro,
wailed, "No Masra Jethro, oh no, look out, let go of me, let
go!"[244]

Sarith, who could not carry on with her beating, yelled at
her child, "Let go, Jethro, or I'll hit you, too!"

"Stay away from her: I'll tell my father, I'll tell papa that
you've hit Mini-mini!"

Sarith, who realized that she could not carry on, shouted,
"Be off with you, both of you, but you, you witch, I'll get
you."[245]

Sobbing, and with a wailing Jethro around her neck,
Mini-mini went outside. There, Jethro said gently to her,
"Come, Mini-mini, come with me: I'll help you." And in his
room, like a little gentleman, he took a cup of coconut oil
and began to smear the wounds with it. "Stay here, Mini-
mini, I'll look after you," he said, and when, around midday,
he heard the sound of horse's hoofs, he ran to the rear veranda to wait for his father, and told him, flustered, that his
mother had beaten Mini-mini.

Julius went quickly to Jethro's room. When he saw his dis-
traught Mini-mini sitting there on the floor, he went and
knelt by her, saying softly, "Mini-mini, how I wanted to
spare you this. She knows, doesn't she?"[246] Mini-mini nodded. Julius went to his wife's room, followed closely by

244 "No no masra Jethro, ke ba, lusu mi masra ke, lusu mi!"
245 "Un komopo gowé. Ma yu dati, yu didibri, m'o kisi yu ete."
246 "A sabi, no?"

Jethro, who perhaps didn't know what was going to happen, but did realize that whatever it was, it was serious. "Mini-mini is pregnant and I'm the father: is that why you beat her?" Julius' tone was measured.

"Yes, I did," said Sarith.

"You, you of all people, you, vile whore that you are," said Julius.

"What? Am I supposed to accept this happening behind my back? Am I supposed to accept this?" Sarith began screaming and stamping.

"Not behind your back; nothing's happening behind your back. I love her and I want everyone to know it, do you hear?" Now Julius was yelling, too.

"Well, keep your bit of fluff and your concubine some-where else, then, but not in my house. I don't have to take that lying down," said Sarith.

"Fine, fine, she'll leave, but for the moment she's staying here, and if you dare lay one finger on her, believe me, I'll flog you 'til you drop! You're warned!" Julius turned and left, again with Jethro, who had witnessed everything, fol-lowing him.

Sarith now began to think things over. "She'll leave," he had said. That meant that he would install her somewhere and then openly acknowledge her as his concubine. He would support her and her child, perhaps buy a house for her, have more children and be with her more and more. But then she, Sarith, had in fact lost out even more. They already had so lit-tle money, now that there was such a huge debt. How would it be if Mini-mini was his concubine in the near future? But Mini-mini was hers, she was her slave-girl. She must act, and act quickly. He must not succeed in making her his concu-bine. She would sell Mini-mini. At the end of the day she could do what she wanted with her property. But first she had to have the papers: the deeds of ownership that showed that Mini-mini was her property. If she asked him, he could refuse to give them to her or he might even give her the money him-self. No, he must know nothing of this, must suspect nothing.

The next day, Julius did not go out to the fields. Obviously he was frightened that something would happen in his absence. Sarith behaved normally, even nicely. Not even a comment when she caught Mini-mini spelling a word. Although Sarith had understood well enough that Mini-mini was learning to read, she had said nothing. Julius could not understand this pleasantness, and really didn't trust this whole Sarith thing, but saw that even the next day she was being friendly, and spoke kindly to Mini-mini.

Sarith asked for help with Eva now and then, because Mini-mini had so much more patience than Nicolette, and Eva was crying so much due to her cutting her teeth. Julius decided that Sarith had chosen to make the best of a bad job, and wasn't so worried any more. He went out to the fields again the next day. The moment he was gone, Sarith went into the office, closed the door, and began to look for the papers.

When, seven years earlier, she had come to live at Klein Paradijs, her stepfather had given Kwasiba's deeds of ownership to Julius. That was it! There was written that the slave-girl Kwasiba had been bought by Jacob A'haron, owner of the Bethel Plantation. At the foot of the sheet there was a note of the children born to this Kwasiba: Caro, born in 1747; Kwassi, born 1749, died 1749; Mini-mini, born 1750.

She hid the paper in her room. For the rest, in the days that followed she was extra kind to Jethro and nice to Mini-mini, and went out of her way to talk to Julius. Then, one afternoon, she said that she would like to go to town in a few days' time, but this time Jethro would have to go along, because she had promised Esther and Rebecca to bring him. They wanted to hold a party for all the family's children, and Esther, especially, was of the opinion that Jethro should see more of his cousins now that he was older. Julius had no objections.

"Of course, Mini-mini must come along in that case," said Sarith. "Jethro can't manage without her."

Me too, thought Julius, but he couldn't say that, and said only, "Don't make it too long, no more than a week. Jethro needs to carry on with his lessons."

Before lunch of the third day after that, Sarith had installed

herself, with children and slave-girls, in the De Ledesmas'
home on the Saramaccastraat, and after the afternoon rest
period she got ready to go out. She told no-one where she
was going and took none of her own slave-girls with her, but
one of her sister's errand boys walked along behind her. At
the stock exchange, where almost all the gentlemen gathered
after the afternoon break and where the necessary negotiations, buying and selling took place, she sent the errand boy
inside with the message that she wished to speak with Mr
Beunekom. Ladies never entered the stock exchange.

When Mr Beunekom came outside and found this lady
waiting for him, the thought crossed his mind that it must be
something serious to have brought her all this way just to
speak to him. She told him that she had a slave-girl for sale:
an expensive one, a mulatto. Beunekom would have to collect
her himself that same evening, from the Saramaccastraat. The
price was not relevant: Beunekom could fix that himself.

That evening Sarith waited for him and led him to the
grounds behind the house where the slave quarters were. The
door opened and Mini-mini saw the misi standing there in
the light of a lamp that was held up high by an errand boy.
Next to her stood an obnoxious, fat man with protruding
belly. She saw the raunchy expression on his face, and the
misi said, "You must go along with this masra!"[247]

Mini-mini's knees knocked as she stood up. No further
words were necessary. She knew what was going to happen
to her.

When he awoke the next morning, Jethro found Nicolette,
not Mini-mini, next to his bed. "Where's Mini-mini?" he
asked.

"Mini-mini isn't here,"[248] answered Nicolette.

"Go away,"[249] cried Jethro. "I want Mini-mini," and
then louder, "Mini-mini," but there was no answer. Again he
yelled, "Mini-mini."

---

247   "Mini-mini, yu a gowe nanga a masra disi!"
248   "Mini-mini no dé."
249   "Gowé!"

"She isn't here,"[250] Nicolette repeated.

Jethro jumped out of bed and ran barefoot downstairs and out to the slave quarters in the grounds. He thrust open the door of the hut where Mini-mini always slept, and called out again and again, "Mini-mini!"

One of the other slave-girls said gently, "She's not here, little masra, she's not here; she's gone away."[251]

Jethro simply did not understand. Mini-mini was always around, wasn't she? He went back into the house, up the stairs and into his mother's room, and shouted to Sarith, who was still in bed, "Mama, where is Mini-mini? Akuba says that she has gone away."

"Yes, she's left, and she won't be coming back. Have Nicolette help you."

"No," screamed Jethro, "I want Mini-mini. Where is she? I want Mini-mini. Mini-mini!"

"Don't scream like that, lad, she is not coming back, never ever. I have sold her." Sarith's voice was very calm. "You can scream from morning to night, she's gone for ever."

"No, that's not right, I want Mini-mini, Mini-mini." Jethro was now howling with every breath in his little body. Just like his mother did in her childhood, he started stamping and throwing things. "I want Mini-mini."

"Now, shut up, Jethro, and get out of my room." Sarith was beginning to lose patience.

"I want Mini-mini, I want Mini-mini. I'll tell papa, I'll tell papa," Jethro screamed again.

"You must do just that. Papa can't do anything, anyway. Mini-mini belonged to me. I have sold her and she's not coming back, however hard you scream," said Sarith calmly.

But Jethro simply started screaming and yelling ever more loudly, "Mini-mini, Mini-mini."

Esther and two of the cousins had come upstairs to see what all the fuss was about, and saw Sarith sitting up calm-

250 "A no de masra."
251 "A no de, pikin masra, a no de, a gowé."

ly in bed, with Jethro behaving like a little savage. "What on earth is happening?" asked Esther, looking in surprise on this scene. "Oh, he's screaming for Mini-mini, but she has gone, I've sold her. He'll simply have to get used to the idea."

"You've sold Mini-mini? No, surely not," said Esther, startled. "Why have you sold her, Sarith? Just look what you're doing to that child!"

"She's expecting Julius' baby, that's why," said a now angry Sarith.

"But that's no reason to sell her, and certainly not in Mini-mini's case," said Esther. "So many slave-girls have babies by their masters. Mini-mini herself was such a case."

"You don't understand, Esther," Sarith had got out of bed. "She is no ordinary slave-girl, she is his concubine, his love." For that was now clear to her: that is what she had noticed. The way Julius looked at the girl. She knew for sure: this was not a passing fancy, this was true love.

"But selling her?" Esther asked again. "Who knows where she'll end up, poor child."

"Poor child, my foot!" screamed Sarith, "Can someone think of me for a change? Am I supposed to accept that my husband's concubine, his truelove, is living in *my* house? Is that what I'm supposed to do?"

"No," Esther shook her head, "No, of course that's not possible. No woman must accept that. But was there no other solution?"

"No, I've sold her, and that's it. I want to hear nothing more about it. I can do what I want with my property. Jethro, shut up now. Nicolette, go and wash him."

But Jethro began wailing even more loudly, as if that were possible, "I want Mini-mini," and when Nicolette brought her hand towards his nightgown, he bit it so hard that blood began to well up in the bite marks.

"Oh, just leave him alone, then," Sarith decided. "He'll calm down, and, oh, in a few days he'll have forgotten all about it." And so everyone left the room, leaving Jethro behind. He had not understood exactly what his mother and his aunt had been discussing. He went and sat on the floor, desolate and despondent, his head against the knees that he had drawn up towards his chest, and he wept, and wept. For if there was one thing he had understood very well, it was that Mini-mini was gone, gone for good.

JULIUS

Julius would never be able to say later what it was in those days that had given him such a funny feeling. Was it premonition, telepathy, a sixth sense? From the very moment the tent boat was leaving he had wanted to shout, "Mini-mini, come back; don't leave!" He had to console himself with the thought that she was going away for only a week, two at the most, and was going because she had to care for Jethro, so he should stop being childish. But still he felt so strange, so restless. He couldn't manage to stay in one place for any length of time, but found himself pacing up and down, going through the house from the front veranda to the rear one, from his office to the next floor, always with the same thought: nothing must happen to Mini-mini. But what could happen to her? This same response always came to mind. Hadn't she been to town so often? And Sarith was being exceptionally kind and calm since making that terrible scene. Was she no longer angry? Or was she planning something? Surely she would do nothing to Mini-mini? And then he suddenly remembered an incident he had heard about.

Long before they were married, Sarith had had the slave-housekeeper at Hébron whipped to death. No-one had ever found out exactly why, but it had been a terrible shock for the family, for the slave in question was the most trusted of them all, the one who had in fact raised the children. But surely Sarith would not be thinking of something like that with Mini-mini? They had known each other from their earliest years, and there was even talk that Mini-mini was the child of the older or the younger A'haron. He tried to console himself, but at the same time had to admit to himself that he simply did not know what Sarith might be capable of. He really did not know her at all.

Even the day after Sarith, Mini-mini and Jethro had left, it was no better. He was still ill at ease and wandered restlessly through the house. On the third day, during his ride through the fields, he decided that he must act quickly. He had been planning to buy Mini-mini free. That would be in about three months' time when the coffee had been harvested and sold. But now he changed his mind: why wait? Why not borrow the money from someone, to be paid back in three months' time, and begin the process immediately? Yes, that is what he would do: wait no longer, go straightaway, the next day, to the town, borrow the four hundred and fifty guilders somewhere and submit the application to the court. She could then already be free when the child was born. Then the child would also be free. Where could she go once she was free? She would not be able to remain at the plantation. But he felt at ease now he had made his plan, and resolved to go to town at the end of the week.

Returning home, he went to his office and opened the drawer where the slaves' papers were kept. He could see immediately that someone had been rummaging around. The papers were not in their usual order. A terrible suspicion began to arise in his mind. Frantically he searched through the deeds of ownership. Where was Kwasiba's? He was sure it had been there at the back. It was gone. So that was it! Good God! Was that what Sarith had been planning? Was she going to sell Mini-mini? The thought sent a chill through his whole body. He called, "Benny, Benny!"

When Benny came, he ordered him to get the small boat ready immediately. "Take twelve oarsmen, so that they can row in two shifts, and straight to the town." Benny wanted to complain that they had to wait for the tide, but Julius had no time for that: they must leave immediately, against the tide.

The boat stopped nowhere along the way. Now and then Julius himself grabbed an oar to help out, but that didn't amount to much, and he therefore had to make do with wringing his hands nervously while the oarsmen rowed with all their might. The whole afternoon and all the night they rowed without stopping, by ebb and by flood, and it was about half past nine the next morning that they reached Paramaribo.

In the Saramaccastraat Jethro had howled the whole day. He had eaten nothing, but had sat all the time in his night-shirt in the corner of his room, shouting for Mini-mini. During the evening he had eventually fallen asleep. Nicolette had put him to bed, but when he woke up and saw that Mini-mini still wasn't there, he went downstairs, dragging his pillow behind him, and sat near a window at the back of the house, asking each slave who went by, "Do you know where Mini-mini is?"[252] Everyone was full of pity for him and they all would answer gently, "No, my little masra, oh dear, no, I don't know."[253]

Jethro had started crying again, silently, when suddenly he stopped. Wasn't that his father's voice? He listened: yes, that was papa! In a few leaps he was in the front room standing with his father. "Oh papa, papa!" He stretched both arms out towards his father, who picked him up. With his arms around his father he screamed, "Mini-mini has gone, papa. Mama, mama has sold her!"

Esther had wanted to have a quiet talk with her brother-in-law, but he wasn't listening to her. He put Jethro down and ran up the two flights of stairs with Jethro on his heels. Once in Sarith's room, he stood in front of her and his voice was hoarse with rage as he shouted, "Where is she? What have you done with her?"

If Sarith was surprised to see her husband suddenly standing in front of her, she didn't let it show, and answered, "I have sold her. She is my slave-girl. I can sell her whenever I want."

"Whom have you sold her to – tell me who."

Julius grabbed his wife by the arm. She pulled herself loose and said, "I don't know. To a trader. He would sell her on. She's probably already on some far-flung plantation or other."

252 "Yu sabi pe Mini-mini de?"
253 "A no de pikin masra, ke poti, mi no sabi baya."

Julius was beside himself. "What kind of person are you?" with trembling voice, "You're a monster, a monster! Her mother saved your life and you promised her on her deathbed that you'd look after her daughter, and then you go and sell the girl! You're a wretch, that's what you are! Julius shook his wife through and through. "A wretch, that's what you are!"

"Do I have to take it lying down that your concubine is in my house then?" screamed Sarith. "Wretched monster!" cried Julius again, grabbing Sarith by the throat. But Esther came between them and pushed him aside.

"Julius, control yourself, control yourself! What Sarith did wasn't right, but indeed a man really can't keep his concubine in his house along with his wife, now can he?"

"No, a man can't do that, eh?" answered Julius cynically. "Not that, but he's supposed to accept that his wife has someone else's baby. That's all right, it seems!"

Esther was embarrassed and didn't know what to say to that. "Julius, calm down now, go and freshen up and take a rest, and then we can always see this afternoon what's what."

She pulled his arm and drew him out of the room, but not before Julius had turned to his wife, saying, "If anything's happened to her, then I swear I'll strangle you with my bare hands!"

Jethro, who had followed all of this in sheer terror, now grabbed his father's hand and said, in tears again, "Will you find her, papa; where is she, papa?"

"Quiet now, Jethro, quiet. I'll bring her back. I promise you she'll come back!" He left the house. Esther wanted to remark on his unshaved face, but he was already gone.

Of course all the slaves in the house knew what was going on, and while his master was inside, Benny had heard in detail how Masra Beunekom had arrived the day before yesterday with Misi Sarith and how he had taken Mini-mini with him. When Benny saw his master come out of the house, he

254   "Masra Beunekom, na en teki en."

said only, "Masra Beunekom took her with him."[254] To the stock-exchange, then. He would be sure to be there at this time of the morning.

Everyone knew Masra Beunekom, a trader who sold mainly salt-water negroes. These newly arrived negroes were first put in a slave depot until they could be sold. The sale was a public affair, usually a few days after the ship had landed. The slaves had to stand on a table and they were examined and pummelled from all angles. But in most cases the more significant transactions had already taken place at the stock-exchange.

Mr Beunekom was, however, not in the stock-exchange. Well, perhaps he was at the slave depot. Julius and Benny hurried to the depot on the Kleine Combéweg, but Masra Beunekom wasn't there, either. The slave who was there at the shed said that Masra Beunekom would certainly not be coming there today, for after all there were no slaves to sell right now: only a few decrepit negroes were there in the depot. Julius wanted in any case to look inside, just to be sure that Mini-mini wasn't there, so the slave opened the door for him with a large, rusty key. She wasn't there. Julius was becoming increasingly nervous and frightened. Every minute that passed without his finding her could mean something terrible happening to her. All right, so now to Masra Beunekom's house. He lived in the Jodenbreestraat. Julius ran there with Benny on his heels.

MINI-MINI

When the misi had suddenly come up with the plan that they should all go to town, Mini-mini had already had serious misgivings, and when the man stood at the door that evening she had immediately understood what the score was. It was over; everything was finished. How could she have ever thought that she would sometime be free, living her life with a man who loved her and whom she loved, too? That was just a dream, never reality for a slave-girl.

The man had taken her to his home and had locked her in a room. Thank goodness, she had thought at that moment, for she had been afraid that he would take her to some brothel or other. At that stage she did not know what was in store for her, for Beunekom was busy considering how this beautiful slave-girl could make him the most money. But in the meantime he would make the most of her himself. So when, a little later, he had entered the room with bare chest and a lamp in his hand, she had understood completely what he was after. She had resisted, punched, kicked, scratched. But that served only to make him more eager, and in the end he had hit her a few times, forced her against the wall and raped her. When it was all over, he had left. The key had ground in the lock and she was alone again in the darkness.

Mini-mini wept. Oh, that this should be her fate. Could the masra know what had happened to her? The following day an old slave had come along with a bucket of water for her to wash herself, a gourd with a few vegetable roots and some salted fish, and another with some water to drink. With pity in his eyes he had murmured, "Oh, poor thing."[255]

The whole day she had sat miserably in a corner of the room, rubbing her ankle, for she had twisted it during the fighting the previous evening. That evening Beunekom came again. He was clearly blind drunk. Mini-mini felt sick with disgust for the man, but she didn't resist this time, knowing it would be no use.

She looked for a way to escape. If only she could do that, and then go into hiding. But the door was locked and the windows had locks as well as grills. She could only open the blinds and just get a hand through, nothing more. Exhausted and miserable, she went and sat on the floor again. And then suddenly she heard something! Wasn't that Masra Julius' voice? Oh, perhaps she was just imagining things. She limped to a window. But the room's windows looked out onto the grounds and the negroes' entrance, not onto the street. She heard how the old slave closed the front door

255 "Keba, ke."

again and she heard departing footsteps on the pavement. With all her might she screamed, "Masra, help me, I'm here. Get me away from here, I beg you, get me away!"[256]

Outside on the street Julius heard this, and with a single leap he was back on the pavement, banging on the door. "Open up, open the door!"[257]

The door opened. Julius pushed the old slave aside and with huge strides he was at a door near the back of the house.

"Mini-mini," he called.

"Yes, masra," came the voice from inside the room.

"Open up," commanded Julius.

But the slave shook his head, scared, "I don't have a key,"[258] he said.

Julius asked no more. He threw his weight against the door, which burst open.

The next moment he had Mini-mini in his arms. "Oh, Mini-mini, dearest, my love, my treasure, what's been happening to you? Forgive me for your having to suffer like this for me!"

Mini-mini could only sob. Julius wanted to get her outside, but when he saw that she could hardly walk he picked her up and carried her through the door. To the frightened slave he said, "Tell your master that I'll bring the money this afternoon, and I'll pay for the door, too."[259]

When they were a few doors further, he suddenly realized that he had no idea where he could go with Mini-mini, and he couldn't carry her much further.

He set her down on a doorstep. She was still sobbing, and he stroked her hair. Frantically he looked for inspiration. Where could they go? The De Ledesmas' wasn't an option. Then he suddenly thought: his daughter, Miriam, was mar-

256   "Masra, kon yepi mi dan, me dya. Kon puru mi, mé begi yu, kon puru mi."
257   "Opo, opo na doro!"
258   "Mi no habi na sroto."
259   "Taigi yu masra dati bakadina mi e tyari na moni gi en, a doro srefi mi sa pai."

ried to one of the tradesman De la Parra's sons and lived in the Molenstraat. Yes, Miriam. She would have a room in her grounds where Mini-mini could stay. But she wouldn't be able to walk that far. Benny would have to hire a carriage, and quickly. In the meantime Julius went and sat next to Mini-mini on the doorstep.

Various passers-by stared in astonishment at the scene of a white man sitting there on a doorstep with his arm round a weeping mulatto woman.

"Masra Jethro," Mini-mini asked, "How is he doing?"[260]

Only now did Julius think of Jethro, who must be told that he had Mini-mini again. Benny came with a carriage. Julius lifted Mini-mini into it and went to sit next to her.

"Saramaccastraat," he ordered. Mini-mini was shocked, but he reassured her immediately. "You won't be staying there: we're going to collect Masra Jethro."[261]

The carriage stopped at the De Ledesmas' door. Julius sent Benny inside to collect Jethro. He must say nothing about Mini-mini. Only that Jethro's father wanted to take him for a ride. Benny went in through the negroes' entrance and saw Jethro, who was still sitting on the step near the window.

"Psst," Benny signalled, and when Jethro came, he whispered something in his ear. Jethro ran up the two staircases, taking his nightgown off on the way. A slave-girl answered Benny's knock on the back door, and Benny said to her, "Masra Julius has sent for Masra Jethro to go for a short ride with him."[262]

Jethro was by this time downstairs again, with nothing on, but with his clothes in one hand and his shoes in the other, and he would have gone out onto the street like that had Benny not quickly pulled his shorts on for him. At the carriage door he threw himself into Mini-mini's arms. "Oh, Mini-mini, you're here, oh you're here; oh Mini-mini never go away again."

And his father, happily watching this, said, "No, Jethro, she'll never go away again. She's staying with us. Forever."

260 "Fa fu en?"
261 "Yu n'e go tan drape, na masra Jethro w'e go teki."
262 "Masra Julius sen' teki masra Jethro fu go rij pikinso."

CHAPTER XIII

OCTOBER 1778

By early 1778 the army, under the leadership of Colonel Fourgeoud and in collaboration with the Free Negroes Corps[263], had managed to destroy nearly all the Aluku villages and farmlands. The Alukus themselves had fled across the Marowijne River and were now on French territory.

In February 1776 a message had arrived from the Prince of Orange that Fourgeoud's troops must return. Many of the colony's residents were, however, afraid that the Bonis would start their raids again, and asked for the troops to stay. A seemingly endless correspondence ensued. In the meantime the French were not particularly happy at having the fearsome Bonis on their land. Fourgeoud was asked for advice. He wanted to cross the Marowijne and exterminate the Maroons there. But Governor Nepveu did not dare to take this step, fearing a conflict with the French. And so the Bonis remained peacefully on the other side of the river. The French did not bother them.

In April 1778 Fourgeoud left the country with the majority of his troops. Of the fifteen hundred men, only about a hundred remained. Fourgeoud complained about the lack of gratitude on the part of the Suriname government, feeling that his good services had not been duly recognized.

By this time, however, the Suriname colonials and plantation owners had fresh troubles to worry about. Because of the war between the English and their North American protectorates there were all too many pirates on the seas. Ships from Suriname carrying goods destined for Amsterdam

263 In contrast to the Zwarte Jagers, this was a corps of free negroes and coloureds who gave their services professionally.

were regularly being captured by one group of villains or the other. As if that wasn't enough, all kinds of diseases were breaking out among both cattle and people. Governor Nepveu was himself ill from June onwards.

ELZA

"I'm going too mama, I'm going too, hey?"

Elza had just reached the bottom of the stairs when the little Abigail in the corridor accosted her with these words.

"Going too? Where to, child?" asked Elza.

"To Ezau's party tomorrow," said Abigail impatiently.

"But of course you're going!" said Elza with a chuckle, and before she had finished talking Abigail was already calling, "You see Jonathan, you see!" poking her little red tongue out at her brother, who emerged from the dining room with a grin on his face.

Elza understood what was going on. "Don't be such a tease, Jonathan," in a strict tone to her second son, who teased his little sister all too often. She ran her hand over the dark-blond hair of her four-year-old daughter. A sharp little thing, was this Abby, as the slaves and the boys always called her.

Elza went into the dining room, pondering on the differences in character between her two sons. On the one hand there was Gideon, now ten, already a big boy, resolute and always nice to his sisters, the four-year-old Abby and the baby of the family, Charlotte, now one-and-a-half. Jonathan was always tormenting Abigail, and Elza or Maisa was always having to come between the two of them when things got too heated. Now he had been telling Abby that she would not be able to go to Ezau's party tomorrow because it was only for boys.

Elza still had a weak spot in her heart for Ezau. Now he would be thirteen and tomorrow would be his Bar Mitzvah. As in all Jewish families, this was the most important moment in the life of a boy. From then on you would be regarded as a man. The Jewish families in Suriname always celebrated this in grand style, and although the financial situation of many of them now left a lot to be desired, there had never been anyone who had scrimped on a Bar Mitzvah feast.

The De Ledesma family, therefore, with five sons, had enough on their plate. The twins, now sixteen, had had their Bar Mitzvah three years previously. Tomorrow it would be teeming there with all the guests. Elza did think, however, that it would be better to leave little Charlotte behind. She was coughing a little, was in any case not all that strong, and often suffered from bronchitis. No, it would be better for Charlotte to stay at home with Maisa. Then just Afanaisa would go along to help. Abigail, however, was really looking forward to the next day. There would be so many other children. Elza thought about the family in the Saramaccastraat and automatically about Sarith, too, for Sarith was more often there than at Klein Paradijs.

What a to-do there had been two years earlier when Julius had installed Mini-mini in a cottage on the Weidestraat! He had had to borrow money for that from Rutger: money to buy Mini-mini's freedom and money to rent the house. Rutger had told Elza that he had taken pity on the large man sitting opposite him and telling him that it was Mini-mini whom he loved, whom he longed for, who gave him love and a sense of security, whom he really had been seeking all his life. And Elza could well imagine this, knowing what a sweet person Mini-mini was, which could certainly not be said of Sarith. Rutger had not been able to increase the loan on the plantation, but had personally lent Julius the money he needed so that Mini-mini now lived in the Weidestraat and already had two small sons.

Julius was now very often in the town with Mini-mini, and Jethro was often there, too. He was sometimes with his mother in the Saramaccastraat, but even if Julius wasn't with Mini-mini, one of the Saramaccastraat errand boys would take him to Mini-mini.

It seemed as if Sarith had resigned herself to all this, though Maisa had heard from one of the slave-girls there that Sarith had more than once remarked that Mini-mini had stolen not only her husband but also her son. Elza felt that there was no talk of stealing in this case. It was after all Mini-mini who had cared for Jethro from the moment he was born. No wonder he loved her more than he did his mother, whom she seldom saw. Tiny Eva was a dapper little thing, completely blond, with light-blue eyes. Of course this gave rise to the necessary whispers, for there had never been anyone blond in Sarith's family or in that of Julius. Sarith herself said that this was all quite normal. Elza's Abigail was almost blond, after all. But that was of course something completely different, for Rutger had light-brown hair, and according to Maisa Abigail was the spitting image of Elza's mother, Misi Elizabeth.

Elza sat by the window. It was hot and dusty. It had not been a good year for the colony. There had been a lot to complain about: so much illness among the people and especially among the cattle. On many plantations cows, horses and mules had been dying quite inexplicably, and even among the wild animals in the bush there had been many deaths: so many, in fact, that even the vultures could not cope. Maisa came in and asked whether the misi already knew which dress she would be wearing that evening. "This evening? Oh, yes, that's true." She and Rutger had to attend a theatrical evening at the Jewish theatre.

In 1775 a Dutch theatre had opened in Paramaribo, but the Jews were not allowed to attend it. One of its most important founders was Hendrik Schouten, a Dutchman who had married a half-cast, Susanne Hansen, in 1772. He had considerable problems with his wife's not being accepted in the foremost white circles in Paramaribo, and took to writing all kinds of satirical poems about this society in which his wife was not welcome. Rutger found it quite incomprehensible that someone who himself suffered so much from discrimination then made such a distinction and founded a theatre bearing the inscription 'Pro Excolenda Eloquentia' followed by 'Jews prohibited'. The Jews, however, had opened their own theatre after that, and twelve productions were being staged there each year.

The next day there was incredible hustle and bustle in the De Ledesmas' home. Carriages coming and going, guests in the large front hall and the dining room, children running up and down the stairs and around the grounds, slaves under the trees who had accompanied their masters' families and were there to lend a hand.

Abraham Cohen was deep in conversation with Rutger. He had a lodger, a certain Joachim Morpurgo from a small town in Italy. The Jews there had been hearing a lot about the colony of Suriname, where the Jews enjoyed certain privileges and where the Portuguese Jews had founded the beautiful village Joden-Savanna: a new Jerusalem on the river. The fame of this place had spread as far as northern Italy, where this group of Jews had ended up after extensive wanderings through much of Europe. A number of well-to-do families, about forty souls in total, now wanted to emigrate to Suriname to establish themselves at this Joden-Savanna, and Joachim Morpurgo had come to see and arrange everything. He had already been to Joden-Savanna and had liked it. Of course he had heard that the place was not what it had been, and he could also see this for himself. Many of the wealthier families had departed for the town and had stayed there. But he and his group would be able to breathe new life into Joden-Savanna. They had enough money to establish plantations and could themselves live at the Savanna. After all, they had everything they needed there: the beautiful synagogue, houses that could be done up, a bakery, a butcher and the famous cemetery.

Joachim Morpurgo had been invited to the De Ledesmas, but had not been feeling himself the past two days and had therefore remained in bed. When they returned home later, could Rutger perhaps drop in at the teacher's home and make an appointment with Joachim? For Joachim wanted to talk business with Rutger concerning the cost of slaves and cattle and in fact everything to do with running a plantation.

That afternoon, when the families began returning home after a busy day with much talking, eating and drinking, Abigail sat in the carriage on her father's lap. She dozed off with a thumb in her mouth, but was wide awake once the carriage drew to a halt at the corner of the Heerenstraat and the Klipsteenstraat, where the house of the Portuguese-Jewish community's teacher was situated. Rutger alighted, and the child stretched out her little arms:

"With papa, can I come with papa?"

With his daughter on his arm Rutger followed the Cohens into the house. The boys also wanted to get out, but Elza said, "No, you stay here. After all, there's someone ill there, and he can certainly do without a lot of fuss and bother."

A little later Rutger came outside. He held Abigail's hand tightly and was pressing a handkerchief in front of her mouth. He was pale, and urged Elza, "Away: get away quickly. I'll walk with Abigail. Have Maisa give the boys a hot bath. You too, quickly; oh dear, it's terrible, it's yellow fever."

Elza was shocked: oh, no, not that dreaded disease! The carriage was already in motion, and a few seconds after they arrived home Rutger was there, too.

"Burn Abigail's clothes, and mine! Quick! Have Maisa bath her, as hot as possible and with herbs, and everyone must take a draught of gin!"

Abigail began crying: did her pretty new dress really have to be burnt? And when she had to drink the gin, well, it was really no wonder that, after a day with so many different things to eat, the complete contents of that little stomach landed in Maisa's skirt.

Rutger was extremely worried. He had got a shock as soon as he had stood at Joachim's sick-bed with Abigail and with little Daniel Cohen on his father's hand. He had recognized the symptoms immediately: blood-red lips and nostrils, bloodshot eyes. And Joachim could say nothing and could only groan. It was as if a kind of rumble was emerging from the depths of his very being. Yes, Rutger knew these symptoms all too well. He couldn't get out of the room quickly enough, and blamed himself for having taken Abigail with him. Elza was also worried, especially after Abigail had been sick and had fallen asleep crying and complaining.

The next day, however, the child was running around as brightly as ever, and this put Elza's mind at rest. Yellow fever was a most serious disease and Abigail had been inside there. But they had taken the right precautions. A few days later, however, the message arrived that Joachim Morpurgo had died, and that the Cohens' youngest son, Daniel, was ill. In the Saramaccastraat, too, Jacob de Ledesma was ill, and it became apparent that the dreaded disease was affecting many families.

And so it was that one morning Abigail was listless. The same afternoon she was running a fever and was confined to bed. The dreaded symptoms were already apparent: the blood-red lips and nostrils, bloodshot eyes, pain all over her body. There was no known cure for this disease. Maisa made a bowl of tepid water containing some herbs to counter the fever. She sat by the child's bed and wiped her face and body with a cloth. A cloth was also laid over her forehead and eyes.

"The other children mustn't go into that room, Elza," said Rutger anxiously. "Have just Afanaisa look after Charlotte and have her stay downstairs in the back room for the moment."

The boys were warned not to go into Abigail's room.

Elza paced nervously up and down in her daughter's room. The child had high fever, was delirious, came to now and then, and cried. She wanted to say something, but could make no sound. It seemed as if a kind of groan emerged from deep inside that emaciated little body, and the next moment a thick, black-red liquid streamed from her mouth. Maisa held her upright for a short time. Elza had to help hold the child while Maisa changed the sheets and carefully cleaned the little girl. Then yet again that groan, moaning, convulsions. Elza could take no more of this. My God, why must her little girl suffer so? Looking at the child, she prayed silently, "God, may she get better. My Lord in Heaven, I pray you, I beg you, please let my child get better."

But the next day brought no improvement. On the contrary, things were getting worse and the day after worse still.

Maisa and Elza took it in turns to be at Abigail's bedside. She hardly recognized anyone anymore. Now and then Rutger would come into the room, looking sadly at his little daughter, lying there helplessly in bed, fighting for breath. Then the message arrived from the Saramaccastraat that Jacob de Ledesma had died. Ezau and Joshua (one of the twins) were also ill, and the next day little Daniel Cohen died.

Elza was at her wits' end and could only pray and pray to God to spare her little daughter. Then at a certain moment she went into Abigail's room and saw Gideon standing next to her bed. "Gideon," she said, alarmed, "Hadn't we agreed that you wouldn't come in here?"

Gideon looked tearfully at his mother, asking, "Why does she have to suffer like this, mama; why?" And he stroked that little forehead and took a fan to cool her.

From the bed there emerged only an occasional groan. After a while, Maisa said gently to Elza that she should go and get some rest. Elza went to her room. Despondent, she sat on her bed, prayed again to God, begging Him to make her daughter better. Then she heard the door slowly open. It was Gideon. He came and stood near her and then leant on her so heavily, it seemed as if he wanted to creep into her body. "What's up, Gideon?"

She looked at her son, but knew what the answer would be before a word had been spoken. "No, oh no!" Elza cried.

But Gideon nodded, throwing his arms around his mother and laying his head in her bosom, sobbing, "She's dead, mama; Abigail is dead."

And Elza could not contain herself any more, and wept copiously with her arms around her son.

It had been decreed that yellow-fever sufferers must be buried as soon as possible, and just the following morning the little Abigail was taken to her final resting place. Elza was inconsolable and Rutger wept too, unable to think of anything but his little daughter.

Father Levi Fernandez had come to the town a few days earlier with Aunt Rachel. She was now in the Heerenstraat, for Rebecca had also been taken ill. In the days that followed more and more cases were noted, and it became known that there had been deaths in nearly all families.

Then Gideon also became ill. Elza couldn't cope any longer. She implored God not to take her son, oh please not her eldest son, who, although she would not admit it, was really the apple of her eye. Not Gideon, no God, please, not Gideon. It was Maisa who sat at Gideon's bed day and night, washed his face, wiped his body with a cloth drenched in water in which herbs had been boiled, changed the sheets, held Gideon upright when the convulsions came. Maisa didn't sleep at all, sitting there day and night, indefatigable. Rutger and Elza came and went in the room, being unable to do much, just look how Maisa was occupying herself with their child. After a while Rutger would leave the room again, totally despondent.

This damned land with all its tropical diseases. He had already lost one child. He begged God not to take his son, too. Elza came out of the room. Fresh water was needed. She had one of the slave-boys fetch it from the rainwater vat and took it to the room herself. When she entered the room she saw Maisa on her knees by the bed. The boy lay very still on the bed, no wheezing and groaning, no convulsions.

"My God, no!" Elza felt that she could only scream, but Maisa turned round and said softly,

"Look misi, look – his fever has gone. Look how gently he's breathing, he's getting better."[264]

Elza hastened to the bed and sure enough Gideon's head was no longer hot, he was no longer gasping, but was breathing regularly.

"Oh Maisa, he's getting better, thanks to you, Maisa, thanks to you!"[265]

She wanted to embrace Maisa, but Maisa put her hand out, saying,

"Don't touch me misi, don't touch me."[266]

264 "Luku misi, luku, a no habi korsu moro, luku fa ai hari bro so switi now, ai kon betre."
265 "Ai kon betre, tangi fu yu Maisa, tangi fu yu."
266 "No fasi mi, misi, no fasi."

And Elza looked at Maisa and saw only now what Maisa had known and felt for the past two days: the swollen blood-red lips, the bloodshot eyes.

"No Maisa, oh no!" cried Elza.

Maisa tried to grasp one of the bedposts, but those hands that had constantly washed, cared and calmed, now had no strength left, and slowly she sank to the floor next to the bed in which lay the boy who would recover due to her efforts.

Three days later Maisa was dead. Gideon recovered. It took quite a while, but he did recover. In the meantime Rebecca had died, and Ezau too, who had just celebrated his Bar Mitzvah. Joshua was recovering, but now Jethro was ill, really ill.

SARITH

In the Saramaccastraat, in the house so engulfed in mourning, Sarith sat in her sick child's room. Everything seemed so unreal. This house, always so full of joy and life, now in mourning because first the father and now one of the sons had died. And now her son was lying there so ill.

Sarith herself could do nothing: she was completely helpless in this kind of situation. She was so scared when Jethro had vomited that deep-red blood, she had run from the room, weeping. Was God now going to punish her like this? Was she going to lose her child?

It was Nicolette who was looking after Jethro along with Julius. Sarith had sent an errand boy to fetch Julius from the Weidestraat. She had never expected that she would do something like that, but seeing Jethro lying there so ill, she had not known what else she could do. Julius had been there by his son's bedside since the previous morning and would hold the child upright when Nicolette changed the sheets. Jethro was almost literally glowing with fever, and now and then he would come to from his delirium. Now, at this moment, too. And his lips formed the words, "Mini-mini."

"Mini-mini isn't here, my boy," answered Julius, laying the child back on the pillows.

Only a groan, that seemed to emerge from the very core of

that small body. Sarith got up from the chair near the window where she had been sitting and came to stand by the bed.

Again Jethro mouthed, "Mini-mini."

Julius glanced at Sarith. "He's asking for Mini-mini."

Sarith nodded. Julius looked at her.

"I'll go and get her," he said.

Sarith nodded again. He could certainly fetch Mini-mini if only that would mean that Jethro would get better. Nothing mattered any more if only the child would recover.

Julius got up and walked slowly out of the room and down the stairs. But before he had reached the front door he heard a stifled scream from above and hear his name being called. His knees trembling, he walked back and came to a standstill under the stairs leading to the next floor, looking at his wife, there above on the stairs with a hand in front of her mouth. Sobbing, she called to him, "It's no longer necessary, Julius, it's no use anymore. He's dead. My God, my Jethro is dead."

JULIUS

Two weeks later the Klein Paradijs tent-boat was on its way to the plantation. Julius sat in the boat with Sarith and with little Eva. He had never imagined that this was how the journey home would be. What grief, what sorrow. His son, his bright, handsome son, was no more. What agony they were leaving behind them there in Paramaribo, where nearly every family now had someone to mourn.

In the Saramaccastraat seven of the twenty-two slaves had died, and with a heavy heart Julius wondered what he would find back at Klein Paradijs. At the plantations where they had to stop now and then there had also been people sick and dying, and everyone knew that their son had died.

Sarith said little during the journey. She was a downcast, sorrowful woman who was asking herself whether all this was happening because God wanted to punish her in this way for all the wrong she had done. She looked at Julius. In the past he had loved her, but now he no longer loved her. He loved Mini-mini. If only she could talk to him. But since the business with Rein Andersma such a chasm had opened up between them that there was no longer any question of their being husband and wife: they were just strangers to each other. Jethro had been the only link that they still retained, and now he was gone, too.

Two days earlier Julius had come to tell her that he was returning to the plantation, and she could see that he was surprised when she had said that they would return with him.

Julius stared ahead while the boat glided along. What was the use of all this? What dreams he had had twenty-seven years ago when he started the plantation. Everything had appeared rose-coloured. A lad of twenty, then. He had started with money from his father, and everything had progressed well and quickly. A coffee plantation. The area was not all that large, but the coffee fetched a good price. Then came the smallpox epidemic of 1764 that claimed the lives of his first wife, his son and many of the slaves. That had actually been the beginning of the end.

Arriving at the plantation, he looked around. Yes, everything indeed looked unkempt. There were not enough slaves for all the work. The harvest the previous year had not been all that successful. He had made less money than he had expected. He had repaid hardly any of the money he had borrowed three years earlier, after the Maroons' raid. Before he had even set foot in the door the supervisor came up to him. He expressed his sympathy at the death of Jethro, but also came to say that twelve slaves had already succumbed to disease. It was almost impossible to work. Even if all the slaves were put to working in the field and in the coffee mill, even then there were too few, and there was no-one left for all the other things that needed doing, such as maintenance, weeding the grounds, keeping the canals clear, working in the carpenter's and blacksmith's shops.

Julius said nothing. What could he say? Hadn't he foreseen all this? In the evening he sat in silence on the rear veranda. He really didn't care any more. He wanted nothing for himself. He wanted only to be with Mini-mini. How he longed to be near her, to feel her comforting hand, to hear her voice. That alone was what he longed for: to be with Mini-mini. He could see her now in his mind's eye, when he had gone to tell her that Jethro had died. He could still see that intense sorrow in her eyes, sorrow for the child she had regarded as her own, the child that had suffered in that way and was now gone for ever. If only he could be with Mini-mini for evermore. Never leave her again. And, in fact, why not? Why should he continue with this plantation? What was the use? He didn't have the money for it. Should he just get deeper into debt? What for? In a few years' time he would be dead, and what then? Jethro, who could have carried on running the plantation, was no more.

Both his daughters were married and had no desire to inherit a plantation that was heavily in debt. And Sarith? Sarith had never liked Klein Paradijs. If he was no longer there she would immediately try to sell off everything. So why should he carry on? He might as well try to sell everything straightaway. The grounds themselves would probably not sell, for it was highly improbable that anyone would now want to buy a plantation on the Boven-Commewijne River. Quite the opposite. The plantations that were still being bought were all much closer to the town. He made his decision. He would not get into debt any more in an attempt to keep the plantation running. No, he would sell everything. If the plantation itself could not be sold, then the slaves, the drying shed, the machines and that kind of thing could be. Of whatever remained after the loan had been settled he would invest a part for Sarith and a part for himself and Mini-mini's boys, and he would go and live with her in the town.

And Sarith? Now, Sarith had after all never been happy together with him and had never really regarded Klein Paradijs as her home. And Eva? Well, sorry to say, he could never think of that child as his own. She bore his name and he would ensure that she was cared for, but she was Sarith's child, not his.

The next day, Julius walked around the plantation, thinking about what he had decided. He then told Sarith. He explained to her that she could leave if she wished, could take whatever she liked, and whichever slaves she wanted. Although divorce was virtually unknown in Jewish families, she could regard herself as 'free', he said, and if she really wanted to marry another man, he would do everything he could to permit that in law. He also told Sarith that he was planning to bestow his name on Mini-mini's boys.

"I shall certainly do that, and you'll hear about it, so I'm telling you myself," said Julius.

Sarith nodded. She had expected this.

"Then these half-cast children will also be called Robles de Medina," she said.

"Your child is called Robles de Medina," he retorted. "These half-cast children, *my* children, will be called Robles, simply Robles."

A few weeks later the tent-boat left the plantation. Sarith left. Little Eva stood in the boat with Nicolette holding her hand. Nicolette was also leaving, as were her own two small children and her mother.

The boat was heavily laden with everything that Sarith was taking in terms of household goods and furniture. They would stop briefly in Paramaribo and then continue on to Hébron, where she longed to be. On Hébron, with her mother and stepfather. In the familiar surroundings of her carefree childhood.

She left. The boat sailed away and the jetty faded into the distance. Away from the plantation, which in time would be empty – empty and deserted. Where only the buildings would remain until they were completely engulfed by vegetation and collapsed. Nature would reclaim what was hers. Bushes and trees would grow there, and after thirty, maybe fifty years there would be nothing to distinguish the spot from the rest of the jungle. Klein Paradijs on the Boven-Commewijne would be forever history.

EPILOGUE

ELZA

It was the last week of February, 1779. Governor Nepveu was now gravely ill. This had been the case for several months, but now his condition was regarded as terminal. 'The fox', as he was called by many, would therefore depart this life, and even the plantation owners who had been so much against him during his life had to admit that he had served the colony well in that time, if only by the creation of the Military Cordon Path, which had given access to a part of the otherwise impenetrable jungle.

It was not a happy time in the colony. Many families were still mourning the passing of one or more loved ones, and there was still much disease among both people and cattle. Even the harvests were poorer. Many things were scarce. Dutch ships did not dare to enter the area because of the pirates. Ships from America with goods for Suriname were being captured by the English.

Elza sat on the rear veranda of her spacious home on the Gravenstraat and looked out over the grounds where Jonathan and Gideon were playing with Amimba's sons under the great mango tree. Gideon was still very thin from his illness, but how tall he had grown, thought Elza. She sighed. That terrible disease. Only that morning she had had one of Abigail's little aprons in her hands and had put it in a cupboard. Her lovely, tiny Abigail, her little angel, who would no longer wear that apron. She missed her, but thanked God that He had not taken Gideon, and who knows she might now be given another little girl, for she had known for a few weeks that she was expecting again. It was Maisa whom she could never replace. How she missed Maisa. She missed her so much that it was almost a physical pain. Maisa!

Only when Maisa had passed away had Elza realized fully how dependent she had been on that one person. Not she, Elza, but Maisa had been the axis around which everything had revolved. The household: that had been Maisa's household. It was then that Elza had discovered that she in fact knew nothing at all. She didn't know how and where things were bought, what was needed. She knew absolutely nothing, for Maisa had always seen to everything.

A few days earlier, Lena the cook had come to say that they had run out of flour. Elza had suddenly burst into tears, to the considerable astonishment of Lena, who could not understand why the misi should be weeping like that just because there was no flour. That was, of course, not the reason for her tears: flour was scarce right now. No, Elza had suddenly felt just how much she missed Maisa. She had always been there to give good guidance. She would certainly have found out where and how flour could be obtained.

It now occurred to Elza that her family was in fact a model for all Suriname society. Wasn't everyone and everything totally dependent on the slaves? Just as she felt so completely lost without Maisa, so the colony would be totally lost without its slaves. They did everything and knew everything, and the whites knew nothing and were incapable of anything. The whites needed the negroes, but the negroes didn't need a single white person: look how the Maroons had managed to create a complete society in the jungle, knowing how to put everything to good use. Without tools and weapons they knew how to survive, feed themselves and defeat the military. And the whites? If they got lost in the jungle, that meant certain death, for they could not survive of their own account. If the negroes were no longer in this colony the whole structure of society would collapse like a puffed-up pudding. There were already enough plantations that had had to be wound up due to lack of slaves.

Elza thought back to what Rutger had told her two weeks earlier. Julius Robles de Medina had come along to his office. He was going to finish with Klein Paradijs. It was simply no longer manageable. He had insufficient slaves to keep the plantation going. He had been unable to repay even half of the loan he had received three years earlier. He would sell everything: the slaves, the coffee-drying apparatus and what remained of the cattle.

Rutger had wanted to encourage him to give it another try, but Julius had looked him tearfully in the eye and had asked dejectedly, "Why, for whom?" His sons were already dead. When he was no longer around, Sarith would simply sell everything, since she had never at all cared for Klein Paradijs. The children he had had by Mini-mini would not be able to inherit the plantation. So it was better simply to sell everything. A part of what was left he could invest to provide for Sarith, and from the rest, albeit a meager sum, he just wanted to live out a peaceful old age with Mini-mini. For that was in fact all he now really longed for in life: to be with Mini-mini and to stay with her in peace.

Elza could sympathize with Julius. Perhaps he was right. Mini-mini would certainly be a loving partner for him now. And what was Sarith doing now? She had gone to Hébron, but she would certainly not stay there for long because she would get bored with it. Actually, Elza was also concerned about her. Sarith had always sought pleasure and entertainment to such an extent that she could never find contentment and enjoy what she did have. What an empty, sad person she had become.

That afternoon Sydni, Pa Levi's slave, suddenly appeared at the back door with a message. Elza was startled: surely there could be nothing wrong with her father? Sydni said that he had been sent by Masra Levi. Grandma Fernandez was ill. The family had already travelled from Hébron to Joden-Savanna. But grandma had asked especially for Elza, her grandchild, and Pa Levi was of the opinion that Elza should go to Joden-Savanna, since it was likely that grandma would not be around for much longer.

When Rutger arrived from the Exchange early that evening, Elza told him what Sydni had come to say, and Rutger said that she should certainly travel as quickly as possible to Joden-Savanna. He himself could not go along. The governor's condition was now such that each day could be his last, and Rutger, who was by now a person of consequence, must remain in the town to attend the funeral.

In fact, Elza was not so keen on going, because it was the first time that she would have to travel without Maisa, and she also considered with some resentment how grandma had spent her whole life commanding everyone and everything, and was still managing to issue commands even on her deathbed. But all right, she would have to go, if only for her father's sake, and Sydni had said clearly that the old granmisi would not live much longer. Grandma had reached the good old age of seventy-eight, and that was really a considerable achievement.

The next day, therefore, Elza travelled with Sydni to Hébron. Rutger had asked Alex to go along, and Amimba went too, along with her eldest son, Rutty. They spent the night at Hébron, in the empty house, for father, Aunt Rachel and Sarith, too, with little Eva, were already at Joden-Savanna. The following day they set out again, and it was afternoon by the time they reached Joden-Savanna.

When Elza saw the old lady lying in bed in her large, old house, her first impression was not of someone who was at death's door. Her body might be weak, her voice was certainly not when she called Elza to her and said that she could have the garnet necklaces, the diamond brooch and two gold chains. The two red-coral necklaces were for her little daughters. Before Elza could say that she had only one daughter, grandma continued, "I know full well that you have only Charlotte now that Abigail is no longer with us, but don't mourn for her. She is with God, my child, and you will surely be given another darling daughter in her place."

She wished to give Elza the porcelain service with Jewish designs and also the hand-woven tapestry. Elza must be careful with all this, for they were very old family pieces. They had been brought over from Portugal to Brazil by grandma's great-great-grandmother and had later been brought to Suriname by her grandmother. It was a pity that Elza wasn't Jewish, but grandma said that she was certain that Elza would hold her ancestors in great esteem. Aunt Rachel and Sarith also received valuables, and Esther and Rebecca's daughters were not forgotten, either.

The next day a messenger arrived by boat from the town with the news that His Excellency Jean Nepveu had died the day before, the twenty-seventh of February.

"So he's gone before me, after all," said grandma.

When the family was getting up two days later, they heard that grandma had died in her sleep. She lay peacefully in bed, and Afi, her slave-girl, had spoken to her for at least five minutes before it occurred to her that the granmisi was exceptionally still. She had then gone to the bed and had seen that grandma was dead.

There were not as many people at the funeral as grandma herself would have wished, because many of her old friends had themselves died, and some other people who would normally have come to Joden-Savanna had had to remain in the town for the governor's funeral.

Elza had not spoken with Sarith all these days. Sarith was lodging with her mother and Eva in Aunt Rachel's house, where only Sarah and her somewhat retarded daughter now lived. Elza was staying in Grandma Fernandez' house.

The same afternoon the elderly widow Fernandez was buried. The site of her grave in the well-kept cemetery had been previously determined. She would rest next to her husband's grave. The marble gravestone had, together with her husband's, also been ordered from Italy at least forty-five years earlier. In line with tradition, the women no longer went to the cemetery. The coffin was carried from the house on the shoulders of eight slaves, and the men followed on, all dressed in black.

Immediately afterwards, Aunt Rachel called the slave-girls to set the chairs aside and mop the floor of the front room and the veranda. Elza went outside. She stood in front of the house, her thoughts centered on grandma. She looked round at the other houses. Joden-Savanna was going downhill. Joden-Savanna, a hundred years ago the pride of Suriname

Jewish society, was being gradually abandoned. Funny how life can be.

Suddenly Sarith was standing next to Elza. "How are things, Elza?" she asked.

"All right," answered Elza, surprised that Sarith, who had not exchanged a word with her in years, was now suddenly talking to her.

Sarith looked at her, and then said, "Elza, can you forgive me? Can you forgive me for everything I've done to you?"

In a flash, Elza saw in her mind's eye what she had seen through the keyhole that fateful afternoon. Rutger and Sarith in bed together. An image that had haunted her for years thereafter. And she saw something else, something she herself had not seen, but knew precisely how it must have been. She saw Ashana tied to a tree and Sarith ordering the basya to whip her. Now she looked at Sarith standing in front of her and said, "It is not I who must forgive you. Look, I have survived it all. It was terrible then, but I have survived. But you, how have you survived it? No, it is not I who must forgive you: you must try to forgive yourself, that's what you must do."

Sarith said nothing. She looked at the ground. Then she turned and began to walk away. Elza thought how Sarith had really made a complete and utter mess of everything. She had lost everything: her son, her husband, the plantation. It was an exceptionally lonely being that was walking away there. But it was also the friend from her childhood years, her sister!

"Sarith!" Elza called out. Sarith stopped and turned.

"Come," said Elza, holding her hand out. "Come on; let's go for a walk together."

A hesitant smile lit Sarith's face, and then she reached for her stepsister's hand.

Hand in hand they walked away from the house, towards the cemetery. The murmur of voices greeted them. They were the voices of the men who were saying the Kaddish, standing there in the cemetery among the graves of their ancestors: the Portuguese Jews, the first colonists, who, after the British, had dared make Suriname their fatherland.

Notes to the various Dutch editions

Upon the publication of this book I would like to thank all institutions and persons who have in various ways made a contribution. I would especially like to mention: the Library of Congress in Washington, DC, the Suriname Museum in Paramaribo, Eva Essed-Fruin, Leo Ferrier, Aunt Emmy and last but not least Helen Gray. The interest shown and assistance given have given me considerable encouragement.

C. McLeod

Paramaribo, October 1987

Upon the second printing
That the first printing of 'Hoe duur was de suiker' would be sold out within four months was something probably no-one expected. I certainly did not!

It is heartwarming and certainly stimulating to note that a novel concerning their own history is so obviously of great interest to the Suriname people.

Upon the appearance of this second printing I would like to thank all those who have so far reacted, in any way.

C. McLeod

Paramaribo, August 1988

Upon the fifth printing
With 'Hoe duur was de suiker' I wished to sketch an image of how everyday life was during an early period in Suriname history. The more than 10,000 copies sold so far indicate that my intention has been well received.

The enthusiastic and sometimes also moving reactions are for me an encouragement to continue my search through the archives.

C. McLeod

Paramaribo, June 1994

LITERATURE CONSULTED

Groot, Silvia W. de, 1978
The Boni Maroon War 1765–1793, Suriname and French Guyana. *Boletin de Estudios Latinoamericanos y del Caribe* 18 : 30–48

Hartsinck, Jan Jacob, 1770
Beschrijving van Guiana of de wilde kust in Zuid-America : betreffende de aadrykskunde en historie des landes, de zeeden en gewoontes der inwooners, de dieren, vogels, visschen, boomen en gewassen... Amsterdam: Gerrit Tielenberg, 11 parts

Hoogbergen, Wim S.M.,1985
De Boni-oorlogen, 1757–1860. Marronage en guerilla in Oost-Suriname. Bronnen voor de studie van Bosnegersamenlevingen, deel 11. Universiteit Utrecht: Centrum voor Caraïbische Studies.

Lier, Rudolf A.J. van, 1949
Samenleving in een grensgebied: een sociaal-historische studie van Suriname. The Hague, Martinus Nijhoff.

Nassy, David de Ishak Cohen (and other learned Jewish men), 1791
Geschiedenis der kolonie van Suriname. Amsterdam

Stedman, Capt. John Gabriel, 1799
Reize naar Surinamen, en door de binnenste gedeelten van Guiana. Amsterdam, Johannes Allart

Wolbers, J., 1861
Geschiedenis van Suriname. Amsterdam: H. de Hoogh (photographic reproduction 1970, Amsterdam, S. Emmering)

GLOSSARY

In view of the relatively limited extent of the Dutch language, the reader may find these notes useful, also for 'visualizing' the pronunciation. Some terms specific to Suriname and similar countries are also explained. Because 'negro' occurs in various combinations in this book, the term has not been capitalized, and the names of other local races are treated similarly for consistency. Most terms are also explained in footnotes.

Alanga tiki	A twig from a citrus tree
Basya	A negro foreman, himself a slave
Boven	Up, upper
Bu...	In Sranan this rhymes approximately with English 'too'
Commewijne	One of the main rivers, flowing from the east and sharing a common estuary with the Suriname River. Approximate pronunciation: Kom muh wine uh
Dram	A highly alcoholic brew distilled from the waste from sugar production
Faya watra	Hot water containing a shoot of molasses
Fiadu	(Fiadoe, or viadoe): a (pastry) tart filled with, amongst other things raisins and almond slivers
Free Negroes Corps	A corps of free negroes and other races who served professionally (in contrast to the Zwarte Jagers)

Futuboi	A young slave-boy who was constantly at the side of his master or mistress to attend to his or her every whim and fancy
Fyo-fyo	(The wicked eye): in folklore and the Winti religion, a curse that could cause a child to become ill or even die; a common cause could be the parents arguing
Gemene Weide	(Village) common
IJ	Treated as one letter in Dutch; 'the approximate pronunciation of 'mijn' is 'mine', 'wijn' is 'wine' (they translate as 'my' and 'wine', respectively); the IJ is the river running past Amsterdam and into the North Sea and serving as Amsterdam's harbour
Inglish boru	(Engris buru, Ingris boroe): a sponge-cake with currants, raisins and sometimes pineapple
J	Is always pronounced as the English 'y'
Joden	Jews (singular, Jood). Pronunciation Yoden, rhyming with the surname Roden in English (the singular rhymes with road)
Karboeger negro	Three-quarters negro, one-quarter white, or a child of a negro and an indian
Keksi	A sponge-cake with currants and raisins
Klein	Small, little; rhymes with 'mine'
Korjaal	An advanced type of dugout canoe (pronounced kor yaal)
Kra	Spirit, or ancestor's soul (term from Ghana), especially in Winti
Manumission	Declaration of Freedom

Maroon	A Maroon (in Suriname, Marron) was a slave who had escaped and lived in the rain forest; whole communities were set up and functioned perfectly in surroundings that were familiar to them
Mees	Approximate pronunciation: 'mace'
Mijn	My; rhymes approximately with 'mine'
Misi	Mistress (also a form of address)
Omhoog	Rhymes with 'vogue' or 'rogue'
Oude Oranjetuin	Old Orange Garden
Paradijs	Paradise (which is also the approximate pronunciation)
Paramaribo	The only town in Suriname and often referred to as 'the town'; originally called Parmirbo; some sources suggest 'para' (water) and 'maribo' (inhabitants) in Amerindian languages
Platte Brug	'Flat Bridge': not actually a bridge, but a jetty on the Paramaribo waterfront where small boats still moor
Pom	A warm dish based on ground taro stem, with chicken and vegetables, eaten mainly on festive occasions
Rein	Rhymes with 'mine'
Salt-water negro	Brought directly from Africa, or born on the voyage
Sapakara	Large type of iguana, living off eggs and small animals
Society	The Licensed Society of Suriname (Geoctroyeerde Sociëteit van Suriname) was established in 1683 by the Dutch West India Company, the City of Amsterdam and Cornelis van Aerssen van Sommelsdijck to manage the new colony, which had been ex-

	changed for Nieuw Amsterdam (later New York) through the Treaty of Breda, 1667. The society was disbanded in 1795 and a colonial government was instituted.
Sranan	Dutch is the official language of Suriname, but Sranan is used by many Surinamers on an everyday basis
Suriname	Pronounced Suri naam uh (so not rhyming with 'name'); sometimes seen as Surinam, but this is not the correct form, even anglicized
Tapu	(Negro folklore): protection through magical forces
Tent boat	As its name suggests, a boat with a tent-like awning for the passengers; rowed by, on average, eight slaves
Th	Always a hard t, as in Thomas, but also in, for example, Sarith ('Sarit')
Tuin	Garden; approximate pronunciation: 'town'
Uit	Out; the English 'out', which is also a very approximate pronunciation
Winti	An Afro-American religion: literally (in Sranan) 'wind' referring to the god-like spirits which can take possession of someone
Wisi	Black magic
Zwarte Jagers Corps	Corps of Black Hunters or Black Rangers; slaves sold to the government to fight their fellow slaves (Maroons) who had escaped into the rain forest